Dark Soldier
The Hunted
Book One

PUBLISHED BY: Aine Carrigan, 2025

DARK SOLDIER | THE HUNTED BOOK ONE

First Edition. April 2, 2025

ISBN: 979-8-9929760-1-4

Prologue

R*un.*
  The panic bounded through me with every one of my racing, erratic heartbeats. As my legs clumsily carried me away, I could feel the sudden cool emptiness along my wrists and ankles where my shackles—*shackles*—had been just moments before. It caused a wave of terror to rise like bile in my throat, the ripe fear squeezing the air from my lungs and making my chest burn with icy fire.

But there was one fire inside me that burned even brighter than my fear, and it was the animalistic rage I felt at being backed into a corner and forced to submit.

Never.

I pushed forward one painful breath, one stumbling step at a time.

I was shaking so hard from fear, and from fury—and probably dehydration and general freaking shock—that I could hardly walk. A painfully sharp ache exploded across my right ankle and shin as I accidentally stumbled into the jagged edge of a dirty wooden crate.

I screamed. My throat was so dry that it just came out as a wheeze.

Suddenly the possibility of being too injured to escape was more powerful than any pain. I glanced down at my leg, noticing the blood.

There was a tiny gash by my ankle and I'd scraped the skin off a little, but I knew nothing was broken or sprained. I could absolutely still run. Adrenaline and terror quickly erased any feeling of pain; it was hard to feel anything at all over the pounding in my chest.

I had to get the hell out of here!

Run.

Then hide.

Where to hide?

1

Run!

A noise behind me made me jump and squeak-scream and I fell over again, but I didn't see anyone chasing me. I gulped the putrid air around me desperately and picked myself back up. The ring of shackle keys I'd grabbed to free myself earlier still dangled around my pinky finger. Tiny flecks of blood were on my hands where a few of the keys scraped into my palm from each time I'd fallen down.

"Here!" I choked out weakly as I grabbed the keychain and threw it into the first room I saw.

Just as I suspected, there was another girl inside of it with identical metal shackles. Her room was also thankfully unguarded.

Our eyes locked just before I tossed her the keys, which had fallen on the floor right next to her severely malnourished form. Her mouth opened, but no sound came out. The poor woman was so filthy and appeared so miserable, but she reached them easily despite her weakened state.

My heart soared in relief when she instantly understood and found her own key to free herself, as well.

I felt so much shame and guilt for not helping her more, but I didn't even look back.

I couldn't.

I was way too terrified to even stop and check if I were being followed by any of the other men here. If I had any damn luck at all, most of them were either dead or dying.

Let their corpses rot in their own stinking shit.

I could hear yells of rage and pain growing quieter from behind me as I continued to flee down the grimy hallway. A sense of ashamed satisfaction simmered wildly within me at the sounds I had caused. Never before had I done anything so violent, but I hadn't had a choice.

I didn't know such evil truly existed until I'd become prey in the hands of these heartless monsters. Their black, merciless eyes were nothing but a gateway into the nightmare I'd been trapped inside.

Those empty black depths held no compassion, no humanity—and neither did those men deserve even a shred of my sympathy.

Violent rage rekindled within me as I recalled exactly how I had come to be here, and how I had been tricked, constantly misled, and manipulated. It gave me much firmer ground to stand on compared to the treacherous quicksand of terror which had consumed me when I'd first woken up a few hours before.

Gunfire erupted continually from behind me in piercing staccato *crack-crack-crack-cracks.*

The sounds caused such a flare up of fear that I could only shake uncontrollably as I hit the ground. Still, I kept crawling and stumbling through the first floor of the filthy warehouse like a lab rat frantically trapped in a maze. That horribly frigid fire of fear burned its way all over my back as I fled. My poor, terrified brain was already imagining those sounds piercing my own flesh, even though they had not.

Guilt and horror warred inside me as I heard more ragged screams and cries of the other women. I worried most were far too sick and frail to run. But I couldn't do anything for them, either, if I didn't get the hell out of here first. From what little I'd seen, some of these women had been here a very long time.

Some of them could barely stand up. At least I could still hear them, and that made me feel a little better.

Keep going keep going keep going...

The monotone mantra helped me focus on reigning in the fear threatening to hijack my limbs as I fled. I glanced at my ankle briefly; it was barely bleeding. Still, I couldn't hurt myself again and risk being unable to escape.

Clouds of smoke gathered thickly around me. It turned the already filthy grey air even filthier as the dirty haze engulfed me, but I felt a little safer inside the foggy cover of smoke. The sickening smell of fresh gunfire grew heavier, assaulting my nose and making my eyes burn and water. My vision was limited but my ears picked up every little sound, desperately straining to hear any indication that I was being chased by the worthless bastards who'd taken me.

The Fat One was already dead. *Very* dead.

After I'd freed myself from the shackles, I recognized his disgusting form slumped awkwardly against the wall outside the filthy room I'd been kept inside.

He'd been surrounded in a river of his own blood. Even in my state of horrified panic and rage as I'd fled for my life, I'd felt a little ashamed for being relieved—no, I'd been *triumphant*—that he was dead.

He was a cold-blooded, heartless killer.

Just moments before my escape I'd been sitting inside that room, in the exact same spot that I'd been for what I thought was maybe a little more than a day. I was starving, dehydrated, terrified, and so utterly *livid* at the complete helplessness of my situation, when there'd been a deafening explosion on the other side of the warehouse.

The other man who'd been guarding me—The Frog Man—had run out of the room so fast, he'd hit his shoulder on the door frame. Hard.

Fucking idiot.

But thankfully, it was enough impact to knock the set of shackle keys out from his belt loop as he continued running toward the other side of the warehouse.

Elated and almost unable to believe my own eyes, I moved toward them so quickly I fell. My trembling hands dropped them several times before I finally managed to unlock first my ankles and then my wrists.

Once I'd removed those metal prisons from my body, there was also nothing left to blunt the sharpened steel tip of my rage. I was feral with it.

I grabbed one of my disconnected shackles and hung it around my neck and shoulders. It was heavy as shit, and it was a weapon I would use on anyone who got between me and my freedom. My hands were still shaking so much it was hard to hold on to anything, but I knew better than not to take it with me.

Before I was able to leave that wretched, filthy room, I heard Frog Man return. Seeing his lanky and awkward form walk through that door caused an inhuman level of hateful adrenaline to spike through me.

Like an animal, I lunged from my hidden corner toward him.

At the same time, I reached my right arm up by my neck, grabbed the chain, and swung with all my remaining strength as I let out a screech that sliced like knives across my dry throat. I aimed my makeshift weapon toward his head, and it had made contact.

Hard.

Harder than the slimy little fucker had hit his shoulder on the door frame.

The inky black feeling of hateful revenge seeped through the cracks of my terror as I recalled the terribly wet, grotesque *crack-crunch* as the heavy metal chain struck soft flesh and hard bone. Blood had spattered and coated the already filthy wall behind him, and he'd crumpled.

Completely exhausted from that tremendous effort, I'd collapsed as well. I'd had to suck in air as I stumbled toward the door, completely uncaring for the fate of the groaning sack of flesh behind me.

I'd banished any remorse for my desperate actions; I could deal with that once I was safe again.

If I were safe again.

It'd been several minutes now since I'd freed myself from that room and found another dark, disgusting corner to hide. I knew I had to be getting close to an exit somewhere.

I wasn't sure if this sudden explosive commotion was from a friend or foe—my guess was on the latter—but I sure as hell wasn't sticking around to find out. Part of me foolishly hoped it really was the American Embassy this time, but doubt clouded my mind as I remembered the Fat One's battered form slumped against the wall. The amount of him missing from all the bullet holes...

That sure hadn't looked like the highly diplomatic American Embassy's style, which meant I was still on my own.

The most important thing right now was escape; the second most important thing I realized was that I could trust *no one*. I desperately prayed that I was not fleeing from one nightmare only to dive headfirst into another version of the same hell—I refused to be caught again by these monsters or any of their soulless comrades.

I kept moving within the shadows as quickly as I could, desperately trying to choose the safest yet fastest route toward freedom. My heart continued to pound wildly within my chest. I was certain at any moment one of the men's grimy hands would grab me and pull me back to hell.

At long last, the hazy grey air seemed to thin and brighten ever so slightly.

My heart soared as the wings of hope fluttered weakly inside of me.

I could see an opening—a wide open hole in the concrete—with wonderful, wonderful sunlight flooding through it like a lighthouse beacon. There was a large, open, *unguarded* area between my safe and shadowy corner and the glowing light of freedom. My heart was beating so wildly in my chest I was sure it would burst, but I tried to steady myself and focus with every gasping, wobbly breath.

My eyes darted across the open area ahead of me, but I couldn't see anyone.

I could only hear the distant sobbing of what I assumed were more women, but something made me wait before I ran toward the opening. I was well-hidden where I sat in a corner amongst a pile of generic warehouse rubble, but I knew I was far from safe. I had to keep going. I gathered every single ounce of courage I had left and prepared to make a run for the open door.

But that's when I heard them, and I froze, completely and utterly unable to move.

Men's furious, booming shouting and yelling out orders—in English—were soon accompanied by a few more *crack-cracks* of gunfire. My mouth was so dry that my tongue was sticking to the roof of my mouth which felt like old sandpaper.

I heard a man's booming, gravelly chuckle from somewhere ahead of me. The sound was so totally void of any warmth it couldn't be called a laugh.

The hair on the back of my neck stood up. My heart sank painfully, furiously, as I instantly recognized the owner of that unhinged, humorless mirth. It was someone I knew I absolutely couldn't trust.

Another man spoke in the same guttural and hissing language as my tormentors, his words thick with rage. That voice was so menacingly quiet that I could hardly hear it, but there was no mistaking the hatred which dripped from every word and again made my heart sink to my stomach in fear.

A third man's voice joined in the captors' language, and whatever he said must have been terrifying because the sobbing got much worse.

I knew exactly who those three men were but had never heard any of them speak with such an ominous and deadly quality. If I couldn't trust the first man, there wasn't even a snowflake's chance in fucking hell of trusting either of the other two men.

I remained hidden, frozen in my flight toward freedom. Certain danger behind me and selfish greed in front of me, and all around me the dusty haze of demolition and death.

I had already come so far.

I would never give up. I would find my way out of this mess.

They were too far away and I was probably too terrified to make out any actual words, but I knew exactly who they were and what—or rather, *who,* they were talking about.

The second man spoke again even softer, and then a brief but heavy silence. That first rough, deep voice sounded again quietly, menacingly, and continued to grow louder.

I desperately tried to overcome the wave of pain I felt at hearing *his* voice again.

Then, a slimy chorus of sobbing and begging from what sounded like several of my captors. Their wretched pleas were soon drowned out by another round of those unmistakable *crack crack crack's,* and then...

Silence.

I couldn't move, my limbs like concrete. And then that deep and gravelly voice roared so loudly, the walls in the empty warehouse seemed to tremble in fear.

"FIND HER! NOW!"

Like a rabbit finally cornered by the hungry wolf, I darted into the open space before me. I prayed desperately that I could make it to freedom before *he* found me again...

Chapter 1

Freya

(Two weeks earlier)

The amount of courage it had taken me to walk into *Caress,* the infamous and extremely risqué upscale lingerie boutique on the Upper East Side, was a little embarrassing.

But once I stepped inside and looked around, the seductive and almost dream-like ambiance of the dimly lit store quickly wove its spell over me. Techno house music added a quietly exhilarating backdrop for shoppers. It was just loud enough to remind us of the seductive promise of the upcoming Friday night.

One of the biggest reasons I had been so intimidated coming into this store had to do with the way they styled their risqué lingerie displays. It was likely the same reason it was such a popular and successful store.

They used live models, posing provocatively as they boldly showcased the designer lingerie.

It gave the place a super-artsy, runway model meets naughty art gallery type of feel. It was a total vibe; they even served champagne for shoppers while they browsed.

Politely nodding thanks to one of the servers, I took a glass for myself and headed toward the center of the store. I was immediately drawn to an edgy black satin and lace bustier with a garter set and matching thong. The material was beautiful and the lace butter soft, and it was also completely transparent.

It was perfect.

It was bold and sexy, and it was totally different from anything I'd usually pick out, so it went in my bag. I tried unsuccessfully not to make eye contact with the model at that display table. When she winked at me and smiled cheerfully, I couldn't help but bite my lip, trying and also failing to prevent the giggle that escaped as I shyly averted my eyes.

Feeling cheeky, I had continued to browse for a few more minutes. I had happily sipped at the delicate bubbles until they were gone, leisurely enjoying this shopping trip as a small reward for a long week at work. I had pranced up to the sales counter with my social media promo QR-code coupon at the ready on my phone screen.

I had chatted warmly with the friendly and very pretty, immaculately dressed saleswoman—who was fully clothed, mind you, as the barely-covered bodies were limited to the display tables, only—complimenting her genuinely on how well she wore the bold red color on her lips.

I'd been in such a good mood, already looking forward to my own Friday night plans for later. I'd been proud of myself for the private little hurdle I'd overcome by braving this store all by myself.

Truthfully, I thought I'd hidden my prudish nervousness well at the checkout counter when the saleswoman asked if she could assemble and test the function of the free mystery item. It was included with my purchase, courtesy of the promo code I'd scanned from my phone.

The free item was a cute little teardrop-shaped mini-vibrator cleverly named *The Panty Dropper*. It was designed to fit inside the front of most of the panty sets without compromising the beauty of the lingerie set, she'd told me calmly. And it also was Bluetooth enabled with a remote control.

Giggling a little, I'd nodded yes to her as I absentmindedly turned my head toward the door, waiting patiently.

And that was precisely when my good mood, my calm and carefree demeanor, died a horribly grotesque and dramatically depressing insta-death.

Dread settled in my stomach as the ultimate peril approached us through the rows of pretty panties.

Horrified, I'd turned to the saleswoman as I frantically tried to stop her from assembling *The Panty Dropper* inside the see-through black thong.

"No! No! Please! It's good, I'm sure it's fine, I'm ready. I'm really go. I mean, I'm really ready to go, so sorry. Can you just...?"

I gestured toward the opened package and the bag desperately, not caring if I sounded like a lunatic.

"Please, Miss; don't worry. It will just take a second or two. Part of our store policy—we just want to make sure all your goodies are fully functional, of course," the gorgeous saleswoman smiled at me serenely, as if I hadn't just had a slightly bipolar mini-meltdown right in front of her.

I watched in horror as she removed the plastic tab by the lithium battery housing and placed the vibe inside the crotch of the black panties. Instantly, the ensemble *"zzzzzzzzz'd"* loud enough to wake the dead, while I sat at the checkout counter in a place where that particular sound could only mean one thing.

I could already feel my whole neck and face was on fire, and when redheads blushed, we didn't mess around.

It was so humiliating.

And still, the danger approached us mercilessly.

Thankfully the buzzing had stopped, but the completely serene saleswoman was not yet finished repackaging my items. She was apparently unphased by my sudden state of panic.

If this weren't in fact a life-or-death situation, I would have been reminded of the scene in one of my favorite Christmas movies, where the salesperson goes to such hilariously meticulous and painfully protracted methods of wrapping an item of jewelry as a Christmas present, almost causing the would-be purchaser to be caught by his wife in the midst of buying said item of jewelry not for her, but for his office mistress...

But this definitely wasn't a charming British Christmas movie classic. It was my life, and that meant that my saleswoman—although she'd been very friendly and nice—was heartlessly holding me hostage. There would be no last-minute exit for me. I tried not to harbor any ill will toward her but wasn't entirely successful.

It wasn't her fault; how was she supposed to know that the embodiment of pure evil itself was on its way toward us this very seco—

"Freya Daniels, what a sur-pri-ise!"

DevLynn Hartington aka "Devi" came strolling toward the checkout counter in her usual snide saunter. Somehow, this bitch managed to throw her voice into three or four different octaves, all sloped into one single word.

I think she thought it made her sound girly; I have no idea.

That or she was secretly casting dark, evil, black magic spells by sing-saying certain words. To be completely honest, as horrible as she acted, the latter was infinitely more probable.

"Hey, there, Devi..." I started weakly, but my attempt to be civil was abruptly cut off as she gestured toward the QR code still open on my phone screen.

"Oh, look at you! I love how you always use coupons, it's so adorable, I just love it," she pretended to share some kind of understanding look with Serene Sally behind the counter.

I simply waited quietly, knowing from almost four years' experience on the university dance team with her that trying to reply to her snooty comment was futile.

"Listen, I'm actually super glad I ran into you. I really wanted to apologize about that night a few weeks ago, you know... when Bryce pretended he was sick so he could invite all of us over."

DevLynn was talking way, way too loud, plenty loud for most if not all of the people in line around us to hear, as well. Shocking.

Her voice trailed off expectantly and I knew she was just waiting for my reaction to the bait. Refusing to respond to her fake as fuck act of compassion, I trained my gaze on the tiny gold flecks mixed into the black granite counterspace in front of me, wanting to disappear.

Eventually I braved a glance up at my only visible ally, Serene Sally, behind the counter of the luxe lingerie boutique. She pursed her lips just enough to barely crinkle the flawless red velvet finish on her perfectly painted pout, but made no eye contact, appearing to be politely disinterested. She discreetly placed my items back into the shopping bag and held up the handles to my outstretched hand.

Her eyes finally met mine, but there wasn't anything cruel in the look she gave me; it was just pity.

Feeling like the rubber scraps of a busted water balloon, I smiled weakly back at Serene Sally. At least she was being nice and pretending not to hear about my humiliating story. I grabbed the handles of the bag, mumbled a quick thanks, and turned to leave.

The She-DevLynn stepped to the side slightly, blocking my way out of the store, and continued.

"Look, it wasn't his idea, it was one of his friends who told him to do it. We all told him to be honest with you and let you down easy instead of just lying to you, but you know Bryce and his buddies," she shrugged her shoulders like it excused his behavior.

Honestly, it was the freaking shoulder shrug that finally made me snap.

If there's one thing that heats my blood instantly, it's being lied to, which is all Bryce McFuckerson, Devi, and their whole little gang was capable of doing.

Normally I hated conflict or any type of confrontation, but there was just something about that feeling of being tricked and swindled that had always made my hackles rise and my claws come out.

Most people knew me as a quiet, soft-spoken rule-follower. The original Scaredy Cat. Never late to class, always ten minutes early to my shift at the university bookstore—even after pulling an all-nighter of studying for my psychology and business administration double majors. I had been the only girl on the university dance team to follow a double major program, and I had never missed a single, mother-effing practice.

So what if it had taken me staying in school basically year-round through every summer, plus an extra year? Did it really matter if I'd hardly *ever* gone out to socialize, too exhausted to do anything but come back home on the weekends and sleep? I was just focused, I always told my peers when they criticized my strict schedule. "Exhausting" and "boring" were how they frequently described my routine.

I wasn't embarrassed to be goal-oriented, even if I'd never be the life of the party. I always tried to be a good person, and responsible, and honest.

But something changed the last semester before we'd graduated.

I was restless, slowly realizing the things I'd poured myself into no longer gave me the satisfaction they had before. I had made very few meaningful friendships at school, preferring to spend most if not all of my free time (which was horrendously scarce) with my best friend Kimberly and her family, although she attended university in another state.

It made me realize how much I'd worked and studied and how much I *hadn't* gone out and enjoyed the college life, enjoyed being young and wild and carefree.

So, right before graduation and feeling sorry for myself, I had accepted a last-minute invite to not just one of, but apparently—according to my coworker from the bookstore, who had invited me as his "date"—*the* hottest party of the entire year—Bryce McFuckerson's annual beach party kickoff.

Technically his last name was McPherson, but I'd liked my best friend Kimberly's version better. It was so much more fitting.

Apparently, if I went to that party, I could go back to any of them over the summer. Rich people rules, my coworker had explained to me jokingly.

The party was actually a ton of fun after I'd relaxed and had a few drinks. My coworker was a nice, attractive guy, if a little handsy. To be totally honest I really hadn't cared that much; that night I'd kind of wanted the attention. I hadn't been to a party since junior year, and here we were about to graduate.

I'd recognized a lot of girls from my classes and some of them even came over to express their genuinely pleasant surprise to see me there. They were playing the *best* music, so I'd done more than my fair share of something I loved, which was dancing. The girls and some of the guys had joined me; I'd felt like the life of the party.

And that's probably where I'd fucked up, by letting my guard down.

That was the first night that Bryce McFuckerson himself had taken an interest in me. *Me,* of all the girls there.

I'd felt so attractive and alive, loving the whole carefree vibe of the party and the people there. I could pretend like I belonged in that crowd, that I wasn't just another poor smart kid attending a fancy university on grant money and the measly scholarship from the dance squad. That I didn't have to stress over every single penny

I spent, spending my free time desperately sorting through the pre-mium outlet malls for something brand-name or maybe even de-signer that I could afford on my practically nonexistent college stu-dent salary. I was the embodiment of champagne tastes on a beer budget.

Bryce had texted me a few days after that party. I'd been elated. We'd had a fake little "relationship" for a few weeks.

I'd acted like a fucking moron, getting all giddy despite him sometimes taking literally three days to respond to a single text I'd sent him. He'd taken me out on a few "dates" where we always somehow managed to meet up with at least three or four of his other friends. I chalked it up to how popular he was, how lucky I was—uggh, gag—to be able to share him with this golden, glitzy crowd.

By the start of summer, we'd been texting and hanging out for a little over a month when he'd made plans for a "real date, just the two of us," for that weekend. On the morning of our supposed date, he'd told me he'd come down with something and felt like crap. There was no way he wanted to give this to me—even if my voice would sound *so* sexy with a cold, he'd told me.

My dumbass had eaten it up with a silver fucking spoon.

By that time in the summer, I'd started working at my first adult job, and I was getting a real adult paycheck. In hindsight I blamed some of my idiotic gullibility on the fact that I was just excited to see the next chapter of my life unfold. I'd been bummed about our first real date night getting cancelled, but fully embracing this new stupidly optimistic outlook, what did my chipper little self do?

Feeling sorry for the lying little rat, I spent an embarrassingly large amount of my first paycheck on a cab to the *fancy* freaking grocery store, bought stupid fu-fu ingredients to make his lying, no-good ass a homemade freaking bowl of my Nana's famous "gets you over everything" chicken noodle soup, then paid for *another* cab all the way out to his parents' summer house in Babylon so I could freaking *surprise* him... all to realize he was absolutely not ill, and absolutely already drunk and making out with not one, but two different girls at the already wild party he was hosting.

I had sat there like a total idiot at his front door, holding this get-well basket I'd put together with homemade mother-effing soup. I realized the red-eyed, sniffly video call I'd received from him hours earlier was more than likely an Oscar-worthy performance where he played off his drunkenness as having a cold.

Judging by the reaction of the guests, they'd seen the whole little show.

"Oh my gosh, I can't believe she actually thought he was sick! I like... kind of feel bad now!"

"Shut up, no you don't!"

"Holy shit, she made him fucking soup, bro! I can't!"

His housekeeper had given me a truly sympathetic glance as she had put two and two together and realized what had happened. She closed the door a little as she tried to shield me from their rudeness. Her eyes had a pitying, annoyed look that only confirmed my suspicions about how badly I'd been played. She opened her mouth like she was going to say something, but then nodded her head sympathetically and closed the door.

In that moment, I realized how freaking stupid I was being.

I wasn't one of them, one of his uber-rich friends and I never would be. His housekeeper and I had more in common than he and I did. She and I were of the same class, the working, normal-people class. We didn't get to have fancy parties, sit around, drink champagne, and pick off charcuterie boards all day while never lifting a finger to do any actual *work*.

We got to clean up after the people who did.

It was on that day, furiously swatting away my tears on the ride home to my apartment, I promised myself I'd never fall into that trap of a bridge between the Haves and Have Nots again. I was who I was, and I didn't need a bunch of fancy bullshit to make me worth anyone's time.

The only people in that circle I could trust were Kimberly and her family. They were the only genuinely nice, yet absolutely filthy rich people I'd ever met.

If I'd learned anything attending university among a bunch of spoiled ivy-league shitheads, it was that the richer the person, the more they lied, and the less they cared about anyone but themself.

None more so than this toxic little tart in front of me, DevLynn Hartington.

It took me all of about three seconds to instantly relive the shame and humiliation of being the butt of Bryce's rude joke before the anger at being lied to took over.

Snapping back to the present of the lingerie store checkout line, I jerked my eyes back up to DevLynn.

This. Freaking. *Bitch*. My claws had definitely come out now, consequences be damned.

"Really? You felt bad, DevLynn? No, you didn't feel bad," Serene Sally's eyes snapped up behind the counter as I spoke, bright with sudden interest. I continued. "You know how I know? Because you," I pointed at DevLynn, "are not nice. Ever. I mean, for fuck's sake, are you people *truly* that bored that you have to literally call someone else and pretend to be sick over video chat? That's childish, Devi. And it's also *really* pathetic."

My voice had this weird wavery kind of quality due to my anger, I was talking *way* too loudly, and I definitely should not have used the 'f' word inside the upscale, classy lingerie store.

But I was *fucking* pissed, dammit.

Besides, this was New York.

People yelling obscenities at each other was just another drop in the bucket.

Serene Sally, my new BFF, sported a satisfying smile behind Devi's back. I once again turned toward my purchases waiting on the counter. Apparently, I'd set the bag back on the counter before my rant. I confirmed that Sally had put everything back in the bag for me along with my receipt, and when she again handed it back to me, she winked at me so delicately I almost thought I'd imagined it.

I offered her a quick, gracious smile as I grabbed for the bag and ran before my temper really got me into trouble.

Being reminded of what Bryce had done with such an audience present was humiliation enough. Keeping my eyes down in shame, I practically ran out of the store...

... and right into a solid brick wall of muscle.

Chapter 2

Freya

H oly freaking shit.

That's all I could remember thinking as I looked up—like, really, really *up*—at the massive man mountain I'd somehow collided with as I tried to leave the store.

He had the sexiest, greenest eyes I'd ever seen, framed by thick black lashes. There was already a hint of a heavy five o'clock shadow along his perfectly square, masculine jawline.

Holy hell, he was so mother-effing attractive.

His deeply tanned skin and thick mass of jet-black hair made such a startling contrast to the deep emerald hue of his eyes that it was impossible to look away.

But I mean, I actually wasn't able to look away from him. He quite literally swallowed me in his embrace so that everywhere I looked he was in my line of vision.

This man was freaking *massive*.

My palm didn't even cover a third of his pectoral muscle, which felt too solid to be real under my hands.

I felt like my neck was going to snap in half with how much I had to bend it in order to look up at him. I could feel the heat pouring out of him from where my hands still rested against his enormous chest from our collision. Before I could stop myself, I curled the tips of my fingernails into his pecs. I felt the power of his muscles stiffen and flex instantly at the light pressure. I wanted to purr in delight at their sheer strength.

In fact, I'm pretty sure one or both of my ovaries had just spontaneously ovulated in his presence.

Was there a legal limit of testosterone emission into the environment?

I have no idea how long I gawked up at him, probably drooling, blinking stupidly and trying to process how delicious he smelled.

What the fuck was wrong with me?! Had I really just plowed into a completely gorgeous stranger in a mother-effing sex store and then groped at his chest like a pervert?!

"...Umm, I—sorry! I wasn't watching where..."

I stumbled awkwardly over my words, feeling every inch of me flush even deeper scarlet. *Awesome, Freya.*

Hurriedly I tried to push against him and step away from his sex fumes, but the mountain didn't move an inch.

Clearly this man had completely unauthorized levels of testosterone. It was definitely not safe to be within a certain distance of him, and here I was trying to grope his pecs like they were metal silly-putty.

Shouldn't he be forced to wear a medical bracelet or something? Notify the neighborhood when he moved somewhere?

"Sorry I'm late, babe. Can't wait to see what you bought, though," when the deep masculine sound of his voice reached my ears, I knew that spontaneous ovulation was indeed possible.

His voice was rough, *deep,* and it washed over me in a rush of heat that immediately pooled in my lower abdomen. I would be lying if I didn't admit my hips may have involuntarily undulated toward him.

Wait, what?

Babe... me?

Holy freaking hell.

Shrill, evil snickering from behind me ripped me free from the sexual haze. He must have noticed it too, because his arms suddenly relaxed enough that I could take a few steps back as I refused to look anywhere but at the floor.

The floor was safe.

The way that the massive expanse of his shoulders was barely contained inside his cobalt-blue *Armani* jacket, the burning teal fire of his eyes along with the totally sexy, delicious way he smelled were definitely not safe, not at all.

The combination was making me dangerously light-headed.

I couldn't even trust my testosterone-soaked brain that he had actually spoken to me.

For all I knew the man could have told me I repulsed him and smelled of stale chicken farts, and I would have nodded my head at him dreamily, also not noticing the drool sliding its way onto my shoulder...

"... my god! I would literally *die* if that were me! How absolutely *mortifying.* She doesn't even realize!"

Devi's sneering words jerked my eyes up and away from the intricate black and white swirls on the floor.

"Pardon me, Miss, I think you dropped your... I mean, I think it's, ahem—is that yours?"

One of the other shoppers had turned to me, discreetly pointing to an area on the floor behind the Magnificent Man Mountain.

Horrified, I realized there was a faint buzzing sound I hadn't noticed before.

The Panty Dropper had apparently launched itself out of the shopping bag during our collision and sprouted to life right there on the polished black marble floor.

But of course—because apparently the entire universe was against me now, dammit—it wasn't only the tiny vibrator that had fallen out of my bag.

Oh, no. Not today, Satan.

The Panty Dropper had remained inserted into the tiny "v" of the black thong panties that matched the bustier, which were both completely transparent. Which meant that not only had the clit vibrator fell out of my bag, but also was inside a set of freaking see-through thong underwear, buzzing and flashing wildly in the middle of a sex store.

I literally could have died from the continual onslaught of humiliation. Desperately I tried to grab for my unruly unmentionables, but again I couldn't move.

I mean, I actually couldn't move. Not at all.

The gorgeous giant had somehow silently replaced his arm—holy hells bells, his *ginormous* and very muscular forearm—around my back.

He flexed more tightly around me when I tried to move toward the scene of the crime. The huge expanse of his hand dipped around to give my hip a little squeeze before he moved toward the tiny teardrop-shaped torture device behind him on the ground. The heat from his grip left a trail of fire across my side which instantly blazed down to pool warmly between my legs.

I gulped, my mouth suddenly completely parched as I stared at him, unmoving. I was mesmerized by the way his muscles so clearly flexed and bunched under his perfectly tailored suit as he moved. It was probably a good thing my mouth was so dry, because it spared me the embarrassment of drooling.

"Please, allow me," as soon as his words reached my ears again, I flushed all over as my ovaries launched another spontaneous egg like a black-ops fighter pilot.

Is this how twins and triplets happened?

His voice was rough, *deep,* and it washed over me in a rush of heat. I would be lying if I didn't admit my hips may have involuntarily undulated toward his direction.

Then I realized he hadn't spoken to me but was looking at someone behind me. My heart sank.

"Of course, sir. Sorry about that, I should have packaged it better! My mistake!"

Sally's voice had increased an entire octave and she had definitely more than crinkled the finish of her red lipstick with that beaming smile as she gazed at him from behind me.

Still trying to decide if I was horrified or turned on, I watched motionlessly as he leaned down to the crazily buzzing and flashing, vibrating panties. The contrast of the skimpy black lace in his darkly tanned, masculine hands had me burning up all over again.

It was a shame I wasn't wearing flameproof panties.

Never taking his hungry gaze off me, he clicked the vibrator off and placed it back into my shopping bag.

"See?! I told you! Literally flew out of her bag and she almost ran over this poor g—" Devi had her phone out in a video chat, snickering.

"There's absolutely no filming in our store, ma'am," Sally interrupted DevLynn coldly. "Please disconnect your video call immediately and leave," she crossed her arms over her chest authoritatively and nodded her head regally toward the store's exit. She looked downright scary.

Mr. Panty Dropper's grip tightened around my waist, and I almost lost consciousness when I realized he was smiling at me. Honestly, the way he was looking at me probably should have sent me running the other way. Like a starving man being served a thick Porterhouse steak, except from the point of view of the steak.

He looked like he wanted to devour me whole.

Everything about his intense gaze screamed super-arrogant-alpha-male-predator, and it called to everything *female* inside me. I could literally feel the heat pouring off him from just his arm at the small of my back.

Then, apparently trying to make me burst into spontaneous sex flames, he winked at me and turned toward my unwanted nemesis.

But before Devi hung up, Mr. Panty Dropper had started walking toward her, and he looked... livid?

Like, super-scary-arrogant-alpha-male type of livid.

She must have noticed it too because her perfectly plastic smile faltered just a little.

Suddenly he stopped, making an odd face.

"That perfume you're wearing, is it sold here?"

My heart sank and a surge of completely irrational jealousy shot through me.

Wow, was I a first-class idiot!

Of course he wasn't flirting with me. He was just trying to get to Devi, the perfect little poisoned plastic blond, and I literally threw myself at him... no, I threw myself *and* my clit-vibrating, see-through panties at him!

"My perfume?! Here?! Of course not, it's designer!"

She still hadn't hung up the phone. Bitch.

"Thank god for that," he turned away from her with dismissive disgust, and my heart did approximately four back flips when his green eyes landed directly on me. "I was worried you may have bought some, babe. But I see you have much better taste, sweetheart. You ready? The car is outside for us; better get a move on or we'll be late," Mr. Panty Dropper stalked toward me as he spoke, placing his massive palm once again on the small of my back as he ushered me out of the store.

Scary Authoritative Sally snickered playfully, loudly, at Devi's expense.

I knew I'd liked her.

"Uh... umm... oh—okay. Sure," I squeaked out weakly.

I couldn't process anything. I could only feel his hot hand on my back and breathe in the wonderful, spicy way he smelled as he guided us out of the store.

I couldn't even appreciate the look of shocked embarrassment on Devi's face as we walked out. Or the shriek of laughter coming from the video call she still hadn't disconnected. I was far too overwhelmed.

Mr. Panty Dropper wasn't flirting with Devi. He'd just told *her* that *she* smelled like stale chicken farts.

At least I think that's what he'd said.

It was pretty hard to concentrate when I watched his mouth move.

I was still trying to keep myself from giving in to the urge to see what the beard stubble along his perfectly square jawline would feel like against my tongue, my lips, my...

He must have felt my hungry gaze, because he gave me a savage smile as he propelled us through the bustling foot traffic of Friday afternoon in the Upper East Side.

And I let him, in a cloud of carnal confusion from the sexual spell he'd put me under.

I didn't even know his first name.

For all I knew, this man could indeed be planning to devour me just like a Porterhouse steak.

What in the holy freaking hell just happened?!

Chapter 3

Brodie

There was absolutely nothing in my thirty-five years that'd prepared me for the way it had felt to have her body thrown up against mine in the middle of that boutique, surrounded by sex.

Every one of the thick curves and contours of her gorgeous figure had been seared into me like a brand.

The scent of her was absolutely intoxicating. I had reached out to touch her, using the excuse of grabbing her arms to steady her after our collision. Quickly I'd pulled her in closer, wrapping my arm around her waist and down the small of her back. I really just wanted to keep her as close as possible so I could continue feasting on the way she smelled.

Clean, feminine, just a hint of something spicy and very, very sweet. It set my blood on fire.

At the time, I also needed her close to help conceal the massive erection currently trying to bust its way through the pant seams of my overpriced *Armani* suit. That shocked, high-pitched little gasp I'd heard when she'd first looked up at me had almost brought me to my knees right there in the store.

Mostly because at six-foot-five, I'd have to drop down to my knees in order to heist her slight form up on my shoulder, out of that sex store, and back to my hotel room where I planned on fucking her senseless.

Which is exactly where we were headed now.

Technically speaking that had been the plan all along—to intercept her and bring her back to the hotel room. Once I'd seen her in that camera feed, I knew I had to have her. But first she needed to be questioned as part of our operation.

Unfortunately for this beautiful woman on my arm, Freya Daniels, her fate had already been decided as soon as the QR code she'd used matched the metadata patterns we had been looking for. I'd already been watching her on the security feed from the minute she'd entered the store.

As smoking fucking hot as her body was—all curves, thick, mouthwatering thighs that led up to an ass that I couldn't wait to watch jiggle as I turned it pink and flushed from my hand, *fuck*—it was her hair that had first drawn me in.

Dark, dark reddish brown, she wore it tied back in a loose braid. It was so long that it dangled down her back, past the curve of her waist. In some of the camera feeds you could see how some of it had come undone around her face. It framed the high set of her cheekbones and kissed the subtle, feminine line of her jawbone.

Just looking at her damn hair through a security feed was enough to make my dick hard so fast that precum was already gathering at the throbbing, swollen tip.

Ffffuck.

As I continued to scan the feeds, I'd actively had to take a deep breath to cool my blood. I leaned back in my seat, pretending to take a break from reading boring emails or whatever the hell these corporate dickheads did for a living.

It was a damn good thing I'd been sitting down, fairly hidden in my corner of the busy café across from *Caress,* or I'd probably have been arrested.

Damn near in shock, I glanced back at the camera feeds hungrily, watching her.

I sent a silent prayer of thanks that I got to exist in a world where skin-tight black sex pants called leggings and yoga pants were a thing. She moved with the unmistakable grace of a dancer, which likely explained the toned thickness to her legs. Belatedly I

noticed the university lettering on her cropped sweatshirt signify-
ing that she was, indeed, a collegiate dancer.

I chuckled darkly at my own expense.

Nothing gets by you, huh soldier...

I'd already started packing up my things for the day as I
watched her through the feeds. I didn't give a shit that I'd been
planning to stay for at least another hour. There was no way, absolutely no way, that I was going to continue working after I'd seen
her. My dick had become so hard it was downright painful.

She'd be with me inside my hotel room within the hour
whether she liked it or not.

As I watched her approach the checkout counter, I held my
breath as she reached for her phone. Clearly visible through the
feed was a QR code.

If over three-fourths of my total blood volume weren't already
trapped within my dick, I'd probably have felt my heart race in anticipation.

When her code came up as a match, I was both elated and furious at the same time. As fucking gorgeous as she was, her beauty
and feminine charms wouldn't save her from the wrath of the Parisi
family if she were ultimately found implicated.

It was no wonder that little blond was such a bitch to her; the
girl whose arm I held like a vise as we walked down the sidewalk
was absolutely. Fucking. Perfection.

The little bitch's jealousy of a girl like Freya, who was such a
timeless, natural beauty, was obvious. It was annoying as hell, even
more annoying than her awful taste in perfume. She also looked
like she'd had more silicone put in her lips alone than my entire
damn computer parts warehouse back in Texas.

This woman in my possession, on the other hand, had likely
just got done working out and had little if any makeup on. She
looked fucking delicious. Radiant.

I'd never seen blue eyes in that shade, with such a faint hint of indigo and lavender around the edges of her irises. A light dusting of freckles was visible nearly all over her body—what little of it I could see, anyway. In spite of her freckles, there was a faint golden glow to her skin. The contrast between my darkly tanned, rough skin and the fair shade of her soft, smooth skin was surprisingly alluring.

Just a glance down her body as we took the short walk down the sidewalk and I needed to feel what it would be like to have those thick, fleshy legs wrapped around me while I plowed into her sweet heat.

Now, as I held her body under my control, I glanced down at her again as we walked toward my hotel. It was just a few minutes' walk from *Caress,* where my team and I had been running surveillance for the last few weeks.

I'd selected that hotel on purpose as it was within walking distance for the case. For the last few weeks, I'd been posing as another overly ambitious generic corporate douchebag in town on business.

And it had been all business, nothing but damn business, for the last several weeks. Which was obviously why I was panting after this woman like a buck in full rut—I just needed to get laid.

It'd been way too long; I hadn't had time for anything besides work since I'd taken this job on for my good friend and long-time business associate, Marco Parisi.

Yes, things were definitely getting *hard* with the busy work schedule, I thought as I glanced back down once again at the bewildered beauty in my arms.

I deliberately wet my lips as I looked down into her pretty, midnight blue bedroom eyes. They were framed by light brown, curly eyelashes that fluttered nervously under my gaze. I bit down on my lip as I ran my gaze boldly down the front of her V-neck shirt, thinking of what else I could lick and tease between my teeth.

She had amazing breasts. I could tell by their obvious bounce as we walked that they were soft, fleshy, and completely real.

A man wanted real tits that bounced and jiggled, dammit, not those fake overinflated balloon looking imposters.

I might have growled out loud thinking about what shade of pink her nipples were as we walked. I honestly don't remember, because I was so focused on not giving in to my urge to sink my dick into her right there in the middle of the street. When she let out another little surprised gasp, her eyes looking right at my mouth, I realized that we needed to get off the street and into a car before I lost control.

Now.

I didn't bother explaining myself. I stopped us abruptly and walked us over to a pickup spot along the busy street. I texted my driver where to meet us as I turned to her.

On second thought, I could start questions now, at least some of them. Everything else could wait until my pulsating dick gave me a chance to come up for air.

"Where did you get that coupon code from? It's very important that you don't lie to me, Freya Daniels."

I smiled wolfishly as I looked down at her, thinking about what I was going to do to her soon. She was so fucking pretty that I didn't know where to look on her face first.

"I need to go, sorry! I um... thanks for... I really didn't mean to see you. No! I mean, I—I really didn't mean to bump into you, I didn't see you," her voice came out as a nervous little squeak.

I couldn't wait to hear what kind of sounds she made when she lost control.

I could see her pulse racing in her neck. I wanted to run my tongue across it, followed by my teeth, and I growled low as my grip tightened around her. She tried to pull herself out of my grasp, but my hand tightened around her upper arm even more, keeping her exactly where I wanted her.

"Please answer the question, ma'am," I said, leaning in closer.

I inhaled her scent as I leaned down, my beard stubble brushing against the slope of her neck.

Her sharp inhale fueled the burning need I had to be inside of her. My cock was so hard it was about to launch itself from my body toward the sweet, hot juncture of her thighs, and I hadn't even fucking kissed her yet. My other hand came up to the side of her face, holding her still so I could drag my thumb across her lower lip.

Her eyes were dazed as they looked up at mine and then fixated back to my mouth. Her lips were swollen as the tip of her pink tongue slid across them, then darted against the pad of my thumb.

I lost it.

I didn't give a shit anymore that we were literally in the middle of the street on a busy Friday afternoon.

With a growl I claimed her mouth. Her taste, so fucking sweet and intoxicating, flooded over me as I sucked her bottom lip between my teeth. I then plundered into her mouth, sweeping past her teeth with my tongue.

I was so consumed by the kiss that I barely noticed when her foot stomped on mine. I pushed my tongue in deeper into her mouth in response, making sure she knew who was in charge now.

When the dull ache in my foot didn't pull me away from her, she kneed me in the stomach.

Damn, but I liked a woman with some fire in her belly. One that liked to get a little rough and dirty in the bedroom.

I immediately pulled away from the kiss as I coughed, trying to recover after she pretty fucking effectively knocked the wind out of me. I didn't want to think about why that turned me on so much, but it definitely fucking did. She was still trying to run away from me, dammit, but she didn't stand a chance as I still held her upper arm tightly as I recovered.

She wasn't going anywhere until I'd sunk my cock into her for at least several hours. I was just arrogant enough to know that she would enjoy every single thing I did to her.

The timing couldn't have been more perfect when my driver pulled into the pickup line and flagged me down. Still slightly bent over—partly because I was still coughing and partly because my dick was still hard as a damn rock—I signaled back to him. By the time he'd reached us, I'd finally stopped coughing and tucked the obstinate fucker back into my belt.

Smiling like a cat that cornered the canary, I walked toward her, grabbing her other arm easily when she tried to run.

"You're going to pay for that, baby. Now be a good girl, Freya, and get in the car."

Chapter 4

Freya

The amount of fear and lust that warred inside me with his words rendered me completely speechless.

If the two emotions could have been embodied, they would have likely appeared as a sleek, black feline cat on one shoulder, and a wrinkly, miserable Catholic nun on the other.

Get in the car this instant, Freya, you prude! Me-yow!

Sure, why not? And maybe he can just drop your body off at the nearest funeral home after he's done murdering you.

I shook my head absentmindedly. Now was not the time for my internal theater department. I was literally about to get murdered. Or fucked. Maybe both, hell, I didn't even know this guy's name!

Extremely delayed fear gripped me from the inside out as I realized he'd called *me* by my first *and* last name.

"What? I—"

"Get. In. The. Car. Now, Freya," he growled the words into my ear as he wrapped his massive paw higher up on my upper arm and dragged me into the back of the black SUV.

His driver shut the door behind us, and Mr. Panty Dropper locked me inside his arm harness while his driver effortlessly pulled into traffic.

I couldn't breathe. My chest refused to expand under the impossibly heavy weight of his embrace. I looked around frantically inside the car, realizing how heavily the windows were tinted. My heart rate plummeted, forgetting to beat at all, then it started again in double time.

"Shhhh, baby. Don't worry, no one can see you inside this car. My hotel is on the next block," he breathed the words into the juncture of my neck and shoulder.

I gasped; my neck was sometimes the most sensitive part of my entire body. The noise drew the attention of his driver's gaze in the rear-view mirror.

Without moving, he growled out, "Miles, screen. Now," the driver's eyes darted away as I watched a completely black panel lower itself from the roof of the car with a gentle humming sound, instantly shielding him from our view.

The dark rumble of his command against my sensitive skin made me shiver.

I was visibly shaking. My throat felt like it was closing in on itself, and despite the heat pouring off his body I felt cold all over.

There were no door handles in the backseat of this SUV. None.

"You smell so fucking good, baby. I can't wait to taste you all over," his other hand grabbed my braid and yanked my head back. I squealed, completely anchored to him as his teeth roughly grazed my neck.

I was so overwhelmed, I started panting. This was bad, this was so bad.

"Pp—please, wh—who are, why are you..." I could barely talk over my fear. It felt like an invisible cotton ball sat inside my entire mouth. "St—stop. Stop! I do—don't know you, I—I..." actual fear gripped me as I started to thrash in his embrace and stuttered over my words.

"Not yet, but we are going to fix that soon."

I didn't know human arms could feel that freaking rock-solid as his wrapped even more tightly around me.

"Why aren't locks?!"

He chuckled at me. It was terrifying. "Why aren't locks what?"

"Your—your car! There's no. None. I mean..."

"Boss, we're here. Where would you like me to drop off you and your guest?" His driver's voice was muffled coming through the privacy screen.

"I'm not a guest! He, umm—he... I don't actually know hi—"

His lips seared into mine, silencing me. A sweat broke out between my thighs when he bit my lip and sucked, hard.

"Careful, baby. You're already in trouble," he warned darkly.

And that was when I totally lost it.

Like a wild thing I twisted and jerked in his arms as the fear finally overruled the lust. The car was shaking as he forcibly restrained me. He must have known I was about to let out an ear-splitting scream because he wrapped one arm instantly around my mouth, while he placed his other hand...

Holy mother-effing hell.

Right between my legs.

Instantly I stopped moving, now trying to figure out if I was turned on or terrified. I think the line between the two had been erased from the minute he stuffed me into his car.

"Listen carefully, Freya. You've suddenly become very interesting to me, and you're not going anywhere until we've... gotten more acquainted," he rubbed his palm firmly against my core as he spoke.

I whimpered into the hot press of his hand over my mouth as tears formed in my eyes. My poor brain had given up. Maybe somewhere along the walk to his car, it had literally said "fuck this" and allowed the crazed demands of my female organs to determine my fate. Which is probably why, despite the tears now streaming down, I rolled my hips into his hand.

"Boss?" His driver's voice sounded again hesitantly from the front.

"Company entrance. Around the back."

His insidious green eyes bore into mine as he reached for my *Caress* shopping bag on the floor by his feet. He still wrapped one of his tree-trunk arms around my head and shoulders like a tightly coiled rope.

"I don't think I can trust that you'll be a good girl and not make a scene when we go inside. How about we make a deal?"

The spicy clean sandalwood musk of his cologne drifted around the backseat as he'd wrestled me down. My eyelids fluttered in response to the delicious scent as I took each shuddering inhale.

I shook my head from side to side, unable to think.

"If you behave and allow me to escort you up to my hotel room, quietly, you can answer all my questions, and I'll have Miles take you wherever you'd like to go afterward," as he spoke, the arm that wasn't snaked around me traced the deepest part of the V on my shirt.

The erratic rise and fall of my chest made his finger dip lower with each breath.

Slowly, he continued to pull the fabric down until it sat below the outlines of my sports bra. He continued touching me, teasing the very tops of my breasts exposed by my black bra. Heat exploded wherever he touched, making my nipples harden instantly.

He growled, the sound deliciously deep and rumbling within his warm, rock-hard chest. I felt the hot vibration warmly purring along my back, and I moaned. I could feel every hot, hard contour of his chest and shoulders as he held me.

"Pp—please, I don't understand! I don't even know you! Just stop, please!"

Even I didn't believe myself that I actually wanted him to stop.

"Shhh, baby... there's nothing to be afraid of as long as you co-operate," he ruthlessly reached for the front zipper closure to my bra.

I had literally just finished my workout a little over an hour ago. I was supposed to go shopping before I got sweaty, but I chickened out, and had walked straight from my last set of stretches and directly into the lingerie store, where I had been ambushed.

I tried desperately to twist out of his hold, but it was useless. I knew what would happen if that zipper came undone.

Newton's Law of Universal Gravitation wins again. Jerk.

The sound I made as the weight of my breasts bounded free of the high-impact sports bra wasn't quite a scream. But it also wasn't quite not a moan, either.

Growling, he used his massive man paws to grope the considerable bulk of one of my breasts. I was mortified at the completely unflattering position he had me in—I had *boobs*, dammit. They were big, heavy, and did *not* sit high on my chest.

I'd seen porn; I knew how boobs were "supposed" to look, and mine definitely didn't look like the cute, perky, perfectly rounded little orbs that all men craved.

I felt so exposed, so vulnerable to his ridiculously superior strength. I knew the way I continued to thrash around in his arms was also *not* doing anything but making my chest jiggle and bounce awkwardly. This was truly mortifying, but I was wild with savage fear and lust. It was surreal; I truly couldn't think, I could only feel.

He growled again as he pinched one nipple between his fingers, tugging on it gently. I whimpered again and I couldn't help but arch my back into his touch. The movement pressed the hot, rigid length of his massive erection into me, and I was absolutely not ready for the tidal wave of desire that swept through me and gathered between my legs. I had to squeeze my thighs together tightly for fear that he was going to make me come, right there in his lap with my boobs bouncing about wildly.

"Please, please..." I choked out raggedly.

I wanted him to stop, and I wanted him to do more, so much more. The hot press of his mouth on my neck sent a jolt of need through me, all the way down to my core. I realized if he put his palm over my pussy again, it would take all of three seconds for me to come probably harder than I ever had in my life. The feeling was terrifying. It was electrifying, and I rolled my hips into him at the thought.

"Boss?" We had stopped moving, I noted weakly as his driver's voice called out again.

"Answer me, Freya. What's it going to be: the easy way, or the hard way?"

His voice was thick with barely controlled energy. He had shifted me to sit with my back flush against his front. The sharp scrape of his teeth along my neck almost sent me into orbit.

I dangled across his massive frame limply while he used both hands to fondle and tease my breasts. I felt like a rubber band about to snap, hot and needy and tipping precariously into a state of complete panic.

Call it the aftereffects of all the shock, lack of blood flow to my brain due to high demand in certain other regions of my body, but I did the last thing I probably should have ever done in that moment.

"I think it's already pretty hard."

The minute the words left my mouth, I clapped my hand over it in abject horror. Why did I always pick the worst time for my idiotic sarcasm?! He really didn't seem like the laughing type of man. The look on his face was indescribable.

There was a muted chuckle from the front seat of the car.

Chapter 5

Brodie

As long as I lived, I would never forget the absolutely sexy fucking picture she made, with her glorious, ginormous tits bouncing inside my hands, dark burnt copper hair coming undone around her face, her head thrown back, eyes heavy with need.

This woman had fucking *tits*. I didn't even realize how well-endowed she was until I pulled the zipper down on that suffocation device she called a bra. They came gleefully bouncing out of lockup, begging to be touched and teased.

I immediately obliged, being such a gentleman.

The rosy shade of her nipples matched the dark pink swelling of her lower lip. Her nipples had pebbled instantly, stabbing into my palms as I toyed with them. It was sexy as fucking hell. I knew if I kept playing with her beautiful body like this, I would blow my load in my pants like a damn teenager.

Now, looking down at her wide-eyed, innocent face as she clapped her hand over her mouth to ineffectively contain the giggles that shook through her, I knew she was going to be more than a little bit of a handful... and I wasn't just talking about her mouth-watering breasts.

Suddenly unbalanced from the unsettling effect those giggles had on me, I barked out orders to Miles.

"Tell Jim and Bryan to open up the interrogation room," I snapped at him.

The dickhead had the nerve to keep laughing until he got inside.

I felt her body instantly stiffen; good, it was time she understood who was in charge. We didn't technically have an interrogation room at this location, which is probably why Miles was laughing like a drunken hyena. But she didn't need to know that, yet.

"Wait, what? Interrogation?! Okay, okay. Look, this is all a giant misunderstanding and it's gone way too far," she moved hurriedly to stuff her beautiful breasts back into their solitary confinement.

Women and their obsession with bras. Boobs should be free to bounce and jiggle at will, dammit. It was unconstitutional.

"Baby, you have no idea how *far* it's about to go."

More uncontrollable giggles.

"You can't just... okay, you can't just *say* stuff like that! I don't even know you. We don't even..."

At least she wasn't stuttering in fear anymore.

I took advantage of her distracted giggling as I remembered why I'd dug into her shopping bag earlier. Before she could react I'd shoved down the front of her black leggings, completely exposing her all the way down to the naked, dripping wet seam of her pussy lips.

Hot fucking damn, but she was absolutely gorgeous. Everywhere.

Her shocked, squeaky little gasp as she frantically tried to stop me from placing *The Panty Dropper* right over her soaking wet folds made me want to howl. I only needed one of my hands to imprison both of her wrists above her head. With my other hand, I ruthlessly held the vibe directly on her taught, swollen clit.

I hadn't turned it on yet. Using my thumb I pressed it against her clit and rubbed it around in circles. At the same time, I used my fingers to spread her response around the entrance to her pussy, teasing her.

"*Fuck*, baby. You're soaked. I bet if I turned this on you'd probably come after just a few seconds. Wanna find out?"

"What do you... what the hell! You can't just... do you have any idea how—"

Her words stopped abruptly as I clicked on the vibrator.

Her mouth formed the cutest little "o" shape as she threw her head back. It was so fucking hot watching her try to hide how close she was to coming. She was so instantly responsive; I could see everything she was thinking as it flashed across her face.

Her hips were rolling jerkily toward, away from, back toward, and then against the buzz of the vibrator. I could tell she was close, so fucking close, from the way her thighs were squeezed together and her hips were digging back into the seat, as if she could move away from my hand and the pulse of the vibrator on her sopping wet pussy.

Just when it looked like she was about to completely come apart in my hands, I clicked the vibrator off. Her body instantly sagged back against mine and she moaned, then started panting and pulling at her arms, clearly trying to remove the device.

"Don't. You. Dare." I breathed into her ear, keeping her arms tightly bound above her.

My dick was so hard it was aching. I could feel my balls clenching, heavy and swollen from being denied release for too long. Slowly I placed the panty vibe back into its place on her clit, then pulled her leggings back into place.

Her eyes bore into mine. Looking into the suddenly very stormy depths of her indigo blue eyes, I brought my other hand up to my mouth and sucked each finger clean.

Her mouth dropped open in the little "o" again as she watched me. She tasted so fucking good, so sweet.

"Listen closely, Freya. I'm going to take you inside now. I'm going to ask you some questions, and you're going to answer them. If I don't think you're telling the truth..." I glanced down to her pussy again, clicking on the vibrator.

She gasped as her hips bucked against the vibe, but her movements likely only increased the sensation and pushed her even closer to the edge.

"You... are... f—fucking ins—insane! Take this shit off me! Who the hell do you think—uhhhh... ohhhh! Holy hell, *ohhhh*—"

The clicking stopped abruptly just before she came apart, and her hips sagged back limply against me.

Tucking my dick back into my pants, I grabbed hold of her upper arm.

"I'm sorry, baby. I haven't introduced myself. Brodie Magnuson. It's a... pleasure... to meet you," I tapped on my watch to open the car door.

I roamed my eyes all over her body as I paused, so she'd know exactly what kind of pleasure I was implying.

"Your name is Brodie motherfucking Magnuson? As in, *Magnuson Security?*"

"Yes. Except the middle name. I'm not sure that's legal."

"So you're like some kind of millionaire then?"

I wasn't sure I liked her tone.

"More like billionaire. We are going inside. If I think you're going to do something silly, like run from me or make a scene, Freya, I think you know what the consequence will be."

"As soon as you open that freaking door, I'm going to yell for he—"

Her hips jerked again wildly as she squealed when I'd clicked it on mid-sentence.

I watched for a few seconds, mesmerized, and clicked it back off. I didn't feel like killing anyone at the moment and that's probably what I would have done if anyone else had seen or even heard her make those kinds of sounds from the open door of the car.

Those were meant for my ears only. I was still trying not to picture my fist going toward my driver Miles' mouth, and I'd been a groomsman in his wedding six years ago, as well as attended his twins' baptisms last summer.

"The only thing that you're going to be yelling is my name. Now behave. We're going inside."

"Who the hell do you think you are?! You can't just... just—"

"Pretty sure I can. And I told you my name. Let's go."

"NO! Are you freaking kidd—"

I clicked the button, cutting her off again.

She tried to pull herself back into the car, but I gripped her arm and pulled her toward me. She was so fascinating to watch, her lithe body jerking and twisting with pleasure.

"Ohhh my... no, please, I... ohh—uhhh..."

I clicked it off as soon as she was completely out of the car.

Glowering and nearly exploding with my need to fuck her, I led her into the company entrance in the back. As we walked, I reminded myself that this was still ultimately a job, and she could very well be part of the problem and not another target.

That only made me angrier. Either scenario was pretty fucked.

Honestly, it would be a little better if she were involved somehow. For one, we would be able to get some more information from her, potentially. For another, I'd rather deal with Marco Parisi than whatever sick son of a bitch was orchestrating this whole fucked up situation. Better the devil you knew.

As a potential target, well... those girls were all missing or dead, or presumed dead. Zero leads, absolutely zero. Only a handful of confused, broken, devastated families left behind, not believing the steady stream of bullshit from law enforcement about suicide or drug overdoses or secret, overly possessive boyfriends.

Finally, we reached the elevator. Once the doors were closed behind us, I immediately shoved her luscious body up against the corner, needing to taste her again like I needed to breathe.

All it took was one look at the stark terror on her face, and I stopped instantly.

Chapter 6

Freya

The change in him as we strolled through the nearly deserted hotel lobby made the hair on the back of my neck stand up. The reality of my situation bloomed darkly in the pit of my stomach with every pair of eyes that hurriedly darted away from us as we walked.

They all looked completely freaking terrified, and I knew it wasn't me that had put those looks on their faces.

I made the mistake of glancing up at him. I wondered what had caused the abrupt switch in his behavior. He looked capable of murder, a cold and emotionless executioner.

I honestly think I would have catapulted into full-blown hysterical panic if he had been wearing anything other than the swanky *Armani*. Somehow the ensemble made him seem slightly less deadly, as if a flashy designer suit could contain and dilute the atmosphere of danger surrounding him.

Armani on a man that large said something like *I play pro football.*

The all-black tactical uniforms with dark grey *Magnuson Security* emblem that some of the hotel staff were wearing said something like *I know three-hundred and twelve ways to kill you with my pinky finger.*

By the time we'd reached the elevators I could feel my legs cramping. His grip on me had tightened so much I probably would have fallen over otherwise, my muscles giving in to the effects of terror and shock. Cold fear washed over me as the words "interrogation room interrogation room interrogation room" kept running through my head.

The teeny tiny little flame of desire still secretly burning within me kept insisting that a man this devastatingly handsome couldn't be that bad, right?

As the elevator doors snapped shut, leaving me completely alone with him, I didn't have enough control of my body to scream. When he lifted me completely off the floor and up against the corner of the elevator, that teeny little flame was put out completely by a tidal wave of scary adrenaline.

I didn't give a shit who watched me do what now, I just wanted someone, anyone else around that would save me from the ferocity that was this enormous man.

I couldn't breathe when he lifted my legs up and out, shifting one of his legs a little to prop open my thighs. I was trembling, and not from desire. He grabbed my face with his other hand and all I could do was wait for the terrifying crush of his mouth on mine.

Suddenly he stopped, moving back from me just a little. He still held me in the same position, my legs spread and held up on one of his oak tree legs. His expression was still scary as hell, but it didn't prevent me from breathing, at least.

How the hell was it possible for him to be so freaking scary and devastatingly attractive at the same time?!

"Freya, baby... breathe. I'm going to make sure you enjoy everything we do, as long as you're a good girl," his palm brushed along the side of my face and down to my neck in slow, hypnotizing strokes.

"I don't know why I'm here. I don't know you. I—I—I just want to leave!"

"Shhh.... and you will eventually, I promise, but we need to talk first, hmmm?"

His hand was doing mysterious things to my brain as it stroked up and down along the side of my face and neckline.

"I don't understand, I don't understand any of this. I'm leaving now, I don't want to go anywhere else with you!"

By the time I'd finished my voice was shrill with stark fear.

The ding of the elevator tore me out of my trance. When the doors opened, I expected some kind of dark, black, metallic themed room with all kinds of horrible devices reminiscent of the Spanish Inquisition. I was definitely not expecting to see the over-the-top uber-luxurious penthouse suite that they'd opened up into.

High ceilings showcased a breathtaking view of the city through the floor to ceiling glass doors. The room was open, airy, inviting. It looked massive, likely taking up the whole floor.

This was an interrogation room?

The doors hadn't even opened up all the way when he yanked me out of the elevator with him. Suddenly the welcoming space seemed much less welcoming as he marched me through the sitting area and toward one of the bedrooms.

We passed by a room in the hallway, and I almost fell over in fear.

Every single cubic centimeter of the room was stuffed with weapons. Handguns, rifles, machine guns, bullets the size of my freaking forearm. Black metal and dark gold glittered ominously as we walked by, and the last thing I remember was opening my mouth to scream, as everything went black.

• • • •

WHEN I CAME TO, I REALIZED I was in a bed. A wave of nausea rolled over me and I tried to run to the bathroom, only I realized this wasn't my bed, or my bedroom, or my anything. Then everything came back in a terrifying rush as I started mildly hyperventilating.

He was sitting on the edge of the bed, and he suddenly moved toward me. He grabbed one of my hands as he kneeled down next to me. I froze at the contact and tried to quell the rising nausea.

"Whoa, whoa... easy now, baby. You fainted. You need to eat something, and drink something too. Food will be here in a few minutes."

He glanced down at his watch like we were talking about the weather, not about how I had just freaking fainted out of pure terror because he ambushed me then mind-fucked me within an inch of my life!

I looked down to where he held one of my hands inside his massive bear paws so gently. It was beguiling given the carnal ferocity he'd attacked me with earlier.

"Bathroom!" I choked out weakly as I placed my other hand over my mouth.

"I'll take you. You're not walking."

I was already in his arms by the time he finished talking.

His massive form took us across the bedroom to the master bathroom in about three steps.

He set me down by the toilet and lifted the lid, then ran back toward the bed. I'd never seen a human move so fast in my life. When he returned with a pillow, he immediately placed it under my legs by the toilet, then squatted down next to me and tried to grab for my hair.

I flinched away from him; there was zero chance I was going to get sick in front of this gorgeous Greek god statue come to life!

"I need to... get sick, please! Uggh! Not with you here! *Leave!*"

"No. I'm staying. You might faint again."

"Get out!"

I frantically tried to shove at him but it was useless. Apparently, this was freaking happening.

He literally held my hair while I got sick. I could have actually died from the shame and degradation I'd felt in that moment. For all I knew, I could have actually died and not realized it earlier that day, because I'm pretty freaking sure this is exactly what hell would be like.

Once I felt better, I leaned away from him weakly. He let me as he stood up to get a washcloth from the linen closet. He placed the warm, wet cloth over the back of my neck, gently moving my hair aside. He left the room again, returning with a small bottle of water.

"Here, baby. Rinse your mouth out. Feel a little better?"

Defeated, I didn't look at him as I accepted his generosity and weakly nodded my head yes. At least he was a thoughtful millionaire arrogant scary kidnapper.

Excuse me, thoughtful *billionaire* arrogant scary kidnapper.

Jackass.

This was one thousand percent all his fault, dammit.

"Thanks," I croaked out weakly.

I really did feel quite a bit better. The wave of nausea hit me out of nowhere; I'd never gotten actually sick from anything like that in my life. But thankfully it seemed to be gone just as quickly. My brain was still spinning as a completely unfiltered thought ran through my mind.

Holy freaking shit balls, Batman.

My eyes snapped up to him suspiciously.

That's how I'd always heard women describe the morning sickness of pregnancy.

Was he some sort of superhuman, top-secret scary government experiment? A larger than life, emotionless killing machine, capable of instantly impregnating unsuspecting, innocent females with simply a glance?! A way to ensure that our government had an endless supply of superhuman man mountains such as himself?

His vivid green eyes... maybe they were superhuman testosterone-shooting laser beams.

I looked him up and down again and took another drink of the water. I had absolutely no clue how or why I was here right now. The cool water sliding down my throat was the only thing that felt real in this entire freaking scenario.

Honestly, I kind of wanted to black out again.

That seemed safer than trying to wrap my brain around what the actual *fuck* of a shitshow I had gotten myself into this time.

Straight from the frying pan and right into the fire, as my Nana would have told me.

"Aftereffects of shock. During my first tour in Iraq, I'd have to blow a few chunks every once in a while after a firefight. It's like your nervous system hits the brakes too hard, then starts up again. Usually passes after a few minutes. Or hours. It's best to get fluids and your blood sugar back up as soon as possible."

I'd noticed he hadn't stood back up after he'd handed me the water. I think he finally realized he was scaring the mother-effing shit out of me with his size, the overgrown ogre.

"You're a veteran?" I asked him quietly, still too embarrassed to look him full on.

"Yes. Marines. Special Forces. I think the food is here. Stay put."

He gently grasped my chin in a teasing gesture as he bossed me around. He was definitely the alpha-male-super-arrogant-I-always-get-my-way type of man.

It also really pissed me off how much his take charge attitude turned me on. Like, a lot.

It was definitely the testosterone emissions. I really couldn't be held responsible for my thoughts or actions around these fumes.

Less than a minute later he returned to the bathroom, holding a small toiletry kit in his hand containing—thankfully, uggh! —a toothbrush and toothpaste. He set it on the bathroom counter, then propped down on his haunches to get closer to my eye level.

On second thought, seeing the massive size of his tree trunk thighs so up close was possibly more terrifying than him towering over me.

"Freya, let me help you up. There's a toothbrush for you."

"No, I'm fine! No. You don't need to touch me."

"I definitely need to touch you, honey. Brush your teeth first so we can eat."

"Are you always this bossy?"

"Probably. Brush, or I'll do it for you."

"You're a jerk, and I'll brush my teeth myself, thank you!"

I snatched the toothbrush off the sink in a fit. At least I said thank you, dammit.

He moved toward me and I squeaked as I pushed myself back up against the bathroom counter in a feeble attempt to escape him. I'd never been so happy to hear the sound of a ringtone in my life, and thankfully his phone call snapped him out of caveman mode as he turned away from me to answer it.

I'd felt a twinge of disappointment, but there was no way in hell I would ever admit it.

I brushed my teeth, watching him watch me through our reflections in the mirror. His tone was short, clipped, all business as he spoke.

"Yes. With me. Not yet. Confirmed match, correct. Nothing so far."

There was a long pause in the conversation as I finished with my teeth, bending over just a little to rinse the toothpaste out of my mouth. I refused to think too much on how it was almost cute that he'd thought to send for a toothbrush. And apparently food.

I rinsed away the last bit of toothpaste. I felt almost back to normal.

When I stood up and glanced back in the mirror at our reflections, I almost passed out again from the purely predatorial look in his eyes. He'd been ogling my ass when I'd bent over the sink and didn't even bother hiding the fact that he was definitely caught when he looked back up at my eyes.

Instead, he smiled even wider when he'd met my shocked gaze in the mirror.

He kept replying in that short, clipped tone while he stared at me. I couldn't look away.

His brilliant green eyes roamed brazenly over my breasts, down my back and again on my ass. He sucked on his teeth again and bit his lower lip, stroking the thick ridge of his erection clearly outlined against his thigh as he continued his phone conversation. His flat, emotionless tone was at complete odds with the raw sexual intent burning in his eyes as his enormous hand moved over his...

Holy freaking shit!

There's no way that was his real dick. No way.

That was a miniature ball-bat that he carried around in a very suspicious location. He was a private security company CEO, right? That was a perfectly likely explanation given his career choice. Right?!

"I need to get back to work. I'll forward you the results when I have them," without taking his eyes off my face or his hand off his ball-bat slash definitely not his real dick, he disconnected the phone.

He took several steps back and tossed it on the table next to him in the bedroom, never taking his eyes off me. I felt like my abdominal organs were on the spin cycle of a washing machine.

He grabbed me again by the forearm and marched me over to where he'd set the food. There were five different trays with all different types of food, and one of all beverages. Juices and sodas, a few bottled waters, even lemon and lime wedges.

"Here, sit on the bed. Eat and drink something," he held out one of the plates of food to me.

"I don't think I can eat right now."

"Do it anyway."

"No! What gives you the right—"

"Fine. We talk first. What were you doing in that store and how did you get that QR code?"

"What? That's none of your freaking business! You're the one who ambushed me and forced me into your creepy SUV and then... well, you know what you did!" I finished in a huff.

He stared down at me, crossing his python arms over his chest. He'd removed the suit jacket and his lightweight dress shirt was practically screaming under the strain of his forearms. I'm pretty sure I heard a faint, high-pitched little sound of distress from the seams of the fine silk.

On second thought, it could have been me that made that sound.

I blamed the testosterone fumes and tried to hold on to my indignation because it was absolutely safer than the other feelings he stirred inside me, mostly at the juncture of my thighs.

Holy hell, the vibrator!

Why the hell hadn't I removed it in the bathroom when he'd left me alone to brush my teeth?! I was an idiot!

In a panic I grabbed for the waistline of my pants to remove it. Honestly, I'd been so scared earlier that I'd completely forgotten it was still there. And then the whole passing-out thing had been more than a little distracting. Foolishly I hoped it had slid down to a more tolerable location inside my leggings, or even that he'd removed it.

Then I remembered how much the universe apparently hated me, and that I wasn't entirely sure this wasn't just some twisted form of hell.

He beat me to it easily, snatching away my hands inside his own dinner plate sized mitts as he made quiet little *tsk, tsk, tsk* sounds at my attempt. Eventually he subdued me with one hand again, dammit. Now he was just bragging. His other hand reached into his pants pocket and...

Click.

"Ohhhh... no, please! Holy hell, I—no, *pppleeeassse*, I can't—"

I'd never been so instantly ready to come in my entire life.

Intense pleasure shot through me and centered around my pulsing clit. I fell back toward the pillows, desperately trying to prevent what I knew was about to happen.

"Fuck yes, Freya. You like that, don't you?! Damn, but you're beautiful like that, baby. I was really hoping you'd choose the hard way," he continued to stroke the appalling length of his erection through his pantleg as he watched me hungrily.

I had to snap my eyes shut because if I kept watching him, I was going to launch into a very powerful and very mortifying orgasm at any second.

"Look at me, Freya," he commanded darkly.

My eyes fluttered open instantly at the authority in his voice. He clicked the remote again, and my hips shot completely off the bed in reaction to the much higher intensity.

"Oh my, I—please, I can't—please! Pp—*uhhhhh*—please! Stop! I can't... please!"

I was literally starting to sweat from the strain of holding back my orgasm.

"That's it baby, hell, yeah. Come for me. Show me how much you like how that feels on your naughty little pussy."

His rough, dirty words sent me into the hardest, most intense orgasm I'd ever had in my life.

My pleas had turned into high-pitched moans and whimpers as my body shook from the sheer force of the pleasure. I jerked and twisted obscenely as I tried to move toward and away from the delicious intensity. When I realized he held my arms so tightly that I actually couldn't move, the sheer bliss between my thighs only intensified.

Wave after wave of pleasure flooded through me as I arched my head back into the pillows and gave in helplessly to his complete power over me. It lasted for an eternity when finally, he took mercy on me and clicked it off. My body instantly sagged in relief.

I lay there on the bed in a complete daze, a surreal sense of satisfaction floating through me. I closed my eyes and tried to stop my panting.

Reality returned abruptly when I felt my hair being yanked back toward the end of the bed. My eyes flew open at once.

Brodie was standing over me on the edge of the bed. The trays of food had been moved to the table alongside his phone.

He was also completely naked, stroking the length of his thickly swollen cock.

Holy. Freaking. *Shit.*

Honestly, I think I would have preferred the ball-bat.

It was probably less intimidating than the swollen, angry-looking firehose he was pumping his hand up and down as his carnal gaze devoured me whole.

A small drop of moisture beaded from the engorged tip. Using his fingers, he spread it around the head of his cock before stroking the entire length again.

I licked my lips before I could stop myself. He growled, the sound low and deep. Primal.

"Open your mouth, baby. You're going to suck on my cock while I play with you some more."

Chapter 7

Brodie

Seeing her orgasm rip through her almost made me blow my load right then and there. She was so damn beautiful, every single curvy inch of her. My dick was protesting almost painfully that it was being forced to watch those hips rolling and convulsing from her sexy release, without actually getting to feel the walls of her hot, wet pussy squeezing and pulsing with every moan.

I couldn't stop touching her. I needed to come so badly I was barely able to get the hell out of that monkey suit—I'd always preferred denim to designers, dammit—and get my cock inside her pretty little mouth.

I wanted to fuck her. I was crazy with it, but once I remembered her actual fear in the elevator, I knew there was no way she'd enjoy it. Not today. She'd need a day or two to become more settled around me before we could have sex.

I liked it rough and acting on my urges would only scare her more.

A little bit of trembly female fear in the bedroom was a huge turn on, but there was a definite line I never crossed.

I could always tell when a "no, please, stop!" really meant "please, *don't* stop!" from the women I'd bedded. The latter made my dick rock hard; the former absolutely did not.

Most of them would never admit it, but I suspected women liked to be controlled, dominated, and overpowered by their men a lot more than they liked to let on. It wasn't surprising their shyness given how easy it was for women versus men to be labeled as promiscuous.

Honestly, it was a bunch of damn bullshit. Mostly because it meant I'd had to work that much harder with some of my previous women to overcome this meek, timid, virginal crap.

It was maddening to be able to detect the strength of a woman's desire, only to hear her deny what she felt time and again. A woman should feel safe enough with her man to let loose and get wild in the bedroom, or that man didn't deserve to bed her at all. Call me an arrogant asshole, but it was how I felt.

I could tell my Freya wasn't entirely unaffected by this bullshit mindset, but I also knew I'd inevitably banish it from her thoughts. I would enjoy every single second of coaxing her out of that suffocating shell.

Back in the store, I'd seen how her eyelids had fluttered when she felt my muscles flex in response to her sexy pawing.

The lioness testing the strength of her mate.

It was sexy as fuck.

There was nothing hotter than watching a woman become aroused, especially when she wasn't shy about it.

And now that I'd forced out some of the tension from her body, she would be more pliable. More accepting of my dominant nature in the bedroom.

The silky, dark strands of her hair felt like heaven wrapped around my fist. Using my other hand, I guided the tip of my aching cock into her sweet mouth. I expected her to hesitate, but my sexy little lioness opened her mouth as she swirled the tip of her tongue around the widest part of my shaft. I saw fucking stars, it felt so damn good.

"*Fuck,* yes baby. That feels so fucking amazing," I watched the perfect image of her lips and tongue as they drove me crazy.

"You like sucking my cock, baby? Tell me you like it, baby," I let go of her hair before I got too excited and pulled too hard.

I felt the faintest little buzz on my dick as she whimpered in protest.

"Look at me, Freya. I want to watch you suck that dick. Damn, but you're so pretty with my cock in your mouth," her eyes opened and shyly looked up at me.

Her jaw was totally extended, cheeks sucked in from accommodating my thick girth, and her indigo eyes were watering slightly from the position with her head leaning back just a little over the edge of the bed.

I'd never seen anything more fucking beautiful.

I tore at the V-neck she wore, easily ripping it in half. Next I threw down the zipper to her bra. I practically howled again as I watched her gorgeous tits bounce free of their prison. Her nipples were dark pink from her arousal. They were so hard and swollen, begging to be tugged, teased, and sucked. I lowered my mouth to one, using my forearm to snake under her torso and arch her up so I could feast.

I couldn't get enough of her breasts. They were so fucking perfect. They more than filled my large hand, and despite their weight were still so soft and fleshy.

Especially in this position, they bounced and jiggled enticingly. I loved the color and shape of her nipples, couldn't stop thinking about putting them in my mouth. They were such a pretty pale pink, but once she was aroused they turned a dark, rosy shade of pink.

I moved my cock out of her mouth to give me better access to her breasts. I pinched and pulled and sucked on her nipples, enjoying the hypnotizing way it made her breasts jiggle. The distressed little whimpering sounds she made were making my blood boil with need. She couldn't stop rolling her hips, still trying to keep her thighs tightly closed.

It wasn't very long before the demands of her needy little pussy won over and she let her legs fall to the side, leaving her center open and exposed.

I continued pinching and sucking on her breasts as long as I could without losing it. My balls throbbed, needing release badly. Her needy feminine moans and whimpers were making sweat pool on my brow. I smiled darkly; continuing to play with her beautiful tits as I wondered if she could orgasm from nipple stimulation alone.

Fuck me, but that thought had me almost doubled over from the already pounding ache in my balls.

I leaned back up and shifted to place her mouth on my cock once again. She took it greedily, her deep blue eyes heavy lidded from her desire. With her hot, wet mouth wrapped around me and her tongue sweeping back and forth, around, and around across the very tip of my pulsating shaft, I was instantly seconds away from coming.

I moved faster than I had in my life, lifting her back a little on the bed so she could turn her head to the side while she sucked me off. My need to come was so savage, I didn't want her to be upside down with my cock in her mouth. I knew I only had a few seconds before the beast inside me took over.

"Hell yeah, baby. Swallow all of my cum. I wanna watch you take it all down that pretty fucking throat, baby."

She moaned around my cock thrusting into her mouth. I lost all control I had when she greedily sucked on me even stronger and took me deeper down her throat. My orgasm tore up from the base of my spine, erupting in white-hot spurts of pleasure throughout the throbbing length of my dick.

I threw my head back, growling in pure sexual satisfaction as I felt the sweet contractions of her throat muscles as she obediently swallowed. My balls pulsed and contracted over and over again from what felt like the most intense orgasm I'd had in a very long time. Maybe ever.

Her hands came up hesitantly to grab one of my balls, and I almost fell over in the twisted pleasure as she continued to suck and lick at the tip of my sensitive shaft while she gently cupped me.

Without warning, a second orgasm tore through me as her hand tightened around my balls.

The sexy little purr I could feel against the tip of my dick was one of the hottest things I'd ever experienced in my life. I was actually lightheaded as most of my blood had apparently permanently moved to my groin.

Once my dick had stopped twitching like a crackhead and my heart stopped racing, I walked over to the trays of food. I grabbed several of them and set them again on the bed. From the corner of my eye, I saw her quick glance down at my still semi-hard dick, lick her lips, then glance away guiltily as soon as she met my gaze.

It was fucking adorable, and my cock twitched again like a crackhead.

"Now, it's time to eat," I told her, sitting down on the bed next to her.

She quickly moved away from me and toward the trays on the other side of the oversized mattress, then obediently reached for one of the fruit, yogurt, and granola parfaits I'd ordered for her. I had absolutely no idea what she liked to eat, so I'd gotten a little of everything.

Unable to resist, I gently took the glass parfait cup out of her hand, setting it on the nightstand next to her. Confused, she looked up at me questioningly.

"I said, it's time to eat. Take off your pants, Freya."

Chapter 8

Freya

"What?! NO! No, we can't. We can't do... we can't do that. Not before I rinse—I mean, not at all, that's what I meant," reality was returning to me in waves after the potent sexual haze started to lift.

I couldn't believe what I had actually done only a few moments ago.

I felt myself flush all over again, the last wisps of my crazy desire fading away with the shame. Quickly I dug into my leggings and took out the evil, buzzing, teardrop-shaped mini-vibe. I shoved it into the pillowcase closest to me and shoved that under me, guarding it with my life.

Deep, heavy, rumbling laughter filled the room as I looked at him like he'd lost his mind.

"It's not funny! We really need to stop. I need to stop, oh my god... I... I need to leave, now! Please," my words did nothing to stop him from laughing.

His ginormous chest shook with each chuckle.

"You are so fucking adorable, you know that?"

He brushed his knuckles ever so lightly against my face as he said it. I was speechless for approximately the eight-millionth time in the last forty-five minutes since we'd met.

"Umm, thanks. I guess. Look, seriously, I really need to go. I'm sorry I uh, let things go a little too far. I wasn't thinking."

"Stop. Talking."

Great, he was back to being Mr. Bossy Pants again. Although, Mr. Bossy Pants wasn't quite as terrifying as Mr. Panty Dropper, to be totally honest.

"I really do need to leave. I have plans. I'm going to be so late," why hadn't I said this before? Nice, Freya. "My friend, Kim, she's expecting me any minute. She's going to be worried sick. And her father is... he's a bid geal. I mean—a big deal."

Like for real, could I not speak English anymore? I was tripping over every other word around this man.

What were the long-term side effects of a testosterone toxicity in the brain?

Was it permanent? Treatable?

The corners of his mouth twitched just a little. He had stopped laughing, thankfully. Each one of those deep, rumbling chuckles were felt right between my still *very* wet thighs.

Hot damn, but he was so. Freaking. *Sexy.*

He had multiple, intricate tattoos spread over his arms and chest, as well as along his back. There was a fair amount of them, but not quite a sleeve. I hadn't realized I was blatantly staring at all the images on his gloriously chiseled body until I heard him clear his throat.

My eyes snapped back up and I blushed. Again. Dammit.

"You're going to eat something—" he chuckled again at the somewhat weary expression on my face, then continued, "and then you're going to drink some of the fruit juice to get a shot of glucose. You can pick which kind of juice," he was back to the bossy business tone again.

"Well, I *was* trying to eat something and *you* took it away from me..." I reminded him pointedly.

The corners of his eyes crinkled a little, then he chuckled and returned my parfait back to me.

I was actually really freaking hungry, dammit.

A girl worked up a big appetite by working out, being publicly humiliated, and then ambushed, and then humiliated again in the same sex store, then abducted and...

Quickly I stuffed a huge bite of yogurt, fruit, and granola into my mouth. I needed the distraction to draw my mind away from all the things we'd done.

My eyes were trying to look everywhere but at his body, which was still completely naked. Like seriously, what was it with guys and nudity?

"Like what you see, baby?"

I started coughing as the bite I just ate took a wrong turn directly into my trachea instead of my esophagus.

"Whoa, whoa! Slow down. I thought you said you weren't hungry," he commented cheekily, moving to sit beside me.

There was a little twinkle in his eye that did a lot of flippity-floppity things to my insides.

"NO! Don't come any closer until you have that *thing* back under lockdown! I mean seriously; did you realize you're still completely nude?!"

I backed up against my pillow fortress which guarded the tiny, vibrating teardrop of terror, my parfait spoon drawn toward him like a tiny round sword.

"This thing making you nervous, hmmm?"

His voice dropped several octaves as he started stroking the quickly growing mass of his shaft, his green eyes burning a hole into me.

"Oh, my god, you... I mean, you can't just. Ahem. That's really not, umm..." I was furiously trying to erase the feeling of that smooth, firm ridge of his erection dragging across my mouth, my lips...

The fumes had consumed my brain. I was doomed, absolutely doomed.

Who did you even call for help in this situation?

The Testosterone Emissions and Regulations Force? *Who you gonna call?! Ball-Busters!* maybe?

It didn't even help looking away from the erotic picture he made with his darkly tanned, muscular, masculine-looking hand wrapped tightly around his almost completely hard cock.

No, looking away from the raw sexuality didn't help at all.

Mostly because I could still hear his deep, sexy, booming chuckle with my eyes closed. If anything, closing my eyes might have been worse. Dammit. I chose to focus on my parfait instead. It was actually really effing good.

Rich people were assholes, but they usually had awesome food.

"Damn, I could watch you use that spoon all day. Reminds me of how you put that pretty little mouth on my co—"

"OH. MY GOD. *STOP!*"

Setting the almost completely gone parfait on the nightstand, I threw my face into the pillow and wrapped it around me, hiding my eyes and ears.

It didn't even come close to muffling his barks of laughter. After several seconds of pure sensual torture, his chuckling faded slightly as he had apparently gone into the other room. I refused to look up from my pillow blinders. If I had to watch that *thing* swinging between his thighs when he walked... or the way his enormous muscles bunched and flexed with every movement...

"It's safe now, my sexy little ostrich."

"I don't believe you," my voice was muffled from the pillow.

More masculine chuckling. Why was that so sexy, dammit!

"Okay, Freya. Playtime is over. Time for your interrogation."

The pillow came down at once. I felt a little surge of self-righteous indignation as I scowled at his smirking, handsomely masculine face. At least he'd covered up the lower half of his body with a pair of dark grey sweats. I refused to notice how sexy they looked on him, hanging low on his very wide but also somehow very lean hips.

Dammit. I mentally shook my head. Wait, what had he just—holy hell!

"You aren't interrogating shit! I want to leave, now. Or... or I'm going to call the cops!"

I dug into my small cross-body purse for my phone. It had been placed on the nightstand, easily within my reach. Given the whole he kind of definitely kidnapped me thing, that seemed more than a little odd.

It didn't seem like something someone would do to a captive, unless...

Of course. No signal.

"Cell-phone jammer."

"The fumes!" I said, at the exact same time he spoke.

"Fumes? Care to elaborate?"

"Nope, not even a little bit."

"Do it anyway."

"Look, Mr. Magnuson—"

"Brodie. My cock's been down your throat; I think we're past surnames. What 'fumes?'"

"Oh, my god, stop saying shit like that! Fine! Brodie! This needs to stop. This was such a mistake, I'm—look I'm already humiliated enough as it is, and I just need to leave, alright?!"

Even I thought I sounded a little hysterical.

"Freya. What. Fumes? You realize I own a security company, right? What kind of 'fumes' would you know of that can interfere with communication devices?"

His demeanor went from playful to predatorial in an instant, and I shrieked back further into the pillows in alarm.

I mean seriously, did he not realize how scary he was already just from being that massive?! Was it completely necessary for him to also growl and glower like a caged lion?!

"Nothing! I'm still in shock is all! Stop stalking toward me like a grizzly bear!"

He lunged for the bed, grabbing me by the ankle. He yanked me toward him, growling. I squealed as he easily subdued me and ran his enormous, hard, *hot* hand all the way up, up, up, past the sensitive skin on my inner thighs, and still higher, toward...

Oh, my god.

It was the fear masking as adrenaline that kept making me respond so strongly. My body didn't know the difference between "scared due to presence of imminent danger" and "hot and horny as hell; take me now and make it hurt a little" anymore, apparently.

So, that was pretty embarrassing, I guess.

His hand moved higher while his eyes never left mine. My breath caught and my throat tightened. Despite my lukewarm fear, I couldn't look away from his raw, masculine beauty. The man was so freaking attractive that it wasn't effing fair.

I wasn't ready for the wave of lust that hit me when he pressed his thumb right over my still highly sensitive and occasionally still pulsating clit. My sharp inhale only brought me closer as I jerked my hips toward him.

Growling, he roughly bit down on the sensitive inner flesh of my thigh. I moaned, and as soon as the sound left my mouth, I knew it'd embarrass me later. But now, I didn't give a damn. I moaned again even louder, needier.

"Freya, What. Fumes."

"Wh—uhh... wh—what? Fumes?"

"Your phone. You said 'the fumes' stopped it from functioning. Talk, or I will make you talk, baby," his slow, deep, rumbly words seared the inside of my thighs with fire.

I couldn't think, all I felt was fire, and need, and him.

"What—fumes? I—well... umm. I just, umm, that is..." yup, complete brain malfunction.

I was warm taffy melting under the heat of his touch. And the scent of his cologne. Or soap. Whatever it was, it smelled like pure heaven and sin combined into one seductive, dark cloud of lust.

"Freya. Talk. Now."

He increased the intensity of pressure on the very top of my pussy. My clit was throbbing, pulsing, so needy. I had never been so close to coming, without actually having an orgasm, in my life. It was pure, blissful, agonizing torture. I wanted him to stop, and I wanted him to do it even harder until I shattered again and again in his hands.

Then, abruptly, the pressure stopped.

I whined, rolling my hips into the very hot, hard palm still placed lightly over my throbbing mound. I felt the pulse beating wildly in my neck as I panted, trying to put out the fire that was still soaring through me, but never quite peaked.

My tongue darted out across my sensitive lower lip. I whimpered as I gently bit down, arching again into his touch like a wanton.

"Freya. Fumes. Talk."

With his gruff, clipped words he started up again on my pussy, and I moaned. He'd instantly ignited me right back up to fever pitch.

"Oh, my god, Brodie. Please... I—mmmm..." I was so close, so close to absolute and utter bliss.

He stopped again abruptly, and I actually slapped roughly at his hands in frustration as I moaned. I was practically frantic with how close I was to coming.

"Freya. If you don't tell me what you were talking about in the next fifteen seconds, do you know what I'm going to do?"

I panted harder. Terrified. Turned on. A little pissed off, too, if I were being honest. I definitely couldn't speak.

"You're going to be completely naked, strapped to this very bed, your legs spread wide, and then... I'll do a cavity search to make sure you aren't hiding anything, anywhere."

"It's your... fu—uhhh. Oh, *fuck*, fu—cking testosterone... fuuu-uuuuuum—mmmes, *ohhhh!*"

I wailed in delicious agony as I came again in his arms, convulsing so hard my torso bended back and shot off the bed entirely. At the very height of my orgasm, he increased the pressure on my pussy and made me come even harder.

He held me roughly, growling and biting softly into my thigh. I almost passed out from the tidal wave of pleasure his touch created between my legs. I didn't exactly scream, but I didn't exactly not scream, either. Again.

Afterward, the sound of his uncontrollable, booming laughter shook me out of my sex coma. Again.

"Stop. Laughing. You. Jackass!"

Chapter 9

Brodie

I couldn't believe what had just happened. Part of me wanted to pound my fists across my chest like a gorilla, then tear all her clothes off and mount her from behind so I could fuck her into oblivion.

Another part of me wanted to sit back against those pillows with her on my lap, so I could drown in the scent of her hair with my arms wrapped around her. It was like a ravenous caged beast had escaped from inside me but was calmed by the touch, feel, scent, and taste of her sweetness.

This gorgeous creature had just had an uncontrollable, sexy as motherfucking *fuck* orgasm. The hottest thing about it was that I was pretty damn sure what sent her tumbling over the edge was the image I'd given her of being utterly helpless, spread eagled, and completely at my mercy.

Fuck. Me. Fucking. Sideways.

And still there was another part of me that shook with laughter at her feisty little personality. Everything she did was so fucking cute and made my dick hard at the same time.

"Damn, baby. That was sexy as hell. You are definitely something else, you know that?"

I couldn't stop laughing at how indignant and embarrassed she was acting because I'd seen her do something so raw and sexual. If she only realized that was probably the hottest fucking thing I'd ever seen in my life... hell, she'd probably run away even faster. Women were the most contrary, perplexing and downright frustrating damn creatures.

"I do have some ropes and zip ties in my tactical equipment, if that'd make you more *com*-fortable," I intentionally emphasized the first syllable, looking forward to how cute it was when she blushed.

"Uggggghh! You are the worst!"

"That's not what your pussy was telling me a few seconds ago."

"Errrrrr!"

She chucked a pillow at me furiously.

It made me laugh even harder, especially the frustrated little roar she made when I caught the fluffy projectile in one hand.

"Mr. Magnuson, I swear to all that is holy, if you don't let me get the hell out of here, right this second, I am going to... to..." she looked around frantically at the luxuriously furnished bedroom.

We were alone inside; this entire floor was part of my private living quarters.

My company owned this hotel.

Nothing and no one to help her, to save her from the big, bad wolf.

"I'm going to... uh..." she was still looking around the room, but there was literally nothing she could do to stop me.

She was at my complete mercy, this gorgeous, sensuous creature.

"How about you answer my questions first, and then you can figure out whatever it is you're going to do to me, hmmm?"

The one-sided eyebrow raise she gave me didn't look like agreement.

"How about no, and how about I'm leaving. Now, dammit!"

"You don't get to tell me no. And not yet. You'll leave when I say you can leave."

"Excuse me?!"

"Which part needs clarification? The part where I ask and you answer, or the exact same version of that same scenario?"

"Anyone ever tell you, you're an arrogant jackass?"

"Frequently. Where did you get the QR code you used in the store earlier? It's important you don't lie to me, Freya."

She was starting to look scared again, but it couldn't be helped. We were running out of time. If what we suspected was correct, she was either a target or involved somehow. All my instincts told me she wasn't involved; I usually trusted them implicitly. They'd kept me alive more times than I could count.

That meant she'd likely been targeted, they could already be working to intercept her. It wasn't likely given other patterns we'd observed, but a possibility nonetheless. It could even happen tonight.

Over my overgrown, stubborn-ass, dead motherfucking body.

The amount of rage I felt picturing my sweet, shy, sensual little lioness at the mercy of these human trafficking scumbags could have leveled continents.

"Look, Freya. Listen. Just listen..."

Suddenly, I didn't know where to start.

The thought of scaring her with the reality of the situation was unpleasant, but necessary. I didn't know what I would do if she started crying. The thought was more terrifying than any black-op or widowmaker-mission I'd ever orchestrated. I took a deep breath.

She stared at me suspiciously, waiting.

"I guess you've heard of my company, *Magnuson Security?*"

"It rings a bell. Why, are you going to correct me on your multi-billionaire status again? It's so hard for us peasants to rememb—"

"Freya, this is serious."

I glowered at her, silencing her sassy reply instantly. She gulped.

Just the way she had when my cock was inside her mouth, swallowing down my...

Dammit, dammit, dammit.

Sweat was already forming on my brow as I recalled the delicious memory.

Clearing my throat and mentally kicking my own ass, I continued.

"The coupon code you used in *Caress* matches a very specific and extremely baffling pattern of metadata signatures my company has been researching."

She stared at me, saying nothing.

Her expression was unreadable. I continued.

"There's a lot I can't tell you, so don't ask. All you need to do is tell me exactly how you accessed that coupon code. I also need your cell phone to extract any additional data that we can."

I hypothesized that last part was not going to go over well; I was correct.

"The FUCK you are! You're not taking my cell phone! Are you out of your mind?! Look, I know we... did stuff... and whatever. But, we're done. I'm done, it's done. I officially don't consent to any of this. I don't want to be part of your investigation, or operation, or extreme couponing reality show, or whatever the hell this shit is!"

As she ranted, she flew off the bed in one leaping, graceful, suspiciously feline motion. She was definitely a dancer, I thought absentmindedly.

I lunged at her. She didn't get very far at all.

"Sit. Back. Down. *Now.*"

I was even surprised by the tone of my voice, but the topic had pretty much killed my sex drive for the moment. The topic pretty much made me want to kill, period.

I growled softly for effect, staring her down as I motioned her toward the bed.

It worked, and she sat down on the edge of the bed with a timid little squeak. I returned to my own post—several feet away from her, where her intoxicating scent didn't fuck with my brain so much—and continued.

I glanced at her, sighed, and braced myself. She looked pretty fucking terrified, but she was paying rapt attention. On second thought maybe a little fear was a good thing. Sure seemed to keep that sassy mouth of hers quiet.

"QR code. Now."

She stared at me for a few seconds, eyes wide and unblinking, then she seemed to collect herself and answered.

"It was sent to me in one of my social media account messages. I get them all the time, literally every other woman my age does. I don't understand why that's such a big—"

"One of? Don't tell me you have multiple accounts?"

"Well yeah, there's Insta, Facebook, Ti—"

"When was it sent? How long since you first accessed it?"

"Hell if I know!"

I growled in response. She got the message.

"Maybe like... ten or eleven days?"

"From initial delivery or point of access?"

"Umm... what? Point of—?"

"Freya. Pay attention; we don't have time for this."

Crossing my arms across my chest, I surveyed her for a few seconds, then nodded in resignation. "I need your phone, now," I'd already decided it would be the fastest way, so I walked toward her with my palm extended.

I didn't have time to gauge her level of hostility as I approached because I was distracted by the power flickering on and off. Even though I knew we had not one, not two, but seven back-up generators for all the essential tech security, I still out of habit turned toward my equipment room to make sure none of the servers or anything else had been disrupted. The amount of power outages in a city this size never ceased to amaze me.

Ever since this voodoo artificial intelligence metadata bullshit that had targeted the Parisi family, I wasn't taking any chances on anything.

I was already out of the bedroom and turning to the right toward the equipment room, when I saw the dark red flash of her hair out of the corner of my eye. She was going left, toward the rest of the living space and the front entrance.

"Where do you think you're going?" I bellowed toward her.

She froze.

"If you take one more step toward that door, I promise you're going to regret it, Freya."

Chapter 10

Freya

I didn't like the way his voice had dropped an octave again, not at all. I froze.

I heard him retreat into one of the other rooms, then return back toward the bedroom. Even if I hadn't heard his steps coming behind me, I would have literally felt his presence. Danger was dripping off him in unmistakable waves.

He must have seen how I shrank back when he approached me because he let out an exasperated sigh, retreated several steps, and propped down on the chaise lounge a few feet away from the bed. I swear the piece of furniture actually cringed in anticipation right before he spread his massive body out across it, propping himself up on one arm.

Using the other, he pointed back to the bed. I sat down, refusing to acknowledge the strange power he had over me.

"I have absolutely, positively, *zero* mother-effing reason to trust you and this is all really freaking weird."

"Freya. Please, I understand this is strange, but trust me when I say there is some seriously fucked up technology associated with the QR code you used today."

"Okay, you're scaring me. This is all a huge, massive misunderstanding! Why the hell am I here and why won't you let me leave?! Because I used a coupon at a lingerie store?! What the hell, man! What—was it expired? Are you the coupon police?! What is this shit?! I'm leaving! Okay?! Leaving!"

I looked around for the scraps of my V-neck he'd shredded earlier. It was nowhere to be found. That was my absolute favorite *Lululemon* V-neck! Some people couldn't afford to go around ripping up perfectly good workout shirts, the jerk!

"As soon as we are done, Miles will drive you anywhere you want," his deep voice dripped over me like hot wax, sending warm chills down the back of my neck.

He stayed where he was across the room, but his eyes never left me as I walked around the bedroom. I shivered, then continued to search for my severely assaulted clothing. Maybe it wasn't as bad as it'd sounded at the time.

Unfortunately, I'd found it completely torn in half from the bottom of the V all the way down to the seam.

"I'll buy you fifty more in every shade they have," he said as I held it up in front of me, disgusted.

"That was my shirt, you dickhead! What the hell am I supposed to wear now?!"

I sighed in frustration, refusing to look his way.

I did still have my university dance squad sweatshirt, I remembered with a rush of relief. Unfortunately, I had no idea where the hell it was.

I was wearing it when I walked in the suite, then woke up with my bare feet, leggings, sports bra, and the V-neck shirt—still intact, dammit—but no sweatshirt.

"It's in the bathroom hanging on the back of the door. Took it off in case you needed to get sick."

Whatever.

I was too embarrassed and frightened at this point for him to not still be an arrogant dickhead, even if he was a considerate one. Even if it made my stomach do a teeny, tiny flip flop that he knew what I was looking for without me having to ask.

Even if some of what he'd just told me scared the mother-effing shit out of me, and all I wanted to do was run into his massive arms and hide while he shot his green-eyed testosterone laser beams of death into whatever it was that was supposedly dangerous.

Even if all that were true, Brodie Magnuson was a literal corporate billionaire, a walking testosterone dripping, orgasm wrenching, V-neck ripping, terrifying heartbreak waiting to happen.

"I want my shoes. Now."

He stared at me for several seconds before he took a long, exasperated sigh. He raked his hands through his thick mass of dark brown hair and then turned toward me again. He opened his mouth to say something, but was cut off by the same phone chime I'd heard earlier. His demeanor changed entirely as he answered the call.

"You have sixty seconds."

My, what a budding conversationalist he was...

Suddenly, he began rifling through a small stack of paper files on the other side of the table as he replied to the caller with one-word answers. He also sounded royally pissed off. I didn't like the way his overlarge, solid frame could move around so quickly and with so much precision.

It was completely unsettling and scary; he was like a machine. A great, big, terrifying, scary, sexy machine.

"You're damn right, it's a fucking problem!"

His loud, barking outburst made me physically jump. There should be laws against voices that deep and that loud.

"You have approximately fifteen minutes to talk some sense into her before I call Marco. Do you understand me?"

I also refused to think about my insane little flare of jealousy when I heard the very female sounding voice protesting loudly through the phone at his high-handed orders.

As he spoke, he opened up several laptops and connected them to a small black box on the table. There were a few red and green and orange lights along the side of the device flashing at random. It looked like some kind of super tiny server.

"What the fuck do you think I'm doing right now? I swear, Laney! One more step out of line, and I'm pulling a code red for the rest of the damn summer, do you hear me?!"

More shrill feminine protesting on the other end. The word "cocksucker" seemed to come up quite a few times.

"I don't give a *fuck* if the two of you are so *bored* you can't see straight. Y'all have a million other things to do. You have fourteen minutes now, Laney. Use them wisely."

He tossed the phone angrily aside and then furiously typed away on one of the laptops. He looked about as approachable as a rabies-infested rattlesnake.

If I knew anything, anything at all in my twenty-four years, it was that I needed to get the hell away from this man as fast as physically freaking possible. Thankfully, I had finally located my sneakers on the other side of the bed.

I quietly let him work, thankful for the respite. Reality was crashing over me in waves.

Cold dread had settled into the pit of my stomach like it was waiting out a weekend blizzard inside a cozy mountainside cabin.

I'd had my crazy, spontaneous, stupid, sexy little adventure, but things had gotten so far past bizarre that I was pretty sure I'd take the details of this misadventure to my grave. I also hoped I wouldn't be going there any time soon.

Told you so. Maybe you can ask if Miles can drop you off at the funeral home whenever Mr. Mountain Murder Man is finished with your body...

I really didn't know why she had to be such a staunch, uptight little witch.

I wasn't even Catholic!

I took a deep breath as a plan formed in my mind. It wasn't a great plan, but neither was anything else I'd done so far today.

My luck was bound to change soon, right?

...right?!

Chapter 11

Brodie

Of all the stupid, hair-brained, idiotic shit my youngest sister came up with. The girl had absolutely no sense, especially when it came to staying out of danger.

When Marco found out about this, he was going to go nuclear. And he would definitely find out. I just hoped I could minimize the damage. We had so many other things to worry about right now, dammit!

The girls had been given strict orders ever since the last incident at the beach house. Several months ago, there was a major security breach that almost led to Gia being kidnapped, or worse, right out from under the Parisi security's mother-fucking noses.

We didn't know exactly what the motive had been, not yet anyway, but it was definitely related to all this shit going on.

So, why in the hell those two girls thought they could just waltz around New York City without a care in the world, was beyond me.

I'd worked alongside Marine Raiders with far less fear of death than those two women.

Apparently, Gia had accepted an online invite for her and Laney to attend a "charity" event tonight at a new nightclub over in Brooklyn.

She had supposedly followed "all the bullshit orders" about informing the security team in advance *exactly* where she was going, so they could act accordingly while she attended. For her own damn safety, dammit!

So, when Laney phoned me just now to inform me that Gia hadn't shown up yet, and then suggested that *maybe* she'd just heard the event details wrong from Gia, I could have wrung both of their stubborn, irritating, apparently suicidal little necks.

I wasn't fooled for a damn second that this wasn't all part of their little plan for Gia to eventually ditch the Parisi security.

Why not throw off all the Parisi family security by sending them on a wild goose chase around the entire city of New York, because Gia "accidentally" mixed up the address? Meanwhile, Laney "accidentally" got the details wrong, tying up half the security team that was supposed to be waiting there for both of them, together, as soon as Gia got off work, *dammit!*

Laney's memory was even better than mine. She didn't forget shit. She also had a nasty temper to rival my own and tended to get extremely angry when she should be scared. Just the same as I did, but I'd never fucking admit that out loud.

I knew my sister better than anyone else. In some ways we were exactly alike—both as stubborn as a damn mule. So of course, I knew that the *only* reason Laney had called me was because something had already gone very wrong in their idiotic, dangerous little plan.

Her equivocation of a lot of the details was proof enough of her guilt—like I said, she didn't forget a damn thing. So was the extremely colorful way she told me off. She was scared for Gia, and I think felt a little guilty for helping her friend into a potentially dangerous situation.

Luckily for both of them, I was the only person who knew about the tracking device that I had put inside one of Gia's favorite pieces of jewelry.

The necklace was a gift from her mother who'd passed years earlier. I knew for a fact that she never took it off. It was the best we could do aside from something biological. My team didn't have access to anything that was safe enough for me to try on the basically kid sister—although they technically had no blood relation—of my best friend, who also happened to be the head of the Parisi Mafia Empire.

I'd already felt like a fucking cockroach when I'd had to covertly sedate her in order to have one of the gemstones replaced with my tracker, but it couldn't be avoided. The only other person who knew about the tracker was the doctor who'd provided the sedative and monitored her vitals, then administered a quick reversal.

She was the wife of a former marine who'd served alongside me, so of course I knew I could trust her implicitly.

I also knew Gia's mother would have supported the reason for my actions, were she still alive.

Once all this shit was over, I'd remove the device, replace the gemstone, and Gia would be none the wiser. Still, the whole process had fucking sucked. I hated lying about anything, anything at all. But Gia's safety would always come first, hurt feelings be damned.

The phone call I'd just received told me I'd made the right decision.

It took me less than two minutes to detect her exact location. Not only was she about an hour away from where she said she was, she was at a strip club over in the East Village in Manhattan.

A fucking strip club!

Mumbling and cussing a blue streak about females and their complete lack of common sense, I almost didn't hear my little captive turn the shower on.

My dick definitely heard.

It was already standing at complete and throbbing attention by the time my brain got the memo. Instantly hard and extremely frustrated, I quickly sent all the necessary texts to my team, and then to Marco.

I felt zero guilt for giving Laney less than a four-and-a-half-minute head start before the both of them got to face Marco and my team's wrath. Maybe it would scare some damn sense into them, because apparently Gia almost getting abducted had just made them "bored." For Christ's sake!

Slamming down my laptop, I stormed over to the bathroom where I could already feel the warm steam drifting through the cracked door.

The only thing on my mind was seeing that gorgeous, deliciously curved body completely naked and soaking wet under the spray of the shower. I nudged opened the door, turning immediately toward the running shower. Steam already filled the room.

I needed to see her beautiful body displayed before me, her pretty, dark pink nipples pebbled as the water ran over her front. I needed to touch her, needed to claim and possess the sweetness of her—

Without warning my foot slid out from under me and I fell down on my ass like a cartoon *King-Kong* slipping on a banana peel.

My head hit the hard tile floor of the bathroom with a *thunk* that rattled my teeth but didn't do any other damage.

Aside from my fucking pride.

Something very slippery, with a pleasant fruity and herbal scent, was all around me on the floor.

I let out a frustrated growl as I pulled myself up and tore open the shower curtain. My little lioness was about to pay for her little prank. It would take more than some shower gel on a bathroom floor to stop me from what I was going to do to her in that shower.

But the shower was completely empty. Confused, I barely noticed the movement by the linen closet on the other side of the bathroom.

The sneaky little fox had been hiding in the closet, then ran out the door when I'd assumed she was in the shower.

It did absolutely fucking nothing to dampen my rage that she'd at least thrown down a stack of towels so I hadn't cracked open my head on the hard marble floor when her plan worked.

With a primal roar, I chased after her.

The last thing I saw as I rounded the corner toward the living space was her beautiful indigo blue eyes wide with terror as the elevator doors closed between us.

Chapter 12

Freya

I didn't let out the breath I'd been holding until I was completely out of the hotel, several blocks away and couldn't see any sign of him behind me. Silver lining to his monstrous size—he would be pretty damn difficult to lose in a crowd. Nevertheless, I almost ran into three different people because I kept looking over my shoulder.

After about five minutes of walking with zero sign of him or any creepy, blacked-out, uber-luxe SUV's, I relaxed enough to get my phone out. It was almost seven o' clock. I needed to get home ASAP or I'd be late for the main event: *Ladies' Night* at a super chic, artsy nightclub called *DiVine* over in the East Village.

It would take me an eternity to get back to our apartment in Soho if I kept walking. I also wanted to get as far away from Brodie mother-effing Magnuson as I could, as fast as possible.

Cringing, I turned toward the closest subway stop and grabbed my train pass. Despite what city officials wanted everyone to think, the train was absolutely not as freaking safe as they claimed. I didn't care; the sooner I got home, the better. There'd most likely be a line, but it was still faster than walking and way faster than a cab this late in the day.

I also *really* felt like I'd had my fair share of danger for the day and attracting any more of it seemed unlikely at this point.

I turned back to my phone once I'd finally found a spot; thankfully the train wasn't as body to body crowded as I'd expected. Five texts and a missed call—I smiled to myself at the thought of seeing my best friend Kimberly tonight. She always somehow knew exactly what to do in situations like this, and I knew she'd never judge me. Suddenly feeling a rush of giddy excitement, I hurriedly texted her.

You will not believe what just happened to me!

Just a few seconds later I saw my favorite picture of the two of us light up my phone. I smiled as I answered the phone call. I should have known better than to dangle that carrot in front of my nosey but loving best friend.

"DETAILS, BITCH!"

Kimberly's voice laughing through my phone was easily heard by the people around me and I cringed at the unwanted attention. A particularly stuffy-looking woman nearby raised one of her eyebrows at me cynically.

Probably not the best conversation to have on the damn subway, but I really, really needed to have the normalcy of my best friend's voice.

I did, however, let Kim know I was on the train and was about to lose her, but I'd call her back closer to home. I laughed along with her as I gave her the very condensed PG version, promising more juicy details when I was safe within the walls of our new apartment in SoHo.

Her family owned the building, and her father was giving us a massive family discount on the rent, just until we "had some money coming in regularly."

Kim's father was probably one of the nicest humans I'd ever met, and ironically also probably the wealthiest man I knew. There was no way we would be able to afford the place he'd selected for us, but it was pointless to argue with Peter Zakharov when he'd made up his mind.

Kim's family came from old money and her father, Peter, was a very successful corporate attorney. He was one of the most generous people I'd ever met, with a warm, charismatic personality. Which was a good thing, because the man was also a total and complete bulldozer. Whatever he decided, happened, regardless of what others thought. Kimberly was a lot like him.

In just a few short minutes I was finally outside our new place and waiting for the doorman to buzz me inside. I was in such a good mood, refusing to acknowledge the potential consequences of the previous several hours. I dialed Kim once I saw the doorman approaching.

I smiled at our doorman, thanking him on the way inside as I waited for the elevator, laughing at the constant stream of ridiculously perverted questions from my best friend. She'd definitely made me feel a little less embarrassed and petrified about the whole thing.

"FREYA! I'm dying over here! I heard the doorman buzz you in! Now tell me what the fuck fucking happened, *moya prodruga!*"

I giggled at Kim's horrible mouth and excited demeanor. Never a dull moment with Kim, which made me even more excited to see her tonight.

Finally relaxed and feeling much safer within the already familiar walls of our apartment, I gave her the juicy details of the past few hours. Taking about two, or maybe seven or eight hits of my vape may have helped, as well.

Thank god for legal weed, I thought ruefully.

I had zero desire to get arrested or shot or worse for such a vice, but did I love a little chill vibe from some "baby weed" as the more hardcore blazers called it?

Hell, yes, I did.

There was a lot of interruption in my story telling due to both of us bursting into fits of uncontrollable giggles at some of the juicier details. Well, I'd told Kim most of the details. There were a few bits and pieces that I didn't even know if I could *think* about again, let alone say out loud.

That would make them real, and I think I preferred to reassign those memories to the 'didn't actually happen in real life' file. Unfortunately, being a psych major, I had to acknowledge that I was engaging in dissociative amnesia to deal with the traumatic events of earlier.

Traumatic?! Oh please! Traumatic for who? Your pussy from coming so hard?!

The wrinkly nun and I both gasped, clutching our pearls, while my sexy subconscious flicked her shiny black tail at us indignantly.

Fortunately, however, I still didn't have to take full accountability for my actions because I was under the influence of completely unauthorized and hella-illegal levels of testosterone.

"More! I want every single detail about this hot mystery man, especially the part where he called DevLynn a crack whore!"

Kim was so excited that I could hear her smiling ear to ear.

"Technically he only said she *smelled* like one, but not that she *was* one," I replied, laughing just as much as Kim at the delectable memory. "And I don't think he used such specific terms, but... I like your verbiage much better, as usual."

Kim squealed in delight and laughed even harder, wordlessly urging me to tell the best parts of the story.

Honestly, by now it all seemed a little less humiliating, a shit ton less scary, and a lot more hilarious. I told myself that there was no way I was ever going to see Mr. Panty Dropper again, and next time I was buying all of that crap *online*.

Chapter 13

Brodie

F*uck.*

That's all I could think as I watched her walk away from the lobby, my palms throbbing with wanting to feel that perfectly rounded ass underneath them.

She had definitely earned herself a very hard spanking and then some for the little stunt she'd just pulled by running away from me. My dick was immediately hard enough to cut granite at the thought of punishing that plump, juicy backside of hers until she begged me for mercy.

Fuck. Me.

I knew I couldn't go after her now, not until Gia had been recovered and hauled the hell back to the Parisi safehouse—a gorgeous, multi-million-dollar estate in Staten Island. Laney should already be on her way there, the damn brat.

I'd always really liked shy, kind little Gianna D'Angelo, but knowing it was her fault that I'd have to wait that much longer to have Freya back under my control and protection again did nothing to improve my homicidal mood.

Like a feral, hungry predator I watched her walk along the sidewalk from one of my first-floor office windows, dazed by the dark red glow of her hair in the late afternoon sun.

I knew by the time she'd hit the first-floor lobby, the cell phone jammer would have stopped working and she could have used her phone, possibly dialed 911.

I did not have time to deal with the damn local law enforcement interfering any more than they already were with our investigation.

It really wasn't their fault; they were just doing their jobs.

Unfortunately, they also had to play by rules that my team did not. That meant they were embarrassingly limited with what they could do compared to what we could. Good old-fashioned playing by the rules never worked against this type of sick, sophisticated, downright evil fuckery—which is where my team came in.

We only played by one rule: we always won.

I'd been forced to follow behind her in a towering rage, having no choice but to watch her walk out of the lobby. I was fucking seething at the situation caused by two apparently *very* spoiled-rotten brats. Thankfully, Freya made no move to reach for her phone before she was out of my sight.

Swearing a blue streak and acting like a jackass around my staff, I barked out orders to notify our law enforcement contacts *briefly* of the situation. They'd cowered and immediately followed orders, which had only increased my anger and annoyance.

I already knew I'd have to take them coffees and cookies all week next week to make up for it, but I absolutely could not calm the fuck down at the moment, so I stormed back toward the elevator.

It was downright appalling how much I'd let my fucking dick hijack my brain for the last few hours. If I hadn't been so damn distracted, I could have gotten the work done first. I could have put the appropriate security measures into place, and then had more than enough time to play. It wasn't like me at all; I always had unwavering self-control. That realization only pissed me off even more.

The next time I saw her, she was getting fucked until she couldn't walk, no matter how scared she thought she was. She wouldn't ever make the mistake from running away from me again, especially until all this shit was over. I'd make damn sure of it.

I just needed to get my dick on the same page—work first and *then* play, dammit.

That part was definitely pretty hard. Pun intended.

That damn hair of hers. It haunted me with every breath I took. It was silky and so fucking soft; I wanted to grab a fistful of it and pull her close while I breathed in the delicious way she smelled. So clean and feminine, so fucking intoxicating. Her scent was burned into my brain, and I wanted to breathe it in while those curves pressed up against me again.

The next time I had her in my control, I was going to grab onto that beautiful hair of hers while I spanked that juicy ass of hers a deep, angry pink.

Ffffuck.

That image made me so hot for her it was painful, but it was absolutely not okay for her to do something so stupid and reckless when she could be in serious danger. Nevertheless, I still had to discreetly adjust my rock-hard dick before another staff member entered the elevator. For fuck's sake, I was acting like a damn teenager instead of my thirty-five years.

After an eternity I reached the privacy of my suite. Her delicious scent still hung in the air, making her absence even more intolerable. I had a feeling I could feast on her body, bury my aching cock inside her for hours and still not get enough of Freya Daniels.

She had the most beautiful eyes I had ever seen, and that mouth! Fuck me, that *mouth*. Deep pink, plump lips that got even pinker and plumper with her desire.

I got hard all over again just thinking about her wrapping those beautiful, juicy lips around my cock as I shoved into the back of her throat.

She definitely shouldn't have run away from me.

Now, I was going to hunt her down and show her what it felt like to swallow the entire throbbing length of me. Those pretty little indigo eyes of hers would fill with tears while I filled her mouth completely. She would look up at me as I fucked her throat, taking in every throbbing inch of my cock.

And I would make damn sure she enjoyed every single second of it.

The sexy little gasp she made when I first put *The Panty Dropper* on her pussy—damn but if it didn't make me want to beat on my chest like a caveman. I also didn't miss how soaking wet her pussy had been from sucking my dick, and the way she'd shyly cupped my pulsing balls, massaging them and catapulting me into a second orgasm.

Fuck me.

The urge to control her, to dominate her, to claim her as mine and mine alone was overwhelming. She was absolute fucking perfection. I wanted her naked, exposed, crazy with need and begging me to use her beautiful body until she screamed and came apart all over me.

My dick had been hard and aching for her for the last few hours. The fucker was throwing an even bigger pity party than I was. And if *anyone* asked how she'd gotten away from me, I was going to shoot first and ask questions later.

My severely wounded masculine pride at having been bested by such a tiny and innocent female was also stroking the fire of my horrible mood. She may think she had the upper hand, but now that I'd had a taste of her, there was nowhere she could go on this Earth that I wouldn't find her.

If we were correct in our suspicions and the beautiful little redhead, Freya Daniels, had been targeted, then she was undoubtedly in a fuck ton of danger. Even if she weren't an intended target, she was close enough now to the situation to be in a fuck ton of trouble with the Parisi family, potentially even the Council.

Either way was fucked, and neither one of those scenarios did anything to cool my anger in the slightest.

My black mood plummeted further when I answered Marco's call several minutes after my little lioness had escaped. I'd been correct in assuming he'd reached nuclear levels of rage. He'd started barking out orders probably before I'd even answered.

"I need you and a full staff over in the East Village," most people probably thought his quiet, emotionless voice sounded calm and focused, but I knew better.

He was barely keeping a lid on his explosive temper. When Marco got quiet, it was time to prepare for landfall.

I lost all of the sympathy I had left for Gia having to deal with Hurricane Marco, Cat-5, when I remembered Freya's beautiful face fade away from me in the elevator.

"Was the lost package not found and re-delivered?"

"Of course it has been fucking found. It won't ever be fucking leaving anywhere, ever again. We have additional problems with a *new delivery*. Added another... stop along the delivery route... and that's where everything must have gotten... *thrown together.*"

"Are you fucking with me right now?!"

Now I was the one who sounded murderously angry, except I'd never been quiet about my temper.

I was already throwing gear into bags and getting ready to leave. I barked at Marco to send me the rest of the details securely and threw my phone on the table. I was packed and ready in less than five minutes; it had fucking taken me forever because I was so distracted by absolute and utter fury.

We didn't say any more specifics on the phone. Marco had just confirmed that Freya was likely the next target.

If we were correct based on patterns from previous cases, the false data trails had already been put in place and she could literally disappear into thin air. Tonight.

The rage I'd felt in that instant about the danger for a person I'd literally met a few hours ago made zero motherfucking sense. I was also too angry to give a damn.

This was mostly my fault, *dammit*, for not staying focused and getting the job done. I absolutely couldn't leave her alone since I'd seen her on that first camera feed earlier that afternoon.

It did little to improve my mood when one of the new employees over at the concierge literally jumped as I stormed past. I didn't give a flying fuck about being civil right now.

I probably needed to set up coffee and pastry delivery for the entire damn staff, for the rest of the year, at this point. And I would do that later.

Right now there was one thing on my mind, and one thing only as I headed to her address in SoHo.

I was going hunting.

Chapter 14

Freya

"**O**kay, my frisky little Feline Freya! Uncle Billie is taking me over there as soon as I grab my overnight bags! The rest of the girls are meeting us there. Meow, go finish getting ready! See you soon!"

Laughing, I told her I was going to go shower right *meow*, and I loved her too. She laughed back at me before we both hung up.

I turned the shower on, almost groaning out loud at how much I was looking forward to the soothing spray.

Kimberly Zakharov and I had been friends since the third grade. At the age of six years old, I'd moved to New York to live with my grandparents when my parents were killed in a car accident back in Southern Kansas.

My mother's parents took me in and raised me like I was their own child instead of granddaughter. They did their best right after the accident, and they were always loving and affectionate. I loved both of them in return but there was always a sense of that first home that I yearned for.

I think that's why I'd always been drawn to Kimberly and her family; they reminded me of the family structure I was first introduced to with my parents. Kim's parents even said that we acted just like sisters, and I'd always felt like we were. Her parents had gotten divorced years ago, but they still had a friendly relationship. I saw Kim's mother rarely as she lived on the other side of the country, but she'd always been sweet to me and she really did love Kim.

I showered quickly. I tried not to think about the guilt I still felt when I'd heard the gorgeous giant hit hard marble bathroom floor.

I mean, I'd put like fifty towels down around the area where his head landed. And he obviously wasn't seriously harmed because he'd immediately bounded after me, yelling like an effing bloodthirsty Viking warrior.

Remembering the savage look on his face as the elevator doors closed made the hair stand up on the back of my neck. It also made me breathless with a puzzling desire to run, if only to be eventually caught by him and dominated completely.

The steamy shower suddenly felt too warm, the soothing stream of hot water was much too stimulating now. My nipples pebbled as I let my head fall back into the steamy water, completely sinking back into the memory of his hands groping and teasing me in his car, on his bed.

I didn't want to think about how much that had turned me on when he totally dominated me and forced me to feel so blatantly sexual. I'd never, ever been with a man like that—who took such total and complete control. It gave me no chance to feel anything but desire, want, need.

Up until today, I had what I thought of as kinky sex. Not turning the lights off all the way. Brazenly rubbing my clit, or even using an actual vibrator during sex because it was usually the only way I could come.

I hadn't even had actual sex with him, and he'd already made me come harder and faster than I ever had in my life.

Despite being in the shower I felt myself blush scarlet from head to toe remembering how hard and fast I had orgasmed when he talked about tying me up, naked, legs spread, pussy swollen and open wide before his hungry gaze.

Something about that crude imagery had turned my blood to fire. The closer I got to coming, the more I couldn't move at all from his grasp and that had only made me even freaking hotter. I had felt like his sexy little bedroom toy, his naughty girl...

When I'd finally given into the pleasure, I could literally feel the wetness seep through my leggings as my pussy pulsed obscenely. I had spread my legs even wider at the thought of him watching me come, watching me *there*.

I had to actually squeeze my legs together in the shower to keep me from teasing myself as I remembered the thick, swollen ridge of his cock in my mouth.

Dammit.

I turned the water to cold as I rinsed the conditioner out of my hair. Hopefully it would also rinse away the insane desire I had to be chased and dominated until I literally screamed in twisted pleasure.

Ahem...

I finished showering, towel dried my hair, and glanced at the clock. Thankfully my fever dreams in the shower hadn't taken up too much of my time.

I applied my skincare and then towel-dried my hair. The familiar scent of my favorite *Oribe* hair products made me feel weirdly secure as I combed through my almost hip-length locks. The luxurious, clean, and decisively feminine *Oribe* scent filled the bathroom as I sectioned it out to do a quick blowout. Once dried, I placed my long hair into my favorite jumbo rollers while I did my makeup.

Finally finished, I admired my efforts in my bathroom mirror with a small smile and a big sigh of relief. I didn't realize how much I'd needed that little confidence boost until I achieved my final look without any major makeup mishaps.

Sometimes no matter how hard I tried, my makeup just didn't turn out well.

The wings of my eyeliner would look like they'd flown through multiple wars. I would have those infuriating, tiny little black flecks on my eyelids after spending almost thirty *ridiculous* minutes trying to get my eyeshadow somewhat even and decently blended, only to accidentally smudge mascara on my lids when I blinked at the wrong second.

The new brand of "maximum coverage" foundation I would try would only make me look like I was wearing a poorly matched anti-freckle mask that faded awkwardly into my neck. It would never give me a "smooth, flawless, pore-less finish," the lying bastards.

Thankfully, tonight I truly felt I'd mastered my sultry, smokey but not *too* smokey cat-eye. I put a subtle pale pink gloss on my lips to compliment the dramatic eye makeup. Oversized gold art-deco earrings and matching necklace were perfect for the artsy, chic vibe of the club tonight.

I gently removed the rollers and applied my favorite *Oribe* hairspray for flexible, shiny hold, allowing the curls to fall naturally around my face. There was just something about the way their products were scented—and performed, sweet Jesus how they performed! —that always made me feel luxurious, sophisticated, and sexy.

It was totally worth teaching myself how to do all my own manicures and pedicures to help pay for the luxury hair products that I had become completely addicted to but *probably* couldn't really afford yet.

Checking the time, I finished dressing quickly as Kimberly would be downstairs any minute now. A little flip-flop of excitement danced around in my stomach; I absolutely couldn't wait to go out tonight. I needed the release of a carefree night out with my girls badly after today's surreal and downright freaking weird events.

I was wearing the naughty lingerie under my favorite little black dress—minus the matching garter set, of course. I wasn't feeling *that* brave. Honestly, I was pleasantly surprised how well the girls were supported, because the skimpy material definitely hadn't looked like it could manage all they had to offer.

A hot flush went through me as I'd gotten dressed in the lingerie set and looked at my reflection in my mirror. I was definitely not getting excited thinking about that arrogant ogre of a man seeing me in these sexy scraps of lace, and nothing else.

I also did not think about what he would do to me if I stood before him with my nipples stabbing through the thin black lace, begging for the feel of his hands and mouth. The sexy, scary literal growl as he pounced on me *definitely* hadn't sounded inside my head before I could stop it.

Nope. Not even a little bit.

Heat pooled between my thighs at the memory of his solid and formidable heat. The spicy, masculine sandalwood scent of his cologne was burned into my nostrils even after my shower.

Too bad Mr. Panty-Dropper was such a crazy bossy scary arrogant ass, I thought with annoyance at my body's lustful reaction to his memory.

Before I could stop myself, images of me straddling his massive thighs and grinding against him swam in my mind and sent the warm rush from between my thighs shooting all over my body. Chills ran along my arms and shoulders and along the sensitive skin on my neck.

The picture was a delectable one, I admitted to myself as I bit my lower lip and then licked it in a suspiciously feline fashion. I had to physically shake to remove the seductive, sexy imagery from my mind.

I was pretty sure the poor, pious old nun had long since passed out in cold shock, and I swore I heard an irritable feline *hisssss* when the blatantly sexual image was finally banished.

Then, a different image doused my desire instantly: the first bedroom stuffed to the brim with guns, rocket-sized bullets, weapons I didn't even know existed.

The way he'd turned to me in the elevator, a cold type of killing rage pouring off him in waves...

A loud buzzing from my front door indicated Kim was downstairs.

I gave myself a mental slap for not staying in the present and reliving things that were never going to happen again.

They weren't real anymore, but tonight was real, and I wasn't about to miss any of it by daydreaming and thought spiraling. I forced a smile on my face until it stayed there completely of its own accord.

Hurriedly, I gathered the last of my things for the evening and slipped on my favorite pair of heels: black *Jimmy Choo* peep-toe booties. They were also sexy as hell and perfectly completed my outfit. Normally close to a thousand bucks with tax, I'd found mine for a significant amount less through a second-hand designer clothing website. They were absolutely stunning.

The way more affordable price I had paid for them made them feel even more amazing every time I'd put them on. If you imagined being full-time student broke *AF* into a game, and counted major discounts, sales, or coupons as huge victories, it made life seem a little less dull, right?

This was my absolute favorite black dress; it seemed to defy physics in the way it perfectly accented my figure. It was cut short in the exact spot along mid-thigh to make my definitely not small, muscular legs look sleek and feminine instead of bulky and thick. The *Jimmy Choo* booties were also definitely helping in the my-legs-are-slimmer-than-they-look department.

In less than sixty seconds I was completely ready, more than ready for anything tonight had to offer. I threw open the door to see Kimberly already heading up the stairs.

We both squealed and embraced in a hug. I helped her bring her overnight bags inside, and in less than three minutes we were already halfway finished with a glass of white wine while we waited for our cab driver to arrive downstairs.

We needed to take a cab over to the East Village for *Ladies' Night*. It was an invite-only event in the VIP section of *DiVine*, a racy, couture, up-and-coming night club. There was no way Uncle Billie, their family's driver and unofficial bodyguard slash chaperone, would have taken us there. Kim's father was *very* conservative.

A little while later, we got out of the cab and walked up to the line outside the door of *DiVine*.

Damn, the line was pretty long—good thing I'd brought my vape.

We'd only waited about five minutes when one of the heavily muscled bouncers nodded at us to come forward. Placed in groups of two or three, they roamed the line as part of the "security," but everyone knew what they were really there for. They preserved the club's image, preventing anyone unworthy from entering.

I'd definitely learned that the hard way on the very rare occasion that I'd gone out clubbing to these types of places without Kim. It was a little ridiculous.

"Invitation only, sweetheart; can I scan your code please?"

He extended the handheld scanner as I pulled up the invite code on my phone. It was for me and a guest, which was of course Kim. I had sent the guest invite link to her earlier on the way over.

She scanned her code, as well. The bouncer nodded to us politely, all business and never smiling. As he stepped aside and we walked out of the line, his partner escorted us inside the club. I was instantly giddy in anticipation of a well-deserved, wild and carefree *Ladies' Night.*

There was nothing, absolutely nothing, that was going to ruin my evening.

As we danced our way toward the VIP-only rooftop bar, we found our other friends Teyanna and Kendrix inside.

I could feel the booming, seductive pulses of the music transport me into the worry-free bliss of Friday night as I sipped my lime vodka seltzer, laughing and dancing with the girls.

A little while later, while trying to pass through a mass of giggling and swaying girls without getting one of their vodka cranberry drinks poured all over my dress, I swore I detected the faintest hint of Brodie's cologne.

I mentally slapped myself and took a long gulp of my drink.

There was zero chance the arrogant, insanely attractive billionaire would waste any more time on a literal nobody like me. I finished my drink as I sashayed back onto the dance floor with my girls.

Besides, he'd probably already forgotten all about me, anyway.

Chapter 15

Brodie

By the time I got to her place in SoHo, it was clear she'd already left for the evening.

The scent of her was everywhere in the cozy, chic space, and my dick was rock hard from the second I stepped inside. I didn't stay long, just long enough to do a quick sweep and let the staff know what to have moved over to my place after they finished the security check.

Now, I was almost to the spot in the East Village where Freya was at. Gia and Laney were already taken care of. Marco's team had both of the girls completely jailed into the 7,800 square-foot safehouse in Staten Island. Their "prison" had a damn indoor spa-style pool, for fuck's sakes!

I'd briefly seen Marco before I headed over to East Village; I'd never seen him so livid. I didn't blame him at all.

Something told me it was the last time Gia or my idiot sister Laney would ever pull that kind of shit again. Not to mention the heat and absolute disrespect it brought down on the security staff, the men who were trained to literally take a bullet for those girls. That wasn't like Laney—or Gia, really—at all. Or at least it hadn't been before all this bullshit started. Still, there was zero fucking excuse for their dangerous and impulsive actions today.

Frankly, I was furious at my own sister for acting like such a selfish, petulant little brat. She fucking knew better. Being rebellious with her friend was cute and funny—to a point.

The strip club I'd arrived at with some of my men over in the East Village was technically speaking a nightclub, but I'm pretty sure the line between the two didn't exist anymore.

Not that I was complaining. The place screamed sex and seduction from the minute you stepped inside. Glowing neon signs of sexy female silhouettes, naughty outlines of juicy asses and different shapes and sets of very female breasts, all in pinks and purples and blues, were all definitely enjoyable.

It was like I'd snuck upstairs to one of the bedrooms in a sorority house back in my school days. Or had somehow gotten invited to a lesbian's bachelorette party.

My dick tingled at that last thought as I placed my feisty girl into the fantasy. It only made me more restless and homicidal that she was not currently under my control.

But that was about to change very soon.

Back at the hotel I'd tracked her cell phone and discovered she was headed straight toward *DiVine*—the same exact damn place that Gia had been earlier. I had a feeling that when Gia found out that the same event she'd snuck off to was nothing but a ploy, another trap set for her, she'd realize how fucking stupid and reckless her behavior had been and never do it again.

We'd told both of those girls, dammit, how sophisticated this technology was. Someone wanted to strike against the Parisi family very badly, and she'd do well to remember that being bored to death was better than being actually dead, dammit!

Mikhail Bychkov, *DiVine's* owner, had later confirmed that Freya scanned an invite that was completely false. He was also livid upon that realization and immediately suspected that Gia's presence at *his* club was meant to be some type of distraction or set-up.

Both of our tech teams were still working to decode the encryptions, but so far Freya's invite was not matching up with the messages to Gia from her "coworker."

Unfortunately, we did confirm that Marco was correct, and Freya was officially a target.

Another wave of ball-busting rage poured over me. There was literally nothing that could have stopped me from getting to her now, so it was a good fucking thing Mikhail's men had confirmed she was still inside the club.

Good for me, but maybe not necessarily for her. When I got done with her, she wasn't going to be able to sit down for a week.

Fuck that, for a month.

Marco seemed to trust Mikhail, but there was absolutely fucking no one I'd trust with her safety besides myself. Not after everything I'd seen in the last few months with this investigation.

In the mood I'd been in for the last few hours, no other male would ever fucking touch her again, let alone be in charge of her safety and well-being.

I'd only met Mikhail Bychkov very briefly. He seemed to keep a low profile. He had a reputation for being absolutely ruthless, if not fair, which I respected.

I absolutely did not motherfucking respect the fact that his motherfucking club was somehow involved in this human trafficking motherfucking *bullshit*.

I took a deep breath to channel the rage into focus before it consumed me.

Marco seemed to trust Mikhail, though, which helped ease some of my fury.

Once I had Freya with me and we decided what to do with her bubbly blond companion, she was getting tied to my bed until the investigation was closed and I'd shot down or blown up every last one of these trafficking low-life fucking bastards. Growling, I continued to search for her in the crowded club.

Just when I was about to throw my fist into the brick wall next to me in a rage because I wasn't finding her fast enough, the unmistakable scent of her hair assaulted me. Instantly I was on full alert, nostrils flared and shoulders drawn back in pursuit of my prey. My pulse quickened when I heard her giggling; I was so close now.

There she was, perched on one of the luxe couches up against a corner table of the upstairs private loft, surrounded by a small herd of other females.

She was effortlessly seductive, the embodiment of sin itself in a black dress that clung to every single damn curve of her body. The satiny black material bunched along the sweet thickness of her muscular thighs as she sat, legs crossed at her ankles demurely.

Black please-fuck-me heels donned her feet at the ends of those sexy, thick fucking legs. Deep red polish was on the tips of her cute little toes.

Suddenly, she and the rest of the herd finished their drinks and moved toward the dance floor.

Holy motherfucking fuck.

I'd thought she'd looked amazing in the black sex pants from earlier today, but seeing her ass practically gift-wrapped in the sleek black dress she wore made me crazy.

Her body was made for pure fucking sin, the sleek muscles in her thighs and calves flexing coyly as she moved with the other girls. I had to flex both of my hands into fists to keep from chasing after her and wrapping those fucking legs around my hips while I plowed into her heat.

Damn, but I needed to be inside this woman like I needed to breathe.

I could already feel the generous, curvy bulk of her ass under my palms. Her long, thick, gorgeous hair was styled in big bouncy curls that framed her face and fell down her back in a sexy mass of shiny, dark red silk. I couldn't wait to wrap it around my fist again.

She was standing on the edge of the dance floor and facing away from me, a very accessible location. Her demeanor was carefree and relaxed.

I knew I needed a minute to cool off before I approached her, so I stayed right where I was, and waited.

Chapter 16

Freya

The club promo event seemed to be going extremely well. The place was packed and the four of us were having such a great time, laughing and enjoying the playfully posh atmosphere.

We'd been trying to flag down one of the bartenders for almost twenty minutes when Teyanna offered to brave the bar front instead. Kim promptly thanked her and offered her card for the tab, but Kendrix stopped her.

"You always pay, Kim! Let me, at least for a round or two."

"No can do, sweet cheeks. You know my dad pays my credit card bills and he doesn't give two shits if I buy the drinks. You know what he says, he'd rather spend the money on 'his girls' than pay the damn government. Besides, you're supposed to be saving your money up for that down payment over in SoHo so we can be neighbors!"

"If you weren't the nicest fucking person I honestly knew, I think I would hate you. Also, we should probably start getting two at a time because it's getting super packed in here, so I'll help Tey carry drinks," Kendrix started toward the bar alongside Teyanna.

I had bought us the first two rounds, already having heard an earful for it from Momma Kim for not allowing her to pay since I'd "gotten us in."

I'd just laughed in her face, shaking my head as I'd handed her the drinks. She'd narrowed her eyes at me, smiling as she took a sip of her usual Moscow Mule and helped me carry one of the other girls' drinks.

If I wasn't sneaky about it, she'd never let me pay when we went out, and we both knew it. Also, Kim had *always* gotten me into clubs before, and then also refused to let me pay for drinks, the hypocrite. Literally, she was just like her father.

Teyanna and Kendrix were soon lost among the thirsty crowd at the bar front. I turned to Kim, but I couldn't remember what I'd been about to ask her because the look on her face stopped me cold.

She was looking at a fairly large, also fairly attractive man walking toward us. He had tattoos peeking out around his neck and along his hands. He was staring intently at our corner table as he approached, authority in every part of his gait.

I felt nothing but dread as I realized Kim seemed to be having a small panic attack, which was getting worse as the man approached.

Scratch that, he was more than just fairly large.

He was only slightly less enormous than—ahem—than the guy I wasn't going to think about again after one more pull on this vape, dammit.

"Good evening, ladies. My name is Mikhail Ivanovich Bychkov, and I am the owner of this establishment. Ms. Zakharova, it is such an honor to meet you. Your father, Mr. Pyotr Zakharov, is an esteemed business associate of mine.

"Please, allow me the privilege to welcome you and your lovely companions to one of my private tables on the top floor. A personal bartender and bottle service is provided, and I've already set out a few bottles of *Dom Perignon* for you.

"Is there anything else you'd like to start with for you or your guests? I'd also like to offer you reimbursement for whatever you have already spent here tonight. Your money is simply not needed here, Ms. Zakhorova."

I glanced back and forth from her to him as he spoke, and Kim seemed to relax somewhat. Her voice was still a little strained when she spoke to him. Honestly, it was extremely unsettling. Nothing, and I mean *nothing,* usually ruffled Kim's feathers.

"That's so very kind of you, Mr. Bychkov. But there's four of us here and I would hate to impose so much on your generosity! I am very flattered by the offer..." her voice faltered and then stopped abruptly at the stormy, dangerous look on the man's face.

Only a damn Russian could smile like that while being absolutely and completely freaking furious and terrifying. It was creepy.

"Please, Ms. Zakharova; I am afraid that I must insist."

His voice had dropped much lower, his accent much thicker as he took a step toward her. Leaning down, he placed one arm behind her back and grabbed her hand with the other as he led her out of the booth. I had a feeling this man wasn't used to not getting his way.

He seemed nice and everything, but also kind of scary.

And he was Russian scary, which was always a thousand times worse. I think it was the accent. That, and they tended to make pets out of things like massive seven-foot bears and full-grown Siberian tigers.

Kim gulped, seemed to shake off the strange trance she was in, and allowed him to help her up. She turned to me, winked, her smile returned, and she looked away. I breathed a sigh of relief.

The wink was kind of like our secret code that "all was good." We'd first started using it in college whenever talking to guys. One wink basically meant "I'm fine, this guy is hot" and two or three or seven winks meant "please save me."

The handsome yet still very scary Russian turned to me, and I shyly allowed him to repeat the same gentlemanly gesture as he helped me up.

He nodded at one of the beefy bouncers along the sides of the room, and then toward Teyanna and Kendrix up toward the bar. Two other bouncers stationed closer to the girls nodded, and then started to approach the girls.

"Ladies, if you'd please assure your friends they are in excellent hands? I'm afraid Leon and Ilya have more brawn than tact and are only scaring them, unfortunately."

Sure enough, I saw the girls grab each other's arms and try to take a step back from the two very enormous, very tattooed men right next to them. Kim waved energetically to get their attention, giving them a blown kiss and the "it's safe" wink.

Teyanna visibly relaxed, tossing a mildly reproachful look at the largest bouncer, who simply smiled at her, bowed his head just a little, and turned to part the crowd for them.

Kendrix, on the other hand, worked closely with a lot of club promoters, so I knew she would have recognized the club's Russian owner at once when she looked our way.

The men escorted us upstairs, and I had to close my hand over my mouth to contain my giddy squeal of excitement. This was such an absolute treat! I'd never, never in a million years be able to afford a freaking private bottle service at a place like this. *And* a private table!

It was almost worth being the ass-end of Bryce's and DevLynn's shitty joke. Technically, if I hadn't gone to that first beach house party, I would never have exchanged contact info with one of the girls at the party, which is how I'd first started receiving all these social media promos.

Teyanna and Kendrix got to the table first and took a seat. The entire floor looked like a sexy, cotton-candy dream in pink and blue and purple neon. Large, beautiful fresh flowers in various shades of vivid colors donned every table. Sheer, elegant ivory-colored curtains wrapped partially around each table made it feel luxuriously cozy and intimate. Live ivy draped around the masts of the curtains, giving an ethereal yet seductive look.

"This place is absolutely gorgeous! And the vibe—is absolutely sick. I can't. It's like... Girls' Night Out meets tropical paradise!" Kendrix was already vlogging everything.

We posed for a quick photo of us all together in the booth, making sure to capture the bottles of champagne between us.

"Come on, my sexy little mamas! This *Dom* ain't gonna drink itself!" Teyanna flagged down a staff member who popped the first bottle for us.

This night could literally not get any better, I thought as I smiled and sipped on the silky, sweet bubbles. The more I sipped, the more I remembered the barely-there bustier set I'd purchased earlier today. It gave me a secret thrill, a weird sort of confidence knowing that I'd worn it out underneath my black dress. No one would ever know, I giggled guiltily.

Turning back to the girls, I raised my glass and joined in on the fun. We'd been dancing and drinking glass after glass of champagne, and I was feeling *awesome*.

Laughing at Kendrix's latest mishap with her apparently super-hot and recently super single boss, I told myself for the millionth effing time that it was not *his* cologne, dammit.

I reminded myself the same thing again, after telling Teyanna how awesome it was that she'd already gotten promoted since starting her job back in May. I cheers-ed with her and promised we'd celebrate for her soon at brunch, almost spilling my drink in the process because I thought I'd seen a dark, massive form moving toward me in the crowd.

I drained the rest of my glass and took another pull of the vape. *Get it together, Freya, for shit's sake.*

"Guess who Freya ran into today?!"

My eyes snapped to Kimberly in horror as I gave her a look that could have melted steel.

She laughed.

If I didn't love her so much, I would have killed her for bringing him up again, just when I had almost forgotten exactly how good he smelled. Forgotten how his massive hand felt around my wrists and on my upper arm...

I cleared my throat nervously, suddenly a little less tipsy.

"Uh, you know, I feel like that isn't the vibe tonight, *Kimberly Anne*," I gave her the crazy eyes, but it was no use.

That cat was definitely out of the bag now, dammit.

"Oh, it's totally the 'vibe,' Frey!"

She winked at me and I couldn't help it, I burst into an obnoxious fit of giggles.

Yup, the alcohol and weed were definitely hitting me right. There's no way I'd be this chill about my ordeal if I weren't moderately tipsy and maybe just a smidgen high.

Welllllp, here goes nothing, I thought, as the girls predictably almost spit out their drinks to get more details.

"DevLynn motherfucking 'the Devil lives within me' Hartington," Kimberly squeaked out victoriously.

Teyanna was not impressed at all, nor Kendrix. There was no way I could ever be good friends with someone who thought highly of that toxic little bitch.

"Uhhh... and just what the mother-effing shit do we care about that stanky ass bitch for?!"

"Uh, yeah, Kim—and exactly how the fuck is that bitch a 'vibe?!'"

Kendrix chimed in, and I couldn't have agreed with her more. Teyanna had a point, as well. Stanky was such an accurate description, it really was.

"'Stanky' is exactly friggin' right!" Kimberly had the same thought I'd just had, and we burst into giggles again.

"Alright, alright, Kimmie... you better have somethin' better than common friggin' knowledge on that bitch to make up for soiling the evening with her stench!"

Teyanna laughed as Kendrix toasted her words.

By now, Kendrix had switched off the champagne and on to the hard stuff. Her glass was already empty when she tried to sip, but she didn't seem to realize as she tipped the glass back further. An ice cube hit her on the face and she jumped, and we burst into another fit of laughter.

Eventually she laughed along with us—but only after we promised she hadn't ruined her eye makeup, of course.

"Girl, you could have poured the whole damn thing on your face and you'd still be the prettiest friggin' girl in the club," Teyanna told her with a blown kiss and a wink. She turned back to Kim, "Okay but for real, how that Devi bitch a 'vibe?!'"

Once Kim had relayed the story to the rest of the group, my sides and cheeks hurt from laughing so much. I had to daintily blot the corners of my eyes to remove the tears and preserve my smokey eye makeup.

Thankfully, everything that happened outside the store—as well as the actual identity of my rescuer slash kidnapper—was excluded.

I think Kim had realized I was going to choose violence if anyone else knew about everything else.

One of our favorite songs came on, and we all finished the last of our drinks and headed to the dance floor. Along the way, I scolded myself for the millionth time that I had *not* just smelled his cologne, dammit.

Chapter 17

Brodie

Hearing the sound of her laughter was almost like a balm to my rage.

Then, the sexy fragrance of her hair drifted over to me. She ran her hand through her soft, dark curls, tossing the silky mass around as she danced only a few feet away from me.

Once her delicious scent hit me, any chance she ever had of escaping from me was gone forever. If she thought she was going to dangle herself in front of me like that and not get snatched up, carried away, and fucked, then I was about to prove her very thoroughly and completely wrong.

I knew she couldn't really see me from where I stood in the darkened corner of the room due to a fancy trick with the lighting. I was also pretty good at hiding in plain sight, in spite of my size, and so were my men.

Watching her gorgeous body in that fucking dress and those damn black heels had made my semi-hard dick instantly rock hard again. The rest of the team had better hurry the fuck up and get into position, because if I had to watch her dancing and literally smell that amazing scent any longer things were going to get explosive.

The song changed to one they apparently didn't like, because the four girls made faces and giggled their way back over to their table across the room.

It didn't matter how far she was away from me. Her intoxicating fragrance had seared itself into my brain even stronger than before.

Finally my team cleared the location and the perimeter. Everyone else was getting into position and then we could move in.

She was coming back to my hotel with me. Tonight.

Once I'd fucked the crazy out of my system and then held her in my arms for at least several hours, we could figure everything else out tomorrow. I was going to go bat shit crazy soon if I didn't get her back within my control and then get her someplace safe.

I had made it exponentially and indubitably clear to the rest of my team that no fucking one was to touch Freya unless her life was in immediate danger, or their own life would be in immediate danger.

I felt myself beasting out again at the thought of any other man touching her, or even seeing her. Luckily, my own men knew me well enough that I meant it.

"Magnuson, you lucky bastard. *That's* the new target?! That gorgeous redhead over there in the little black dress and the fuck-me-heels?!"

I'd never been more thankful for Bryan, who had the good sense to slap the newest member of Marco's tactical team very comically across the face before he got himself killed running his fucking mouth.

"Gabe, you better shut the fuck up if you want to keep your head attached to your neck and shoulders," Jim piped in, too.

I really needed to increase their bonuses; it would have been such a pain in the ass to have to cover up a murder with this many witnesses present. The thought of any kind of serious violence in front of Freya also made my stomach turn pretty fucking instantly.

Gabe at least had the decency to look terrified as I stepped toward him.

"Her name is Freya, and if you even think about her like that again, I'll spoon feed your fucking spleen to you one bite at a time. That fucking clear, soldier?"

He nodded and kept the hell quiet, proving he apparently wasn't a complete fucking moron.

Unlike my own team, apparently.

"What?! I thought you said you'd do that to my kidneys earlier if I called her pretty again? What the hell, Magnuson. Thought we had something special."

"Just wait 'til you hear what he said he was going to do to my spine."

I pinched the bridge of my nose and closed my eyes, trying to remember why the hell I was friends with these degenerates.

"I'm starting to think this boy's all talk; just guess what he threatened to do with my still beating heart."

Taking the safety off my gun and pulling back the slide only made them laugh harder. Idiots. I really should have just shot them, witnesses be damned.

The bastards were still laughing as they retreated back to position so I could intercept her. The girls had returned to the dance floor as soon as the current song had started playing.

I had to admit, *Cardi B* was one of my favorites, too.

Completely unaware of my presence, she continued laughing and moving that body in ways that probably weren't legal in some states. My dick was trying to eject itself out of my pants, demanding that I pounce on her immediately. That evil little black dress and those damn fuck-me-now heels were making me want to rip out the eyeballs from every other man in the room.

I stalked toward her slowly, willing my anger to simmer to a more containable level as I approached. The rest of the girls smiled alongside her—Mikhail's team informed us they were all four to-gether—dancing and doing very stereotypical female things. Freya threw her head back as she tried and failed to stop the infectious giggling from something one of the other girls had done.

Damn, she was cute.

Smiling like a predator finally having cornered his prey, I wait-ed patiently for her to realize exactly how much trouble she was in.

My grin widened menacingly as her friends noted my presence. They also noted my sudden, very intense interest in their redheaded friend. Their giggling got even worse as the other three girls gave me the once over.

I'd probably watched her dancing for at least half the song before she realized something was off. When she'd first turned around to see what her friends had been staring at, she was still laughing.

I'd never forget the way she looked in that moment.

She was the most beautiful sight I'd ever seen, the beaming warmth of her smile glowing across her face and shining through her smokey indigo eyes. Her long, dark hair was tousled and there was a fire in her eyes, a purely passionate joy. Need to claim her, hold her, and protect her all soared through me as I stared down at her hungrily.

The instant she recognized me, she tried to run.

She didn't get far.

I grabbed her upper arm easily and her mouth formed that tiny little "o" again. Still smiling darkly, all I could think was how my dick was going to be in there soon.

Very soon.

"Baby, you're in So. Much. *Trouble*."

Chapter 18

Freya

As I turned around, my heart literally stopped in my chest and the smile died on my lips.

Brodie had found me. *He was actually here.*

I bolted.

He grabbed my arm, instantly trapping me.

"Baby... you're in So. Much. *Trouble*."

I stared up at him, completely lost. His firm grip around my upper arm had set my entire body on fire.

"Ummm... what? Wh—why are you here?"

Fear, panic, raging lust, embarrassment, fear again... my head was swimming a little drunkenly. I was abruptly glad I'd skipped the booze and chugged a water during our last dance break.

Why the freaking hell was he here?

And how?!

He chuckled, looking down at me, and I ovulated again.

At this rate I was going to go straight into freaking menopause by the ripe old age of twenty-four. A few more hours around this man and I was bound to run out of oocytes.

"Honey, why didn't you tell me you were going out tonight? You look... good enough to eat," as he paused, his eyes roamed down the length of me, back up to my lips, then directly into my eyes.

By the time he'd reached my eyes again I was almost pissed at the girls for not pouring their drinks on me to help put out the flames that had obviously enveloped my entire body.

On second thought, the drinks were back on the table. Still, they could have at least looked concerned!

I couldn't even speak at this point; I could only burn.

Kim recognized him instantly because she'd searched his picture during our conversation earlier. She gave me a little shove toward him and grabbed the other two girls, signaling toward the table.

Teyanna passed by, giving me a wink and a very loud cat-like "Rawr!"

Kendrix raised her eyebrows at me crookedly, grinning like an idiot.

Some freaking friends they were! Feeding me straight to the hungry, psychotic lion!

"No! No! Wait, I—I need to use the ladies' room. Yeah, can we all uh, go together? All of us *together*? As in no one gets left *by themselves?!*"

But it was absolutely no use. They'd quickly deserted me, giggling and catcalling like a bunch of maniacs. I was alone with the angry giant.

"I'll take you, baby. Let's go."

Brodie's grip on my arm was like an iron shackle as he led me toward the back where the facilities were located.

He then stood outside the ladies' room door like an angry, scowling oak tree, inclining his head toward the entrance. When I just stared at him, he crossed his arms expectantly and stared back at me, turning his back toward the door. He was literally guarding the only entrance and exit.

Stunned, I turned to go inside.

Before I got far, he grabbed me again, then reached into my purse for my phone. He pocketed it, then nodded his head behind him toward the bathrooms.

"Hey! You can't just—"

The words died on my lips at the look he gave me. I ran into the bathrooms, closing the closest stall door with a loud *bang!*

I locked the door behind me.

Because the tiny metal lock on the bathroom door would stand a freaking chance against the giant growling grizzly bear, yup.

What the hell was I supposed to do now?!

I dug around in my purse for my vape. I definitely needed to take a hit—or seven—to calm my racing heart. I was just sober enough to realize how freaking scary and probably insanely dangerous it was for me that he was here. How impossible it was, and how it made absolutely zero sense.

This was bad. This was really, really bad.

I was also still drunk and high enough to feel instantly turned on the second he put his hands on me back on the dance floor, despite the fear that came right after.

It was like the memory of him had been slowly simmering in my subconscious all night, teetering between a daydream and a much darker, sinister type of dream.

When he actually appeared in front of me, it was like a sexy monster had somehow escaped from the depths of my nightmares to follow me back home and finish the job, uncaring that I was now fully awake and supposedly in control.

I took another pull of the vape as I tried to get the image of that room full of all those weapons out of my mind.

It absolutely didn't work. Annoyed and completely out of sorts, I roughly shoved it back into my purse.

I wasn't even wearing my digital watch, dammit. I'd accidentally broken it earlier that week. Which meant that I officially had zero ways to contact the girls to help get me out of this mess.

What was worse, I was pretty sure I was by far the most sober of the group. And I felt pretty damn drunk, actually, now that I was sitting in this bathroom stall with so much really bright lighting.

A loud banging on the door told me that Brodie had grown impatient with my frantic stalling. Without thinking I jumped to obey his command. I quickly washed my hands, then placed my wet hands along the back of my neck to cool my flushed body. Too much dancing, that's what was making me so warm and shivery at the same time.

Yup.

I quickly checked my reflection in the mirror—I mean seriously, this new foundation was *amazing*—and headed out to face my fate.

When I was almost out of the bathroom, I glanced back at the soap dispenser. Maybe I could make a run for it again...

Chapter 19

Brodie

"Freya; if you aren't out in three minutes I'm coming inside and I don't give a damn for the consequences," I didn't mean to growl but I was having a very hard time controlling my rage.

I heard the *clickity-clacks* of her heels on the tile floor, the sink running, and then the door was thrown open. I met the beautiful purple fire in her eyes with my own darkly feral smile.

"Are you sure you can handle yourself? The last time you ran into a bathroom after me—"

"Don't. You. *Dare.*"

I grabbed her shoulders and lifted her face up to mine as I breathed the words into the sweetness of her barely parted lips. The little squeaky sound she made right after I'd put my hands on her had set me on fire, and I feasted on her little tremble of fear as she looked up at me. I loved the way her lips were already swollen, already turned a deeper shade of sexy, glittery pink.

"Let's go. Now."

Letting go of her shoulders, I grabbed her by the arm again and marched us toward the elevator. I couldn't get her back to my hotel fast enough. I also couldn't stand to not be touching her somewhere, even if it was only her shoulders or her arm.

"What? No! I'm here with my friends! I'm not going anywhere with you!"

"It's already taken care of. My men will stay with each one of them until they are ready to leave. They'll also see them safely home. Judging by how fast they were hitting the champagne, that won't be very long," I told her darkly as I practically launched us inside the elevator.

I pounded my hand against the keypad for the ground floor of the club. Immediately I closed and locked the doors using the program on my watch, completely barring other people from getting inside.

Or any pretty little redheads from getting out.

She turned toward me with deep indigo sparks practically flying out of her eyes. Gorgeous, yet more than likely combative.

"I don't want to go anywhere with you! And how the hell are you here, now?! How did you even..."

I moved toward her the instant the elevators locked us inside, forcing her up against the wall. I almost passed the fuck out when I saw the way her breath hitched and her eyes half closed. How she arched into me, not away from me, when I'd handled her so roughly.

Fuck me, but this woman was perfect.

"Baby, I'm trying really hard not to shove my dick inside that sweet, tight little pussy of yours right this second. It's all I've been thinking about since you pulled your little prank this afternoon. So, I suggest you behave, unless you want to get fucked like a wild animal inside this elevator," I breathed the words against her face and her neck as I held her close to me.

I was mistaken about her intoxicating scent. It was definitely way sweeter and a hell of a lot more sinful in real life.

Her eyes looked more blue now as they stared up at me, dazed from alcohol as well as desire. She was much easier to read after she'd been drinking, I'd noticed.

Her eyes wandered farther and lingered longer. Her bottom lip kept getting pulled inside her mouth, then captured softly between the flash of her white teeth. Her dark pink shimmery lips were constantly teased by the tip of her cute little tongue. There was an obvious flush to her pale cheeks, and I knew it wasn't just from the drinks.

Especially while she was a little tipsy, the purely female way she arched her back and gracefully moved her hips as she walked was like a calling card meant for my cock.

"I... I... umm," the way she stuttered breathlessly only made her lips appear more swollen and needy.

I descended on her like a starving man, pulling those lips between mine and sucking.

I bit down gently, then plundered inside her mouth when she gasped in reaction to my dominating kiss. I could not get enough of the hot, wet sweetness of her mouth. The delicate hint of the champagne she had been drinking mixed with the cotton candy sweetness of her lips, and the combination made my dick throb.

I pushed my hips into her softness, letting her feel the rigid outline of my cock pressed into her core. I wanted her to know exactly what she did to me, every heavy, swollen inch of it.

I held her up against the wall of the elevator and spread her thighs even wider. I watched in fascination as she whimpered and trembled while I thrust my cock against her once, twice, three times. On the third time, she threw her head to the side and tried to suppress a very sexy, whimpery little moan.

I grabbed her roughly along the graceful slope of her jaw, forcing her pretty face back toward me.

"No baby, don't hide anything from me. I want you to show me how much you want it."

"I—I—I don't know. I'm not..." her words stopped instantly as I swung down on her backside with my open palm.

"Fuck, baby... keep acting up. I am already going to punish this juicy ass. So. Fucking. Hard," my words were cut off by her moans and the hard cracks of my palms on her ass with each word.

"Ow! What the—hell?! Fucking hell! *Owwww...* you fuckhead! Owwww! That fucking hurts!"

She was trying to twist away from me, but there was no escaping. The sweet, fleshy bounce of her ass was like a drug. I couldn't get enough.

Suddenly I turned her around, her back flush against my front as I ground my pelvis against her deliciously rounded backside. She moaned, throwing her head back, eyes completely closed, her mouth forming the little "o" that I was officially fucking obsessed with.

"That's it, baby; you like a little sting, don't you," I nuzzled my face against the curve of her neck.

My dick was so fucking hard, throbbing almost painfully against the fabric of my black tactical pants.

Her only response was a whimper that quickly turned into a moan when I gently nipped the juncture of her neck and shoulder.

"I bet your pussy is wet for me, hmm? Damn, baby. You're driving me crazy, Freya."

I groped the generous bulk of her breasts as I molded her body against mine, cursing the barrier of the black dress she wore. I wanted to feel the soft, supple weight of her bare breasts in my hands.

Through the thin material of her dress, I traced along the sensitive edge of her torso and along her ribcage. I touched the firm, curved edges of what felt like underwire cups and a small strip of fabric attached below.

My heartbeat tripled and my mouth started watering as I slowly reached to her front, searching right between her breasts for the outline of the pretty black lace rose that was burned into my memory from earlier that day.

My dick almost exploded when my fingers brushed across black lace petals...

FUCK.

Growling, I grabbed a fistful of her gorgeous hair and yanked her head back to look up at me over her shoulder. I was honestly astounded at the sheer self-control I was exerting when very little blood was available to my actual brain.

"You're wearing it now, aren't you?" I growled against her lips.

She whimpered into my open mouth, held so close to hers.

"No! I—of course not—no, it's a different one. It's not that one!"

Her face and neck deepened in a beautiful blush as she tried to lie, but her breathy voice and the way she kept arching up into me gave her away.

My other hand fell down again, hard, on her ass.

"Baby, don't ever lie to me. Are you wearing the same naughty lingerie from earlier today?"

I could tease this woman for hours. She was made for pure fucking sinful pleasure, every sweet, mouthwatering inch of her.

"I—ahem, ahem—that's really none of your business, dammit!"

She tried to struggle against my hold, but it probably only heightened the brush of my pelvis against her stinging backside. She was breathless, moaning, and whimpering. I tightened my hold around her, loving how it made her arch into me even more.

I used my other hand to slowly raise the hem of her black dress. Still leaning into me, she frantically grabbed at my hand as she tried to stop me. It was like a butterfly trying to beat up a boulder.

Higher and higher my hand pulled up her dress, exposing the muscular curve of her thighs, the sexy as fuck flare of her fleshy hips, and eventually...

...the edge of the tiny little black thong that she'd purchased earlier.

I have no idea how I remained standing when my entire blood volume was pounding through every inch of my aching cock.

She moved her hips into me again as my fingers moved closer and closer to the burning heat between her thighs. I moved aside the miniscule scrap of lace and ran my fingers across the soft seam of her pussy lips.

She was absolutely, completely, and utterly *soaked*.

Growling, chuckling, pulling her so close to me that every single curve was pressed against me, I leaned down to nibble gently on her ear.

"Baby, the things I'm going to do to you tonight, you naughty little girl..."

My blood pounded in my ears as I thrust her dress back into place and practically flew us out of the club, onto the street, and into the back of my black SUV.

Chapter 20

Freya

There was nothing that prepared me for the insane amount of lust that was surging through me in the backseat of that SUV. I could barely breathe because my mind kept replaying what he'd growled in my ear back in the elevator.

Baby, the things I'm going to do to you tonight, you naughty little girl...

"Boss, make sure you get that package in the backseat. It's from Jim. Said it was important."

I vaguely recognized the same slightly muffled voice from earlier coming from the front seat. It almost sounded like he was shouting, but his voice wasn't very loud. The same blacked-out privacy screen was drawn; it was apparently some level of soundproof.

I didn't know if that made me feel safer or not.

Brodie retrieved what sounded like some kind of plastic package on the floor of the SUV. His handsome face was drawn in a ferocious scowl and had been since he'd drug me out of the elevator. When he grabbed what looked like some kind of padded fabric from inside the package, he let out an extremely terrifying bark of laughter.

"Fuck both of you fuckwads. Are these what I fucking think they are?"

His voice boomed toward the front seat and I jumped. Yup, soundproof. Or maybe he thought his driver was partially deaf.

"You betcha; Jim was worried about those sharp little kneecaps doing any more damage. He heard you'd choked to death the last time you tried to get fresh with her."

"I call bullshit, Miles. Sounds like a cover story. I bet Jim got you a pair of knee pads so you wouldn't bruise each other while y'all sucked each other off."

Muffled barks of laughter were audible from the front of the car.

"How about you just fucking drive instead of trying to run your own damn comedy show?"

"Funny you would mention that; I'm actually considering uploading the video of her kicking your ass to *YouTube*... consider it my early Christmas bonus. Whadya think, eh Boss?"

"I think dead men don't have much need for Christmas, or bonuses."

Even louder laughter from the front seat.

"You know, I don't blame her one bit, Boss. I've always heard you were a fucking lousy kisser."

Who the fuck were these guys?

Brodie glanced at me, then burst out laughing again at the expression on my face.

"Nervous, baby?"

He blatantly stroked the rock-hard thickness of his cock as he stared at me. His voice was so low, so deep, I could almost feel it more than hear it.

"Nervous doesn't even begin to cover what I'm feeling right now," I tossed the words at him as I hugged my purse closer to my midsection.

I was not looking over at him when he was doing that. Nope, nope, nope.

He moved toward me again, his vivid green eyes shining darkly as his other hand still stroked. I froze, very confused between fear and the strongest surge of lust I'd ever had in my life. I couldn't look away from the pure sexual fire in his eyes.

"Are you nervous because of how fucking hard I'm going to make you scream tonight? Or how much I'm going to enjoy spanking that juicy ass of yours until it's dark pink and angry?"

He imprisoned his arms around me again as he spoke. The dirty, filthy way he talked sent desire soaring through me to pool hotly between my legs. My hips rolled involuntarily as I whimpered, which quickly turned into a definitely not quiet moan.

He placed his other hand over my mouth to stifle the sound, and something deep in the corners of my mind blossomed to life. I'd never admit it out loud, but in a twisted way that huge, rough palm over my mouth made me feel ridiculously secure.

"Shhhh, baby. We're almost to my hotel, Freya, I promise. I can't have you making any of those sexy noises in here. Miles is extremely skilled at what he does. It'd be a real pain in the ass if I had to replace him because I had to kill him for overhearing you," the deep timbre of his voice stroked the fire inside me.

I felt hot literally all over and my head was spinning wildly.

I was pretty far from sober at this point, at least I told myself that it was alcohol and not testosterone that was making my head swim.

I was also about to be under the complete control of this terrifying man, this total stranger. I didn't want to think about how much that really freaking turned me on, mostly because it was getting a little hard to think at all. Thinking could wait for tomorrow, or later, or maybe never.

But he'd literally ambushed me, again, and kidnapped me away from my friends!

How the hell did he even know where I was?!

The longer I was in his SUV, the less sober I felt. I absolutely knew I wasn't in driving shape—to be fair I normally wasn't in driving shape, definitely not in this part of the city. But I could also tell I wasn't anywhere near blackout drunk.

Whenever I got close to that point, it wasn't even fun anymore.

Still, the buzz I felt was strong. It made me just foggy enough to not be actively screaming because his grip on me was so tight yet left me just wary enough to recognize that I was probably making *really* dumb choices.

And he was so warm, and so impossibly strong. The way his tattoos were peeking out from his tight black shirt, the ink wrapped around his bowling ball sized biceps made me flush with dark desire.

What would it be like to let him take complete control, knowing he'd keep me safe while I let him use my body? Giving in to the relaxing effects of the alcohol and weed, I sighed as I eased back into his grip.

He growled in response, flexing his arm just a little harder around me. I moaned behind his hand over my mouth. Why the hell did he have to smell so freaking amazing?

"Fuck baby; I'm not going to make it to the hotel. I need to taste that pussy. Now."

He kept one hand around my mouth as he moved his other down the length of my dress.

Once again he lifted the hem, this time much more forcefully as he pulled the satiny black material all the way above my hip. In practically the same movement, he ran his thumb down the front of my pussy, spreading me open for the savage thrust of his fingers inside me.

I was actually glad that his hand was over my mouth because it helped cover the sound of my desperate moan when he'd instantly found my G-spot.

He curled his fingers up wickedly, and I couldn't help but open my mouth behind his palm so I could glide my tongue along the salty roughness of his skin.

Oh my god, his hands; they were so massive, so freaking *manly*, just like the rest of him.

I wanted to lick and suck on his fingers, twirl my tongue around and around while I watched his emerald green eyes burn with need. I felt the raw feminine power of my desire heating up from his fingers twisting and thrusting inside me. The sounds he made were quiet but they were absolutely feral, and they were only making me hotter.

I have no idea how long the drive was. All too soon he removed his fingers from inside me, and I immediately wanted them back.

He obscenely sucked on his long, tanned fingers exactly as he had this morning. It made me want to pounce on him.

"Damn you taste so good, baby. *Fuck.* I'm going to feast on your pussy until you scream."

I couldn't speak. There wasn't enough blood flow to my brain because it had all pooled between my thighs.

"We're here. You're already getting another spanking, so I suggest you don't do anything stupid on the way up to my room, Freya."

He was running his hands through my hair as he spoke. It felt so amazing, his words barely registered. By the time they did, I was already out of the backset of the SUV and being marched toward the private entrance.

One look at his face, and whatever sassy retort I'd tried to throw at him died on my lips.

Chapter 21

Brodie

If I didn't get my aching cock inside the sweetness of her pussy soon, I was going to lose my mind. My body was burning way beyond fever pitch for her. I couldn't ever remember a time when I'd needed to be balls deep inside a woman so badly.

Probably because there hadn't been one.

I couldn't stop touching her. Even though I knew she wasn't completely sober and there was no way she'd escape me, I still needed to hold her. To make sure she was close, real, and finally fucking safe.

While waiting an eternity for her when she'd been in the restroom at the club, I had seriously contemplated storming inside and laying claim to her right then and there. But something made my stomach turn at the thought of our first time being inside a public fucking bathroom.

A fancy-schmancy bullshit luxury nightclub public bathroom, but still.

That was when I'd pounded on the door. I'd been about to storm inside when she'd emerged.

Honestly, I thought I'd compromised extremely well given the circumstances. They were lucky that door was still attached to its hinges.

The elevator doors finally opened and I couldn't get her inside fast enough. The doors closed behind us, and she visibly jumped. Abruptly I noticed a slight change, a tension in her posture that hadn't been there before.

Good. I wanted her to be a little bit afraid.

She really had no idea the kind of fucking danger she'd put herself in tonight. She should have stayed put dammit, and listened to me instead of running off without a clue as to what kind of evil was looking for her.

I'd never allow her to do something so foolish again, ever. I couldn't fucking help it, I knew she was already scared and I was acting like a psychotic jackass, but the thought of how differently this night could have ended for her made me let out another growl of frustration and rage.

She visibly trembled in my grasp. Her skin felt cold and clammy, not flushed and heated like it had been before.

"Are y—you... what are you going to do to me?"

Shit.

That was fear, real fear. Dammit. Not trembly submissive female super turned-on bedroom play fear.

I turned to her, wrapping my arm around her back and bringing her up close.

I used my other hand to gently play with her long, silky hair.

"Mmmm, you have the prettiest hair, Freya. I love the way it smells," I leaned down, brushing against the curve of her neck with my lips.

I took a long, slow inhale and blew it out gently across her neck. She gasped, but her voice cracked a little too much to be only desire. I kept my touch gentle and very slow.

I knew she was feeling the roughness of my beard along the super sensitive spot. I've always had more of a two o'clock shadow and a five o'clock beard. The way her skin instantly flushed pink from the slightly abrasive contact made me glad I'd not shaved since yesterday morning.

Damn, but I loved seeing my mark on this woman.

"Freya, baby. Why are you so scared?"

I kept teasing the spot along her neck with my beard stubble and tried to keep the savage, growling need out of my voice.

"Because you're... we don't even know each other, and—you said that you were going to—to—"

She started panting a little when I gently nipped the skin along her neck. I immediately soothed the little sting with a soft swipe of my tongue, and she moaned.

"Going to what, baby? Tell me, honey."

"To... you said... I can't say it, okay?!"

She was starting to sound much more breathless than scared.

Fucking finally. I was a man, not a damn monk!

"Why can't you say it, hmm?"

I was probably going straight to hell for the way I loved to tease her so much. I couldn't resist the sexy way she responded so boldly to me, then acted shy and guilty, like she'd been caught being naughty. It was so motherfucking sexy.

"It's, I don't know, it's—messed up. Embarrassing. Demeaning, and dirty."

"No, baby; it's so damn sexy. It's naughty. And you've been a very, very naughty girl."

I probably wasn't playing fair, but I couldn't trust myself much longer around her if she didn't submit to me soon. One of the things that'd instantly turned me on about her was how much she liked when I talked dirty to her. As I'd expected, she whimpered huskily, then relaxed a little into my arms.

"But... I was scared. You scared me, I didn't know what to do! Look, I'm sorry about the whole body wash, uh, shower thing, alright?! I didn't know what else to do! You didn't have to—have to track me down and kidnap me again!"

She was starting to struggle more in my grasp.

I sighed. So be it, then.

"Freya, the only thing you should be scared of right now is how fucking hard I'm going to spank your juicy little ass for putting yourself in so much danger tonight. Now get on th—"

"Danger? DANGER?!"

She interrupted me, squeaking at the top of her lungs in little tornado of fiery indignation.

It was so damn cute, I had to bite back a grin.

I was supposed to be punishing her, dammit. Making her understand that whether she liked it or not the rules had changed, and she was in a very treacherous world now. A dark, lecherous world that would swallow her up without my protection.

She started actively struggling against my hold. Good, she seemed angry now. Not scared. I could deal with angry.

"Yes, baby. Danger. And you'll never do something so stupid and reckless again. I'm going to make sure of it."

"You have *got* to be kidding me! *Errrggh!* Let me go, you fucking buffoon! This is so hella-illegal!"

I chuckled at her, enjoying the way her body pushed into me everywhere as she struggled uselessly. I easily subdued her, crossing both of her arms behind her back—damn she was *really* flexible, that was so sexy—using only one of my hands.

She wasn't going anywhere. Not until she'd learned who was in control.

"Buffoon? What are we, distinguished English gentlemen trading parlor-room insults?"

She really was adorable. I'd never had so much fun with a woman before.

"How about cock sucking asshole-er fuck shit dickhead bastard *fucker?!* Now let me *motherfucking* go, you dick fucker!"

I laughed even harder at her nonsensical yet creative string of profanity. I shifted her easily, giving me better access to her curvy backside. She must have known what I was going to do before I did it, because she let out an angry shriek and tried to flex her hips away from my hand. The first blow was aimed right below the curve of her ass, close to the center of her thighs.

The way she gasped and then whimpered made moisture bead on the tip of my pulsing cock, and I groaned hungrily. If I kept this up, just spanking her ass was going to make me blow my load in an instant.

"No! You jackass! Stop! It hurts! It—"

"What did I tell you about lying to me, hmm baby?" I growled into her neck as I gently bit down, then licked away the sting. I gave her a few more hard swats to prove my point.

"Screw you, I'm not freaking lying! It hurts, dammit! Stop!"

She probably didn't realize she had started to lean into the blows, instead of away from. Her body had started to take over.

I stopped spanking her ass long enough to roughly grope each one of her wonderfully rounded cheeks. I loved the way her whimpers were turning into deep, sexy moans.

"You're not lying, huh? So if I check your pussy right now, it won't be soaking wet? Your clit won't be swollen, peaking out between the top of your pussy lips?"

"Oh, my... holy hell, I'm... no, I'm not. I'm definitely not, it hurts! You can't, it's—"

The deep red flush that enveloped her face and neck told me otherwise. Her eyelids were also half-closed, as if they were too heavy with desire to keep open anymore.

"Why are you lying to yourself? When you know how good it feels when I put my hands on you?"

Her only response was a short moan, which she quickly tried to muffle by biting her lips.

"You... scare me. You're so freaking intense, dammit! And bossy! I can't think!"

Her breathing was heavy, erratic.

"Maybe you're thinking too much, hmmm?" She was so fun to tease, I couldn't help it. "Baby, I'll be honest with you. My dick is way too fucking hard right now for me to be gentle. You're safe, baby. You're always safe with me, Freya. But..." as I spoke, she couldn't stop trembling.

I leaned down to kiss the soft skin along her collarbone before I pulled up her dress to see for myself. I could taste the frantic pulse beating along her neck and feel her goosebumps with my tongue.

Delicious.

"...but, if I check your pussy and find it so wet for me that it's dripping down the inside of your thighs, I'm going to spank that bare ass with my leather belt, then fuck you like we both know you want me to."

Chapter 22

Freya

My body was singing, every inch of me on fire and burning with unbridled pleasure as he held me in his iron grip.

It was wrong, so wrong the crude way he talked and roughly handled me. I should be absolutely appalled, terrified, disgusted. I should be thinking of any and every possible way to escape from him.

I should definitely be thinking how psychotic and over-the-top controlling it was that he'd tracked me down at the nightclub, then hauled me halfway across town and drug me up to his private lair to torment. I should be thinking a million other things right now, but all I could think was *more,* and *hell, yes!* Those were the only coherent thoughts I could conjure.

I fully suspected after this much testosterone exposure that my brain resembled a sad, pitiful hunk of slightly green Swiss cheese.

I should probably be thankful that I still had basic body functions at this point. My ability to pant was completely unaffected, if not enhanced. Which was all I could do as his hand moved straight toward my aching center, because I knew what he'd find.

"Mmmm, my naughty girl, you're fucking drenched, hell yeah," his fingers thrusted into me and I moaned shakily, already horribly close to orgasm.

He pulled his fingers out of my pussy and then slowly drug them upwards toward my clit. I almost screamed from the intense pleasure. If he weren't holding me, I would have fallen over.

I felt wetness between the very tops of my thighs, exactly as he'd said. I tried to close my legs tightly, but the iron strength of his hand moved relentlessly in search of the soaking wet heat between my legs.

When he'd discovered my secret, he growled as he roughly shoved me toward the bed.

There was literally no part of me that was capable of moving away from him; my body was screaming at me to let him take over. I watched the movements of his powerful masculine hands as they reached for his belt buckle.

Fuck, that was so sexy! I wanted more.

"Get out of that dress. Now. I want to see you in that lingerie."

There was no mistaking the authority in his voice, but I was so drunk on lust that all I could do was whimper and bite my lip as I drew my legs closer to my body. The slight sting of the soft black fabric of my dress rubbing over the super sensitive skin on my ass was making it hard to think.

"Freya, take it off. Now. Or I'll rip it off, baby."

He'd already taken his belt out of the loops and folded the thick, worn strip of leather in his hands. Suddenly, he snapped the belt loudly between them. The ominous *crack* of the black leather made me whimper again helplessly in spite of my racing heart.

"One," he slowly moved even closer toward me on the bed.

I remained immobile.

"Two," he moved even closer yet and leaned down on the bed, putting the belt in one of his hands as the other reached for my ankle.

My favorite *Jimmy Choo* booties still covered each foot.

"Baby, if I get to three, you know what's going to happen."

I definitely knew what was going to happen. But I couldn't move, couldn't look away from the beautiful green fire of his eyes.

My body was practically screaming for his touch.

"Three."

He moved so fast I could barely process as he flipped me over onto my stomach.

I felt the material of my favorite black dress scream as it was torn down my back. Goosebumps were all over me from the sudden cold rush of air. Normally, the needless destruction of my *favorite* dress would have made me angry enough to choose violence instantly, but the only thing I could do was whimper and pant and arch my back like a freaking cat in heat, begging for more.

"Hot fucking damn, baby. You've got the nicest ass I've ever seen," he growled as he grasped each one of my cheeks in his massive hands.

I moaned brokenly at how the rough skin of his palms brushed against my angry, sensitive flesh.

"Yeah, fuck yeah baby. That's it. Push that pretty fucking ass up for me, yes."

I did as he asked, arching my back as I looked over my shoulder at him.

I'd never felt like this with any guy I'd slept with, ever. My entire body was on fire and pulsing with need. I probably would have started doing the *Macarena* at any point if he'd told me to.

His hands grabbed my hips, squeezing firmly, then ran down along my thighs. His hands were so hot, rough, and they covered almost the entire width of my sizeable thighs. The monumental size of this man as well as his even larger fuck-around-and-find-out personality made me feel ridiculously small and feminine. I arched my back even more into his touch.

I felt his hands grasp each one of my cheeks and spread me open. The cool rush of air over my most private place made me gasp in surprise as I tried to wiggle a little out of his hold. He growled in response, giving each of my ass cheeks a hard slap.

"Keep this ass up baby; I want to look at your pretty little holes," as he spoke, his thumb traced the outline of the thong all the way from my clit and back toward the cleft between my cheeks.

He held me completely still with the rest of his body. Slowly, he moved the lace strap of the thong aside, thrusting his thumb inside my pussy and then dragging the moisture up and around my clit.

I had never been so close to coming, so fast, in my entire life. But a deep, dark part of me wanted to hold back my orgasm. It was the same part of me that only wanted to come while that thick, massive cock of his was thrusting deep inside me.

"Oh my god, I—I—that feels... *uhhhh!* Please, Brodie! Please, yes..."

I was a helpless sexual clay for him to mold and play with as he wanted. I melted further into the bliss of his hands on me. I didn't recognize the needy sound of my own voice; I was floating.

"Fuck, baby. You look good enough to eat," as he spoke, I felt the rough scrape of his beard stubble between the very bottom curve of my ass cheeks.

Before I could pull away, he'd wrapped his iron grip around my hips, holding me open for his mouth. I went wild; no one had ever really done that... *there.*

"Wh—what—no! Oh, my god, what are you—*ohhhh!*"

I couldn't let him see how much I liked what he was doing; it was too mortifying. I didn't exactly feel sober, but I definitely was not drunk or high enough for... that!

Without pulling his mouth away from me, he spanked one side of my ass. Hard.

I moaned, shaking, trying to control the wave of pleasure that spiked through me with the sharp sting of his hand. My legs were shaking with the effort of trying to hold myself closed against what his mouth was doing.

"I love the way your fucking ass bounces baby. *Damn,* but you're sexy as hell," his words tickled against the sensitive flesh between my legs.

The motion of his hands around my hips was enough to make my nipples brush deliciously against the bed, even through the torn shell of my dress. I almost couldn't stop myself from rubbing back and forth on my own to chase after more of the delicious pleasure.

He straightened, and I heard a smacking, sucking noise as he brought his thumb and fingers up to his mouth. He gave my ass a very hard parting slap, then flipped me over onto my back. My head was spinning with how fast and efficiently he moved.

I felt my nipples harden even more, begging for him to touch them again. His hungry gaze lingered over every inch of me in the completely transparent black lace. I didn't realize I was rolling my hips up toward him until the unconscious movement became too strenuous to remain unnoticed by my muddled Swiss cheese brain.

Flustered, confused, and super turned-on, I glanced around to see what was weighing me down from the sexual haze. Some of the remnants of my little black dress were twisted underneath me, pinning me tightly to my own self.

Brodie must have noticed my struggle. With a purely predatory smile, he freed me from the sex-induced straitjacket in one ominous flick of his wrist. The growling sound he made as he completely revealed my breasts in the black lace had me biting my lip and moaning. I felt a heated blush over every inch of my skin.

"Now it's time for your punishment, baby. Spread your legs for me. I want to hear how loud I can make you scream."

Chapter 23

Brodie

I couldn't hear anything from the pounding in my ears. My dick was so fucking hard for her, demanding I plunge into that soft, wet heat between her thighs. There was already a fine sheen of sweat forming on my overheated body from the energy it took to not let my cock completely hijack my brain.

This woman was going to be the death of me, but I'd gladly feast on her delicious body until the flames sent me straight to hell. That's the only place a body like hers could have come from. Every inch of her was made for pure, delicious sin.

When I ripped the rest of the black dress from her body, I knew that damn lingerie was going to send me over the edge. I had to take a step back from her or I would have tackled her right then and there, and then pinned her down underneath me.

The way her dark pink nipples were clearly visible through the transparent material, already pebbled and begging to be tugged and sucked on, had more precum running down the tip of my cock. But instead of following my orders and parting her thighs so I could ravage her, she just stared up at me, her blue eyes heavy lidded with desire.

"I said, spread your legs, baby. *Now.*"

More precum collected over the tip of my painfully throbbing dick. I was seconds away from losing the last shred of my control. Her eyelashes fluttered as she tried to hide her arousal, the puffy peaks of her nipples practically stabbing through the delicate black lace. Her breasts bounced gently with each of her inhales, making my balls clench almost painfully.

Then, she did exactly what I'd wanted her to do.

She tried to run from me.

I let her get almost out of the bedroom, enjoying the angry pink flush on her ass so much I saw stars. I caught up to her easily, snatching her to me as I breathed her in. There was nothing in this world that smelled better than she did.

"I was hoping you'd try to run from me again, baby. I love to watch your ass in that thong," her eyes were still heavy with desire, but there were little lavender embers burning around the edges again.

"You—you tore my dress! Uggh! I *loved* that dress!"

I felt the little whimper she let out in the pit of my stomach then instantly in my dick as she pouted toward the scraps of shiny black fabric.

"I'll buy you fifty more, sweetheart."

I couldn't wait to spoil her. She was just so damn cute. I also had a feeling we'd need a lot of back-ups.

She was still trying to escape, but I sensed her desire like I sensed my own thoughts. I knew she'd been drinking and wasn't exactly sober, but she should have fucking thought of that before she'd run from me earlier.

Fuck it.

For the foreseeable future, I would be the shadow she'd never be able to shake. She wouldn't be leaving my side, period, not until I'd blasted every one of these low-life trafficking fuckers into pieces with a few AT4's.

If she had any female regrets in the morning, she could damn well get over them, because I was planning on fucking her every chance I got. If I had it my way, she'd never leave my damn bed until this fucking shit was over and it was safe.

And maybe not after that, either. As hot as I was for her right now, I didn't see how I would ever not want to bend her over and sink my cock into her until neither one of us could walk.

I moved swiftly, kissing her back on the bed so she was lying on her back. I couldn't get enough of the addicting way her mouth tasted, so sweet and soft and wet. She had the softest lips, and they turned the exact same color as her pretty pink nipples when her pussy was wet and begging for me.

She was too busy trying to hide how turned on she was to notice I had wrapped one of her wrists into the straps on the side of the bed. I'd had my staff discreetly install them while I'd been gone. Before she'd realized what I'd done, her other arm was also tightly secured so that both her hands were now tied above her.

Growling, I stared at her gorgeous body as her breasts bounced and swayed from the efforts of her struggling. It was no wonder she'd accused me of acting like a grizzly bear. The way I was feeling, I'd gleefully take on a herd of them if they stood in the way between me and her.

"Hell fucking yes, baby; keep doing that. Damn, you have the prettiest pair of tits I've ever seen, Freya."

She stopped struggling immediately at what I'd implied, glaring daggers at me.

I continued to stare down at her, smiling, my eyes roaming all over her beautiful body. She let out a frustrated yell as she kicked out one of her legs, which I immediately grabbed and secured using the strap on the other side of the bed. Her other leg followed into its own prison in another second and a half.

I ripped the clothes off my own body as I feasted on the glorious sight of her, spread-eagled, hot and ready for me. Completely under my control. Furiously I stroked up and down the entire length of my aching cock, almost coming from the sensation of my balls bouncing up and down along with my strokes.

But this was a punishment, after all. My own pleasure could wait.

"Please... pl—pl—ease don't hurt me... I—I don't want to... I don't want to do this anymore. Please, I..." she frantically twisted in her bindings.

"Freya, baby. What did I tell you about not lying, hmmm?"

I was impressed at the gentle, cajoling quality of my voice given the violent storm of lust that was raging inside me.

"I... please, I'm—take these off, let me up. I—I'm scared," there were tears at the corners of her eyes now.

I stopped and scanned her body, seeing everything.

The rhythmic, almost undetectable undulation of her hips. The shining, irresistible wetness seeping from her pussy and onto the insides of the very tops of her thighs. The tightly drawn peaks of her nipples. The flushed, swollen appearance of her lower lip, constantly hidden behind the shadows of her pretty white teeth. The position of her heels on her feet and the way her muscular legs were flexed as she curled her cute little red toes under in blissful anticipation.

The only thing my little lioness was afraid of was probably how turned on she was.

"Naughty girl, Freya," I growled at her, turning toward a variety of shopping bags discreetly placed on the side table on the other side of the bedroom as I'd also requested earlier; I really did need to give my staff a raise.

"What... wh—where are you going? I—" her words stopped on a sharp inhale when I turned toward her, holding the cutest little neon pink, tear-drop shaped panty vibe between my fingers.

Chapter 24

Freya

I almost came right then and there when I watched him walking toward me. His sexy, insanely muscular forearm was flexed and straining under his tattoos as he fisted the thick, swollen length of his cock. He looked right into my eyes while he savagely pumped up and down.

In my tipsy, desire-soaked mind I boldly admired the sheer size of him, from the base all the way to the almost purple, throbbing tip. It was shiny from an almost steady drip of precum; I wanted to smear it around with my tongue, then close my lips over the largest part of him and *suck*.

He continued moving toward me slowly, with one hand on his magnificent cock and the other holding a neon pink version of *The Panty Dropper.*

The only true fear I had in that moment was how freaking fast I was ready to be fucking him like an animal.

He said he'd wanted to make me scream.

A wave of extremely powerful lust hit me and I started panting; this man was absolutely ruthless.

What if he left that vibe on for hours after I'd come? Leaving me in a twisted, hot, moaning, and helpless heap from some kind of seizure-like orgasm? Hot chills erupted all over my body at the thought, and I moaned shamelessly.

Transfixed within the grips of that dark fantasy, I watched him hungrily. Our eyes locked when he saw me watching him and he smiled at me, his expression completely feral and blatantly sexual. I felt myself blush all over, but I was too far gone to look away. It only took one thirsty, tortured moan and a blatant roll of my hips for him to pounce on the bed, growling.

It made me even hotter.

His masculine fingers deftly slipped the panty vibe into the tiny slot sewn along the thin wisp of fabric covering my clit. Just the light pressure of the vibe against me felt like heaven. Another desperate, breathy moan escaped as I rolled my hips toward him.

He clicked something he still held in his hand. Instantly, my hips shot off the bed as white-hot pleasure exploded between my thighs. I could hear his sexy, rumbling growls as he watched me, and it made me even more wild.

To my horror, he set the tiny pink remote on the table with the other bags. After a short series of taps and swipes on his watch, he'd set the vibrator to a terrifying, pulsing setting.

"Ohhh... oh fuck yes that—feels... ohhh!"

Normally when I was about to come, I felt that delicious, warm rush of sensation stemming from my clit and radiating outward.

This was completely different.

My entire core felt hot, needy, and unbearably empty as I tried to process the intensity of pleasure.

The panty vibe was centered right on top of my clit, and when it reached the most intense setting I wanted to scream. Just when I thought I was going to come, it would slow down to a soft, lukewarm tickle on my pussy that was much more bearable. Then, it would shut off, and I'd realize it all felt much better than I thought it had.

The next series of pulses would be so strong I would feel like I was actually coming, but the sensation was too intense to actually break through. Instead, I just continued to pulse and clench my pussy hungrily, experiencing the intensity of an orgasm without actually getting to ride the crest of the wave and float back down.

"Please, I... I'm so close, Brodie pl—please..."

I was dimly aware of how breathless and needy my voice sounded, but I also didn't care.

I needed to come so badly, and I didn't care how I got there as long as he made it happen. The sounds of his growls made me even hotter, and I licked my lips as he continued to pump his fist up and down on his cock.

"Do you want to come, baby? Is your pussy wet for me?"

His deep rumbling voice poured over me like an actual touch.

I couldn't speak. I kept panting and moaning, throwing my head wildly from side to side.

Absentmindedly I noticed I'd put my mouth around the only thing I could reach, which was the inside of my own arm. I didn't have any idea how long I'd been licking and sucking on my skin until I felt the little sting of my own teeth when I'd given myself a love bite.

"Mmmmm, fuck yes, baby. Tell me how much you want to come," I could barely hear his voice, it had become so low and deep.

My only reply was an unintelligible type of panting grunt, really not some of my best work. However, there was zero part of my brain available to filter any of the sex sounds before they came out, to make sure they still sounded decently coy and feminine and alluring.

I probably sounded about as sexy as a hairy female gorilla in full-blown heat.

Without warning, the horribly delicious pulses stopped completely. I couldn't prevent the frustrated, moaning whimper when they'd ceased.

"Tell me how wet and ready your pussy is, baby, or I won't let you come," Brodie's gaze was burning green fire, sending little viridian embers over every inch of me.

I had to shut my eyes to keep from rolling over the edge, knowing how hungrily he watched me.

"I can't... I... oh, my god. Please, I... it's—"

My words died on a high-pitched wail when he'd turned the vibe back on.

I had zero control over my body as my back arched and I uselessly tried to pull my tightly bound legs closed. Pleasure soared through me from my pussy all the way into the pit of my stomach and up into my brain. I was so close, so close to absolute bliss...

Again the pulses stopped. I protested in a whiny, breathless moan that didn't even sound like my voice.

"*Tsk, tsk*... naughty girl. Tell me how wet your pussy is and how much you want to come, or I'll use my belt to prove it to you."

As he spoke, I noticed he held his thick black leather belt in one hand.

I almost started hyperventilating from the desire that soared through me. Every inch of my flesh sizzled with ticklish, delicious heat. I could actually feel moisture dripping down between my ass cheeks from the wetness of my pussy. I was so freaking hot for him, instead of being mortified it only made me roll my hips toward him more.

I loved the deep, hungry way he growled as I watched his response to my body, to all of me tied up and spread wide for his use.

My desire had become so consuming that my embarrassment had turned into a delicious type of thrill. Even as totally and utterly helpless that I was in this position, the most instinctual and divinely feminine part of my brain dared to challenge who held the real control with every roll of my hips, every breathless whimper, every drop of wetness that emerged from my swollen core.

I screamed when I felt the soft crack of the leather belt on the inside of my upper thigh, leaving a trail of heat in its wake. It was dangerously close to my desperate and tormented pussy. I started panting wildly at the thought of him doing that, *there*. Lukewarm alarm seeped through the haze of my desire as my eyes snapped open.

"Tell me, Freya. Tell me how wet your sweet little pussy is."

"It's... it's wet!"

The tiny after-sting of the belt was doing strange things to my already throbbing pussy. If he turned that vibe on, I was going to shatter instantly.

"What's wet, baby?"

He passed the strap of the belt very lightly across my clit. I instantly shot off the bed from the bliss, then moaned in misery when it wasn't quite enough pressure.

I screamed again when he placed another soft leather bite across the skin on my other thigh, directly in the sensitive crease between my pussy lips and my leg. I felt my pussy and ass clench helplessly, both totally open and exposed to him. I shuddered as the light sting quickly morphed into something much more sinister and delicious that was redirected completely between my legs.

With some more of that sexy growling, he threw the belt across the room and yanked down the flimsy material of my bustier. The rough yet totally capable way he handled me kept me panting and trembling, like he was in control of not just his own body, but mine as well. In one move he'd placed his massive thighs on each side of my upper body, straddling me.

I couldn't look away from the heavy swing of his veiny, swollen cock. The broad tip of it slid across the skin of my abdomen, leaving a hot, wet trail of precum. I moaned desperately at the contact as I involuntarily rolled my hips up toward him.

He rolled my nipples roughly between his finger and thumb, then tugged on each one. I felt the twisted pleasure spike instantly between my widely spread thighs. The sensation of being so helplessly spread open for him to play with made me burn uncontrollably. I felt even more wetness drip from my swollen core as he continued the ruthless torment.

There was something so fucking sexy about the sight of his darkly tanned, rough fingers teasing my dark pink nipples, the obscene way he appeared to be almost milking me. It made me feel so dirty in the best way when I watched him tug on my nipples, the hungry, dark look in his eyes while he made my breasts jiggle and bounce.

I was floating along a rough river of pleasure, helplessly thrown about in the wild current.

I always shyly liked my nipples played with during sex and sometimes it helped me come faster, but I'd never actually had an orgasm from it. And I was definitely not brave or confident enough to touch my own nipples during sex. The most brazen I'd ever felt was shyly placing a guy's hand on one of my breasts. They usually took over from there.

"Baby, I want to hear you say the words. Tell me exactly how wet your fucking pussy is right now, or..." he pinched both my nipples, hard.

I screamed from the confusing pleasure-pain.

"Oh, my god! Oh my—*uhhhhhhhh*, please, I—"

"Say it, Freya. Tell me how wet your pretty little cunt is for me."

Normally I hated that word. *Hated.* The fact that it made me even hotter was probably concrete proof of the whole Swiss cheese brain matter theory.

"I—I—it's wet. My... my p—pussy is wet! Please! It's so wet, please!"

The way I felt when he made me admit it out loud was not something I was prepared to think about unless I had about four or ten more drinks.

"Oh, fuck yeah, baby. You like when I tug on these gorgeous titties? You like your nipples played with, Freya?"

"...oh, fuck... I—oh my god, yes! I—" I was so fucking close to coming, I felt as if I'd faint from the sheer force of the orgasm.

I had never felt so absolutely feral with lust in my entire life. It was wonderful, primal, absolutely delicious. I cried out again when he pinched my nipples, a little harder than before.

"That's not what I asked, baby. You know what I want. Tell me now, Freya."

He was twisting each one of my nipples, the sensation getting dangerously close to actual pain. I panicked slightly, then fully gave into the delicious shame of his naughty game.

"Yes, I—I like when you tease my nipples, it... makes my pussy so wet! Please, please fuck me! Brodie, please... I'm so close!"

"*Fuck, yes.* Baby you're so fucking sexy. I love watching you squirm. Do you want me to make you come like this, Freya? With your legs spread and your titties bouncing in my hands?"

"Oh... *ohhh*... fuck, yes. Please... please make me come!"

"How, baby? How do you want it?"

"Oh, my... *ohhhh—uhhh,* please! Please make me come with my legs spread... and—and my titties bouncing!"

He let go of my nipples long enough to tap a button on his watch. The intensity was centered on my swollen clit and I moaned, blatantly rolling my hips. I desperately missed his hands on me, tormenting me.

"Mmmm, fuck yes, baby! You are so fucking sexy, Freya. *Fuck.* Suck my dick while I make you come, baby. I want to feel your screams around my cock."

I almost came just from hearing his filthy commands barked out in the rumbling bass timbre of his voice.

I know I should have been appalled, offended, turned off from the way he'd—not even asked, but commanded—that I suck his dick. If anything, it made me feel insanely desired, important.

I really hated being a psych major sometimes.

He shifted slightly as he forced his magnificent cock into my mouth. He reached for my nipples again, rubbing the roughness of his palms around them in small circles. The combination of his rough hands on my oversensitive breasts and the furious vibration on my desperately swollen pussy was everything I needed, but I still wanted *more.*

My needy moans were muffled by his cock pumping in and out of my mouth. I swiped my tongue along the tip of his shaft, then sucked my cheeks in hard, just like I'd imagined doing to him earlier. There was so much precum coating the tip, for a minute I'd wondered hungrily if he'd started coming already.

"Holy shit. Freya, baby... your mouth feels so fucking good. You look so damn pretty with my cock in your mouth, fuck!"

He rolled my nipples around and around between his index fingers and thumbs. It felt so amazing that I let out a low, strangled type of groan that turned into a weird high-pitched sort of whimper.

I continued to moan and pant, making obscene slurping noises while I licked and sucked the entire length of his cock. The way it was so freaking hard, yet so soft and slick was such an intriguing combination that made me want to swirl my tongue around the tip again and again.

"Yes, Freya... fuck, baby. You suck that cock so good. Are you ready to scream, baby?"

Several things happened at the same time.

I moaned into his cock at his dirty words. The clit vibe was set to the highest possible speed, and I wasn't even finished with a single moan before it turned into a ragged scream as white-hot pleasure burst through me. I wailed around his cock, sucking him even further into my mouth. He continued tormenting my sensitive nipples and it only amplified the insatiable power of my orgasm.

I could hear his savage, masculine sounds as he played with and teased my body while I jerked and twitched and trembled from the sheer power of the bliss soaring through me.

At the same time, threw his head back and yelled, the thick muscles in his neck flexed and strained from his efforts. The view of him like that made my pleasure spike to cataclysmic levels.

I was dimly aware of the obscene thrusting of my hips toward nothingness as I rode out each wave of sheer, agonizing, wonderful pleasure. It was endless. The bliss kept bursting behind my closed eyes in warm, brilliant colors that softly fizzled and faded into a million different iridescent sparkles.

"Fuck, yes, baby... scream all over that cock. You're so fucking pretty when you come."

I writhed and moaned on the bed as the pleasure slowly subsided from my body, the warm glimmers slowly fading back into a muted twilight behind my closed eyes. I whimpered a little in protest when he pulled his thick, swollen shaft from my mouth.

Distantly I realized he must not be completely inhuman because I didn't feel the buzzing on my horribly sensitive pussy.

Honestly, I was pretty sure I actually passed out a little after coming so hard. I had officially never, ever, ever come that hard in my entire life.

Including the other times he'd made me come earlier that day—which had also been the most intense orgasms of my life.

And he hadn't even put his massive ball-bat cock inside me yet.

"Now, Freya; tell me how you want me to fuck that pussy."

Chapter 25

Brodie

W atching her pretty pink lips say such naughty, dirty sexual words for me was one of the hottest things I'd ever witnessed in my life.

At least that's what I'd thought until I watched the sheer power of her orgasm burn through her, all while her pretty mouth was full of my cock. I honestly don't know how I didn't blow my load all down her slim, graceful throat. Probably because every slick suck of her mouth just made me want to ram my cock so far into her pussy that she'd never think to run from me again.

I could tell the exact instant when the hottest, most consuming flames from the firestorm of lust had died down, because her body finally rested limply between my thighs.

Earlier, I'd planned on torturing her with the panty vibe for at least an hour. Of course I was going to let her come, but not before bringing her to the very edge of orgasm and then stopping short, leaving her to burn in her own lust until she was just as crazy as she made me.

As soon as I started teasing her into talking dirty, I realized there was no way in hell I possessed that kind of self-control.

The way her body had jerked and thrashed and the wild sounds she was making tested the absolute limits of the authority I had over my painfully hard dick. At the moment, I was picturing myself spraying cum all over her beautifully bouncing tits.

I absolutely had to shut the vibe off just as she was fading from the highest peaks of her orgasm. I'd also planned on punishing her some more after she came, keeping the vibe on the highest speed at least five or ten minutes while she moaned and cried from the force of the twisted pleasure.

Now I realized there was no way in fucking hell I'd make it through another minute before my balls erupted all over her gorgeous breasts. Or down her beautiful throat.

I'd visualized those exact scenes about a hundred times, each with a few minor variables, on the entire way to the East Village earlier tonight. In my fantasies, I had furiously stroked my cock as she struggled and screamed with her legs spread wide before me. I had pictured her just like she was now, moaning and shaking uncontrollably from the steady onslaught of pleasure.

There was no way in motherfucking hell I would have ever lasted as long as I thought I could. That was pretty clear as soon as I started teasing her.

If my dick weren't currently hard enough to slice through my femoral artery with one wrong slap against my thigh, I would have been more ashamed of the amount of power she had over me.

It made me crazy when she acted so shy. I didn't want her to be able to hide any of her arousal from me, but I also loved the way she blushed when I forced her to play the naughty, dirty-talking game with me. Watching her slowly come apart and lose control like that had fried most of the circuits in my brain. The only one still functioning worth a damn was the one that controlled putting my cock directly into her pussy until I'd loaded her full of my cum.

I looked down at her mouth-watering body, all the curves and swells of her breasts, hips, thighs, and stomach.

"Damn, baby... you're so fucking gorgeous. Everywhere. Are you ready for my cock, Freya?"

I nuzzled the skin along her neck again as I leaned down, slowly releasing her from the binds around her arms. I loved touching the sweet softness of her skin along the inside of her wrists. There were a handful of dark pink lines from the ties, but they were already fading.

"I—I, um... I can't come again, it's... too sensitive!"

She hadn't even moved her arms from above her head after I'd released her, and she was panting the words rather than saying them.

So fucking sexy.

More precum oozed from the tip of my dick, my balls clenching in anticipation.

"Oh, yes, you can, Freya. I'll make sure this cock fits nice and deep in that soaking wet pussy."

She started panting again and rolling her hips as I removed both of her ankle straps. She immediately drew her thighs closed, twisting her hips to the side and pulling her legs in to her stomach. The sex-me heels were crossed over the view I should be having of her pussy in that position.

That was unacceptable.

I grabbed each of the black heels and removed them in practically one motion. Her cute little red-tipped toes were already tucked under as she tried to pull her legs back toward her.

I wasn't having any of it.

Growling, I flipped her back over on her stomach. The hungry sound she made had me smacking both of her ass cheeks in quick succession. She moaned in response, arching her back into the blows.

I wanted the stings to bring back all the blood flow to her pussy. I wanted her soaking wet heat to stretch around my cock, her clit throbbing and protruding from the tops of her pussy lips greedily, begging to be teased.

My own vision was blurry from needing to come so badly.

"Oh, my god, Brodie! Owww! But that hurts, please, please, I—"

She continued to arch into the blows, her legs squeezed together tight.

Naughty girl... she couldn't hide her arousal from me, especially not like this.

The faint outline of her pussy glistened through the soaking wet black lace of the thong. She had her thighs closed tightly together, but it did absolutely nothing to block the view I had of those cute little pussy lips barely covering her swollen, shiny clit.

Suddenly I wanted her totally and completely naked. I wanted to see every single part of her gorgeous body. I made quick work of the bustier fastenings along her back, then threw it over my shoulder across the room.

Before she could stop me, I'd grabbed both sides of the black lace thong and snatched it down her legs. When I was just past her knees with the tiny black scrap of fabric, she immediately started twisting underneath me, trying to prevent me from getting her completely naked.

My cock lengthened and twitched painfully at the thought of how I'd soon be sinking into her wide open, spread legs.

After a very brief, mostly nonexistent struggle I held the delicious, wet fabric in one hand and both her arms above her head in the other. She lay on her back again, panting. I groaned in pleasure watching her breasts jiggle and bounce, her nipples already distended and wanting more.

Looking right into her stormy, purplish-blue eyes, I smiled as I brought her panties to my face.

Grinning evilly, I closed my eyes and inhaled the absolutely amazing smell of her sex, which was now all over them. I brought the wettest part of the black lace to my mouth and sucked, trying to get more of the fucking intoxicating way she tasted.

She gasped at my crude sexual gesture, the look on her face utterly adorable.

"My dick is too fucking hard right now to lick your sweet little pussy, Freya. But next time we fuck you're going to straddle my mouth. You're going to grind that swollen clit against my tongue until your pussy juice runs down my face. *Fuck...* I can't wait to watch your tits jiggle while you come all over me like that."

It was fascinating to watch her desire bloom across her cheeks, lower her eyelids, and plump up her lips as I spoke. Fucking beautiful.

She moaned as she closed her eyes and rolled her hips up toward me. She was instantly back at fever pitch. I fucking loved her response to my filthy, dirty sex talk.

"These are mine now. I'll buy you another pair. These are irreplaceable."

I winked at her, the teasing gesture at complete odds with the savage sex beast inside of me that needed to fuck her like an animal.

I placed the heavenly scented panties into the drawer of the nightstand. Putting my body over hers on the bed, I shoved her thighs apart with one of my own.

I growled at her when I felt the hot, soaking wet core of her desire against the skin of my upper thigh. It left a shiny wet mark like a brand seared onto my skin and I groaned.

She was soaking wet and more than ready for me. It made me want to beat on my chest in triumph.

Savage, unslakable lust tore through me as I roughly placed the tip of my throbbing cock against the entrance to her pussy.

Finally, I thrust my entire throbbing length inside her with one savage pump of my hips.

She screamed into my embrace, then started moaning brokenly. I felt the hot, sweet fucking wetness of her pussy as it choked down on every single inch of me. Her tight, hot sheath was squeezing my dick so hard I was seeing stars burst with my eyes wide open.

My balls were clenched so hard against the base of my cock from the way her pussy felt. If I moved a single inch inside her, I would have come. She was so fucking wet, so fucking hot and tight.

I could feel her cum dripping down around my balls with every flutter of her pussy as it adjusted to being filled so full of my cock.

"Holy hell, it's so... it's too big, I can't! Brodie! Oh, my god..."

Her hips twisting wildly below me tore the last shred of my control. I slammed into her at an obscene speed. Her thick, fleshy thighs took every single one of my thrusts, and I felt her body relax a little more against the bed at my brutal rhythm.

"Yeah, baby... take that cock. Fuck yes, Freya, baby. You feel so fucking good on my cock, damn!"

I pumped my hips even harder, slamming my cock back and forth into her tight sheath.

It had been a while, but I knew for a fucking fact I'd had sex with virgins that weren't this tight.

There was a small part of my brain screaming at me to slow down, that I was going to bruise her sweet pussy with my thrusts. I was straining with the effort of trying to regain control and slow my furious pumping when she suddenly responded.

"Oh... my... *Brodie.* Fuck, yes! Fuck me, oh my god... please, right there! Don't stop, don't stop, *yes!*"

Her eyes were completely closed and her brows drawn tightly together, her voice desperate and needy as she whimpered and begged me. A hint of a smile played across her sexy, shimmery pink mouth. She was total fucking perfection.

I felt her pussy clamp down around the entire length of me as her desire built even higher. There wasn't enough blood flow left in my brain for anything else besides pumping my cock into her tight, wet heat as I watched her lose control again.

"You feel so good, Freya. You're so fucking tight," I was so close to coming I could feel the orgasm starting to build at the very bottom of my spine just behind my aching and throbbing balls.

As close as I was to losing control, I absolutely refused to allow my own release until I'd felt the hot pulses of her orgasm milking my cock for the first time.

"Yes, fuck, yes! *Brodie*, that feels so... oh, my god, yes! I—I'm so close, *please!* Don't stop!"

Her pussy was clamped down so tightly around my shaft that it tugged and pulled on the very tip of my cock. I kept her legs spread wide for each one of my pumps, enjoying every inch of her bared before me.

With my thumb, I reached down to rub circles around the very top of her puffy, slick little bud while I fucked her. I could feel the swollen ridge of her G-spot against the tip of my cock with each thrust inside her, and I knew her orgasm was close.

The sounds she made were wild and fucking primal as her entire body tensed, and the pleasure finally shattered over her.

She was so damn sexy; screaming, whimpering, and sobbing while I forced her to feel every little ripple of pleasure from her orgasm. Her pussy muscles clenched violently again and again, all over the length of my aching cock. I roared like a man possessed when I felt the sweet, hot juices of her release running down all over the front and sides of my furiously bouncing balls.

"*Yes,* fuck yes, Freya! Come all over that cock. Tell me how good it feels, baby," I reached up to pinch one of her nipples.

It made her scream even louder, clench down on my dick even tighter. I only plowed into her harder.

"Your—your cock feels so good, Brodie! Oh, my—oh my—*uh-hhhhhh-uhhhh!*"

She was sobbing with the force of her release. Her pussy was clenching down on my dick so hard she almost pushed it out.

I pinned her down to the mattress and plowed into her until I felt my own release explode from my balls and all the way to the tip of my cock. The entire length of me was pulsing with electric pleasure. I threw my head back and yelled as I thrust every last ounce of my cum into her pussy.

Panting and heart hammering like I'd just run a six-minute mile, I gently pulled my still semi-hard cock out from inside her. I fucking loved the little sound she made and the way she still gripped me so damn tightly on the way out.

I leaned over her on the bed as I grabbed both her thighs and kept her legs spread wide open. She trembled and let out a sexy as fuck little whine when I kissed the soft skin along her inner thighs. She tried to close them, but one little smack on the inside of her thigh and a dark look from me, and she relaxed back on the bed with a weak little moan.

I winked at her, then burst out laughing again at the look of shocked surprise on her face at how I held her open. She was so fucking adorable.

"Keep your legs spread wide, Freya. I want to watch my cum drip out of your pretty little pussy."

Chapter 26

Freya

It took a few seconds for his words to register, but once they did, any remaining sexual buzz I had quickly evaporated.

His cum. Inside me. He'd freaking come inside me.

He hadn't used a condom.

Holy shit, had I really freaking messed up this time!

I'd just had unprotected sex with a man I'd known for less than twelve hours!

An arrogant, super scary, alpha male type of man... who'd also somehow known *exactly* where I'd been in a city full of millions of people.

The delicious fire I'd felt just seconds before fizzled away as I tried to calm myself.

What in the freaking hell had I been thinking?!

He could have knocked me up, or even given me an STD! I'd never, ever done anything so impulsive and reckless.

There was zero part of this situation that was anyone's fault but my own, and a wave of shame collected in the pit of my stomach instantly. It burned through nearly all of the buzz from the alcohol and weed. My throat felt tight, my once languid and satisfied muscles now felt cold, clammy, and stiff.

I also realized that my head was spinning as if the mattress were on some kind of merry-go-round, and I was *really* effing exhausted.

"No, I'm done now. Stop."

My voice sounded way more in control than I was feeling at the moment. The sides of my vision were getting blurry, but it definitely wasn't from tears. Nope.

The soft growl that had once made me feel hot all over now made me feel even colder. A secret tear escaped from the outer corner of my eye, running a warm, wet path down the side of my temple and along the back of my neck as I lay on the bed. From the corner of my vision, I could tell he was moving toward me again.

"You don't get to tell me no, baby. I wan—"

His words stopped abruptly.

Suddenly he was sitting on the bed leaning over me, pinning me to the mattress between his thighs. He was scowling down at me. My throat was burning too tightly to care. He roughly grabbed my face and held it still as he looked all over me. His thumb lightly traced my lower lip and I bristled, trying to move away from his touch.

He scowled even darker, the muscles at his temples bulging as he clenched his jaw.

"Freya. What's wrong."

He didn't even have the decency to ask; it was more like an implied command that I answer.

I remained silent.

With an arrogant male sigh, he turned toward the bathroom. I turned over on my side away from the door and pulled the impossibly fluffy, soft white comforter around me to hide my nudity.

Just a few minutes I'd lay here and let my head stop spinning. Then I'd figure out how to get myself out of this mess.

Where the hell was my self-control? Where had this reckless, impulsive behavior come from?

This wasn't me, at all. I typically only had sex with guys I'd been dating, or at least going on dates with—plural. I didn't throw shade to anyone who had one-night stands, it was just something I'd never been interested in.

I wanted to enjoy the sex, not be too nervous to relax with some stranger I didn't know.

I hadn't even slept with Bryce McFuckerson after a few weeks of pseudo-dating, a fact I was thankful for during every single second of every single day.

I laid there and focused on breathing in, and out. Then doing it again, and again. I just needed my head to stop spinning, then I'd find my phone and—

The cell phone jammer. Awesome.

I wouldn't be able to use my phone anyway. The thought made the spinning even worse. I pulled the cover more tightly around me and drew my legs up into my chest. I didn't even have a chance to finish the movement before the cover was yanked off of me.

"Freya, come here."

He held what looked like a wet washcloth in his hands as he reached toward my thighs.

I tried to jerk away from him. He easily subdued me, sending me another glare.

I stared blankly back at him, unwilling to be so easily manipulated by him again. He ignored my reaction as he gently placed the warm, wet cloth between my legs. The feeling sent another wave of shame over me, a reminder of how stupid I'd just been. I turned my face away from him, even more humiliated that I didn't seem to have any control over my emotions.

I was a grown-ass woman, dammit. Not some weepy female that couldn't stand on her own two feet. I didn't need him to take care of me.

I could almost feel his irritation at my defiance to his high-handed commands, but he just continued to clean between my thighs in slow, gentle strokes. The act of unexpected tenderness from him when I was feeling so unbalanced just made my throat burn even more. To my continued humiliation, I felt a few actual tears streaming down from the corners of my tightly shut eyes.

The tightness in my throat and the hot slide of tears down my face almost took my mind off the constant twirling and spinning that got worse when I shut my eyes.

I opened my eyes instead. Making a weak attempt to ward off the sudden feeling of fatigue, I stared at the intricate patterns carved into the wood of the coffered ceiling as I tried to sit back up.

I turned away from him again when he'd finished between my legs.

He tossed the rag toward the bathroom. It landed in a soft, wet *plop* on the tiled marble floor. In practically the same motion, he'd pulled back the comforter and slid into bed. When he tucked himself in right behind me and then pulled the cover over both of us, I was surrounded in a solid wall of clean, spicy, sandalwood heat.

I really had no idea why I felt this way, because I usually had way better control over my emotions. One thing I did know was that being around him was not good for my health.

So far, my ovaries were probably going to go on strike if they hadn't already, my brain had been morphed into decomposing Swiss cheese, and I could already be freaking pregnant!

I mean, the last part wasn't likely as I was on the pill. And I usually remembered to take it at the same time every morning when I drank my coffee as I got ready for work. That being said, having a baby was absolutely freaking not something I wanted to do as an unmarried, barely out of school, almost but not quite broke twenty-four-year-old.

I sat there stiff as a board while he wrapped his scalding-hot python arm around my waist. It immediately pissed me right the hell off that the gesture melted away some of my prickly unhappiness and made the tightness in my throat a little less constricting. Unfortunately, when I relaxed into him the spinning got worse.

"Can you tell me what happened, Freya. Did I hurt you?"

His voice was gruff, low. Almost angry, but not quite.

I tried to talk, but I couldn't think of anything to say to explain my likely confusing behavior. I wasn't even sure how I was feeling at the moment. The longer I lay there in bed, the more I noted my head swimming and total exhaustion were both getting a lot worse.

The silence stretched, but he didn't push it. I was grateful. He just held me a little tighter for a few minutes, leaning his face into the back of my head. He took a deep, long inhale, clearly smelling my hair.

"Mmmm. *Oribe*. I had my staff put your hair stuff in the bathroom."

I hadn't realized I'd almost dozed off when his words shook me back into alertness.

"You... hang on, you did them had what? I mean... you had them did—do—what?!"

Great. I was back to Dyslexian again, my own made-up version of English.

He wrapped his arm around me tighter, taking a deep inhale into the crook of my neck where my hair had fallen.

"Your hair. It smells so fucking amazing. It's gorgeous. I wanted you to have everything you needed when I brought you back here."

"Your staff? My hair stuff?! What do you mean, my hair stuff?! They were—who's 'they?!'"

"I told you babe, my staff. There were a few bottles in the shower and some more in the bathroom cabinet back at your place. I told them to bring it all. If they missed anything, I'll have them go back. Or tell me what you need, and I'll have it delivered here," the calmness of his voice was at complete odds with my frazzled nerves.

"You... how? Why?!"

"Freya. I have no idea what happened a few minutes ago but you're obviously upset about something," he sighed deeply. "And unfortunately, now is a really shitty time to explain the how and the why."

I suddenly needed to be away from him. It was all way too much. I tried to remove his arm from around me, but it was like trying to bend a telephone pole. I was already so freaking tired.

"Let me... up. Now."

Even talking seemed like entirely too much effort.

"No. You're upset."

"You're damn right... I'm upset!"

I thrashed weakly in his grip, then stopped when I felt the unmistakable hard ridge of his cock against the curve of my very naked ass.

He groaned softly as he wrapped both arms around me and pressed his hips firmly into my ass.

I whimpered. It was still a little tender from him freaking spanking me, dammit.

"Freya, baby... I'm trying really hard to be patient. But if you keep moving that perfect fucking ass against my dick, I'm going to be shoving it inside that tight little asshole regardless of how pissed off you are," he punctuated his threat with a light slap to each of my cheeks.

"*Errrrgggh!* Ow! Dammit, that... hurt! And this—this is you trying hard... to be patient?! Are you freaking... kidding me?! Try harder, dammit!"

It was even exhausting being furious with him.

Perversely, lust burned with every slap against my tortured backside at the same time the spinning threatened to pull me into the dark promise of his dirty words.

"Oh, baby, I can definitely do it *harder* for you."

The hot rush of air from his deep chuckles tickled the crook of my neck right before I felt the light scraping of his beard. Goose-bumps erupted all over my skin from the rough contact. A tiny gasp escaped from me and I failed to prevent my hips from rolling back into his hardness.

I also had to bite my lip to keep from grinning at his ridiculous sense of humor. It was very disarming when he made jokes like that. I was supposed to be reminding myself how much danger I was in by staying around this probably unstable, very wealthy, very bossy and manipulative, *very* powerful man.

But he didn't really seem that dangerous when he made boner puns like he was starring in a raunchy teen movie.

"Well... I need to... use the bathroom," I actually did have to pee pretty badly, and it was the perfect excuse to need to get away from him.

I was getting way too relaxed in that bed, and it was getting harder to talk.

All I wanted to do was shut my eyes and spin with him on the bed, but the still sane part of me was desperately screaming at me that my bladder was precariously full.

Besides, everyone knew if you didn't pee after sex, you could get a UTI. Hard pass on that.

Chuckling, he gradually released his hold on me and stood up from the bed. His now almost completely hard, monstrous dick was bobbing crazily between his massive thighs as he sauntered around the bed to my side, extending his open palm. I gulped and looked away.

I ignored his outstretched hand and tried to move to the other end of the bed myself, but he apparently wasn't having any of it. He said nothing, just moved his massive form directly in front of me on the bed, blocking my entrance.

I glared back at him. Frankly, I was getting really sick of being bullied by his arrogant masculinity.

When I still didn't take his outstretched hand, he sighed rather dramatically. Before I could even form a retort to his high-handed attitude, I was suddenly being hoisted up off the bed and over the enormous bulge of his shoulder toward the bathroom. I really didn't understand how the hell I couldn't move when he'd secured me with less than a fourth of his body.

It wasn't even freaking *fair* how much stronger he was. I had never considered myself very small, but I was quite hilariously out-matched by just his size and testosterone fumes, I thought bitterly.

"Put me... down, dammit!"

He was moving us so fast toward the bathroom that I had a hard time talking. I felt as if I were doing constant somersaults as we flew across the room.

My head was still spinning when he set me on the edge of the jacuzzi-style tub across from the walk-in shower. Weakly, I noted the white cloth shower curtain had been removed.

"Do you need help, Freya?"

I had to blink my eyes once or twice to make sure I hadn't imag-ined him asking me that. I was a little confused why he was also spinning.

"No. I'm good. Just... spinning. You... move fast."

He continued to stare at me, both of us stark naked. When I didn't reply he raised his eyebrows like this was the most normal situation in the world, and that I was the weird one for not reply-ing. Arrogant pain in the ass, he was.

"I can pee... by myself, thanks," my mouth had a weird sort of metallic taste, and it was suddenly quite dry.

Total exhaustion from the entire weird, surreal, and terrifying day was hitting me hard. Fatigue that was no doubt only enhanced by the champagne and vape, I had to admit. At least I'd had enough sense to seriously hydrate as I'd gotten ready earlier, drinking al-most two liters of water. Still, I could already tell this hangover was going to suck, badly.

He continued to stare at me as he crossed his arms over his chest. I raised my eyebrows back at him. I would absolutely not budge on this one.

If he thought I was going to sit on that toilet, butt-ass naked, and *pee* in front of him...

"Alright, alright. Message received. You have two minutes, Freya. If I knock on this door and you don't respond in the next second, I'm coming in. Understood?"

He didn't even give me a chance to reply as he slowly turned, shutting the door behind him. I moved cautiously toward the door as I navigated through the spinning so I could lock it. The tiny metallic click gave me a small sense of security.

Suddenly very dizzy and unable to stay on my feet amongst the constant twirling, I braced myself over the edge of the sink on my way to the toilet.

I really did need to pee, badly.

Doing a weird 360-degree spin move where I pivoted along the edge of the sink toward the toilet, I literally had to use my grip on the marble countertop to keep my balance or I would have spun down and crashed into the floor.

I could have cried in relief when I made it to the toilet. It was one of those stupid luxury type designs that sat super low on the ground. On the ridiculously long way down, I lost my balance and I grabbed onto the counter on the other side of the toilet so I didn't fall.

For fuck's sake, I was on a roll tonight. Literally.

Apparently, I was not only mentally paralyzed by my own stupidity, but also physically.

I could see it now; after my death they'd make some sort of super edgy indie-docuseries about the odd and unexplainable circumstances surrounding my death. They'd call it something over-the-top dark and artsy like *The Girl with the Swiss Cheese Brain.*

When I'd almost fallen into the damn toilet, I'd also accidentally knocked down a bottle of something that was sitting on the counter next to me. It hit the floor and a high-pitched plastic echo rang around the room. The sound still felt odd as it reached my ears.

"And don't even think about trying anything with those toiletries, babe. There will be consequences," I heard his arrogant, slightly muffled orders through the door and shrieked in outrage.

Deep booming laughter made me even angrier. I threw the nearest thing I could at the door, which was an extra roll of toilet paper. It felt like a lead paperweight as I clumsily picked it up and launched it toward the door.

It didn't go far at all.

It landed on the floor, not even making it the distance to the door. It rolled in slow motion as it bumped the wooden door with a pathetic little *thud*, nowhere near satisfying enough. The soft sound echoed between my ears strangely, my arm still feeling the sensation of throwing despite it being rested on top of my thigh.

"Go... away! I have... to pee," I was so tired, so freaking tired.

All I wanted to do was curl up in a ball in that soft, fluffy white comforter back in the bed and go to sleep. I felt like it took physical effort to tell my brain to pee, which I felt was super weird given how badly I needed to go. My body finally cooperated.

I tried to coordinate my clumsy hands with the spinning button on top of the tank. Finally, it flushed.

This really didn't feel like drunk and high from legal weed.

Alarm bells were going off in my very foggy brain, but the spinning was getting so loud it was hard to focus. My mouth tasted so odd, as if I'd been sucking on an iron bolt like a lollipop. Confused, I tried to smack my lips together, but it felt as if rusty metal shavings were inside my mouth.

I managed to turn the faucet on just as Brodie opened the door.

I remember being so confused about the flow of the water down into the sink, and up into the mirror, making his reflection wet and rippled. It was almost if I could smell it, the cool crisp scent of fresh water, flowing into the mirror and beyond. Alarmed, I reached out to touch his wavy, wet reflection but it kept getting further and further away from my outstretched hand.

I heard what sounded like a grizzly bear screaming into a thick, see-through pillow before I melted down into the confusing, strange darkness.

Chapter 27

Brodie

What the motherfucking fuck!
I moved so quickly toward her I almost sent us both back into the sink, but I caught her limp body before it even got close to the floor. I was furious as I turned toward the bedroom.

This was completely my fault; I never should have let anything get this far. I shouldn't have left her alone in the bathroom—here, or back in the club.

Dammit, dammit, fucking *dammit!*

In a few strides I'd carried her back over to the bed and laid her on top of the comforter against the pillows. I grabbed a blanket for her, making sure I could still easily monitor the rise and fall of her chest.

I didn't bother dressing her more. It would just be in the way for the medical team or ECG leads, if needed. A morbid, angry sense of déjà vu washed over me as I realized this was the second damn time that I'd had to carry her unconscious form onto my bed, and we'd known each other less than a damn day.

Now if that wasn't the start to a healthy and perfectly normal fucking relationship, I thought sarcastically. One more reason I needed to get my head back in the game and fucking keep it there. Distractions and mistakes in my world were deadly; neither of which were acceptable.

I scanned her vitals, noting her pulse was steady if a bit slow, and her breathing was deep and even. Her capillary refill time was normal. The skin on the inside of her bottom lip looked a normal, pale pink. Her pupils were light-responsive and consensual, but mildly delayed.

I told myself the variation could be appropriate for many different non-life-threatening reasons, such as the alcohol she'd consumed earlier. There was a reason a flashlight in the face was a tried-and-true if technically unofficial part of most field sobriety tests.

Unfortunately, my gut instincts raged at me that something had been slipped into her drink at the club. This wasn't normal drunk behavior. We also strongly suspected that all the previous victims had been sedated when they were taken. It was an extremely common practice in these trafficking rings.

The thought boiled the blood inside my veins. I cracked my knuckles to release some of my restless agitation as I turned to get my phone.

The knuckle-cracking didn't work in the slightest. It just made me angrier there was no soft flesh to pummel between them.

Marco might trust Mikhail Bychkov, but I needed a whole fucking hell of a lot more convincing, especially after this shit!

I didn't have enough history with the Russian to put someone else's safety in his hands. Each time I closed my eyes I pictured the man's orbital bones shattering under my fists.

He better have the world's best fucking explanation for this shit. I furiously threw on another pair of dark grey sweats and dialed out for emergency medical services.

My gut instinct also told me if she'd been drugged, it had fucking happened in *his* club because of the timing.

"Pack your medical bag and meet me upstairs. Now," I barked orders at my chief medical staff through my phone.

I'd have to apologize to her later, but for now I didn't care. I needed to make sure Freya was safe.

Now.

I had pretty sophisticated medic training and combat experience but none of that shit mattered in this scenario. I'd never compare my knowledge with that of a practicing trauma doctor, and I happened to have one of the best in the world on my staff.

There was a damn good reason you didn't bring a knife to a gunfight, unless you wanted to lose.

I wasn't the type of man to lose a fight.

A million different scenarios went through my mind as I waited a fucking eternity for Dr. Briggs to show up. All of them scared the motherfucking shit out of me, so it was safe to say I was in a towering rage by the time the highly skilled, gentle yet very formidable woman showed up in her pristine, cream-colored scrubs underneath her immaculate white coat.

I was about to berate her for taking—I glanced at my watch—almost five and a half minutes to get here, for fuck's sake!

But before I could get out a word of my temper tantrum, she came marching into the room with her heavy black medical bag on her shoulder and stethoscope around her neck. The look she gave me screamed *fuck around with me and find out.*

"Save it, Magnuson. I'm not in the mood for your useless barks and growls tonight. Where is my patient?"

Her calm, no-nonsense, I'm-in-charge-now attitude was one of the reasons I liked her so much.

She'd also never put up with any of my bullshit. Like I said, the woman had skills.

"In here, Dr. Briggs," I muttered angrily as I turned toward the bedroom, taking the bag from her to carry.

She responded with an authoritative raise of her eyebrows as she followed me.

"Set up my STAT chem and blood gas machines. Get me two green tops, one purple, and two tiger tops. History?"

She nodded her head toward the big black medical bag as she sat on the bed, placing her stethoscope into her ears and then on Freya's chest.

Her eyes fluttered slightly at the doctor's soft, assessing touch, but otherwise she didn't stir.

It made me want to strangle someone.

Dr. Tanya Briggs could bark out orders like any commanding officer I'd ever had—including myself—but I'd never seen more gentle, capable hands with patients. I knew Freya would be in excellent hands.

I set up Dr. Brigg's machines immediately and gathered the different types of blood tubes she needed while I updated her regarding Freya's condition.

I didn't miss the narrow-eyed scowl she gave me when I summarized our earlier activities as being "intimate." I didn't blame her one bit, I realized furiously. Given the situation from someone else's perspective, I would think I looked like a psychotic asshole, too.

"She was coherent and responsive up until about thirty-four seconds before I called you," I replied with a growl. "Trust me, I know the difference." Really though, I couldn't blame her for acting reproachfully toward me.

"Neurologic symptoms? Nausea? Stumbling? Light sensitivity? Speech difficulty? Excessive drooling?" I raised my eyebrows at her on the last one.

She raised hers back, her face riddled with impatient annoyance.

"Well, Magnuson? Any of those symptoms? You're not giving me anything to go on. For all I know she could have popped a pill containing who knows what at the club."

"You don't think I fucking know that?!" Even I flinched a little at the tone of my voice.

"If you *fucking* know that then you better start talking and telling me something useful, and do it fast," she was absolutely unphased by my tantrum as she turned to her medical bag.

In a few efficient motions, she turned back to Freya with a handful of syringes and the things she needed to place an IV catheter. She quickly organized the items around her in into a miniature assembly line and continued seeing to my girl. Every one of her movements was smooth, confident, and competent.

Thirty-seven minutes and eighteen seconds later, all of the preliminary labs were completed.

We'd confirmed there was definitely alcohol in her blood but it wasn't anywhere near alcohol poisoning. Her blood oxygen levels were acceptable and steady, and there also weren't any detectable amounts of fentanyl, roofies, or other types of known dangerous narcotics in her blood samples.

I didn't realize how ridiculously tense I'd been until I let out a sigh of relief so forcefully, it cracked a few joints along my spine.

Nevertheless, I was still in a blood-curdling rage. Clearly, someone had drugged her. Dr. Briggs also agreed that the timing and progression of her symptoms meant that it more than likely occurred when she was in the club.

I was having a very difficult time not seeing Mikhail's face explode when I closed my eyes. If he had anything at all to do with this, he was a dead man.

"I'm going to need to run these on the big mass spec machine in the lab with a few other tests. I'll put a STAT on it. All results in sixty or less. There are numerous amine groups in her serum sample, which could be a lot of different narcs. But the big ones, the dangerous ones, aren't showing up."

Dr. Briggs packed up her things as she spoke, taking one last look at Freya's IV line as she adjusted the rate on the small, white digital pump.

Before she turned to me, she gently patted Freya's arm and gave her hand without the IV catheter port a little squeeze. There was a kind expression on her face which was gone by the time she turned to face me.

"Will I need to pull the sample results from the Anderson case for reference?" Her voice was flat and emotionless, an icy look within her soft brown, intelligent eyes.

"Yes."

The word was like acid in my mouth. I didn't fucking like it any more than she did, dammit.

She nodded, her entire body tense, already turning toward the staff entrance with the samples. Our lab was on the next floor. The private staff elevator in the other side of my suite would take her directly to it.

"Very well. I'll be back in an hour or less with the results; I'll check on her again. All her vitals are being recorded and sent to my monitor in real time. They have been and remain to be within normal parameters. The machine will alert me—as well as Esmeralda and Cassie downstairs—if anything becomes questionable. Cassie is just putting the baby back down, and she'll be up in a few minutes to help monitor.

"At this point I have no reason to expect any long-term damage, but I want her full report from the lab. And I want to run another blood gas on her in a few hours. Possibly run some imaging or scans in the morning, depending on her symptoms and how she feels when she wakes."

She pushed the keypad on the staff elevator, then entered in her thirteen-digit employee code. The elevator doors opened as she turned to go inside.

"I'm not leaving her side again until she wakes up."

She turned toward me at the gruff sound of my voice.

She looked at me, saying nothing as she let the doors close without getting inside the elevator. She took a deep breath, looking at the floor before she asked, "It's the same *MO*, isn't it?"

I nodded. I was too fucking furious to speak.

She pursed her lips and clenched her jaw, looking down at the floor again.

"She's only a little older than the last one," her words sounded muted, distant somehow.

Her face was an unreadable mask. I simply nodded, still too angry for words. She turned toward the elevator again, stepping inside for real this time.

"Brodie Magnuson, so help me, if you bring me another body to examine without first telling me you have found every last one of those *fucking sons of bitches* and turned them into a pile of fucking fertilizer... I'm going to go find the sorry motherfucking bastards myself. And then, I'm going to fine-tune my surgical skills on the lot of you."

Her eyes were shiny with emotion, but only a complete and total fool wouldn't take that threat of hers seriously.

I'd seen how skilled she was with a scalpel.

And possibly even better with a gun, expertly taught by her husband who was also a former MARSOC Marine.

"Doc, trust me; when we're done with them, there won't even be enough of the motherfucking bastards left to use for fertilizer."

Dr. Briggs nodded in morbid approval, her face an icy mask as the elevator doors closed between us.

I turned back to the bedroom immediately to check on Freya. I had to be near her. I focused on the steady rise and fall of her chest, the dark copper beauty of her hair, anything instead of the helpless rage.

Someone had tried to fucking take her right out from under me. I'd find every single person involved in this and end them. Loudly, and violently.

I sent out encoded updates to my team. They all responded immediately and confirmed the other three girls, Freya's friends, were safely home. I'd activated a code red, level-one security protocol on all three of them while I'd been forced to wait a thousand damn lifetimes for Freya's tox screen test results.

I'd already activated the same one on Freya Daniels as soon as I'd gotten back to my hotel room earlier that afternoon, when she'd run from me.

Somehow, even a red level-one didn't seem like enough as I watched the infuriating stillness of her body.

I was thinking more along the lines of, code *touch-her-and-I'll-rip-out-your-beating-heart-and-feed-it-to-your-mother*, level *right-after-I-feed-your-broken-limbs-to-your-father* type of protocol.

Chapter 28

Freya

My head was pounding. This was undoubtedly the worst freaking hangover I'd ever had in my life.

My mouth felt like I'd been chewing on tin foil, and it was so dry I was afraid my skin would tear if I tried to open my lips.

When I'd first opened my eyes, I immediately shut them again. They watered painfully from the blinding bright light in my bedroom. It made my head hurt even more.

The next thing I realized was how badly I had to pee.

Like, right now.

Suddenly worried I'd literally pee in my own bed like a child, I tried to sit up. There was some kind of cord pulling on my arm and around my hand. It was probably my phone charger cord, I realized as I tried to tug and wiggle myself free.

The-I-have-to-pee-right-now situation was getting dire. My whole body felt heavy and sluggish, like the sleep hadn't completely left me yet.

And why the hell was this cord not coming loose? Everything was so foggy. Besides the fact that I had to pee... that part was becoming exceedingly clear to my sluggish and still mostly sleeping brain.

"Whoa, whoa, whoa... easy, now. What do you need? Nauseous? In pain?"

I couldn't make sense of the deep masculine voice barking orders at me.

I tried to blink him into focus through the medium-sized herd of elephants stomping about inside my skull, right behind my tender eye sockets. Then, like a wave of ice-cold water being dumped over me, I remembered exactly where I was.

"Pee! Now!" I croaked out in a total panic.

It made me even dizzier watching the machine-like efficiency that he used to untangle my—

IV catheter?!

"What the fuck?!"

Screeching, I tried to move myself away from his hands, needing to see for myself what the hell was going on as I woke up.

It was like trying to play tug of war with a cement wall.

His jaw clenched and unclenched, but he kept doing whatever it was that eventually freed me from the IV set.

The freaking IV set!

"Why the hell do I have an IV, Brodie!"

I was so far past pissed off at this point, I was starting to sound like him. Growling and grunting instead of talking.

No answer, just more jaw clenching. Fine; he could just crack his stupid, perfect white teeth for all I cared!

I stayed silent as I allowed him to help me to the bathroom. I went into his arms without protest because I honestly wasn't sure if I could move fast enough. I was too freaking pissed off to talk and my urge to pee was reaching emergency level.

What the freaking hell was wrong with my bladder? At this point I was glad I hadn't actually pissed in the bed.

As soon as my head stopped pounding a little less—and my bladder wasn't about to burst, dammit—all of this whole shit show giant circus freak marathon fuck-up of mine was going to be dust in the pan. I'd get my things as soon as I was feeling better, spend the rest of the day doing self-care, and then tomorrow I'd deal with everything else.

"Can you stand, babe?"

His deep, barking voice just pissed me off more as he lowered my feet to the ground.

I nodded tersely, refusing to look at him. He set me by the counter and lifted the toilet seat lid. The weird intimacy of this moment between two essential strangers only pissed me off more. Unfortunately, my urinary predicament took precedence over all else, including my rapidly rising anger.

He went to pull down my pajama pants—wait, what the *hell?!*

They were mine, as in from my new place in SoHo.

I had definitely not packed them in my tiny shoulder bag last night! The fact that they were here, on my body, without any recollection of how they got there, was the spark that breathed the fire of life onto the slowly burning embers of my anger.

The very delicate hold on my temper snapped.

"Get. Out."

He stopped instantly when he heard my tone.

His face was drawn in a tight scowl as he stared down at me. He looked absolutely furious.

I didn't give a shit how angry he looked. I could assure him that at this moment, I was absolutely and positively freaking angrier. When he turned away and shut the bathroom door behind him, I could have cried in relief when I could finally freaking pee.

Feeling a lot better, I flushed the toilet and sat on the edge of the jacuzzi. My heart dropped into my stomach when I started to remember all that we did last night.

Some parts were actually a little blurry, but the part where I came screaming from his ball-bat cock was pretty clear. As well as the dirty way he'd made me beg for it. The space between my thighs warmed instantly at the memory, followed by shame, followed by very potent anger.

I stayed in the bathroom for a few minutes longer, trying to feel human again. I was also trying to convince myself that taking the empty shower rod down and using it to beat his arrogant ass with as I came lunging out of the bathroom was probably not a great idea.

Mostly because on second thought, the thing would probably snap in half like a paper straw when it his rock-solid body frame.

The mental image of him grabbing my makeshift weapon and twisting it into a pretzel shape before my eyes only made me angrier.

After washing my hands and splashing some water on my face and neck, I felt a teensy bit better. My stomach did a confused little flip when I saw my toothbrush and toothpaste—as in, my own toothbrush from my own bathroom in my own apartment back in SoHo—but my mouth felt too gross for me to not be at least a little grateful.

I brushed my teeth with much more fury than was necessary, feeling more and more energy as I moved my body around in the bathroom. When I rinsed my mouth out and looked back up in the mirror, I saw he'd opened the door and was glaring down at me.

I glared back at him through the mirror, then took a deep breath and turned to leave the bathroom.

He remained silent, still glowering at me as he stepped aside to let me pass.

"Where are my things?"

My voice cracked a little; my mouth was so dry. I *hated* being hungover, dammit. I still refused to look at him, but I could feel his stare on me as I walked toward the bed.

That's when I noticed what looked like lab machines and monitors.

"Freya, you need to listen to me. You're in danger, and—"

I wasn't sure why *he* sounded so angry. This whole freaking thing was his fault!

"Don't give me any more of your psychotic bullshit. I don't know you; I don't want anything else to do with you! We had sex now, you got what you wanted, we're done. And why the *hell* is my personal shit here, Brodie?! What the shit is that about?!"

It was hard to yell at him the way I wanted because my throat was so dry.

"Freya, I'm warning you," he kept glaring at me, standing completely still across the room.

"Warning me? *You* are warning *me?!*"

I didn't care how dry my throat was and how crackly my voice was as I yelled even louder back at him.

I was so far past the boiling point and close to hysteria. Most of my anger was directed toward myself, but he was the much more satisfying target at the time. His arrogance was starting to grate on my nerves so much I wanted to claw his gorgeous green eyes out. My chest was heaving with the force of my breathing.

He started moving, stalking toward me slowly.

I lost a teeny, tiny little bit of my anger.

"Freya," his deep voice was almost shaking it was so quiet.

He kept walking toward me, scowling. "I'm trying really, really hard to be patient. I understand you've been through a lot in the last—"

"Patient? *Patient?!* This is you being patient?! I want answers, Brodie freaking Magnuson and I want them now! I don't care how much *freaking* money you have—" the room started spinning a little as he moved toward me.

"Stop yelling, and Dr. Briggs will be here in a few minutes."

"Dr. Briggs is already here," a very pretty woman with soft, silvery blond hair and kind eyes was standing in the doorway to the bedroom.

"I'm sorry but... what? Who?"

My head was literally spinning again. I didn't protest when Brodie helped me back to the bed.

The woman—Dr. Briggs, apparently—approached the bed with a small smile. She gently offered her hand to me, and I took it hesitantly.

"My name is Dr. Tanya Briggs. I'm so glad to see you're awake and moving around, Freya. I want you to know you're completely safe here. Please, I insist; what questions can I answer for you?"

There was nothing but kindness in the way she looked at me.

Something about her motherly demeanor doused the fiery sparks of my anger. Before I even realized it my throat had tightened as tears started streaming unfettered down my face. She reached out for me again, taking one of my hands and holding it between hers as she squatted down by the edge of the bed, a calm smile on her face.

"Magnuson, leave us. Now. I'll call you back when you're needed. Do not come back before then," she didn't even look at him as she barked out her orders.

He nodded his head tersely and abruptly turned to leave.

If I weren't already lying in bed, I probably would have fallen over again. I looked back to her as if she were some kind of warrior goddess, commanding the arrogant gorilla around like a well-trained puppy.

Yeah, so I was *definitely* going to need lessons on how she did that.

She laughed softly at the expression on my face.

"Let me guess, he doesn't let you boss him around like that?" There was a warm twinkle in her eye.

"Er... umm, no. Definitely not," I didn't even know where to begin.

She sighed. "Well, Freya; what can I answer first?"

I took a deep, steadying breath. I tried to talk but instead cleared my throat a few times. Patting my hand, she instantly popped up and grabbed a bottled water and a straw from one of the room service tables. She placed the straw into it and handed it to me, still smiling calmly.

"Thank you," I mumbled weakly.

After I took a few sips, it was a lot easier to talk.

"Why am I here?" I searched her face for reaction as I started asking questions.

She sighed again quietly, her calm and reassuring demeanor never fading. "Are you aware of Mr. Magnuson's company, *Magnuson Security?*"

"Yes; he's already corrected me on the billionaire status," I couldn't help rolling my eyes a little.

She copied my gesture as she chuckled softly.

"Sounds like him, alright. Do you also know of his service in the military?"

"Yeah, I mean—no, not really. He said he was a veteran when I'd asked. Special ops, marines or something. Why?"

My stomach felt like it was doing back handsprings. The only thing scarier than a super-arrogant alpha-male billionaire was a super-arrogant alpha-male *former special-ops combat veteran* billionaire.

"Well, Mr. Magnuson is technically my boss. He has hired me to offer my medical care for one of his newest... contracts," I didn't like the way she hesitated before saying the word 'contracts.'

"What does any of that have to do with me? How did he even know who I was, or where I was?!"

I was getting a little hysteric again. I took another sip of water, taking a deep breath.

"Freya, Mr. Magnuson worked under my husband's command for several years in the marine corps, and eventually MARSOC, which is what the marine corps special operations command is called. Despite his horrible temper and gorilla-like demeanor, he is one of the best men I know aside from my husband," there was a warmth in her eyes as she spoke.

"That's very good to know," I offered calmly, "but that still doesn't explain why I'm here."

"Of course," she nodded, taking a deep breath. She gently took my hand again in her own as she spoke. "Freya, I'm so sorry to tell you this, but Mr. Magnuson has very good reason to suspect you've been targeted as part of a very sophisticated human trafficking system."

I stared at her, dumbfounded. I physically felt the coldness of the blood flushing out of my face and neck as her words rebounded around inside my still slightly aching head.

"Wh—what? How? Are—I—how? Are you sure?"

This made zero sense. Didn't that shit happen to ignorant rich girls on vacation? What the hell would they want with me? I was literally nobody, a broke orphan! I didn't even have anyone who would ransom me, or whatever the hell kidnappers even did!

"Yes, I'm sure," came an angry growl from the doorway.

Dr. Briggs sighed and rolled her eyes at him. "Follows orders well, this one."

"We don't have time for this, Doc. I have four other meetings to set up, and—"

"Don't talk to me about meetings, Magnuson. You have hundreds of employees at your disposal; use them," Dr. Briggs fired back like she was his mother, not his employee.

If I hadn't already liked her, I would have fallen in love with her right then and there. She had a seriously impressive set of lady balls.

"What do you think the meetings are for, Doc?! I still need to confirm her tox samples with Raffaele; I'm waiting on the—"

"Don't you start your barking and growling at me, Magnuson. You took this poor girl away from her entire life and probably didn't even bother to explain why."

Dr. Briggs might be even scarier than Brodie, on second thought. She definitely had that FAFO type of energy.

At least he had the decency to look sheepish at her tone.

My head was swimming. I had so many questions I didn't know which to ask first. Suddenly, I remembered the question that Brodie had been so adamant about asking me when he first brought me up to the hotel. It still seemed like an extremely odd thing to care about, and it didn't make very much sense, but at least it was a good place to start.

"Is that why you were so obsessed with the QR codes? The coupon that I scanned at the store?"

As soon as I asked the question, I immediately felt like an idiot for asking. It was such an insignificant detail.

"Yes. We've also confirmed that the invite you used last night at *DiVine* was similar, if not identical, to the metadata characteristics we've been assessing. It's been a very consistent part of the investigation regarding the targets' online activities," he sighed. He seemed to be deciding whether to continue, then asked, "Are you familiar with the Fiona Anderson case from Chicago?"

Fear washed over me so violently it was hard to breathe. I felt cold, then hot, then icy-hot at the same time.

Of course I knew that case.

It'd been all over the news as the case unfolded for almost the last two years. About a month before we'd graduated, they'd reported her remains had been found washed up off the coast of a small fishing town in Texas.

Fiona Anderson had been the picture-perfect daughter, student, friend, sorority sister. She had beautiful long, curly dark brown hair and a megawatt smile. When she'd disappeared seemingly out of the blue in the beginning of her junior year of college, her family and friends had been not only devastated but also at a total and complete loss. No history of reckless behaviors, no angry boyfriends, literally zero leads.

As the case unfolded, it became a circus of conspiracy theories and fake disappearance videos. Law enforcement was reportedly bombarded with the amount of fake data trails to sort through, not knowing what was real. It ranged from idiotically amateur photo-shopped videos to completely fake texts from ex-boyfriends—as in, the texts as well as the entire *person* had been faked, down to a false but still very convincing birth certificate that had somehow even been registered through the State of Illinois, according to the news.

Long story short, when her body was found, it took several weeks for her to be definitively identified. It was over a thousand miles from Chicago, where she'd been last seen alive.

Emaciated. Multiple broken bones. Missing fingers. Evidence of severe sexual trauma.

My stomach turned all over again as I remembered hearing the news report during my treadmill warm-up at the gym. I'd had to discreetly wipe the tears on my t-shirt as I'd watched the clips from interviews of her family and friends. I'd never met her. I didn't know any of her friends or family personally. It was all just really, really, really freaking sad.

It made me so freaking angry that such an innocent, beautiful life was pointlessly stopped so short.

The world around me slowly came back into focus as Brodie slowly approached me, leaning down by the edge of the bed. His face was unreadable as he spoke.

"Freya, I want you to know that I will do everything in my power to keep you safe. I'm going to find whoever is responsible for this, and I'm going to put every single one of them in the ground."

"'In the ground?' Is that some kind of military term?!" I felt like a vise-grip had been applied to my chest and someone was cranking it tighter and tighter with every breath.

"No. It means I'm going to kill them. Every last one of them."

Chapter 29

Brodie

I was so glad to have Dr. Briggs there as we answered all of Freya's questions. Never in my life had I felt more helpless, more furious than when I saw the steady stream of tears rolling down Freya's face. It didn't matter at all that we'd just met; she was mine, and she was crying, and at the moment I couldn't really do a fucking thing about it.

She was obviously terrified, and it made me want to shoot someone even more.

I wanted to hold her, to make sure she was safe. I also really did need to shoot someone so badly I kept absentmindedly reaching for the gun holster on my tactical belt. It wasn't anything I was proud to admit. Losing control of your emotions was a deadly and unforgivable sin in my line of work.

In the last several hours she'd had a few visitors.

Kimberly and her father, Peter Zakharov, had been here the longest and had just left. I had to stop the insane sense of possessive jealousy when they'd first arrived, and she immediately ran toward the other much older man. They embraced in what was a very affectionate, father-daughter type of hug. His daughter Kimberly joined them an instant later, kissing both her father and Freya on the cheek. I already knew from the intel we gathered that Freya's birth parents died in a car accident when she was six years old.

As insane and ridiculous as my possessive anger was, it softened a little when I forced myself to picture how differently her life could have been without the affection of this man and his family. Even though Freya's elderly, maternal grandparents were primary guardians after the accident, it was clear that Mr. Zakharov and his daughter were like family to her. I was grateful for her sake to have them here to provide the support that she needed.

I didn't know if it was the fact that another man was touching her, or that she willingly ran into another man's arms instead of my own that made me angrier.

Probably both.

My jealous reaction was absolutely embarrassing given how upset she was, which of course did nothing to improve my mood. Mostly because I knew the man that hugged her so tightly could give her the affection she needed right now, when I couldn't.

Like I said, I really needed to shoot someone.

Now, it was late into the afternoon and we were completely alone together.

Earlier, when Kimberly and her father had insisted that Freya come stay at the family estate, I adamantly refused. I didn't miss the murderous and very fatherly glare from Mr. Zakharov at my bold refusal.

That had definitely been an interesting conversation, I recalled sarcastically.

I didn't give a fuck about Marco's warning to not get into a confrontation with the Zakharov man who did business for Mikhail, the head of the Bychkov international crime syndicate. Mikhail Bychkov was also a member of the Council. Peter Zakharov was one of his chief attorneys, and the man had a heavy influence in his own right.

I didn't give a flying fuck about any of that.

Freya was mine, and she was going to be within arm's reach until I had every last one of these low-life, worthless, scumbag bastards blown to smithereens. As far as I was concerned, if anyone had a fucking problem with that then they could take it up with the barrel of my gun.

Not that she had a say in any of it, which Freya had very color-fully shouted at me before they left. I didn't care; she could be furi-ous at me if she wanted, as long as she was furious and safe. If I had my way she would stay in this very room for the foreseeable future.

Call me an asshole, but I'd be a lying asshole if I didn't admit that I selfishly liked her angry and spitting mad as opposed to silently crying and utterly terrified.

"How're you holding up, Freya?"

Her head snapped up angrily from where she sat on the over-sized sectional in the main living area, curled up like a cat in her big, fluffy grey blanket. It was one of the things I'd had my staff bring from her home; I told them to make sure she would be comfort-able.

"Angry enough to spit nails; tired enough to pass out standing up."

"Well, it's a good thing you're not standing up," I tried and failed not to laugh at her outraged cry of frustration from my teas-ing comment.

"I really don't feel like making jokes right now, Mr. Magnuson. So, if you'll excuse me, I'm going to go to bed for the evening. Good night."

She wrapped the fluffy grey blanket around herself and stormed past me haughtily.

"It's Brodie, Freya. Call me Brodie," I called after her darkly.

She stopped and whirled back toward me, her fluffy grey cape twirling around her like a disdainful queen addressing one of her unruly subjects.

"Excuse me? Look, pal. You don't tell me what to call you. You don't tell me anything, understand?!"

"Freya, sweetie, I'm trying really hard to be patient right now."

I could feel the angry growl of the beast inside with every word. The claws were shredding at me from the inside out, stripping away my control with every step she took away from me.

She was mine.

"Listen, *Mr. Magnuson*, I—"

"*Brodie.*"

Her eyes darted down to where my hands rested on my belt buckle, then back up to my face. Her mouth formed the cute little "o" again about a half second before she bit her lower lip, then turned her face away from me.

Too late. I saw how she was really feeling despite her contradicting words. She drew her fluffy cape around her regally, hiding the mouth-watering beauty of her body from my hungry eyes.

"No. I'm not calling you by your first name. It's too personal. And that," she pointed to the bedroom, "is never going to happen again."

I lunged for her. She must have been expecting it because she squealed and took off a split second before I grabbed for her. My hands came up with a fistful of the grey blanket and none of her sweet, soft flesh underneath. I left it in the floor of the hallway as I took a deep breath, trying to tame the beast.

"Freya, listen carefully."

I stalked toward my bedroom, not surprised to find the bathroom door shut. I heard the little metallic *click* of the bathroom door and chuckled darkly.

So, my little lioness wanted to play rough, did she? My dick lengthened and became rock-hard so fast the corners of my vision seemed fuzzy again. I stroked myself roughly through my black pants as I walked toward the closed door, practically licking my lips.

"Piss off, Brodie! Leave me alone! I agreed to stay here, but I'm not going to be your personal little sex doll. Last night, yesterday—it was all a mistake. I'm not—we're not—doing any of that again!"

I considered myself a man of fierce, unquestionable self-control.

There were few men alive who could do what I had been trained to do. I'd looked into the black eyes of death more times than I cared to count. Had dared to challenge and conquer it time and time again. I had been pushed to the absolute physical, intellectual, and emotional limits of man and emerged not only victorious, but hungry for more.

But to hear her say out loud that there was basically nothing between us other than sex, after what we'd shared the night before, was the final nail in the coffin of that exceptional self-control. I took a long, deep breath and exhaled.

It didn't help.

I lurked outside the bathroom, the beast ready to pounce on the gorgeous yet contrary creature whose delicious scent was already fading away through the barrier of the door.

"Freya. Open. This. Door. *Now.*"

"No! Fuck off! I have a right to say no, dammit!"

"One."

A rumbling growl came from deep within my chest. The beast was clawing free, and he was famished.

"Don't you dare do that stupid counting thing like I'm a child, dammit!"

Her words were punctuated by a soft *thud* as the door rattled slightly, as if a wad of towels had been thrown toward it from the other side. Despite the blood pounding in my ears, I had to smile. Damn, she was feisty.

"Two. Don't throw things like a child, and I won't have to treat you like one."

"Congratulations, you can count. Now go storm off somewhere else with your arrogant male caveman bullshit! Leave me
alone!"

"*Three*. Baby, get back from the door. Now."

I barely heard her outraged, muffled yell. I could tell she was on
the other side of the bathroom from how her voice echoed, or I'd
have never done what I was about to do. I just couldn't resist teasing her, she was just so damn cute when she was mad.

I placed my booted foot firmly against the sweet spot on the
door, right by the handle, and it came swinging open.

She was over by the shower, just as I'd suspected.

"Don't come any closer!"

She kept glancing up at the shower curtain rod with desperate
interest. My deep, predatory chuckle echoed in the bathroom as I
cornered her against the sink, placing a hand on each side of her.

"Or what, baby? Are you scared I'm going to make you come
screaming again? Hmmm?"

I couldn't stop touching the softness of her skin as I traced my
fingertips up her arm. It felt like ages since I'd been able to touch
her, which was unacceptable.

"No, please, I—just stop, okay! Freaking stop!"

Her tiny little fists beat against my chest and it made my dick
even harder. She was such a fighter, my pretty little fiery-haired
warrior. She could pound her cute little fists against me all she
wanted if it took her mind off being scared.

She was so much smaller than me, she'd wear herself out eventually.

"I love it when you pick the hard way, baby," I growled into the
crook of her neck.

I inhaled the sweet nectar of her scent, instantly drunk on the
breathless little whimper she let escape. I felt the fight leave her as

I savagely pushed my hips into the softness of hers, using my hands to hold her in place while I let her feel exactly what she did to me.

"Fuck you, Brodie!"

I chuckled. Well, most of the fight had left her, anyway.

"Gladly, baby," growling again, I bent down to capture her lips between mine.

I sucked hard, gently biting the soft flesh before I plunged my tongue into her mouth. She tasted so good, so sweet. The hot wetness of her mouth reminded me of how she's sucked my cock earlier. The thought made me growl into her open mouth, and suddenly I couldn't wait any longer to be inside her.

I easily lifted her over my shoulder, giving her ass a firm spank on the way out. The little jiggle of her juicy ass cheek made my balls clench in anticipation.

I carried her to the bed, kissing the rest of the fight from her with every step. Eventually I subdued her on her back with her arms held above her head and her body between my thighs. My eyes roamed over her body, everywhere, especially the soft jiggle of her beautiful tits in her soft white tee shirt as her chest rose and fell angrily. She noticed my gaze and let out a growl of her own, struggling against me wildly.

"Freya, you and I are going to come to an understanding, right here and now," she was still thrashing about below me.

Sighing in frustration, I easily flipped her over so that her stomach was on the bed, and that perfect ass of hers was up in the air, right where I wanted it. I placed her crossed arms behind her back as I anchored her to the bed with one of my legs. I felt the submission of her body to my will, and I wanted to beat my chest in male triumph.

Eventually I wanted to look at her face, to be able to see directly into her deep blue eyes when we had our chat. But first, apparently, my little lioness wanted to be taught a lesson.

She threw her head over her shoulder, hissing and spitting like a bobcat.

My dick almost exploded when I saw the little flush on her face as I reached for the hem of her leggings, yanking them down in one thrust. Her ass cheeks bounced with the rough motion, making my mouth water. She'd changed clothes earlier which was also probably why I was hot enough to fuck her into next year.

It should be illegal to have legs as sexy as hers. I didn't know which was worse, those sexy, toned *thick* thighs exposed in her cute little pajama shorts, or every single curve covered yet emphasized in the second skin, charcoal grey sex pants.

"Fuck yes, baby. I love spanking this juicy ass of yours. I'm gonna need you to keep acting up," I wanted to be inside her so badly I could feel my temperature raise by the second.

Her feral cries had turned into broken little whimpers and moans as I continued to rain little sparks of fire on her quickly pinkening skin. Once again, she started moving her hips into, not away from, the blows.

I yanked down the leggings even further, wanting to see if her sweet pussy was wet for me again.

I chuckled quietly as I saw the shiny wetness from her swollen pussy lips peeking through the juncture of her closed thighs. Damn, but that looked good.

She sobbed out loud when I placed a firm swat right on top of her gorgeous cunt. I could barely hear her response over the pounding in my ears and my own grunts and growls at her sexy as fuck reaction.

"Let's get something settled, Freya. Right here and now. Your life is in serious danger. I'm here to keep you safe. Tell me you understand this, or I'll get my belt instead of my hand," it was getting really hard to control the savage force of my lust.

But I needed this, and I think she did, too.

"Okay! Fine! I believe you, alright!"

Her breaths were coming out in short, desperate pants.

"Good girl," I purred, using my thumb to spread her pussy juices all around her cute, pink pussy lips.

She squealed, trying to move away. I swatted each cheek again. My balls were about to burst with every one of her cries.

"Okay, okay! I understand, I'll listen, please! Stop! Please!"

She was practically shaking with need. Her hips moved jerkily as I rubbed her puffy, swollen little clit with the very tips of my now soaking wet fingers. Smacking my mouth obscenely, I sucked her sweetness from my fingers as I continued.

"Starting now, you're going to let me protect you, Freya. You're going to listen to me, obey me if I say something isn't safe. Is that understood?"

I rubbed my palms over her backside, enjoying the low and very sensual moan she tried and failed to hide from me.

"Y—y—yes, I'll be good, and I'll listen! Please, I don't want... oh my—"

Her hips were rolling into the mattress in timid little thrusts. I felt every single motion down the length of my aching, pulsating cock.

"Shhh, baby... I'm going to let you come. But not until we finish our little chat, mmm?"

I slowly brought the tips of my fingers back to her soaking wet folds. She moaned raggedly, arching into my touch.

On second thought, maybe she'd be more receptive to the situation after I'd made her scream and shake with pleasure again.

I gave her ass cheek a hard slap with my hand. She squealed, then whimpered as her pussy lips fluttered around my fingers. My cock jumped hungrily as I lost a little more of my self-control watching her become aroused.

"Answer me, Freya."

"Yes! Okay, we'll talk! I'll talk, please!"

"Mmmm, baby. Are you sure you don't want to keep misbehaving? I could play with this ass all day, fuck," I moved my fingers toward the cleft of her ass cheeks.

"I... wait, what? Oh, my... no! Not there, umm... I haven't ever... I don't really want—"

"You don't want what, Freya? Me to keep playing with your soaking wet, swollen cunt?"

I pushed my thumb into the hot, wet sweetness of her pussy as her hips thrust back toward me.

"Holy hell, I—"

"Use my name, baby. Call me what I want. I love hearing my name on your lips."

I curled my thumb toward the swollen ridge of flesh along the wall of her vagina, stroking her G-spot wickedly.

"Oh, *fuck,* oh my—Brodie, holy hell! That feels—oh my god, so good," she was so fucking sexy when she panted like that, her words all jumbled into cute little high-pitched squeaks.

"Your pussy gets so wet for me, baby. You make my dick so damn hard I can't see straight, just being around you," I increased the pressure of my thumb as I used my fingertips to tease her clit.

"Oh! Brodie, fuck, *yes!* Please, I can't—I'm... I'm so close!"

Growling, I removed my thumb from the tight, wet sweetness of her cunt. I put two fingers in its place, thrusting in and out like I wanted to do with my cock. And I would, soon. But first, she needed to understand that I was in control, and that she'd never be allowed to deny her reaction to my touch.

My thumb was still soaked with the sweetness of her arousal. I continued to fuck her juicy cunt with my fingers as I pressed my glistening thumb onto the tight little pucker of her asshole. She immediately tensed, and I almost came thinking about how her tight little ring of muscle would feel clamping down on the length of my cock while she screamed with uncontrollable pleasure.

"Have you ever come with something inside both of your sexy little holes, baby?"

Chapter 30

Freya

Once his naughty words registered in my brain and I recovered from the shock of where he'd put his thumb, I violently tried to escape his hold.

It was like wrestling an oak tree.

I didn't know if I could survive the complete mortification of what he was doing. It was so wrong, so dirty, but at the same time I was too hot to care. When my brain finally realized that he was in control, and that I couldn't escape, all I wanted was more.

However, there was no freaking way in hell I was going to admit that out loud.

It was already bad enough that he'd made me a sopping wet pile of needy female goo, *again,* when I'd told him I didn't want him to do those things to me. He'd made a liar out of me from almost the first touch of his hand as he spanked my ass.

"No! Oh my god! Brodie, not there, take it out!"

"Mmmmm... now why would I do that when your pussy is getting even wetter? Damn, but that's a pretty sight, baby! Have you ever come with a finger in your ass, Freya?"

The deep growl of his voice was going to send me into another spontaneous orgasm.

"No! No one... I've never done that. I don't, it's dirty! Please, I don't like it, stop—*ohhhh!*"

I couldn't breathe when he started thrusting both his fingers and his thumb violently into me. I could feel my pussy and ass cheeks shaking from the force; it was absolutely delicious.

"Fuck, yes, baby. You are so fucking sexy, Freya. Are you ready to come like this, baby? I want to feel your asshole clench around my thumb and your pussy juices drip all over my fingers."

Holy unicorn dicks.

The power this man had over my body.

It didn't matter that we were basically strangers when he talked so dirty in that deep, rough voice. The way he took complete control and demanded I respond.

My orgasm hit me like a tidal wave. I came so hard from what he was doing, the deliciously twisted pleasure flooded through me as I jerked and thrashed in his hold. The sensation was endless and totally consuming, and I screamed as I felt bliss erupt from somewhere deep inside my pussy. I had the strangest sensation that I was either going to come so hard I died, or so hard that I peed.

Either way, death by orgasm or orgasm-induced embarrassment seemed imminent. My befuddled and sex-saturated Swiss cheese brain didn't know whether to panic, or pant.

It chose both.

"No, please I—I think I have to—umm, I—Oh, *ffff*—*uhhh*... *yes!*"

Without warning, a second orgasm crashed through me. I felt it erupt everywhere between my legs from front to back. I was drowning in the bliss, my entire body being carried along in another wild wave of pleasure. I could feel hot wetness coating the insides of my thighs; it kept dripping everywhere.

Suddenly it was too much, all of it, and I collapsed weakly into the mattress.

"Freya, *baby,* you came so hard for me. Fuck, you're absolutely gorgeous squirting all over my hands, *fuck!*"

I tried to bury my face in the mattress as the shame washed over me. His words sounded dirty now, which was instantly what I felt, and I hated it.

"Please, let me up," I couldn't hide the hint of tears from my voice.

I was flipped around on my back so fast I squealed, almost catching him square in the jaw with my elbow as I tried to cover my face in my hands. I couldn't look at him, not after that. Not after he'd made me freaking piss myself! That was too much for me, way too much.

"Freya, what the hell is wrong?"

His tone was laced with incredulous impatience. It immediately grated on me. He grabbed my jaw firmly and brought my face to his when I refused to look at him. I did the only thing I could as I squeezed my eyes shut, trying to shut out the embarrassment.

"No, baby. Open your eyes. Talk to me," his tone was more soothing, which perversely made me more upset.

I refused to look at him, trying to turn my head to the side. Eventually, he let me, and started stroking my hair gently in spite of his heavy and excited breathing.

I was so angry, unbalanced, sad, shocked, and whatever. I wanted my old life back, my comforting and ridiculously ordinary life. I didn't want to be under this man's control, even if he was just as insanely hot as he was scary. I didn't want to have to look over my shoulder for the next who knew how long. To not even be able to go out with my friends, or even buy groceries, for fear that I'd wind up dead.

Or worse.

They'd told me it could be more than a year before I'd be out of the woods.

I couldn't even handle five minutes alone with this man before I was swept away, burning in the fire of his lust. What the hell would be left of me if I had to stay with him a year? I'd be a sorry little pile of ashes by that time.

It was like being swept into a thunderstorm. It's addicting, exciting and wild being at the mercy of so much raw power. That's all wonderful until the storm spits you out when it's done, leaving you a crumpled, broken, and mangled mess of torn fabric and confusion.

Speaking of which, I was still pissed as shit about the two items of clothing he'd already destroyed.

It was all way too much. I was absolutely not about to cry right now, dammit. But in my defense, it *really* was the best little black dress ever, the jerk.

He wrapped his arm around me and threw his massive thigh over my legs, prisoning me to him with his body. It felt too good to resist his strength, so I finally admitted to myself how scared I was. What the hell had my life turned into?!

"That was fucking beautiful, baby. You're sexy as hell. Why are you so upset, Freya?"

He sounded off-balance. His deep, growly voice sounded less growly. His tone somehow less arrogant.

I couldn't talk past the tightness in my throat. I couldn't believe I'd just let him put his finger in my ass, and then actually peed. I'd never done anything so wild, even with guys I'd been dating! I barely knew him, yet I was wallowing in my own guilt at the same time I settled back more into his arms.

He sighed, completely back to his normal arrogant self.

"Don't even try to pull this 'I didn't want to' with me. It's pretty hard for me to believe that when your pussy is so wet it's dripping down between your thighs," he nuzzled his scratchy beard along my neck as he spoke.

I shivered, moaning at the contact and unable to retaliate to his infuriating masculine arrogance. Because I was too angry to think of a retort, not because it made my toes curl a little when he was so bossy and weirdly sweet at the same time. Yup. Too angry. I started to panic a little.

"Please let me up, I want to shower! It's, umm... I'm a little embarrassed, and it's a lot right now, and I need to shower," my voice cracked a little on the last part.

"Freya, what the fuck? Are you serious? What do you mean, 'embarrassed?!'"

His teasing voice was like rubbing salt in the wounds.

"Brodie, screw you. Let me up. I want to freaking shower."

"Gladly, sweetheart," he kissed my forehead before continuing. "But only about the screwing you, not the shower. I don't think I'm ever going to shower again, to be honest," he winked at me as he sucked on his fingers, then laughed at the expression on my face.

I didn't know why he was being so callous about the whole ordeal and teasing me. He's the one that made me totally lose control and piss the damn bed!

"You know, you're a real asshole for making fun of me. It's not my fault that—"

He threw his arm over me, pinning me into the mattress again.

Why the hell did he have to be so massive and so fast at the same time?! I mean, pick one or the other!

"Making fun of you, Freya? Explain. Now," he growled quietly into my face.

"If I wasn't supposed to do... *that*... then you shouldn't have done... well, *that!*"

His eyes were like two burning teal gemstones as they gazed into mine. He didn't say anything for a few moments. I felt the heat of his gaze all over me as his eyes roamed over my entire body, then locked in on my face.

"Freya, what the fuck. *That* was the hottest fucking thing I've ever seen in my life. I'll do *that* to you anytime and every time you want, baby."

"Look, I've never... done that before, alright? I didn't know it was happening. And I told you to stop, and you didn't!"

I could feel my face and neck burning with shame as I scowled at him.

"Of course I didn't stop, Freya. I knew what you needed, baby. I wanted to give it to you."

He was stroking all over my body, squeezing the sensitive space along the crease of my hipbone. He grabbed me there, holding me still to rub the steel length of his cock along my sensitive backside, and continued arrogantly. "Stop overthinking it. You liked it. I liked it even more," he resumed his touch along my hips and back.

"I don't want you to do that again. Ever."

It was getting really difficult for me to remember exactly why, though.

I could feel the whole length of his thick, completely hard cock pressing against me. He really needed to stop that hypnotizing way he was touching my back, my waist, my hip, everywhere. It was confusing.

I didn't realize how close I was to drifting off again until I felt the rumble deep in his chest all along my back when he spoke, and I jumped.

"Hang on. Freya. Have you never—you know that wasn't pee, right?"

The look on his face was indescribable.

"I don't, um... I'm not sure I know what you're talking about," I lied, feeling my skin turn beet red as he looked at me.

"Is that why you're upset? You think I'm making fun of you because you came so hard that you pissed yourself?"

He looked like he was about ready to burst out laughing.

"FUCK YOU, Magnuson!"

Maybe Dr. Briggs had taught me a thing or two when she'd visited earlier, because before he could do anything else I'd grabbed a pillow and smacked him upside the head.

I completely ignored the fact that it was probably his own laughter that had been distracting enough for me to escape from him and into the bathroom, and not how hard I'd hit him with the fluffy hotel pillow.

A girl's pride could only take so much.

I went to lock the door before I remembered that he'd kicked it in—like for real, what kind of psychotic control freak kicks a bathroom door in?!—then I furiously turned on the shower, anyway, ignoring my lack of privacy. It's not like he hasn't seen me naked, I thought sarcastically.

I also completely ignored the little twinge of something warm I felt in my stomach when I saw all my *Oribe* products waiting for me in the promising tranquility of the natural stone shower enclosure.

Now that I had been convinced by the Zakharovs that this crazy shit was real, and that Brodie and his team really were highly trained to protect me, that gesture seemed impossibly sweet.

So did the pair of my own pajamas that I'd woken up wearing. So did the soft, cozy, and comforting fluffiness of my favorite *UGG* couch throw which I'd donned as a protective shield while I tried to absorb this drastic new twist in my life.

Angrily I grabbed an oversized bath towel from the hook and wrapped it around myself. I sat on the built-in bench across from the spray from the numerous jets of the luxury shower enclosure, seething. My complete lack of control of my own situation was making me throw one very large pity party, but at the same time I realized I needed to feel what I felt, deal with it, and eventually I would find my way forward.

Right now, my way forward was a nice long, hot shower.

Within a few minutes the entire space was blanketed in a fine mist from all the jets in the shower. I didn't even glance back at the door as I placed the towel on a hook by the bench and stepped around the side of the stone wall into the soothing, warm steam. I'd been looking forward to this moment almost the entire day.

There really wasn't anything a nice long, hot shower couldn't fix, I thought as a let the warm water run its way over my scalp, down the back of my neck, back, and all around my body. I sighed contentedly, the water instantly melting away a little of the nervous tension. I took another slow, deep inhale, trying to focus on being present and enjoying this peaceful moment after such a damn circus-freak shit-show of a day.

A deep, rumbling growl interrupted my peaceful moment and made me squeak in alarm as I opened my eyes.

"Fuck yes, baby. You look just like that when you're coming."

Brodie was sitting on the shower bench, stark naked, legs spread arrogantly as he pumped his magnificent and rigid cock up and down with one hand. The other hand was propped lazily on his tree trunk thigh holding...

...the pair of panties I'd been wearing today.

Smiling wolfishly and looking right at me, he held them up to his face again, closing his eyes as he inhaled obscenely.

Words were useless against the firestorm of lust he'd instantly reignited inside me with his raw and blatantly sexual gesture. The scalding water was starting to feel cold compared to the burning temperature of my skin. I turned away frantically, hiding him from my view so I didn't do something really freaking stupid, like walk over to him and put the thick, throbbing length of his cock into my mouth.

"Damn, Freya; you smell so fucking good."

I jumped a foot in the air when I heard his voice suddenly right behind me.

"Stop sneaking up on me like a freaking panther! Jesus, Brodie! You're going to give me a heart attack!"

Laughing, he wrapped the warm iron band of his arms around me from behind as he pulled me in close, so that my back was pressed alongside his front. I felt the searing hot, rock-hard length of his cock along my lower back; it was making me lightheaded again.

He just held me like that, both of us under the hot, soothing spray of the water, for what felt like a long time. For some inexplicable and probably really screwed-up reason that I wasn't going to acknowledge anytime soon, something wild and restless calmed inside me when he held me like that.

Even while my pulse still raced in anticipation of what he was going to do to me with that monstrosity swinging between his thighs.

"Freya, do you remember what I said you were going to do the next time we fucked?"

His deep, rough words sizzled hotly over the crook of my neck and down my spine, then immediately set me on fire.

I gasped, leaning into him and shaking my head *no*.

He chuckled darkly, the sound like the purr of an engine before it explodes to life.

"I told you you're going to sit on my face and fuck my mouth with that sweet pussy until you came, remember?"

He massaged each one of my breasts as he spoke, teasing the tips of my nipples with his rough palms.

I moaned brokenly, unable to say anything. He continued to play with me, his hot mouth all along the crook of my neck and collarbone.

"Now that I know how much that sweet fucking pussy of yours squirts, I'm not going to waste a single drop, sweetheart."

He chuckled, the thin patch of hair on his solid chest tickling my back as his shoulders heaved. The sound was promising in the most sinister way, and it made my toes curl. His hands turned rough, grabbing me everywhere and holding me so close to him that there wasn't a single place our skin didn't touch.

"Freya; do you know what I'm going to do to you after you come all over my face, hmmm?"

I could only pant and shake my head again. He growled menacingly at my response, placing a weak slap on each ass cheek.

"I'm going to fuck you until neither of us can walk."

"Oh... holy hell. I—no, we can't. It's not a good idea, please Brodie, we have to stop. This is craziness!"

He sighed. I could literally hear him rolling his eyes just as well as I could hear him chuckling softly at my refusal, the arrogant bastard.

"Then, after you come all over my cock, you're going to tell me why the hell you keep pushing me away when you and I both know that's not what you really want."

...*busted.*

Chapter 31

Brodie

The last time I'd heard that shower running, I'd vividly pictured her dripping wet, completely naked body inside of it and almost came from the fantasy.

Unfortunately, I'd also almost sustained a concussion in my rush to get to her, only to discover how she'd tricked me. That had been the last of the shower curtain.

By the time I strolled into the bathroom she was already in the shower. She was even more beautiful than I'd imagined, my fantasy not even coming close to the real thing. When she let her head fall back and sighed in sensual bliss as she enjoyed the warm water, she looked just like she did right after she came.

The beast inside immediately came clawing through, howling with need.

I couldn't resist teasing her again with her panties. There was probably something a little fucked up inside me that I wanted to scare her a little with how much she turned me on. My little warrior liked to bear her ferocious little claws at the beast before she gave in. I loved how that turned her on, made her pussy dripping wet for me. It was so damn *sexy*.

I had needed to hold her in the shower.

She needed to understand that even though we'd randomly been thrown together, everything happened for a reason. She might as well get used to it because she wasn't going anywhere without me by her side.

I didn't give a shit that I'd only known her for a little over a day, I'd never felt this attracted to a woman in my entire life. She was like an obsession, like being around her was the final clarity I needed in my life.

Her personality was so feisty and warm at the same time, every movement she made graceful and feminine. Being around her was like a shot of a drug I was never going to get enough of. From the minute I'd seen her, I'd wanted her, and I was going to have her. It was that simple.

If she had any idea how the crude panty sniffing was only just the tip of the very large iceberg, she'd probably run away screaming.

But what a sexy fucking view it would be watching her ass sway as I gave her a head start, I thought as I looked down at her.

I finished showering before she did, kissing her on the forehead as I left.

I tried to watch her as she shaved her legs, but my guilt won over when she kept sending me glares and I let her have the time to herself. I started to sense her tension. I would take care of that for her as soon as she got done soaking her entire body in the *Oribe*, or whatever she did to always smell amazing.

The domestic way I felt was shockingly comforting. I just wanted to be around her.

"Babe, I'm starving. What do you want to eat? Are you thirsty?"

"Umm, what? I thought—oh, um, never mind! Yes, a little hungry I guess."

"What do you want to eat? Steak? Salad? Pasta? Seafood?"

"Yes? Any of that sounds great. I'm not very picky. Whatever you eat is fine, please and thank you," her voice sounded a little more confident and relaxed now.

I smiled, knowing she probably suspected I'd been kidding about her face fucking me, and then actual fucking me as soon as she got out of the shower.

She'd be wrong, of course; I simply wanted to have food ready and waiting for us because I was starving, and afterward I wanted to cuddle. Maybe watch a movie on the couch. Or take a bottle of wine to the rooftop terrace when the sun set. All of the above sounded amazing, as long as I got to touch her.

I had stopped questioning the things my dick was getting hard over sometime Friday night.

It didn't even bother me in the slightest that I wanted to fuck her brains out and then hold her all night long while my cum stayed deep in her pussy. I wanted to watch it drip out around her thighs as she slept peacefully. That I wanted to make sure she was comfortable and happy, and safe. If someone would have told me that I'd feel this insane about a woman, one woman, a few days ago, I would have laughed in their face and then thrown one of my fists into it.

When she'd run away from me Friday, her pretty blue eyes fading from sight as the elevator doors closed, something inside me had snapped. I had felt like a starving man dying from hunger who'd been given nourishment for the first time, only to have it snatched away again cruelly.

She was different from the moment I'd first laid eyes on her. The savage way I felt when she screamed out her release all over my cock just cemented that fact. My fucking *soul* had temporarily left my body when I came inside her pussy.

I knew sex would never be the same for me again unless it was with her.

I didn't know exactly why she'd frozen up on me earlier, but I was going to find out one way or another. Then, it was going to be dealt with. It wasn't just her body that I needed to have control of, but also to know that she trusted me enough to submit, to obey my every command until things were safer.

She was in my world now whether she liked it or not. And in my world, you didn't always get the luxury of time to adjust to the situation. Sometimes you had to skip a few steps, or maybe even all of them.

I peeked into the bathroom and saw she was almost done combing out her dark copper hair. When it was wet, the purple hue was more prevalent. I didn't realize I'd probably been staring until she cleared her throat sarcastically.

"Did you need in the bathroom?"

Her tone was relaxed and detached. Professional, polite. I could fix that soon.

I wanted her naked, moaning, screaming underneath me while I held her open for every one of my savage thrusts.

"Since you're asking about my needs, I am pretty sure I need inside that sweet pussy of yours," I stalked toward her in the bathroom.

I was hypnotized by the way her indigo eyes sparkled within the dark frames of her long eyelashes. She was blushing furiously. It made her eyes appear an even deeper, more intense shade of blue.

"But I thought... aren't we going to eat now? I mean, the food will get cold, and I'm sure you're probably super hungry, right?!"

She'd done exactly as I suspected and assumed I was joking about the face fucking and then fucking.

"Who said we weren't going to eat?"

I winked at her wolfishly as I pinned her hips against the sink. I rubbed my cock into her softness as I'd done earlier, enjoying the way her eyelids fluttered shut and her head rolled to the side before she could hide anything from me.

"And I am absolutely starving, Freya. I want that pussy grinding all over my mouth."

Her breath hitched and she moaned brokenly. The sound was like a lightning strike of pleasure to the tip of my dick. My balls clenched while I kept teasing her.

Her skin was so soft. I kissed her face, all the way down the side of her neck just below her jaw. She smelled so fucking good; I couldn't be around her without that scent making my dick immediately stand at full attention.

Finally, I moved to her lips and plunged my tongue deep inside her mouth. She moaned brokenly as she opened her mouth more to the kiss. I greedily absorbed her cries, needing more.

I had to tear myself away from her lips because my need to be inside her was excruciating. Gasping like I'd just run a mile, I yanked off the towel she'd wrapped around herself. I wanted to see every inch of her gorgeous body, for her to be completely exposed to me.

She'd squealed in surprise once I'd gotten her naked. Her eyes darted around nervously as she tried to cover herself and play innocent. It was almost like a challenge to the beast raging inside me; he wanted her just as crazy with need as he already was.

"You said we were going to eat now, right? And we can't really do that in the bedroom," her voice was breathless again, panicky.

I chuckled darkly, tracing her bottom lip with my thumb.

Good; she should be a little scared. If she thought she came hard earlier, she was about to learn what being with me was really going to be like.

"Oh, I'm definitely going to eat in bed tonight."

I smiled at her, the sheep finally showing its wolf's teeth to the unsuspecting prey. I could see the pulse beating wildly just above her collarbone, and it made me want to nip into her there, then kiss away the sting.

"Now get on the bed, Freya. I'm... starving."

I grabbed her around the waist and lifted her to me, her legs wrapping instantly around my hips. It felt so fucking good to have her thighs wrapped around me, her pussy hot and wet along the lower part of my stomach. My balls clenched desperately as I carried her to the bed.

"Brodie, I—"

"Freya, I swear, if you open that pretty little mouth of yours and lie to me..." I set her down on the bed, then spread her legs open wide so I could see all of her.

"I don't know if I can do that, Brodie!"

She tried to hide herself from me, but I snatched away her hands before they could block my view.

"Naughty girl, Freya. Stop fighting me. Baby, I'll keep you safe."

I looked into her eyes as I teased her clit. When she blushed all over, I winked at her right before I closed my lips around her and sucked lightly.

She was so fucking beautiful; I wanted to see the fire burn in her eyes again for me when I forced her to the very edge of sanity. Seeing her lose control had quickly become like a drug I couldn't do without.

"This is so fast, Brodie. I don't even know you!"

"I have a great way for us to get to know each other better."

I traced the entrance to her soaking wetness with my fingertips. I felt precum dripping down the tip of my cock when she moaned, pushing her hips up into my touch as her eyes burned into mine.

"Keep your hands above your head, Freya, or I'll tie them up again. Understood?"

She whimpered, biting her lip and nodding her head weakly. I took her mouth in mine again for a punishing kiss. I couldn't handle the way she bit her lip like that while she was practically begging me to fuck her brains out with her eyes.

"Freya, answer me," I reached around and gently swatted her backside, drinking in the sound of her tightly drawn breath at the sting.

"Yes! I'll... I won't move my arms!"

She was already breathless; there was no way she'd be able to stay put. I smiled greedily. I could already feel that juicy ass jiggling under my palm.

I kissed all the way along the inside of her thighs, paying special attention to the crease right between her pussy lips and her inner thigh. She went wild when I licked her there, her arms falling down to her sides as she grabbed a fistful of my hair, tugging not quite gently.

All thought of reprimanding her evaporated and I growled into her soaking wet core, enjoying every single feral sound she made as I feasted.

I flattened my tongue and ran it all the way up and down from the entrance of her pussy and up against her clit. Lust clawed at me as I willed my aching balls not to explode, not before I'd sunk the entire length of my cock into her. Her moans and whimpers were driving me insane. All I could think about was fucking her and filling her full of my cum.

"Fuck yes, tell me how good it feels, Freya. Tell me how good your pussy feels when I lick it."

My balls were drawn so tight against my body I felt like I could come at any second, but I refused to give in. Not until my dick was sucked up tight in the hot sweetness of her pussy.

"Oh, my god, yes! Brodie, that feels so good! It's—it's... oh *fuck,* yes!"

I could tell she was almost at the breaking point, her words tumbling out between her frantic, high-pitched moans. The sounds made my dick throb, but I wanted her to be even louder, more desperate. Her clit was so swollen and puffy it was completely exposed from its hood. Her arousal was all over her pussy lips and dripping down around the tiny little pucker of her asshole. My dick was so rock-hard, throbbing painfully at the view.

I couldn't resist dipping my tongue into her there, smiling at the way she squealed and almost shot off the bed in her shock.

"Brodie! Oh, my god! That's not my vagina!"

Holy fucking adorable.

I laughed out loud at her shocked tone. I honestly couldn't think of a time where I'd genuinely fucking laughed when my cock was hard enough to pound nails into concrete.

"I know, baby. That's why I put my tongue into it. Pretty soon I'll get you a cute little jewel to wear in your bottom while I fuck your pussy. It will make it easier when I fuck your tight little asshole with my cock, Freya."

"Oh! What? Brodie, that's... you can't! I mean—I've never really, umm... I don't like that type of thing, it's, uh, not *made* for that!"

I couldn't believe she was still trying to hide her sexy responses when her pussy was literally pulsating wildly into my mouth from the vision I'd likely just created in her head. Again, I was too far gone with lust to reprimand her for being dishonest. I was having a pretty hard time with the image I'd just created as well.

Definitely fucking hard.

I grabbed her hips and held her up, then slid my upper body underneath her spread thighs. Spinning us around, I locked her into position on top of my face with her pussy lips spread right in front of my mouth.

It was the absolute hottest fucking thing I'd ever seen, especially when I glanced up at the delicious view of the underside of her tits. Her rosy pink nipples were drawn into tight little buds as her chest jiggled and swayed. She was absolute fucking perfection.

"Oh! Ummm... that's really, like... are you sure you still want to—*ow!* Dammit! Oh, god, Brodie! It's really—"

"Mmmm, bad girl, Freya. Naughty girls get spanked. Now do as you're told. Put that sweet pussy on my mouth and fuck my face until you come."

Chapter 32

Freya

I had never done something like this with a guy before, had barely had my pussy licked during sex. It was always something I was curious about but I'd never felt that comfortable with the guy to actually orgasm from his mouth. There was just some kind of connection that was missing for me before.

Perversely, "comfort" might be the last word I'd use to describe how I felt around Brodie Magnuson. He simply demanded that I submit to his raw, dominating sexuality.

I didn't have time to go through all of my pre-conditioned hang ups, like *does this angle make me have a double chin?* Or *are my thighs jiggling too much?* He gave me zero time for any of that.

Sex with him was like a wild ride down a steep water slide.

Once I hopped on, there was no turning back. There was only falling at the speed of light, and then an explosion into that all-consuming pool of pleasure. I stayed there, suspended in sheer bliss, until my brain resurfaced from the wild ride.

By now, my body was probably physiologically hooked on the twisted sexual rush that only he could deliver, and I'd known him barely twenty-four hours.

He made me so crazy with lust that I spread my legs wider at his dirty words, brazenly grinding my pussy into his tongue. I felt his low moan vibrate against the hottest and most swollen part of my clit. The pleasure made my head spin.

"Fuck yes, Freya! Rub that sweet fucking pussy on my mouth."

His python arms were locked around my thighs so tightly, there was no other choice as I greedily followed his orders. My body was singing with pleasure, more than happy to obey.

I moaned, leaning back a little so I could play with him. Lust curled the tips of my toes when I felt how freaking thick and hard his cock was already. The tip of it was covered in precum, and I used the palm of my hand to spread it around while I obscenely rolled my hips into his mouth.

He growled into my pussy as I stroked him up and down. The low, rumbling feeling sent white-hot pleasure directly on my clit.

I was so fucking close, but there was a little nagging thought in the back of my mind that kept pulling me back from letting go to the pleasure completely.

What if the same *thing* happened again, and when I was literally directly on top of his mouth?! The mild panic made me hesitate and then stop my movements all together, the lust sizzling away like water dumped on a fire.

"Brodie, I can't... please, I—maybe we should... I can't come like this, I'm too nervous," I felt so exposed like this. He tightened his arms even more around me, bringing me even closer to his mouth. I gasped at the contact, trying to reason with him, "What if that thing happens again!"

I felt another soft vibration right on my clit as he growled into my pussy again.

"Hell, yeah, baby! *Fuck* yeah, grind that pussy all over my mouth. Squirt all over me, Freya. I want that pussy nice and wet when I fuck you. I want every last fucking drop of your cum all over me, baby."

Holy freaking hell.

My concern faded into nothingness. I let the crazy lust completely take over, grinding and rubbing my swollen clit against his tongue and his open mouth. I felt wild, reckless, desired.

He moved suddenly, wrapping one of his arms around my waist and completely anchoring me to the sinful attention of his mouth. With his other hand he grabbed both of my arms and twisted some kind of strap around them. I hadn't even processed what he'd done before I found my wrists tied together and hooked to some kind of soft strap on the bed frame in front of me.

The crude position brought back some of my concern, because there was no way in hell that I looked good like this at all!

I was still straddling his mouth, but now I was leaning forward with my arms above my head and my definitely *not* small, *not* perky breasts jiggling obscenely right above his head.

Even worse, the way I was leaning forward now made my lower tummy look even poochier. Uggh.

Inwardly I cringed, but he'd started sucking and licking on me so wildly that it was hard to focus on anything besides how amazing it felt at the juncture of my thighs. There was no way this was a flattering angle, but I couldn't move away from him, either. I couldn't move much at all.

That made me even hotter.

I squirmed as I tried to adjust to the intense pleasure that was quickly building from his mouth. My movement only caused more unsightly bouncing and jiggling.

"Keep those gorgeous tits where they are. I want to watch them bounce and jiggle while you come. Now be a good girl and fuck my mouth with your pussy, Freya."

I could literally come from listening to the crude sexual way he talked. It was so blunt and honest. Unapologetically filthy, yet weirdly reassuring.

He yanked on something by his head, and suddenly I was leaning down even further over him. He used both of his hands to reach up as he teased and tugged on my nipples. I was frantic with the need to come. When he continued groping and squeezing my breasts relentlessly, I was quite literally forced into a brain-melting orgasm.

I came apart all over his mouth. The growling, guttural sounds he made into my pussy caused that wonderful tickling buzz directly on my clit. It only made me come even harder. The pleasure was so intense it made me scream, my body trembling and twitching like I really was having some kind of orgasmic seizure.

I could feel the hot moisture running down between my thighs and ass cheeks but there was nothing I could do to stop the orgasm ripping through me. It felt endless. I moaned and wailed brokenly as each shattering wave of pleasure washed over me, from my throbbing pussy to the tingling intensity as he played with my nipples.

Afterward his hands rubbed all over on my body, giving me goosebumps. My skin felt like it was hooked up to an electric fence, every touch of his hand sending delicious yet slightly painful zings all over my skin.

My world was still spinning slightly when he moved like a flash of light, pinning me underneath his massive upper body as his thighs thrust between mine. He roughly spread me open, and I rolled my hips up to him hungrily.

I hadn't even noticed he'd removed my hand ties from my wrists. I'd been too consumed by my soul trying to return to my body after he'd made me shatter.

I craved the feeling of his massive cock inside my pussy. As hard as he'd just made me come only a few seconds ago, I still craved the fullness of that enormous thing thrusting up wickedly inside me. It was madness.

His mouth claimed mine. I could taste my own arousal as he kissed me, and it did funny things to my insides.

"I can't last a damn minute when I sink my cock into you, baby. Your pussy is so fucking tight! You like my cock in your pussy, Freya?"

He threw one of my legs up and around his hips as he pumped all the way inside me with animalistic intent. I took every one of his thrusts, wanting more.

"Fuck yes, Brodie; it feels so good!"

"Mmmm, baby. Hell, yeah. Come again on my cock. I want to feel that pussy juice drip down around my balls!"

I barely heard his vulgar words. The end of his massive dick had a slight curve to it, so that the impossibly wide tip rubbed directly against my G-spot with every single thrust. It was everything I needed to completely shatter with bliss. A second orgasm tore through me from the inside out, and I wailed like some kind of mentally unstable banshee as the pleasure burst deep within me.

Shortly after, he threw his head back and let out a primal roar as his hips hammered into me like a wild animal.

The view of his massively powerful frame with his muscles all bunched and flexed above me was such an intoxicating picture that I couldn't look away. It was so raw and sexual, the way I could feel his massive cock twitching and jumping inside me, spreading me wide for him. The way his hot cum was dripping out of my pussy as his hips pumped into me made me moan.

We lay there for a few minutes, both of us panting and completely spent. He was still inside me. When I tried to move my hips a little, he growled at me and held me tighter. I got the message and stayed put.

A few seconds later, he gently pulled his literally *still* semi-hard cock out of me and laid down on the bed behind me. He placed one of his massive arms around me and pulled me into him. I could feel every single inch of the solid wall of muscle that was his chest and shoulders along my back. His massive chest hummed excitedly with his still rapidly beating heart. It was actually really nice to lay with him like that, I realized reluctantly.

It was only a few minutes later and my sanity returned with a million questions and reasons why I should not be doing what I was doing. Instead of relaxed I felt on edge.

"Don't even think about it, Freya," he warned.

"Don't even think about what?"

It was eerie how well he seemed to know my mood.

"Whatever female bullshit you're coming up with again that made you get all tense just now, and probably what made you upset the last time we had sex."

My mouth opened in shock and my hackles immediately raised at his absolutely unapologetic mansplaining.

"Excuse me?! 'Female bullshit?!' What the hell is that supposed to mean?!"

He still wouldn't let me move from under him. Suddenly I didn't want to be anywhere near him. Who the hell did he think he was?!

He sighed irritably. I wanted to punch him.

"Yes, female bullshit. There's no other way to put it. Tell me I'm wrong; tell me what made you so upset earlier? You were crying."

"Wow. You know what? Piss off. I'm the one that was wrong, we shouldn't have done this again. Screw you, screw this. I'm done! Let. Me. *Up*."

Anger was coiling tightly in the pit of my stomach, quickly getting ready to strike.

"Hell yes to screwing you. No to everything else. I'm not letting you up. You're going to tell me whatever female nonsense is going on in that pretty little head of yours."

"You want to know?"

"Yes."

"You really want to know?"

"Yes, Freya. That's why I asked."

"I'm thinking what a total and complete freaking moron I've been acting like in the last day and a half. I'm thinking you're a manipulative bully who probably always gets what he wants and doesn't care who he hurts in the process. I'm thinking you don't truly value my opinion or getting to know me as a person other than someone to have sex with, because if you did, you wouldn't have called my being upset earlier 'female bullshit.'"

My heart was beating rapidly in my chest by the time I'd finished. If he weren't holding me, I probably would have lunged at him by now with my claws unsheathed and thirsty for blood.

"Okay. Anything else?"

The calmness of his voice made me see red.

"You know what? There is. You keep throwing your sexuality at me and overwhelming me to the point where I can't think clearly and make any of my own choices! You're completely taking advantage of me and of this situation, because now I'm seriously doubting that you'll 'protect' me if I'm not putting out for you!"

I was so pissed by that point that I actively started fighting him, shoving my elbows against the solid wall of his chest.

It didn't help my anger whatsoever when I totally felt like I'd bruised myself on him while attempting to escape the prison of his massive arms.

"Freya, enough."

He roared so loudly that I actually was a little scared of him in that moment. It stopped my fighting pretty effectively. But so did those stupid pythons he had the nerve to call arms.

"Then let me the fuck up, you overgrown jackass," I threw back at him over my shoulder.

I wasn't *that* scared.

"No. You're going to listen to me first," he nipped the side of my neck lightly.

I growled more ferally than he ever had since we'd met. He had the decency to jump back a little, but then he ruined it by chuckling and holding me closer to him.

"I like how feisty you are. It's fucking adorable," he paused to laugh again. I growled at him, but he continued, "and I'd already started packing up my shit the second I'd seen you on the footage across the street. Whether or not you'd be involved in the investigation was irrelevant at that point. I'd already decided I wanted you, and that I'd be getting your number before you left the store."

"Wow! Lucky me. You decided all this for me? Great. No one actually likes making their own choices, anyway, right?!"

I seriously considered biting into one of his rock-solid forearms, but then I realized I'd probably break my teeth because his muscles were so freaking rock-solid. I also realized a split second later how much the hardness and sheer size of his veiny, tattooed arms turned me on.

And then I just got pissed off all over again.

I really was not doing great, not at all. Murder was typically a state of mind I'd always tried to avoid, but I was starting to seriously reconsider the concept.

"I figured I'd be able to change your mind. Every squirrel gets an acorn eventually, right?"

"Am I the acorn or the squirrel in this scenario?"

Prince freaking Charming, he was.

"I'm the squirrel, and you're my acorn. That means I have official nutting rights to your body. It's in the paperwork, baby," he made kissy noises that tickled the crook of my neck. I was still pissed.

"You're delusional."

"That's already been ruled out by a team of psychiatrists."

I immediately tensed. I didn't know why someone would need an entire team of psychiatrists, but I was pretty freaking sure there weren't very many reassuring reasons.

More barking laughter at my obvious unease made my stomach keep doing its flippity-floppity thing. For fuck's sake, I was going to need my own team of psychiatrists after I finally became free of this man!

His arms tightened around my body a little more as his laughter faded.

"Why haven't you asked me what else I'm really thinking about all of this? Since almost every word of what you said earlier was, indeed, female bullshit," he breathed the words quietly into the crook of my neck.

It wasn't fair that he knew exactly how sensitive that area was and used it against me. It also wasn't fair that his voice was so deep and rough that his words buzzed across my skin like an actual touch.

Nevertheless, I was still pretty torn between murder and moaning. I remained stubbornly silent. He did the arrogant male sigh thing again when I didn't respond. I started counting to ten.

"I'm thinking I've never been so fucking turned on by a woman in my life, and I'm a hundred percent sure I've never laughed this much with a woman while my dick is literally hard enough to pound nails into concrete. Did you know your eyes turn purple when you're angry?"

I was speechless. I absolutely hadn't expected him to say anything like that.

The way he talked was so blunt and crass. But at the same time, it was also strangely genuine, almost caring. I couldn't see him being anything less than unapologetically blunt with anyone about anything.

In all honesty, I'm sure he would flat out tell a woman he was not interested in her, or that he was done with her, straight to her face without a thought to her feelings.

Which was exactly why I was never, ever letting my guard down around this man. It would be the end of me.

"You could just be saying that so you don't have to expend so much energy convincing me to have sex with you."

I wasn't ready to give in yet. I still wanted to be angry with him.

At least I think I still did, anyway.

"Freya, do you have any idea how much it turned me on when you threw your knee into my stomach on the street? Damn, baby. I couldn't even breathe and my dick was still rock-hard for you," he started grinding his hips into me as he spoke. "It's so fucking sexy how strong and feisty you are."

"Wh... what?"

My brain was getting reluctantly warm and fuzzy as I tried to moisten my suddenly dry lips.

"When you try to fight me, it just makes me want to dominate you even more. And I don't understand why you keep feeling bad about how wet it makes your pussy when I unleash the beast."

He started teasing my nipples again while he spoke.

"Umm, well, I barely... I hardly even know—*ohhh!* I don't know you at all!"

I really couldn't think when he started doing that, especially with his hot mouth so close to my neck and his solid heat along my back.

"Freya, here's what's going to happen. I'm going to make you come again because you're the fucking prettiest thing I've ever seen when you lose control," he used his thighs to spread my legs wide. I barely put up much fight when I heard the steel in his tone. "Then, you're going to let me hold you for as long as I want afterward. The only thing you're allowed to think about is how fucking hot you are when you come all over my cock, Freya. Understood?"

He'd started playing with the very top of my pussy while he spoke.

"Umm, I... yes, okay. I—oh, *ohhhh*, holy hell, Brodie. I seriously can't again so soon, and it's too big!"

Even as I protested weakly, I couldn't help but move my hips toward the tip of his cock. He used one of his hands to guide the swollen tip to my once again soaking wet entrance.

He imprisoned my hips within the iron grip of his hands, anchoring me to him. I lay completely on top of him, my back along his front. My legs were wrenched wide by his tree trunk thighs. I could feel the rigid smoothness of the tip of his cock as he guided it to my center, getting ready to plunge into me from below.

The whimper I let out immediately turned into a loud moan as I felt every inch of his thick cock shoved up inside me, all the way to its base. It made my pulse beat in triple time the savage way he held me and used his thighs to keep my legs wide open for each savage thrust of his hips.

I screamed as he pushed in, the curved ridge of his cock stroking directly on my G-spot.

"Fuck, yes! Fuck, yeah, baby. Your pussy feels so amazing. So fucking tight and wet, *damn*. Do you like that cock pumping into your pussy, baby?"

"Oh, god, *yes!* Please... Brodie, please... fuck me! It feels so... *yes!*"

I felt the wave of pleasure wash over me but it faded just short of total bliss. My moan of disappointment was more like a hiccupy whimper.

He moved one of his arms to lay directly between my breasts, the roughness of his palm wrapped around my neck. A carnal haze of tepid alarm made me stiffen in his embrace at the same time I arched into him. His grip wasn't tight enough to scare me, and *exactly* tight enough to make me want to purr in submissive approval of his enormously superior strength.

"Mmmmm, yeah. That's it, baby. Tell me how much you like my cock in that sweet pussy, and my hand around your neck," his voice was so low and guttural I could barely understand him.

I felt the tension in his body underneath mine like I was strapped on top of a log of dynamite.

"Yes... I like it, Brodie, please don't stop!"

"Yes baby. Does your pussy want to come all over my cock?"

I screamed my release as I thrashed and twisted within the storm of the powerful orgasm. My pussy was clenching so hard on his cock, I was almost afraid I would push it out as I was coming and ruin the divine intensity of my bliss.

He instantly erased that fleeting concern. His grip on me tightened even more as he bellowed and grunted, pumping his own release into me. I could feel the hot spurts of his cum deep inside me with every twitch and jerk from the tip of his throbbing shaft. I moaned boldly at the naughty, purely primal sensation.

Afterward, I was too utterly exhausted to argue when he pulled me in close to him and wrapped his massive arms around me. He pulled the fluffy comforter around us both.

The last sane thought I had about how bad this situation was for me bounded about frantically in between the numerous holes of my mostly malfunctioning cheesy brain matter until finally, it gave up completely.

Irrevocably defeated, that last plea to choose the path of sanity melted away into the nothingness inside my head as I, too, faded into the seductive heat of his embrace.

Chapter 33

Brodie

It was only about eleven minutes that I had tricked her into cuddling with me, but it was about seven and a half more minutes than she'd let me so far. It was a start.

I sighed defeatedly as I threw back the comforter that I'd wrapped around us earlier.

"Fine. I can hear how tense you are now. Let's go rinse up for supper."

"Supper? You mean dinner?"

"Don't even get me started, Yankee. It's supper because it's evening. Everyone knows that."

When I turned toward her to help her out of the bed, the last thing I thought she was going to do in that moment was tear up. I was instantly off balance.

I didn't do off balance.

She didn't seem angry with me. I had no idea what had caused the abrupt change in her mood. Her eyes seemed distant and not just from the way they were a little glassy from the sudden tears.

I panicked.

It definitely wasn't my proudest moment.

"I'll uh... turn on the shower for you." I couldn't retreat fast enough.

Magnuson, you chicken shit pussy. I heartily berated myself on the way to the bathroom. Tears weren't something I was well-equipped to deal with.

I'd faced down some of the most sinister evil in the most wretched corners of the world with more level-headed bravery than I did a weeping woman. There wasn't a material strong enough to deflect the kind of damage it did to a man watching his woman's eyes fill with tears.

I was the first to admit that my entire plan of action around tears was evasion.

Most people assumed evasion just meant running away. Regarding the instance of distraught female tears, they were probably half-ass correct.

There was more to evasion than just running away; it was about survival within a hostile enemy territory. It was about using the resources in your environment to your advantage, to change and manipulate anything and everything in your favor to gain advantage over the enemy and gain access to a more favorable vantage point.

I'd always found it important not to engage directly with the crying female if apparently hostile.

In my experience, a neutral expression and confirmatory head nods or negatory shakes, where appropriate, tended to be the most placating. I knew I wasn't great at offering words of comfort to normal people. Action was my go-to in most situations anyway, which helped compensate for my lackluster ability to administer soothing words.

To me, comfort was the familiar weight of a loaded gun in my hands and braced against my shoulder, ready to fire. For reasons I had accepted but will never begin to comprehend, distraught females tended to get even more upset when things like going shooting, having sex, or a sparring workout were suggested to lift their spirits. Not that I would seriously suggest any of those to an upset female.

Not since my early twenties, anyway.

It was my experience that females in distress tended to prefer things like flowers, *Disney* movies, chocolate, bubble baths, fuzzy and child-like clothing, and chivalrous gestures. I surveyed the area for any available resources.

Since the shower was already on, I turned on the jacuzzi and tossed in a eucalyptus and Epsom salt bath tablet for some bubbles. The bubbles seemed to be an essential part of the gesture. Using my watch, I turned on the tv and was headed out to ask her what show to put on when I saw her standing in the doorway to the bathroom, watching me. She'd put on one of my favorite *Texans* tee shirts. It dwarfed her, reaching down to just above her knees.

Only the slightly panicked state I was in could have prevented the blood from flowing directly into my dick from the sexy sight of her in my shirt. The woman could wear a trash bag and she would still look like sex on a silver fucking platter.

I couldn't read her mood from the expression on her face. That only increased my mild panic.

Her eyes were still a little shiny. She looked at me and the corners of her eyes creased slightly while she took in the running shower and jacuzzi tub filling behind me. She looked back at me again as she pursed her lips, then looked to the tv on the bathroom wall. Her gaze turned back to me. She tilted her head a little to the side, squinting at me a little.

"Have you ever heard of water conservation?"

I didn't trust the unsettling neutrality and curiosity in her tone.

Teary-eyed women weren't usually capable of reason. This was definitely uncharted territory, but I remained vigilant in spite of my rising panic.

"I wasn't sure which one would work better."

The corners of her sexy mouth crinkled as she squinted her eyes a bit more.

"Work for what, exactly?" She sounded torn between skepticism and humor.

"Look, Freya, I don't know what happened but the jacuzzi tub is almost ready. Or the shower. You can watch whatever you want on tv. I can upload any *Disney* movie you want."

I really didn't like the way she continued to smile as I spoke. It was absolutely unnerving given the still slightly shiny appearance to her pretty indigo eyes.

This was serious, dammit.

"So both the shower and jacuzzi are running because you didn't know which one would work better to... get me clean again?"

The way her eyes were still a little teary despite the warm smile on her face felt like someone had punched me in the gut. With a sledgehammer. Repeatedly.

Which one was she, happy or sad, dammit!

"No. Well actually, yes. But use whichever you want. I did both just in case. Movie?" She'd progressed to a full smile, and then she did something completely unforgivable.

She bit her lip as she tried and failed to hide her chuckle, which quickly turned into full on giggles.

It was fucking adorable, but I was still apprehensive.

I stared at her, completely dumbstruck and speechless for probably the first time in ten years.

"That's the second time it's happened. I didn't believe it was possible," she kept smiling and eventually laughed quietly as she indulged in her private joke.

I wasn't sure what the hell was so entertaining.

"Second time what has happened? Didn't believe what was possible, exactly?"

I asked her cautiously, wary that the enemy may return at any point to dampen those beautiful blue eyes.

"For you to look nervous," she gazed at me, still smiling.

I couldn't tell if she was teasing me or simply making an observation. It was fucking unsettling.

I cleared my throat and looked at the notification on my watch.

"The food is here. I'll go get it."

I moved toward the door so I could regroup and regain control over the situation. I still wasn't sure what the fuck just happened, but I knew it wasn't safe yet.

I turned back immediately at the sounds of her giggles returning. My midsection took another direct hit. I stared at her, absolutely dumbfounded, which only seemed to make her giggle even more.

"Care to let me in on the joke, Freya?" I asked her darkly.

More giggles, and she clapped her hand over her mouth now to help control her mirth.

"Freya, I'm warning you..." what was supposed to be an intimidating growl from me only made her laugh so hard she snorted.

The little surprised squeak she made right before she started laughing again made my dick instantly rock-hard.

She kept laughing as I lunged at her, taking both of us to the bed. She let out another squeal of laughter as we both landed on the softness of the mattress. I pulled her to me.

"Tell me what the fuck is so hilarious or I will find a better way to distract you than giggles, Freya," I breathed into the curve of her neck, enjoying the way her voice cracked sexily in the middle of a laugh.

"You looked... scared of me!"

The admission brought an even louder round of giggles from her as her words sunk in. Apparently, the idea was so hilarious to her that she couldn't speak past her laughter.

"I'll show you scared!"

My fingers dug into her waist mercilessly as I tickled her. I was instantly rewarded by another adorable snort and more laughing.

"Okay! Okay! Uncle! I give up, stop! Stop!"

She could barely get the words out between her pants of laughter. Finally, I took mercy on her and stopped my tickling.

That turned out to be a huge mistake. It gave me nothing to distract from the massive erection I'd gotten from having the sweet sounds of her laughter in my ears with that delicious body of hers so close. I groaned quietly as I drank in the scent of her hair. I pulled her in even closer as I nipped at her neck.

"Oh, no you don't!"

She started struggling in my grasp, but her words were teasing as she giggled some more.

I chuckled, easing my grip on her. I was instantly rewarded when she turned toward me on the bed. She suddenly seemed shy and avoided my gaze as she spoke.

"My dad used to call it that. Supper, not dinner," she smiled again weakly, still not meeting my eyes.

She was preoccupied with tracing one of my tattoos along my waist and up toward the side of my chest. My brain was transfixed between lust and the morbid anticipation of the enemy's return. Something told me she didn't require a response from me, just a quiet audience.

"I don't remember very much of my parents. I was only six years old when they were killed," she paused again as the tattoo she was tracing ran up towards one of my pectoral muscles.

The muscle flexed instantly as soon as she neared. She looked up at me briefly, then gestured again to the tattoo. "Did this hurt?"

I shook my head no. I couldn't look away from her face, she was too damn pretty.

She paused a few moments longer, then kept talking quietly. She resumed her initial path with her fingertips as she started tracing the path of ink again. I started sweating, the blood pounding in my ears from her touch. It was pure and delicious torture.

"Sometimes a memory comes back to me out of nowhere and it catches me off guard. Even if... even if they make me sad sometimes, I feel like I always have to acknowledge them. I don't have very many to choose from. If I don't feel each one and give it a space in my mind, I guess I'm afraid that someday I'll stop remembering them altogether," her voice drifted off quietly.

I died a thousand deaths watching a tear roll down her cheek as she continued. "And that, I think, makes me the most upset. Not remembering," she smiled, her expression calm.

I didn't know what to say. I kept quiet and stroked her hair because I sensed she wasn't done yet.

"My father had a pretty strong Southern accent. He and my mom used to argue and tease each other about whether it was called supper, lunch, or dinner. He used to call her a Yankee, too. It always made her laugh. They used to laugh together, all the time. I hope I always remember how much they laughed..." her voice trailed off, but I didn't detect any tears.

Thank God. That had been terrifying.

I hugged her tighter, having no fucking clue what to say. There was a very uncomfortable yet glowing feeling in my stomach that I really wasn't familiar with.

Hunger, that's what it was. We needed to eat. I cleared my throat.

"The food is ready; where do you want to eat? The sun should be low enough now that the rooftop will be comfortable."

She started laughing quietly, then looked up at me as I spoke. She was still smiling slightly and there was a twinkle in her eyes.

"What about my shower slash jacuzzi slash movie?"

She was definitely teasing me as she tried to hide her smile by biting her lip again.

She bounced up from the bed and floated gracefully into the bathroom. I watched the slight jiggle of her rounded ass cheeks and the mouth-watering sway of her hips as she walked away. My hand immediately went to my dick, which was already completely hard again. I'd been inside her less than twenty minutes ago and already I was ready to fuck her again.

I stepped into the shower and immediately turned the temperature to cold. It was absolutely necessary because of the exaggerated sighs of carnal pleasure coming from the jacuzzi. It didn't help cool my blood in the slightest.

I showered quickly and stormed out of the bathroom. A man could only take so much temptation, dammit.

The sounds of her laughter sounded downright demonic as I headed into the closet to get dressed.

• • • •

ABOUT AN HOUR LATER we'd enjoyed a comfortable meal on my rooftop terrace as we took in the twinkling glow of the city. We had almost finished a bottle of red wine. Although the view wasn't near as beautiful as the one on my ranch back home in Texas, it wasn't a bad way to experience The City that Never Sleeps.

"The wine is going straight to my head. It's delicious, thank you. But are you sure Dr. Briggs said it was okay for me to drink again?"

I lowered my eyebrows at her disapprovingly in answer.

As if I'd even let her smell the damn wine if Dr. Briggs hadn't given her explicit medical clearance beforehand.

She gave me her own stern look in a mocking response, then started giggling. I couldn't help it and smiled along with her. I was surprised at how easy it was to relax and laugh around her. I really couldn't remember when I'd ever wanted to spend this much time around one female before.

Ever since I'd met her, I felt absolutely restless whenever she wasn't within arm's reach.

I simmered quietly with barely contained frustration as I watched her walk around the ivy-covered tresses of the pergola across the rooftop. She slowly sipped her wine as she took in the twinkling lights of the city below us. The restless feeling inside reached fever pitch as I watched the way the shimmering lights danced across the dark fiery beauty of her hair.

My mind switched gears abruptly as I recalled the most graphic and heinously evil details we'd come across while on this case.

Whoever was behind this operation had apparently crawled up from the most wretched and rotten fucking corners of hell. I wouldn't be able to find any sense of peace until I had personally sent every last fucking one of them right back to the burning, festering pit they'd slithered out from.

There was a job to do, and there wasn't time to sit around idly enjoying a bottle of wine. Not for me.

I was instantly ashamed of my lack of discipline. Her safety at all times was my primary objective, for multiple reasons. Clearing my throat, I stood up to grab the remainder of our dishes as well as the now empty bottle of wine.

"Freya, thank you for having dinner with me. Unfortunately, I have a lot more work to do tonight."

"Of course. It was a pleasure, thank you as well."

I hated the way her tone had changed into what I was now referring to as the business casual voice.

I followed her back inside and held the door open for my security team. I wasn't taking any chances where she was concerned.

I'd placed a team of four of my men along the rooftop as we'd dined. It grated further on my barely contained temper when she'd only nodded her head in solemn understanding as they'd taken their posts. She seemed to be accepting her completely unfair circumstances with much more poise than women twice her age. Her apparent strength of character hardened my own resolve to focus on what needed to be done.

With more determination than I'd felt since I first bumped into her in *Caress*, I steeled myself against the constant temptation of this intoxicatingly beautiful woman.

This was a job, I reminded myself, and I was a soldier first and foremost. I couldn't let her beauty and intoxicating allure take up any more of my focus from what I'd been hired to do—which was ultimately to keep her alive and safe.

For the first time in my life, I was worried that the man I needed to be in order to do what needed to be done would end up scaring her off. Or disappointing her, once she realized what I was truly capable of.

It was a chance I was more than willing to take; the alternative option was unthinkable.

I'd hunt every last one of those cockroaches to the ends of the Earth before they'd ever lay a fucking finger on my woman.

Chapter 34

Freya

A week had gone by in a surreal blur.

Now it was Friday evening and I sat alone in my keeper's fortress, halfway through a bottle of wine. He'd apparently left it out for me with a hastily scrawled note. I kept insisting that I was glad to have the time to myself and that his gesture was thoughtful.

It didn't matter that he wasn't physically here to spend time with me. It wasn't like we were dating.

I sighed as I took another sip, determined to see the good in my circumstance.

In all honesty, I didn't even know how the hell to describe the situation. The random but not-so-random meet-cute that turned into a crazy-hot, borderline stalker type of one night stand that never ended? With the awkward "morning after" that lasted an entire week—or maybe even weeks, plural—instead of a few hours?

Somehow the phrase 'it's complicated' didn't even scratch the surface.

I'm pretty sure I had whiplash from the complete change in his behavior after we'd had dinner together on Saturday evening on the rooftop. We'd both gone back inside but he'd gone into his office and seemed busy, so I'd kept to myself for a few hours until I was too exhausted to keep my eyes open.

I hadn't seen very much of him the entire week.

He'd been working late every night. When he did sleep, which appeared to not be very often at all, it was on the oversized couch in his office.

This man had been a complete stranger to me a little over seven days ago, I reminded myself. It felt presumptuous for me to draw any conclusions from his schedule, whatever they might be.

My own schedule had remained mostly unchanged apart from my new security entourage. Each day I'd gone to work, and each day I'd been followed like a shadow by a team of Brodie's armed security staff. There was even a female bodyguard that accompanied me to the restroom.

To the mother-effing restroom!

Thankfully, she was one of the most enjoyable people to be around. She stood around six feet tall and if she weren't so insanely muscular, she probably could have been a supermodel with her high cheekbones, absolutely flawless skin, icy blue eyes, and bow-shaped mouth.

Actually, screw that, she would have made a kickass supermodel. Her name was Bridget and she had quickly become my unabashed girl crush. She was a total badass and a welcome break from the gloomy testosterone that shadowed the rest of the male security team. For as freaking intimidating as she appeared, she had a very warm and engaging personality.

If any of my coworkers had anything to say about one of the new girls at work suddenly having an entire team of blacked-out, beefed-up, super-intimidating and armed muscle following her around, they'd done a good job of hiding it.

No one had so much as batted an eye about Bridget taking me to every single bathroom break. Or the other three men that followed me around literally everywhere else.

It actually wasn't all that surprising that no one had seemed to notice considering the size of the company I worked for.

I'd been ecstatic to get this entry-level job within the human resources department of *Gerulte, Inc.,* the energy company that had hired me in May. The position provided great potential for upward movement within the company, and I really respected my supervisors. They'd been great mentors so far and I was genuinely enjoying the work. Even so, I was still super glad to be done with such a long week.

This wine really was delicious. I took a long drink, enjoying the decadence of the smokey-sweet red blend.

Ultimately, I wanted to be a clinical psychologist, but I knew I needed a break from school for a year or two. Being a totally broke, full-time student for another four to five years sort of seemed like a prison sentence at this point in my life.

I sighed, taking another sip. I only hoped this completely unbelievable circumstance I found myself thrown into wouldn't prevent me from my long-term goals.

What had been Fiona Anderson's five-year plan?

My heart sank to my stomach miserably at that thought.

Whenever I was feeling like complaining about the steaming pile of shit that had been served to me by the universe, I made myself think about her. I immediately felt guilty for not having a better attitude. Soon after came totally righteous anger that someone could have ripped away her future like it was ever *freaking* theirs to take; and now they were trying to do the same to me.

Considering everything that had happened to me in the last week, I still felt like I was doing a decent job staying positive. It was the only thing I felt like I had any control over.

When Brodie had taken me to work on Monday morning, he'd barely looked at me on the drive over. I tried not to think too much of it.

Something had changed since we'd had our rooftop dinner and he'd become distant ever since. He was still extremely polite, thoughtful, even, but he rarely if ever even looked at me. He hadn't intentionally touched me since. It was absolutely unsettling given the downright obsessive caveman behavior he'd initially approached me with.

And they said women had mood swings. Yeah, right.

I told myself I had way bigger things to worry about than whether he was trying out some sort of Cavemen Anonymous twelve-step program, or if he'd simply lost interest in me.

I couldn't even feel guilty about it.

Some memories of last weekend still made me blush furiously and get warm in very private places, but it was some of the best sex I'd ever had. I told myself that I didn't care if he hadn't felt the same way.

He was an uber-sexy, tall, dark, and handsome, tatted-up former super-soldier turned billionaire; I had to be realistic. I probably didn't even land in his top ten, especially with my obvious lack of experience in the bedroom compared to him, I thought pitifully.

Damn him, anyway. I took another drink of the wine. It both pleased me and pissed me off that he'd selected something I enjoyed so much.

The reasonable part of my brain reminded me that I should be damn grateful that he'd been able to intercept me before someone else had. His level of interest in me personally or romantically was not near as important as my life. I felt ridiculous every time I caught myself pining after something that should have been my last concern.

I hadn't been able to eat anything at all the first day I'd gone to work—and I was someone who tended to turn slightly green and perhaps a teensy bit hostile if I ever skipped a meal. I got almost nothing out of the entire workday because of my frazzled nerves.

By the end of the day I was utterly exhausted from the mental strain, but I'd still had to catch up on meeting notes and emails for most of the evening. If not, I would have been completely behind for work the next day.

Tuesday had been a little bit better. I'd gotten hungry by the end of the day and only had to catch up that night for about an hour. The rest of the week got better a little at a time. It was actually quite therapeutic for me to stay busy and retain a sense of my normal routine.

So therapeutic, in fact, that on my way out of work earlier tonight I'd subconsciously started to text Kim to make weekend plans. I'd almost hit send before I'd snapped out of it, then immediately deleted what I'd typed.

Not only had someone apparently hacked into my phone several weeks ago, but also now it had been digitally cloned by Brodie and his entire security staff for the investigation. I'd given up arguing at this point.

So, basically anything and everything I said or did on my phone was being and had been monitored by who knows how many stuffy, middle-aged, judgy, arrogant men from the FBI to local law enforcement to the entirety of Brodie's security team. It probably wasn't fair of me, but I felt like if there were more women involved in my situation, they'd be monumentally more understanding and sympathetic.

Annoyed and angry, I had put my phone back into my purse with a petulant sigh as I'd walked out of the office with the security. I hadn't even tried to pretend like I wasn't pissed. I'd let my temper simmer for the first part of the drive back to the hotel before I'd been able to calm back down.

At least I was still here and not... well, somewhere else.

When it came down to it, I was pretty damn willing to sacrifice some of my privacy in return for safety.

Still, it wasn't easy dealing with that total invasion of my privacy, of my entire life. It was so unsettling. I shivered as I rubbed my hand along my arm, trying to remove the chills from my skin and calm the racing of my pulse. I took another sip of the full-bodied, smokey red sweetness.

I hadn't gone to my gym since the lingerie store collision.

I didn't really understand why, but just the thought of being at the gym had my stomach in knots. Something about just walking past the cardio area by the front entrance made my heart race so violently I hadn't even considered staying to exercise.

Maybe because that's where I'd been when I'd first watched the news of the young Anderson woman's remains being identified. I'd been sweating on my favorite treadmill that had the highest incline and almost no broken buttons on the display screen.

Now, it was like my brain had automatically rewired that memory into something terrifying that my conscious refused to identify. Walking past the physical space that the false memory took place made it seem as if I'd be swallowed up into some sort of alternate reality time-warp.

Instead of Fiona Anderson's face on that tv screen, it would be my own. And then it would be very real. I wouldn't be able to escape that kind of fear.

Besides, the hotel had an amazing gym a few floors down.

I'd gone along with Brodie and the rest of the security team to work out last night on his suggestion. Despite it being a fairly large space with adequate room, I couldn't take more than a few steps without almost bumping into him because he'd stayed so close.

A few times I'd actually bumped into him and had to endure the hot, heavy grip of his hands around my shoulders as he'd steadied me. It had annoyed me how distracted I'd been during the rest of my work out because of it.

At first, I'd just smiled up at him, getting ready to politely say, 'Oops, my bad,' or something like that. I really hadn't meant to run into him.

But once I'd caught a glimpse of his scowling face, the semi-automatic apology died on my lips.

I was torn between throwing one of the dumbbells toward his head and asking him what his effing problem was. I was almost done working out when I realized that he very well could be annoyed that I had to tag along in his life because of his work.

After that unpleasant thought, I'd just avoided him as much as possible. I realized how much I didn't want to find out if he'd changed his mind about whatever the hell he and I were to each other.

Going by his recent behavior, I was pretty sure he'd completely moved on. That being said, it seemed like he was always working and that he truly wanted to keep me safe. It was difficult not to be pretty damn glad about that, at least.

But what about the woman he'd spoken with on the phone earlier, last week? The one who'd yelled at him and called him a "cocksucker" so many times?

What if that was his angry girlfriend or wife?! Stuck in some fancy house somewhere and apparently bored out of her mind?!

I didn't like the way jealousy twirled crazily inside my stomach—as well as guilt—when I thought of who that other woman might be to him. For all I knew about this man, he could literally have a wife and kids.

Now very annoyed, I downed the rest of my glass of wine and headed toward the living room area. I got out my laptop and absentmindedly sorted through my personal emails. I had almost dozed off when I realized my phone was ringing.

I didn't recognize the number, so I let it go to voicemail. Stupid scam phone calls, I thought as I closed my laptop.

I'd been on my computer most of the week trying to be productive. Maybe what I needed was some brain-numbing screen time, instead. I strolled through the available streaming apps on the tv in the main room and selected one of my favorite series to binge-watch. As soon as I'd pressed play, my phone rang again.

Same number. I rolled my eyes and sent it to voicemail as I turned back to enjoy my show.

A few minutes into the latest episode, I heard a series of pings on my phone. Three text messages from the same number. A cold feeling of dread settled in my stomach as I looked at my phone screen.

A little sense of relief washed over me when I remembered that my phone was being monitored. Most of my unease went away as I opened the texts. I smiled, thinking how ironic it would be for some dickhead scammer to get caught because they'd hacked into the one person's phone being monitored around the clock by some of the most sophisticated technology in the world.

Freya. It's Brodie. One of my work phones.
Head to the gym if you want. We already started working out.
That is, unless you're already too tipsy.

As soon as I read the texts I realized maybe another workout was exactly what I needed. So what if I'd just drank about a half bottle of wine? If I started working out now, maybe I'd work off the alcohol before it affected my work out.

That was a thing, right?

I quickly went to change into workout clothes and tennis shoes. Yesterday at the gym, Bridget had shown me a ton of self-defense moves. It was super fun, and I wanted her to see if I'd mastered any of them yet. She was an excellent teacher.

My spirits lifted so much at his invitation that I ignored the way my head was spinning pretty noticeably by the time I'd stepped into the gym.

For some reason, the elevator had skipped the gym's floor the first two times. The extra stops felt like they'd taken forever, and I blamed the increased head spinning on the constant internal flippity-flip thing that happened to everyone's insides on elevator rides.

On second thought, maybe I'd just accidentally pressed the wrong floor a few times. That's probably why my head was spinning so much.

I took a long drink from my water bottle. I hadn't felt tipsy at the gym since the spring semester finals of my junior year of college. I took another drink of water; my mouth was already pretty dry.

I walked through the gym which was almost completely deserted at this time on a Friday night. Most people were probably already drunk from happy hour or getting ready to go out, not work out. It was also one of my favorite times to be at the gym because I never had to wait for machines or weight racks very long.

I started walking toward a small group I'd thought was them. But after only a few steps, I realized that the men were way too small. I turned around toward the opposite end of the gym to keep searching, but I stumbled a little when I accidentally brushed by a machine too closely.

I giggled, looking around me, but no one seemed to notice. The gym really was empty.

My head was really foggy from the wine. I took another sip from my water bottle as I walked because my mouth felt even stickier. I smacked my lips together clumsily, then I covered my mouth as I giggled again; this was not going to be a great work out.

There was a flash of movement on my side that made me jump. I turned toward it, but I couldn't stop my vision from spinning long enough to focus on anything. I felt like I was still moving as I grabbed onto the metal frame of the lat pull-down machine closest to me. My knuckles turned white with the force of my grip, but the spinning wouldn't stop.

"There; over that way. Now! Move!"

As soon as I'd heard him, the hair on the back of my neck stood up in stark fear.

The unfamiliar voice sounded muffled and there was an accent I couldn't place. Somehow, I knew he was talking to me as I felt an adrenaline rush so forceful that I thought I might vomit. Even as the very floor moved beneath me, the blood froze in my veins when

I saw a large man, dressed completely in black tactical gear, running toward me through the swirls.

I tried to grab for my phone as I turned to run away, but something massive knocked into me from my other side.

All the air in my lungs was ripped away as my shoulder crashed onto the floor painfully. My heart hammered in my chest as I heard the stranger's surly voice again. I felt someone grab my other arm roughly from behind, yanking me partly upright in a low stance, and yelling at me in a language I didn't understand.

Bridget's voice popped into my head at the same time my body subconsciously followed the hip toss move she'd shown me the night before.

Use that ass, girl! Then grab, pop and pull!

As much as my head was already swimming, I have no idea how I actually managed it but somehow the man who'd grabbed me from behind ended up on the ground on his back.

Unfortunately, I also landed on the ground, mostly on top of him.

I tried to jump up and run away despite feeling like I was on a carousel ride, but an iron band grabbed me around my waist.

I screamed so loud that my own ears hurt, but it must have worked because the chain-like grip around my waist suddenly slackened. I tried to leap up and run away but my limbs felt like they'd been filled with sand.

My ears were ringing and everything sounded distorted, as if I were partially underwater. I desperately tried to move my limbs, but they wouldn't budge. I tried to open my mouth to scream again but all that came out was a strangled type of squeak that turned into a gasp when I felt myself being lifted up.

The delicious scent of spicy sandalwood surrounded me as I tried to open my eyes. I felt like there were fifty-pound weights attached to each of my eyelids, but I finally focused on the face of my rescuer.

A pair of bright green laser beams shone down into my face and then shot bright teal sparks all around me.

They were so pretty, like little green fireflies. I could hear tiny little *pew, pew, pew* sounds as each one danced above me. I tried to lift my hand to touch them, but my limbs were fixed in some kind of warm concrete.

The concrete started to rumble and shake around me, but I still couldn't move my arms or legs. The last thought I had was that even though I was stuck in some kind of cement, it was okay, because that deliciously masculine sandalwood scent meant that I was safe.

I watched lazily as the sparkly gray haze of his intoxicating aroma enveloped the little green fireflies, bringing them along with us as we all floated down into the warm embrace of the cement.

Chapter 35

Brodie

The amount of unbridled, furious rage that was still coursing through my veins was undoubtedly in direct violation of all types of TSA regulations.

Fortunately, we were pretty fucking far past having to worry about civilian bullshit like passports and security clearances.

Which is why I was currently trying not to crack the steering wheel in half as I drove to my private hangar in upstate New York, with an unconscious Freya, Dr. Briggs, and two other fully armed men with me.

At this point, spending upwards of twenty million on a fleet of various types of tactical and military armed transport vehicles was absolutely nothing. It was the best we could do in a few hours' notice and they'd more than serve our purpose.

Marco, Bryan, Gianna, and Laney were in the car directly behind me. Three more vehicles in front and back completed our entourage, their occupants also mixed with both Parisi and Magnuson security teams working amiably alongside each other.

There were also three other seemingly identical vehicle trains heading in three completely different directions. One of those *Rezvani* tanks contained Freya's actual phone which was held in the hand of a very convincing, life-like robotic soldier we called *Forrester1*, or *F1*. He was one of many that *Magnuson Security* had created.

That entire vehicle train was heading south toward a fake safehouse. There wasn't a single living human within that group of seven armored cars. I was taking zero chances.

I had never seen the type of technology that I had last night. It shouldn't be possible.

I gripped the steering wheel even harder.

I'd been in one of the offices on the floor just below my hotel room, checking the camera system in the main living space instead of reading through the reports from my cyber security team. It had been like that all fucking week. I'd never felt this restless, distracted, furious and downright useless in my entire damn life.

The more we dove into the data from her phone, the more furious I became. Every single one of her online accounts had been hacked into. It went all the way back to the beginning of the summer.

It was almost August. She'd been spied on by these sick fucking bastards for almost the last two months. That fact alone made me want to crack skulls.

I'd almost exploded with jealous anger when I found messages from one of her online dating apps. I'd had to take a shot or four of my favorite single-malt scotch before I'd felt calm enough to ask her if the conversation actually happened.

In summary, she'd supposedly agreed that she wanted to meet up and have crazy wild sex with someone named Wyatt a little over a month ago. As if that weren't already enough to put me into a killing state of mind, the messages had been sent from an account associated with the same IP address as her fake invite for *Ladies' Night*.

That had been Tuesday evening.

I instantly believed her when she blushed furiously and shook her head no, that she'd never sent any of the messages. After a few more questions it was pretty clear that we'd found another thread of fake data trails just like in the previous cases. Once again, the metadata we'd analyzed from the fabricated conversation had the same impossible inconsistencies.

The only way to determine if that conversation were genuine would be to ask either participant. Which was of course, conveniently hard to do when one didn't exist and the other is missing, or dead. It was essentially indiscernible if the data were real or faked.

I'd never wanted to reach out and comfort her more when I saw her try to hide the angry tears that threatened the corners of her pretty blue eyes. She'd taken a deep breath, angrily swiped at one of them, squared her shoulders back and bravely asked me how else she could help.

"If it means finding these assholes sooner, I don't care how embarrassing it is at this point. What else do you need to know?"

Her calm and determined resolve had once again hardened my own.

It also made my dick even harder for her. I'd never been all that attracted to women who were quick to back down. Probably because they couldn't stomach my personality. My baby girl, on the other hand, was a natural born fighter.

I'd nodded to her instead of holding her in my arms like I wanted to. I was furious again with the situation and my lack of control over it. I knew what would happen if I touched her, and I couldn't live with myself if the distraction somehow compromised her safety. My dick was so hard for her it ached, and I felt like an actual loaded gun every second of my consciousness because of it. I was an absolute shit show.

The rest of the week had dragged on with not much new information.

Finally, on Thursday morning Mikhail had located the source of the sedative slipped to Freya at the club. The man responsible had been caught switching the straws of the first drink she'd ordered at the bar. They'd found it while combing through the security footage. Of course, he'd never shown up to any shifts after Friday night.

It had taken my men a little over an hour to find him and bring him in for Mikhail's team to start with. I'd been called shortly after to carry out the rest of his interrogation, which had been maddeningly uninformative.

The scumbag fucker hadn't even known Freya's name.

He'd almost died instantly when he'd started off by referring to her as 'some stupid slut.'

Before the last word had exited his mouth, the heel of my boot had entered into it. When he sputtered and coughed up blood and teeth and probably bone, I shoved it in further, all the way up to my fucking ankle.

Not only was he lucky he was still breathing, but also that his face was still fucking attached to his own skull. It wouldn't be for much longer, though.

He'd never even seen the actual person who'd given him the orders, he'd sobbed to me pathetically through his fractured jaw. I wasn't sure if it were possible for anyone to be that fucking stupid, yet here we were.

Nevertheless, it had only taken a few more broken bones to get what I ultimately knew was the truth from him. Apparently, he'd been promised a few million dollars from her sale and they—the big, bad, text-message-only bad guys, for fuck's sake—had threatened his life if he didn't comply.

The minute that rat bastard had uttered the words *"her sale,"* I fucking saw red. Blood pounded in my ears and I'd jumped on him, pummeling his body like a cheap piñata.

I'd attended the memorial service for Fiona Anderson.

I'd read every single line of her autopsy report, seen every photo of the deplorable state her body was recovered in.

I'd seen her mother collapse onto her closed casket, heard the sounds of her wails echoing through the shoulder-to-shoulder crowded church as her father shook with his own devastated sobs.

It was their faces, twisted with unimaginable grief and anguish, that I saw with each one of my swings. I didn't see the man in front of me. My fist was met with the satisfying shattering of bones with each blow, but it wasn't enough. It would never be enough, especially for them.

After a minute or so I let Marco pull me off of the broken, blubbering little fuck.

What was left of him, anyway.

Most of the dislike I'd had toward Mikhail went away when I'd realized he hadn't moved an inch to stop me. I'd tossed him a half-ass look over my shoulder, seen his own murderous scowl fixed on the soon to be dead man, and thrown one last punch.

Mikhail only told me I couldn't kill the man, but everything else was apparently fair game. It was more than the worthless, sobbing sack of fucking shit deserved for what he could have done to my beautiful Freya.

Mikhail nodded his head to the man on his right, who promptly drew his own gun and shot the battered piece of shit in the head. I told myself I couldn't actually feel the fucking evil that had just escaped around us as I looked at the man's now lifeless form.

My only consolation was the tragic loss of life we'd undoubtedly prevented by disposing of such a monster.

Even if I'd had to become a monster myself in order to take him out. I'd pay that price over and over again if that's what needed to be done to keep her safe.

We'd all gone to the gym later that night. I'd instructed Bridget to start teaching Freya some basic self-defense moves. I was actually surprised she hadn't done so already. Bridget was one of the best tactical training instructors on my task force, man or woman.

I'd gotten hard so damn fast watching Freya execute the moves with the tenacity of a soldier and the grace of a dancer. I wanted to be the one touching her, dammit. If it were anyone other than another female so close to her, I would have gone nuclear.

I had seriously questioned my own sanity when I'd had to walk by her constantly throughout our workout, her delicious fucking scent teasing me with every movement she made.

By the time we'd finished training it was a miracle I hadn't already pushed her up against the wall and buried my throbbing dick inside her slick heat until neither one of us could stand.

I'd taken an ice-cold shower, but it hadn't helped in the least.

I honestly didn't know how much longer I could keep her at a distance without inadvertently pouncing on her. If I came on too strong and pushed her too far, I had no doubt that she'd run from me. I simply couldn't take the risk.

Friday morning, I'd received a frantic call from Laney.

What eventually turned out to be a false alarm had taken me away from reviewing my teams' reports for most of the day, which was why I'd been working in the office below the hotel room so late instead of returning upstairs. My need for her was so fierce, I didn't trust myself not to jump on her as soon as she was within my reach.

I'd glared at the security footage streaming the main living room area of my personal suite for the millionth time.

She'd been curled up on the couch with her fluffy gray blanket. I was trying to convince myself not to go up there and fuck her brains out when I realized the pattern of ruffles on the blanket looked different on my computer screen. The pattern looked off, but I couldn't place why or how.

I tried to zoom in on the security feed to investigate, but the program wasn't responding to my commands.

In the next second, I'd flown out of the room with one waiting in the chamber of my gun as I activated the emergency response team and coded for a building-wide breach.

I took the stairs five at a time to the next floor, but it felt like I was moving in slow motion. When I'd stepped into the hotel suite and found it empty, I'd let out a roar so loud I wouldn't be surprised if it created a small seismic spike. The amount of sickening rage I experienced at not finding her safely tucked inside my hotel room made me feel capable of leveling entire cities to the ground until I had found her.

I wasted no time as I cleared the rooms, shouting like a maniac at the same time my mind raced for any clue to where she was. Thankfully my team had located her within minutes after I'd first signaled the breach.

When I had seen the man from across the gym room floor running toward her, my heart stopped in my chest. I'd never moved faster in my entire fucking life. Garrison had immediately signaled to me as he took out the first assailant that had dared to touch her.

The bastard was dead within a few seconds after he'd hit the floor, Garrison's knife embedded on the left side of his chest between his fourth and fifth ribs. He never missed.

I didn't pause when I watched my amazing little warrior execute a near-perfect hip toss on the second assailant, bringing them both crashing down to the floor with her on top. The raging beast inside me was almost upset at the sight of her besting him. That fucker better still be conscious and able to feel every single thing I was going to do to his body before I killed him.

That had been his fate as soon as he'd so much looked at a single fucking hair on her head.

It had taken a few hours but eventually he talked late last night before we'd left for my private airport. I always made them talk, one way or another. What I'd learned from him made me want to sever his head from his body, and that was only after I'd calmed down for a few seconds.

He was to receive fifteen million dollars for her successful delivery, and he was just a glorified errand boy. For him to actually get that kind of pay out, she must be bringing in close to fifty million.

It was unheard of. A number that high would only draw out the cockroaches even faster.

Marco and I had exchanged a look before I'd ultimately put a bullet in the sick son-of-a-bitch's head.

He had no more useful information to be extracted, nothing else that we needed him to be alive for.

I wasn't a man to waste time on anything. My team would take care of his mangled body so that he'd never be found, never be identified. Afterward, I'd send an encrypted message to my contact in Interpol that he'd been un-alived.

No point in wasting resources to hunt for dead men.

I liked to throw them a bone every once in a while, it helped them looked the other way. A lot. After all, we were all on the same team... even if we played very different roles.

It had only taken several hours to secure everything we needed for our flight. I couldn't do what needed to be done on American soil with so much restriction and witnesses and factors I couldn't control.

We were going to Sicily, my private jet already fueled and ready, and we were finally almost to the private airspace. Marco would be taking his as well; he always kept a jet in my hangar here for last-minute trips.

I made eye contact with Dr. Briggs in the rear-view. She pursed her lips angrily and shook her head. Freya still hadn't woken up from whatever fucking sedative they'd placed in the bottle of wine.

Something cracked slightly inside the mechanism of the steering wheel as I recalled the forged handwritten note and laced bottle of wine.

When I found whoever was responsible for luring my girl into danger under the false guise of my own fucking protection, I was going to rip out their worthless insides through their own throats, then feed it to them again as many times as it took until they finally died.

After an eternity of driving, we arrived at the airport and got everyone ready for takeoff.

I had her safely tucked into my arms in one of the two bedrooms on my plane before she woke up. I had no idea what she'd remember from the ordeal, and I would have physically fucking cut off one of my arms before I'd let anything scare her again like that.

I wanted her to know that she was safe in my arms, and I also wanted Dr. Briggs to be one of the first people she saw.

When her eyes first opened and she looked up at me, every dark, rotten corner of my soul suddenly sprang to eternal life as she leaned into me, intentionally seeking the comfort of my embrace.

Chapter 36

Freya

"*Saluti!*"

Gianna and Laney giggled as they clinked their pink flower and pineapple-rimmed glasses together. They both turned and clumsily repeated the gesture to me, cackling with glee as they leaned back into the cushions on the cabana. I laughed along with them and repeated the Sicilian phrase as I took a sip from my own drink.

These girls could drink me under the table, which I had quickly discovered the first day I'd laid out by the pool with them, soaking up the sun and way more than my fair share of alcohol.

It was just about all we were permitted to do for the foreseeable future. That, and go down to the beach, but only with the armed escort. I wasn't even mad about any of that. I'd never felt so weirdly comforted by the presence of such rough, massive, tatted-up and intimidating men. It was as unsettling as it was reluctantly reassuring.

It had taken a few days for me to—sort of—get used to the hundreds of armed men walking around the resort. They were visible from everywhere within the interior and all the way out to the coastline.

But even their constant foreboding presence couldn't mar the sparkling cerulean beauty of the crystal-clear water that surrounded us. The Sicilian coastal landscape was a wild yet sophisticated mix of tropical palm trees, spindly cactus, and flowers blooming in every shade of color imaginable.

Truly, I had very little to complain about.

The Parisi resort and massive private villa on the southern coast of Sicily was without a doubt the most beautiful place I'd ever seen in my entire life. Ever.

Everywhere I looked was an ethereal sense of effortless luxury, but my favorite place was the natural stone oasis of the Parisi private pool, which is where I was now with the girls. There was a main swimming area that was almost Olympic-sized, with numerous stone waterfalls and an infinity-style design which boasted a stunning view of the coastline.

I sighed indulgently, loving the feel of the breeze. It gently swished the white linen curtains of our cabana and lazily ruffled the palms around us in the partially secluded area. The cool ocean air felt so wonderful in the hottest part of the Sicilian summer day as I marveled at the sheer amount of luxury around me.

The absolutely breathtaking view of the Mediterranean Sea was visible from almost every point of the Parisi family's ginormous private wing, but the pool view was by far the most spectacular. The ocean breeze whispered through the entire place seductively, carrying along with it the tranquil scent of the turquoise beauty of the coast. I took a deep breath and willed the beauty of my surroundings to calm my churning thoughts.

"Freya, aren't you going to get in the pool? It's getting hot as balls out here!"

Laney was already finished with her pink flower drink and was stepping out of the pool as she walked back toward me. Gianna followed not far behind, ringing the water from her long, dark hair and setting her own empty glass on the table next to Laney's.

I laughed at Laney's choice of words. She sounded just like Kim.

"Yes! Absolutely. But I feel myself burning; I need to put on a little sunscreen first. Dang ginger skin," I sighed theatrically.

"Ooh, good call, babe. Your shoulders are a teensy bit pink! Sunburns are the worst. You better put some on. We might as well have another round while we wait for your sun lotion to dry, right?!" Gianna's grin was infectious as she affectionately waved down a member of the staff.

I sipped on the dangerously delicious cocktail as I reapplied sunblock. I had zero intention of getting sunburned again like I had two days ago. Now, my skin had a nice golden glow that I'd never be able to attain back home in New York. Even the smell of the pearly white, silky lotion felt pampering as I rubbed the toasted coconut sugar all over me.

It was hard to find a reason, any reason at all, to be anything but ecstatic that I was here in this moment.

Nevertheless, every other thought was a thinly veiled attempt for my subconscious to replay the foggy events of almost being abducted back at the hotel gym.

It was a constant game of mental trickery that left me exhausted after each day. I fell asleep almost immediately after my head hit the pillow each night. Brodie stayed in the attached office until late, working.

I'd shyly asked him to please keep the door open while I fell asleep on the first night we'd been here. The sounds of his irritable typing, clicking, occasional frustrated growls and irritated sighs made me feel strangely safe and protected as I'd dozed off.

Brodie had informed me on the plane ride over that the Parisi family territory spanned most of Sicily, as well as parts of Southern Italy. The Parisi empire also worked closely with other branches of Sicilian families that had since established their presence back in the States, mostly in the South. The Parisi name was akin to royalty here in Sicily, and Marco Parisi was the undisputed king.

It was beyond unnerving being around that many people with so much effing *money*.

I'd heard Marco's name multiple times throughout the previous several days, but I hadn't met him until we'd gotten to the private airport in upstate New York. I'd only woken up shortly before take-off.

Marco Parisi made Brodie Magnuson look like an overgrown teddy bear.

The man was dark, sinister, and terrifying despite being physically a little smaller than the arrogant green-eyed giant. Tattoos were visible in ominous dark swirls, dashes, and menacing looking symbols along his hands and wrists. They likely extended up the length of his arms underneath the bespoke Italian suit he wore.

Reluctantly, I'd noted that Marco was undeniably handsome in a lethal, bulky panther sort of way. However, I was pretty sure the man had some sort of disease that only allowed his face to be fixed in an absolutely terrifying scowl.

Maybe his face had never formed a smile in his life, so the muscles responsible for the normal human expression had simply atrophied from severe lack of use.

He'd never been anything but calmly polite and respectful to me, but it didn't stop the tiny burst of fear that fluttered in the pit of my stomach whenever I'd had to speak to him.

On the very first evening at the resort, when I'd tried to tell him how much I appreciated his enormous generosity letting me stay here, he'd given me such a stern look of dismissal that I simply stopped talking and nodded. He seemed almost offended that I had thanked him instead of just expecting to be taken care of.

It was entirely unsettling.

I'd been glad to keep our interactions brief, infrequent, and pleasantly polite over the last few days. I always breathed a little sigh of relief when the interactions were over.

Gianna seemed to be the only one completely unaffected by his menacing presence. You could almost see the heat radiating off Marco's skin whenever she was near him. It was fascinating to see the amount of neutrality that she managed under the constant scrutiny of his gaze.

It wasn't my business, nor would I judge either of them, but it didn't seem like Marco's interest in her was purely platonic.

They'd kept referring to Gia as his "kid sister," but there was nothing very sisterly in the way he stared. There was also, I'd quickly discovered, less than zero blood relation between them. Apparently, Gia's family had worked for the Parisi empire for generations, and their families had been intertwined since.

Laney had informed me that Marco was still monumentally pissed with the two women for successfully shaking the security detail a while back. It had been the same Friday evening that I'd gone to *Ladies' Night* with Kim and the other girls. That night, Gia had made a slightly tipsy spur-of-the-moment decision to accidentally, ahem, flash her bare chest at her three male guards in order to distract them long enough for her to slip past them.

I mean... was it *really* Gia's fault that it had worked? Uggh, *men!*

That night seemed like an eternity ago, like it was a completely different lifetime. It may as well have been a different lifetime considering how much had changed, and in less than two weeks.

I took another sip of the pretty pink drink followed by two sips of water. Dehydrated, hungover, and out in the sun all day was a very bad combination for normal people. Unfortunately for most ginger folks such as myself, that combination was a death sentence. I'd learned my lesson since the first day and had been drinking water like a camel since. As well as applying sunscreen on the regular.

I really had no idea what the hell was in these drinks, but they were dangerous.

Each sip tasted like a fresh flower squeezed into sunshine-soaked citrus with a smooth burst of berry sweetness. I couldn't even pronounce whatever name Gia had rolled off her tongue as she'd handed it to me the first night we'd arrived.

I took another delicious sip. A few more minutes to let my sun-block sink in before I'd go cool off in the pool with the girls. It was almost worth my life apparently being in constant danger to get to experience this level of paradise.

Fiona Anderson's face flashed behind my eyes.

Almost worth it, but not quite.

However, if I had to hide out somewhere for the next year or more of my life, I literally couldn't think of a better place. Staying here on the private wing of the Parisi resort kind of felt like a prison sentence to heaven on Earth.

The totally unsettling part was being at the complete mercy of people I barely freaking knew, to literally trust them with my life.

One day at a time.

Dr. Briggs had told me that back in New York before the plane had taken off, holding my hand gently between hers as she spoke. I was so glad she'd been near when I'd woken up.

They'd confirmed it was likely the same type of drug as before that had been placed into the red wine bottle. That's when I'd discovered that Raffaele Parisi, the youngest Parisi brother, was apparently not only a medical doctor, but had also earned a PharmD, or Doctor of Pharmacy.

He'd been the one to analyze my blood samples and had collaborated with *Magnuson Security* many times over the last few years. Together, they'd been able to conclude it was the same sickos somehow involved in Fiona Anderson's disappearance and murder that were still trying to take me.

And they were getting *really* freaking bold about it.

There weren't enough pink fruity cocktails in the world to completely drown out that terrible thought.

But you couldn't blame a girl for trying, right?

I'd been about to turn the shower on and start getting ready yesterday morning when he'd apparently found out how the drugged red wine bottle and fake note had gotten into his Manhattan suite, completely undetected.

I'd never truly felt scared of him until I saw his explosive reaction to the news.

His security team back in New York had discovered four staff members at the hotel that were unauthorized. They'd somehow snuck past the insane level of hotel security to get inside Brodie's suite and pose as cleaning staff, placing the bottle along with the note inconspicuously as they'd tidied up the kitchen area.

He'd been deceptively quiet after ending the phone call as he'd run his big paws through his hair, letting out a long breath. Then like a bomb going off, he'd exploded up from the chair and completely upended the table along with all his equipment.

I wasn't sure which was louder, the crashing sound of the heavy wooden desk or his savage outburst as he'd thrown it like it was made of plastic.

Cheap plastic.

I'd stared at him from the open bathroom door, a little terrified and also a little hot from the raw display of power, but I'd never admit that last part out loud. When his burning emerald eyes had met mine, the breath stopped in my chest as I felt the sheer intensity of his fury.

Like a coward I'd instantly retreated into the bathroom and closed the door.

I turned the shower on and put on my favorite morning playlist to drown out the echoing of his outraged roar inside my head. I'd taken a longer shower than usual. By the time I came out of the bathroom, everything had been put back into place in the office space as if nothing had ever happened. He hadn't been around as I'd finished getting ready.

Before I left the room, I saw him out of the corner of my eye, swimming laps.

He was just beyond our patio in the swim-out area which wrapped around the private quarters. He swam almost the entire length in practically one breath. I was glad he hadn't been around to see the way I bit my lip as I watched his darkly tanned muscles bunch and flex as he moved through the water.

I ignored the smirk from the guard stationed across the terrace when he'd seen me watching Brodie swim.

I was pretty sure his name was Jim. Or Bryan. To be honest they kind of seemed like the same person to me every time I'd met them.

Turning away from Jim's slash Bryan's annoying male smugness, I'd hurriedly grabbed my pool things from the room and went to meet the girls for brunch. After brunch, it'd be the pool and then beach as we'd done the last several days. Even the most routine part of my new routine, if you could even call it that, was surreal and totally different from what I'd normally be doing.

Alcohol had already felt very necessary for the day, and it hadn't even been ten a.m. yet when I'd sat down at brunch.

I almost felt guilty for still feeling scared, but to be honest I really didn't understand how I was actually feeling about anything anymore. It'd been nonstop emotional whiplash since I'd woken up in Brodie's arms right before we'd taken off for Sicily.

I felt safe, but at the same time terrified and uncertain. Comforted, but at the same time pushed away and held at a distance. It was unnerving. Almost as if my sense of mental, physical, and emotional safety had been extracted from within me and divided into three parts, forever in constant disagreement and imbalance.

My entire world had been thrown so far off balance I didn't know which way was up or down, high or low, danger or desire. I recognized how unhealthy it was, but all I wanted to do was catch a little brain-numbing buzz from these flowery drinks by the pool and focus on the beauty surrounding me.

That way, it was much easier to pretend this was some kind of weird, surreal, uber-luxe vacay and that I was doing fine.

Yup.

Drugged—twice—in less than two weeks; had unprotected sex with a totally random, terrifying, arrogant billionaire bully who was now completely ignoring me and that I was also now pathetically pining after; and a group of men who kidnapped and tortured women had also apparently made not just one, but two attempts to abduct me—also in less than two weeks.

Yyyyup. Everything was freaking *groovy.*

The night in the hotel gym was the first time I'd truly felt that my life was in danger. It was a petrifying and very humbling feeling. My memories from the whole ordeal were a little patchy even going back to before I'd left the hotel suite, most likely from being drugged again. The one thing burned into my memory was the bone-chilling feeling of being hunted.

It was something I won't ever forget.

I finished the drink and reached for the second round, courtesy of Gianna. My life was madness. Someone tried to abduct me—like who the hell does that actually happen to in real life? I sighed again quietly as I sipped on the berry-pink citrus sunshine.

Gianna and Laney were awesome company the last few days. I felt so lucky that they were here with me, and that I wasn't ever really alone. It was probably due to the weird circumstance we were all randomly in together, but I felt like I'd known them for months and not just days.

From the first day we arrived I'd easily let them convince me to party with them to keep my mind off being hunted for my insanely sexy bod, as Laney had teasingly told me. It felt so natural to relax around her lighthearted and fearlessly carefree personality.

It was uncanny how much she reminded me of Brodie, who was apparently her oldest brother.

I'd weirdly known the instant I'd seen her because she had an almost identical pair of piercing aquamarine eyes. She had the same perfect symmetry in her high cheekbones and straight nose as her brother, but in a distinctly feminine way. She was so pretty; I'd been instantly intimidated by her.

That feeling hadn't lasted very long, thankfully. As soon as she'd seen me sitting on the couch in the Parisi's private wing of the resort, she'd grabbed Gianna's arm and squealed while she marched both of them toward me. That had been the first evening that we'd arrived, and I was barely awake.

"Gia, look! There she is! Let's go talk to her!"

She'd rambled the words out so fast that her equally pretty, petite brunette friend looked dazed as she was yanked toward the couch where I sat.

Brodie sighed in exaggeration and tried to intercept her before she reached me. It hadn't worked.

"Out of my way, shithead. I want to talk to your girlfriend. She's probably traumatized from having to put up with all of your growling and grunting."

"Behave, Laney. And she isn't a 'girlfriend', dammit. This is a job. This is real, this is important shit, okay Laney?! She's been through enough without all of your drama and shenanigans."

"Rude. Now I *am* going to tell her the story about your invisible friend Mr. Piddlesworth."

"Oh, for fuck's sake, Laney! I was barely four years old!"

Gianna had been smiling and chuckling as she watched the two siblings' back-and-forth. She made eye contact with me and smiled, shaking her head as she playfully rolled her eyes.

"Hi; it's Freya, right? I'm Gianna. Marco's friend," she'd extended her hand out to mine gently.

"Hi, umm, yes that's right. I'm Freya, it's nice to meet you, Gianna," I'd taken her hand and returned her warm smile shyly.

"Likewise! Laney and I have been dying to meet you!"

She lowered her voice and held up her hand to her mouth as she leaned in closer.

"Marco said Brodie has been an asshole all week. He's got it so bad for you he can't see straight, girl," she winked at me as she cleared her throat toward the still heartily bickering brother and sister.

I'd been beyond stunned when she'd said that. I think it had taken me a full minute to process what she'd meant by that or if I'd heard her wrong, because other than silently holding my hand or dragging me around by my upper arm, Brodie still hadn't freaking touched me.

Sometimes it literally seemed like he couldn't even stand to be in the same room with me. It wasn't fair; he'd melted my brain with his arrogant alpha-male caveman bullshit and then he totally ignored me.

I hated myself for the way the bottom dropped from my stomach and my eyes almost teared up when I'd heard him say I wasn't a girlfriend, without even stuttering. Because I *wasn't* a girlfriend, and it was totally unwise for me to see myself as such.

I also hated myself every time I thought I smelled that wonderful, masculine sandalwood musk of his cologne throughout the day. Because every time my heart did a flip into my stomach, and I had to actively stop myself from looking around for him.

It was all absolutely ridiculous.

As we'd headed over to our room to unpack, I'd broken the stony silence between us that had started the minute we'd landed.

I tried to hint that since we were basically inside the equivalent of a private military compound here in the Parisi resort, it would surely be safe if I had my own room. Really all I needed was one of the smaller, single rooms in the main area, and I'd be out of his way so he could work...

The rest of my words died on my lips when I'd glanced up at him over my shoulder and seen his narrow-eyed glare.

The only response he gave me was the cranky scowl and an even crankier growl. I'd turned my head away from him as I rolled my eyes weakly, determined not to fall prey to his dark mood. It wasn't like I'd asked for any of this, dammit.

Uggh. Stupid arrogant alpha-males and their mood swings!

On that first night after meeting the other girls, his staff had checked us both into the same suite with a private office attached. He'd apparently stayed in the same room numerous times before when he visited Marco over the years.

He made it quite clear, once again, that we would absolutely be staying together in the same suite. Period, end of story.

However, he'd slept every night in the attached office with the door propped open—at least he'd been nice about my shy request on the first night. It made me feel safer, but I was glad he hadn't asked why as he went to engage the door stop.

Still, if I hadn't been so exhausted when I'd gotten into bed every night, I'd probably have cried myself to sleep waiting for him to stomp over and growl at me as he wrapped me up in his stupid python arms.

I shook my head for the millionth time about the direction of my thoughts.

I took another sip of my drink and forced myself to laugh at Laney and Gia's tipsy conversation next to me. It worked, and soon the laughter felt genuine. Really, I couldn't have been luckier they were here, and that they were so nice. They'd welcomed me into their friendship instantly.

Last night, I'd accidentally confessed to them that Brodie and I had slept together.

Even with the slight buzz from the wine the three of us had been enjoying down by the beach, I'd been blushing beet-red after it slipped out of my mouth. It was beyond super weird talking about a guy I'd slept with to his own sister, but Laney seemed completely unphased. She was way more upset about the fact that it was no longer happening, and probably wouldn't happen again.

I'd gotten a little uneasy feeling in my stomach when Laney and Gia shared a very doubtful and then conspiring look when I'd explained how his feelings had probably just changed. It made total sense with everything going on, I told them.

They'd both told me not to worry, and they'd 'snap him out of it' soon. I'd just smiled and shrugged my shoulders in a non-committal way. There was no reason to burst their bubble and let them know that there wouldn't be any snapping anybody out of anything.

As far as I was concerned, it was your typical case of boys will be boys; although that didn't stop me from feeling a little abandoned by him, dammit. The girls didn't seem to agree with me in the slightest. They insisted he was just being a stubborn male idiot and that he needed a little "nudge."

That was probably why earlier this morning before we'd headed to the pool, they'd drug me along to one of the boutiques within the resort after we'd had an obnoxiously luxurious breakfast. The entire time we'd eaten, Laney had tried to convince me again that Brodie was obsessed with me. She insisted that I should be using that power to my advantage, and I couldn't help but laugh at her silliness.

I'd still been laughing when we'd strolled into the cute little shop and the girls made a beeline to the swimsuit section.

It still felt weird to have Laney telling me to tease her older brother into making a move on me. Super weird. But before I'd even finished laughing, she'd snatched up a barely-there black thong bikini and held it up to me. As soon as I looked at how much material wasn't there, the mirth died instantly as I'd felt myself flush from head to toe.

"Freya!! You HAVE to get this. He'll go freaking bonkers! Girl! Your ass, this swimsuit. NOW!"

"Oooh, let me see... Oh, my god, Laney's right! It's so cute, you have to get it, Freya!"

Unfortunately, I'd forgotten just how much brain matter I'd lost to the testosterone exposure. Consequently, I had made the very poor choice to drink the exact number of mimosas with breakfast to allow that sort of selection to become a reality.

Even in my boozey state, I still tried reasoning with them by pointing out the insanely high price. Honestly, the amount of sticker shock I experienced took away a little of that mimosa buzz.

I was not, nor would I probably ever be, the type of person who could allocate over a thousand US dollars on a swimsuit that I'd only be brave enough to wear in another country, and only while I was slightly drunk.

"It's super cute, but it's super outside my budget..."

They'd stared at me like they were waiting for more. When I didn't say anything else, they looked at each other and then burst into laughter.

"Oh, my gosh. I love her so much! How is she so nice?!"

"Freya, sweetie—you don't pay for anything while you're here. You're Marco Parisi's guest. That's all that is needed. Now get your sexy butt in that suit, girl!"

Before I knew it, I was walking out to the private pool area with the other two girls and trying not to panic at the feeling of my naked skin hitting the sunlight.

I chided myself at the same time I tugged the front of my sheer black swim dress more tightly around me to prevent any breeze from revealing the miniscule black *Gucci* swimsuit. The girls had insisted I immediately put it on and wear it to the pool, and it wasn't hard to convince me at the time.

But as soon as we settled into the cabana a few hours ago and my champagne brunch buzz had worn off, I began to feel panicky in the scathingly thin scraps of the shimmery black bikini.

Every time I imagined Brodie's response, I was torn between anxiety that he'd remain indifferent and the terrifying yet irresistible anticipation that he'd revert to caveman mode and pounce on me. I'd had to have two more flower power drinks, or whatever they were called, before I'd felt brave enough to even consider getting in the water.

I took another sip and was startled when I realized my drink was already gone. Shrugging, I set it up on the table next to the cabana bed. It clinked with two other almost empty glasses containing deep fuchsia petals floating drunkenly in the small amount of melted ice water.

Oops. Make that three more flower power drinks.

I took a few more gulps of water, and then I couldn't lie to myself anymore; I was stalling. I was having a hard time staying calm as I continued to delay walking almost freaking naked into the pool. The sunblock was a conveniently true excuse to prolong the delay, but it had been at least twenty minutes and I was feeling overheated.

It really wasn't a big deal.

Gianna was wearing a thong. Laney's suit was definitely on the cheekier side of bikini cut and they both looked great.

Besides, the majority of females here wore thong swim bottoms anyway. Not to mention the eastern side of the resort had a designated and very secluded area permitting complete nudity for beachgoers and sunbathers. I wasn't sure why I was acting like such a prude about a little thong swimsuit by a pool.

I pretended to act natural, like I wasn't being a huge wimp, as I carefully stood up and discreetly untied the black sarong from my hip and quickly—but not too quickly—walked the shortest possible route to the water.

As soon as I'd reached the ledge, I realized there was no way in hell I was bending down to get into the water.

Shit.

I was losing my nerve and feeling extremely overexposed. I turned toward the opposite end of the pool where the water turned much shallower, like a natural shoreline. I'd get into the pool there, which would allow me to remain standing.

No freaking way was I bending over that other ledge with my bare ass in the air.

Even though I couldn't see Brodie, I knew he wasn't ever far away from me. That's how it'd been since we'd arrived in Sicily.

I had no idea why, but suddenly I had a strong and unyielding instinct that Brodie was going to be angry when he saw me in this itty-bitty suit. I felt the hair stand up on the back of my neck in warning. I looked around nervously, but he wasn't anywhere to be found.

Yet.

Sure enough, I'd barely gotten past our primary guards as I headed toward the other edge of the pool when Brodie came stomping around the corner behind them, headed directly toward me.

I started walking at a much more reasonable pace because I was definitely too far away from the concealing water for my comfort. He looked absolutely furious, his nostrils flared and shoulders squared back as he scowled at me. The guards hurried to jump out of his way so fast that one of them tripped.

I mean seriously, how the hell did someone so large move so damn fast?

Laney looked over at Brodie and then back to me as I double-timed it toward the shallow end at the complete opposite end of the enormous pool. The way she smiled triumphantly at Gia made me instantly nervous, but there wasn't any time to waste. I was less than halfway there.

I could feel the bareness of what the suit wasn't covering more than what it actually did. I could physically *feel* his hot gaze on every single inch of my bare skin. The way he was storming toward me could only be described as predatorial.

My heart fluttered nervously; I wasn't going to make it!

Laney must have known Brodie was about to reach me, and that he looked capable of murder. I could hear her giggling evilly right behind me, the traitor.

This was totally her and Gianna's fault.

To be fair, I also couldn't stop the hysterical, giddy laughter that bubbled out of me when I realized what she was about to do. I felt like I was in middle school again or getting chased around the playground by the boys at recess. Right before she gently shoved me into the deeper part of the shallow end, she squeaked out, "Deep breath, girl!"

Brodie had been one step away from grabbing my upper arm. I felt the phantom touch of his iron grip on my skin as I was submerged in the safety of the blissfully cool water.

I could hear Laney laughing as she jumped in after me. Gia wasn't far behind. I came up for air, sputtering and choking on my own laughter. The water was like a cooling balm to my overheated skin.

Brodie had stood along the edge of the pool, glaring down at us with his pythons coiled angrily over his massive chest. The sight of that tall, powerfully muscled and tattooed frame all dressed in black tactical gear was like a shot of ecstasy to my ovaries. I quickly swam my way to the other end of the pool, trying to contain the crackhead butterflies in my stomach that were throwing a freaking rave.

"What the hell is she wearing, Laney?!"

Brodie's deep rumbling voice sounded like a thunderclap, and it made me jump even from the tentative safety of the water.

"Why the hell are you asking me, you asshat? I think she's perfectly entitled to wear whatever the hell she wants."

His only reply had been a simmering type of growl and some angry mumbling as he'd stormed over toward the corner of the pool area to grab a chair. He'd sat in the corner by the outdoor kitchen area with his massive arms crossed furiously over his chest, staring at me and occasionally harrumphing.

His glare had been so potent I could see it through the black *Ray Bans* he wore. Laney and Gianna had elbowed me teasingly, winking and blowing kisses my way. I'd hidden like a coward in the water for almost an hour before he finally left.

The guards hadn't so much as looked in my general direction since he'd stormed back off to whatever cave he kept retreating within. I didn't think it was possible, but he looked even angrier leaving.

· · · ·

IT WAS ALMOST SUNDOWN, and us three girls were feeling the effects of so much sunshine and boozey poolside cocktails.

The girls had wanted to have a stereotypical girls' night and watch chick flicks in our pajamas. I almost teared up when Gianna had suggested it as we'd taken one last dip into the pool before drying off and heading to our rooms to rinse off.

I was walking into the suite I shared with Brodie when I found a note on the inside of the door in his slanted, cranky handwriting.

Gone out until after dark. Work. Stay put or else. -B.

I yanked the note from the back of the door and crumpled it in my hand with a petulant little groan. Annoyed and suddenly restless with anxious energy, I threw it into the trash can as I looked around for the remote to the speaker system.

I needed the pounding music and carefree release of dance.

It was the way my soul healed from every painful event I'd ever experienced. Whether I was happy or sad, I needed to dance. I picked a music channel and turned the volume up to max. I needed my body to burn, bend, twist, and stretch, and for my heart to beat so fast that I didn't have space to think about anything else swimming miserably around and around in my head.

I would stay put, alright. And he could kiss my black-thong-wearing ass.

But first, I was going to jam out, then have an awesome shower, then go put my most comfy damn pair of pajamas on and watch the best damn chick flicks until I turned into Reese Witherspoon herself.

I remembered our earlier pool conversation. The girls were amazing, but I was shocked that neither one had seen *Legally Blonde,* or even *Sweet Home Alabama.* Blasphemy! They were classics! We could remedy that very soon, though.

I had been dancing for about twenty minutes, totally losing it to the best and growliest parts of *Walk This Way* when the volume suddenly dropped way down.

Startled, I turned around.

My heart dropped into my stomach and then exploded.

I saw a massive, dark figure creeping toward me from around the corner of the room that led to the swim out terrace.

Steam was rolling off the dark, powerful body as the ginormous chest and shoulders expanded with each breath. It was definitely a man, and he was definitely soaking wet. The sliding glass door that led to the pool was partially ajar behind him, giving the man a hellish, golden-red glow from the setting sun as he came closer, and closer, and closer.

The man was Brodie, and he looked capable of murder.

It wasn't even dark out yet, dammit!

Chapter 37

Brodie

S he stopped mid-body roll when she saw me, letting out an adorable squeak and dropping the pink hairbrush she'd been using as a microphone.

It clattered noisily as it hit the Carrara marble floor in the suddenly much quieter room. She drew her arms over herself—it was a little late for that, dammit—and tried to back away from me as I closed and locked the patio door, then clicked the button for the blackout drapes.

I was livid.

I couldn't think. Couldn't eat. Couldn't sleep, couldn't get any fucking work done to save my life. I was distracted, and I fucking knew it, and it pissed me off. I didn't get distracted.

I had been taking cold showers and either working or working out until I could barely stand up. I'd used every single bit of self-discipline I possessed to keep from pouncing on her like a man starved.

Unfortunately, none of that shit was helping.

I knew it was only a matter of time before our combined task forces combed out some physical locations to strike, but until then I felt like a bomb waiting for the slightest excuse to detonate. I couldn't stand being away from her, and I couldn't stand being so close to her and not be able to do anything to all those fucking mouth-watering curves.

"Freya, what do you think you're doing?"

She didn't answer me, just stared.

My dark gaze roamed all over her, from the flush on her cheeks to the way her pulse was beating rapidly along her collarbone. I growled hungrily, clenching and unclenching my fists as I stared back at her.

I was shaking with the force of my anger. I didn't dare get any closer to her, not yet.

I'd seen the expression on her face when she'd watched me throw the table across my office yesterday. She'd scurried back into the bathroom like I was the boogeyman. That really wasn't even close.

I was the boogeyman's worst damn nightmare, especially the mood I'd been in lately.

If she thought she was going to parade around basically naked in front of me and not eventually get fucked so hard she couldn't see straight, then she had another think coming.

It was a miracle that any of the guards were still alive after the way I'd seen them staring after her as she walked to the pool.

They'd gotten the message pretty damn fast that if they looked at her again, they'd be minus their eyeballs.

I'd sat there as I glared at every droplet and splash of water that got to touch all over her amazing body. I wanted her so bad my fucking balls were about to explode. I could sit back and watch the way her generous breasts bounced in that pathetic excuse for a swimsuit all day, but the fact that there were other men watching made me batshit motherfucking crazy with jealous and insanely possessive anger.

I wanted to throw a long-sleeved, hooded, floor-length black parka over her and go tear into the men with my fists.

There was one thought that had been raging inside me as I'd glared her down, daring her to get back out of the water and let me do something about that barely covered body she'd been dangling in front of me.

It was the same word that had been on repeat in the back of my mind ever since I'd first seen her.

Mine.

The only reason I'd left earlier was to deal with a semi-emergency situation. Apparently, Mikhail had news so important that he would be here by the morning to deliver it in person. That meant several things needed to be completed if it meant what I thought it did, and I sure as fuck hoped that it did—the time for a strike was drawing nearer.

I was elated when the necessary preparatory tasks took less than half the time I'd expected, and I was able to return to our room long before dark. In all honesty, I'd underestimated the size and power of the empire Marco Parisi commanded. It was impressive.

I'd been almost back to the private pool area to finish what she'd started when I'd heard the music and switched directions. It was coming from the room we'd been sharing, and it was absolutely blaring.

I'd fucking panicked and immediately went into fight mode.

Everyone knew that really fucking loud music was the best way to cover up broken glass, furniture crashing, and screams if you were trying to kidnap someone. And the music was way louder than really fucking loud.

The logical part of my brain denied any kind of breach were even possible because the Parisi territory here was undoubtedly more securely protected than the Pentagon. However, none of that mattered and I'd instantly gone to a very dark place where one of my favorite *Aerosmith* songs was only a backdrop for evil deeds done to an innocent soul. My gut twisted with fear that immediately morphed into murderous rage.

I'd soundlessly entered the darkest part of the swim out pool outside the private quarters and gave the signal to the guards nearby for possible force-on-force. I crept like a shadow toward our room.

The guard closest to our patio terrace immediately drew his weapon and went to clear the area. When he glanced into our room through the sliding glass doors, his jaw dropped in apparent shock. He stepped back immediately as he turned away from the view inside. He kept his eyes downcast. He looked increasingly terrified as I'd gotten closer.

I didn't miss that he'd taken several more steps and actually placed himself behind one of the other guards, and I really didn't like how he suddenly looked so nervous. When I'd reached the outside patio by our room, the view hit me like a punch to the gut. I knew instantly why he'd panicked.

Freya was dancing to the music, her softly toned body rolling, twirling, shimmying, and shaking like there was no one watching. Her hair was a wild mass of dark coppery silk all around her. With the pulse of the music, she threw her head around in that boneless and fluid way that only natural-born dancers could pull off. Long wavy strands were sticking to parts of her bare torso, stomach, and arms as a fine line of sweat formed on her flushed skin.

The look on her face was pure and indulgent contentment. It took my breath away watching her.

Fuck. Me.

Even through the sheer coverage of the curtains that were drawn over the sliding glass door, I could see she still had on that damn black thong swimsuit and absolutely nothing else.

The raw and blatantly sexual way her body moved made my dick lengthen instantly. I'd silently waded up the steps to our terrace, uncaring that I was still fully clothed and now soaking wet. Soundlessly I crept inside, which was pretty damn easy considering the volume of the music, dammit.

There was nothing and no one that could have stopped me from doing what I was about to do to her.

Now she was going to see what happened when she pushed the beast beyond madness. She still hadn't answered my question, and the beast could smell her carnal fear. He was ravenous.

"Freya. I said, what. Are. You. *Doing*."

She squeaked, taking a stumbling step backwards for every step I took toward her.

I'd backed her all the way up against the wall outside the bathroom door. My already throbbing dick hardened even more when I saw the muscles move in her throat when she gulped, gazing up at me.

"I—I—I was just dancing, I didn't think—"

She was so fucking cute when she was nervous.

Good, she should be fucking nervous. She'd almost given me a damn heart attack!

Not to mention putting those men's lives in danger by allowing them to see her like that.

I threw both of my hands on the wall on either side of her face, blocking her in completely. I looked down at her in the swimsuit that hardly covered anything at all. I growled when her nipples hardened even more as I looked all the way down to her cute little painted toenails, and back up to her face.

I was going to enjoy this very, very much.

"Do you have any idea what it looks like to the men outside the door, watching your sexy little dance party?"

I could barely get the words out; I was so far beyond furious.

I had over a week of pent-up sexual need for this woman that I had refused to act upon in order to keep her safe. I'd had the longest and most severe case of blue balls I'd ever had in my damn life.

Her eyes opened even wider, and she gasped as she jerked her head over to the patio door. A frantic blush erupted all over her face and neck. She even looked guilty as her eyes darted hesitantly back up to mine. I saw a little flutter of actual fear across her face, but an instant later it was gone as her gaze lowered to my mouth. Her whimpery little moan was whisper-quiet, but I heard it anyway, and my balls clenched in greedy anticipation.

I couldn't wait anymore.

I shoved her up harder against the wall, grinding my throbbing dick into her sweet softness through my drenched clothing. My mouth descended on hers as I forced her to take every bit of my possessive kiss. I needed to taste her, claim her. I needed to feel the firm softness of those curves pressed up against me, everywhere. I couldn't touch her enough.

I grabbed both of her arms. With one hand I held them above her as I pressed into her even further, holding her body against the wall with my own dripping wet form.

I felt precum dripping from the tip of my cock as she arched her back and immediately submitted to me.

She let out a high-pitched gasp as I stripped her out of the miniscule bikini top. I swallowed every bit of the sound as I shoved my tongue even deeper into her mouth. Her heavy breasts came spilling out and I groaned at the way they bounced with her shaky breathing. With the hand not holding her wrists, I groped and squeezed at their delicious softness. Her gasps and whimpers only spurred me on as I used my finger and thumb to roll around and tug on each one of her pebbled, dark pink nipples.

"Do you have any idea what you've been putting me through this last week, Freya?"

I growled into the curve of her neck right before I bit down.

The sound she made at the slight sting had my balls drawn so tight it was almost painful. I licked away the sting, and her head fell to the side as she moaned. I kept teasing her nipples in turn, groaning at how wet and swollen her pussy was going to be for me soon.

"I... Brodie, I'm sorry, I—"

"Do you have any clue how many times in the last two weeks that I've wanted to bend you over and watch my cock sink into that perfect fucking pussy?"

Just the thought had me almost ready to come as I wrapped my hand around her throat.

When she arched up into my grip, I saw stars. I could see her desire making her eyelids flutter, but I also saw the violet embers burning at the corners of those pretty blue eyes.

"And they say women have mood swings."

Even her deadpan humor couldn't stop me from doing what I was going to do to her. She'd awakened the raging beast in me, and now she was going to deal with the consequences. I tightened the grip around her neck, enjoying the way her eyes widened in fear and then darkened even more with desire.

My dick throbbed painfully. She was fucking perfection.

"That's pretty brave talk for a girl who has her tits and ass out for all to see—"

"What?!"

"—parading around like it's not a huge fucking distraction!"

" I never had... no, I didn't! It was just a damn bathing suit, Brodie! Literally every other girl here is wearing that kind of—"

"I don't give a damn if every other girl is fucking naked, Freya. *You're fucking mine*; do you understand me?"

Her mouth opened and closed several times like she didn't know what to say.

It made me want to stick my cock into it.

She was panting in little gasps that I felt along the entire length of my dick. I ground my hips into her even more, loving how damp I was making the front of her body with my own soaking wet clothes. The ample curves of her breasts were pushed up against the very top of my abdomen like this, and with every breath I could feel the imprint of her pebbled nipples against me.

It was the sweetest kind of torture I'd ever experienced.

The rough material of my wet shirt was making her dark pink little buds swell up even more as she moaned with each pump of my hips. Her head lolled to the side and her eyes closed as if she were trying to fight against her desire.

I wasn't having any of that.

She was going to show me every single thing she did when I made her lose control, just like before. It was only fair after the way she'd tormented me all fucking week.

Tightening my grip on her wrists, I reached around and gave her ass a hard slap that echoed around the room. I fucking loved the way her ass felt under my hand, so rounded and juicy. I was going to turn her ass such an angry shade of pink that she wouldn't be able to bare that perfect backside of hers again in public for at least twenty-four hours.

The way I felt right now, the only way I'd let her sit by the pool again was in a parka.

I continued to spank her glorious backside, feasting on the sight of it jiggling with each strike. In no time at all, her ass had turned a pretty shade of light pink. I didn't know where to look, between her beautiful face and bouncing tits to the way her hips flared out thickly to meet the perfectly rounded curve of her ass. Every inch of her was perfection.

When she opened her eyes again, they were so heavy-lidded with blatant desire that I almost plunged my cock into her right then and there.

I let go of the grip I had on her arms and started to really tease and torment her nipples. They were already pebbled and a dark rosy pink as I gently tugged and toyed with the sensitive buds. I groped their weight and enjoyed the way her softness filled my entire hand when I made them bounce provocatively, her nipples stabbing greedily against my palms as I rubbed around in circles.

Damn, but she had the prettiest pair of breasts I'd ever seen.

I wanted to howl when she didn't even try to move her arms from above her head and leaned into my hands on her body. One was teasing her gorgeous tits, and one I'd wrapped around the feminine length of her throat again. I couldn't wait to taste the sweetness of her pussy as she lost control.

I loved the way her nipples got even harder as the wetness was transferring from my body to hers. They were practically begging to be sucked on and licked, so I bent down to taste them.

The sound she made when I gently pulled her nipple between my teeth and flicked my tongue over the tip was felt all along my cock as it lengthened again painfully. She continued to pant and whimper as I tormented her with my mouth and my hands, pinching and pulling gently on her tiny buds until they'd almost doubled in length.

Fuck, but that was sexy as hell.

"Do you know why I'm angry, Freya?"

She moaned brokenly, then finally realized her hands were free. I couldn't help it and smiled darkly at how responsive and wild she was. She made a feeble attempt to remove my hand from her throat. Growling, I tightened it even more. She submitted again instantly, but her eyes were full of purple fire. I pressed my hips into her even harder.

"Because you're an arrogant alpha-male dickhead bully who thinks the world revol—"

Her words ended on a shriek as I gave her another stinging swat on her juicy ass.

The sound she made was barely audible over my savage grunt. Part of my fingertips had grazed against her soaking wet pussy lips underneath the tiny scrap of the thong she still wore.

My dick twitched like a fucking junkie, but I furiously ignored it. I needed to make her understand whose world she was in now.

Mine.

"Let's try that again, baby. Do you understand why I'm angry?"

"The things I don't understand about your mood swings could fill a textbook—*owwww!*"

"I'm going to show you 'ow,' baby. I'm going to spank this naughty ass so hard you won't be able to sit for a week," I punctuated my threat with another sharp slap to her ass.

"Why! Why, Brodie? What the freaking hell did I do this time?! You're the one who can't even stand to be in the same room as me! I didn't ask for any of this shit, okay!"

Her voice was wavery and breathless; I could tell she was right on the edge of giving in completely to the desire that exploded between us. I could also tell she was pissed, probably at me, which for some reason made my dick ache even more.

I loved how she challenged me with that fiery temper. It made her eventual and inevitable submission all the more electrically satisfying.

Roughly I spun her around in my arms and walked her toward the open bathroom door, holding her arms behind her back so her gorgeous breasts were totally exposed. I held her tightly, right in front of the bathroom mirror as I murmured quietly from behind her.

"Look, baby. Look at this sexy fucking body. Do you see how fucking perfect your tits are?" I spun her around again so I could see the angry pink flush on her fleshy backside through the mirror. "Mmmm, damn Freya. Do you have any fucking idea how nice your ass looks with my handprints all over it?"

"Stop. You're doing it again! I can't do this hot and cold bullshit!"

She wouldn't stop thrashing in my hold and it was only making me hotter for her. I had a feeling she was angry with me, and figured she needed to fight me a little.

I would always let my beautiful little lioness sharpen her sexy little claws on me.

The thought had me lightheaded with the need to be inside her and pumping into her tight, wet heat as she scraped those claws across my back until she was satiated.

"Mmm, yes, baby; keep fighting me. I could watch those tits bounce all day, *shit*," I couldn't help teasing her.

I grinned at her look of shocked outrage.

"Then let me go and behave like a normal human being, dammit!"

She was trying to avoid looking at her almost completely naked reflection in the mirror as I'd spun her back around. I pumped my hips into her ass and enjoyed the tiny whimper she made when the rough, wet fabric of my pants scraped across her likely stinging backside.

I wrapped one arm around her and grabbed her throat again, and she moaned as her upper body went limp in my arms. She closed her eyes and let her head fall back and to the side with a sexy little whimper. I could see the goosebumps over every inch of her skin.

"Open your eyes, Freya. Look at this gorgeous fucking body. I can't think when I'm around you unless it's thinking about fucking you. Tell me how the hell I'm supposed to be in the same damn room with you and not even touch you?"

Her eyes popped open immediately as she glared at me through the mirror.

"You're the only one who decided not to touch me again, Brodie. Let me go."

I really didn't care for the tone of her voice.

Like I had any other fucking choice until I'd found and killed the ones after her! It was making me crazy, like I couldn't completely claim her until it was safe. I refused to compromise regarding her safety.

"Listen carefully, Freya. You're *mine*. Just because I have a job to do first doesn't mean—"

"Yeah, alright. Save it, Brodie. It doesn't mean anything, and to you it's 'just sex.' I've heard it all before, Brodie. No, thanks. I don't—"

"What did you just say to me, Freya?"

Her words made me see red instantly.

I wouldn't tolerate her denying the connection we had, or the fact that she was mine and no other man would ever touch her ever again. Period.

She glared at me in the mirror and stubbornly stayed silent. She was so angry now that her hair almost turned a more brilliant shade of red and it drew my attention. I moaned out loud at the sound she made when I yanked on her pretty locks, forcing her to look up at me. I wouldn't let this go.

"Baby, tell me what you just said to me."

I could tell she was close to the breaking point of her anger. I wanted her to lose control; I needed an excuse to get even rougher with her and satisfy a primal need to dominate her completely, once and for all.

Those blue eyes of hers were dark, stormy, and just a little bit shiny as I watched her reflection. When one wet, hot tear landed on my other hand that was wrapped around her throat, I snapped.

Growling like a fucking maniac, I threw her over my shoulder with one hand.

Still soaking wet and fully clothed, I headed toward the bed and deposited her on it with a quick smack to her ass. I was rewarded with a high-pitched moan that made my balls clench. I couldn't wait to hear the sounds she was going to make when I turned her ass an angry, dark pink from my hand.

I turned the music up just a little louder, but not near as loud as before, dammit. The sounds she was going to make were for my ears, and mine alone.

As soon as her bouncy backside hit the bedding, I knew she was reminded of my hand on her ass when she couldn't hide her breathless gasp. Her arms had crossed over her chest protectively as she glared up at me from the middle of the bed.

"Freya, you need to understand that you're mine. I don't give a fuck if I've only known you for less than two weeks. You. Are. *Mine*."

"I get it, I'm your responsibility. I'm not blind; I can see how important your job is, Brodie. So don't worry, I'll behave. I won't embarrass you again, I really didn't think anyone was... I mean, I really didn't think anyone could see—"

"You think *this* is about a fucking job?"

I couldn't help the angry edge to my voice as I pointed from her to me.

"Umm, I—well, yeah, that's exactly what you told your sister when we got here. 'It was a *job*, it was *serious*, blah blah blah.' Did you not say that?"

I closed my eyes and took a deep breath. I pinched the bridge of my nose, trying to find some control before I jumped on her. Females had zero damn logic or common sense, none at all!

"Freya, I have a job to do, and it's to keep you safe, dammit. Because you. Are. *Mine*. Apparently, you aren't understanding, so I'm going to have to show you just how *serious* this is between us. And after tonight, you better not ever doubt it again."

Chapter 38

Freya

There wasn't a cell in my body that wasn't screaming for him to fuck me like an animal by the time he'd thrown me onto the bed. By the time he'd got done growling at me about how *serious* this was, I was going to combust from the inside out.

I currently had no idea, none at all, why I'd ever been upset with him or confused about how he felt. My body was responding and telling me that this man in front of me wanted me with a ferocity and possessiveness that should have scared me. Not that it didn't, but that was probably the most screwed up part.

I liked that he scared me a little.

Instinctively I knew he'd never really hurt me. I felt so ridiculously safe whenever I was near him, but also when he turned those burning green eyes to me and growled, my heart forgot to beat. I knew what that look meant: conquer and dominate. And I was most definitely freaking here for it, so help me but I was.

I was so scared slash turned the hell on for him that I couldn't talk. My mouth was dry, my breath felt constricted in my lungs as I breathed in and out shakily. I felt hot all over, more than ready to be touched.

The force of my lust must have rekindled some of my frustration, because by the time he'd come back to the bed I suddenly couldn't stop the words coming out of my mouth.

"Brodie, no. I'm not yours. I'm not anything. You fucked me, then fucked with my mind and then... nothing, I guess. I don't understand what I did, and it's not fair. I appreciate the enormity of you're doing for me, I really do. But... this. This shit has to stop. I'm scared enough as it is, and—"

The more I talked, the more furious I became. I was so choked up that my voice cracked, and I stopped talking altogether. My emotions had been all over the freaking place lately.

That, and he'd scared the shit out of *me*, too, when he'd come creeping into my room, soaking wet, like some kind of demented, beefed-up *Ninja Turtle* warrior!

"Freya, I'm warning you. To stop. Talking."

"Brodie, no. You're going to do this shit again and then ignore me, and it's really... I dunno, okay. It's shady. Makes me feel like shit. So I'd rather you'd simply be up front with me and I'll stay out of yo—"

My words turned into a squeak as he lunged toward me.

He moved so fast I didn't have time to react. He pinned me down on the bed with my ass in the air, right over his lap.

Holy hell, he really was going to spank me. Like, *spank me, Sir* type of spank.

My Swiss cheese brain melted even more when he handled me so roughly. The more I thrashed, the more I realized I couldn't move. His soaking wet tactical pants were rough against my throbbing nipples and the sensation made me gasp in secret pleasure.

I whimpered when his rough palm squeezed my sensitive backside. His hand roamed back and forth across my ass. I was utterly helpless as I laid awkwardly in his lap, my ass up in the air just waiting for each slap of his massive hands. A carnal chill ran through my entire body when I realized just how helpless I was like this, and how much I liked it.

"I told you to stop talking, baby. Now it's time for your punishment. When I'm done spanking your ass, you're going to be begging me to fuck you. But first," his palm came crashing down on one of my cheeks so painfully, I forgot to breathe, "the rules. There's actually only one rule. You can't come during your punishment. I'll take care of that after, trust me. And the only fucking reason I've been ignoring you all week, is because I can't get a damn thing done when you're around, Freya!"

I gasped in shocked pain when the first blow had turned into a very sinister type of ache that I felt directly between my thighs. I whined brokenly when the second slap hit right below the curve of my ass toward the inside of my thigh. I didn't want to like the stinging pain, but my pussy had a mind of its own.

He kept them coming, one after the other, and a primal haze fell over me as I once again forgot why I was ever angry with him. A wave of white-hot pleasure surged through me when the very tips of his fingers brushed against my throbbing clit.

Even through the barrier of the swim bottoms, his touch felt like heaven and hell combined.

"Mmmm, yes. Tell me how good that feels, baby girl. I fucking love the way you sound when you lose control," he started to slap my ass so hard I couldn't tell where the sting began and the throbbing ache of my clit started.

He kept going, grunting at the obscene noises I was making with each slap. He stopped the spanks suddenly, and I sobbed out loud when he gently rubbed his palm across each angry cheek.

"Please, I can't—it hurts so bad, please!"

I didn't care that I was sobbing and begging. I couldn't let him see how much such a dirty act had made my pussy absolutely sopping wet for him. I'd never even had a spanking fantasy before. If any guy before had ever attempted to do anything like this, I'd have laid them out flat.

I was so close now to jumping over the edge into the confusing pleasure that I couldn't think. My pussy ached so badly to be filled, I could feel my entire core clenching hungrily. I knew the black thong suit I still wore would be absolutely soaked with the force of my arousal. And I knew he could see that, too.

My heart raced wildly at that thought, and I had to squeeze my thighs together tightly to keep from coming, right then and there. I couldn't lose control, not like this. It was entirely too overwhelming.

My entire ass was on fire, but not just my rounded cheeks. No, I was sore and throbbing all the way from the tops of my actual cheeks to the tops of my thighs. I could feel my sizeable backside jiggling with every blow, and as sensitive as my skin was it felt like every little movement was an electrical zing that shot across my angry flesh to land directly on my clit. The pleasure crested traitorously, wonderfully, with each frantic heartbeat.

"Tell me, baby. Tell me how sorry you are. Admit that you were teasing me, and you need to have your naughty ass spanked, and I'll stop your punishment," his hands felt like static electricity as they continued their light caress.

"Brodie, please, I—don't make me... don't make me say that, it's—*ohhh! Ohh-uhhh!*"

The blows started again, and I gave him what he wanted. I was so wet I could feel it gathering on the tops of my thighs.

"Please, I'm sorry! I'm sorry! I wanted you to... *please*, Brodie!"

I was so close, the throbbing ache between my thighs and the fire across my entire ass was all I could think about.

"You wanted me to what, baby? Lose control?"

Yes!

"N—n—no, I—"

He chuckled darkly as he stopped, and then started petting my sore ass again.

"Your punishment is almost over, baby girl. Tell me you won't do it again."

"I... you're not going to tell me what to wear, Brodie. That's messed up!"

He let out a deep bark of laughter in response. It startled me, then made my toes curl in delight. The sound of that impossibly low, rough rumble he called a laugh was almost more seductive than an actual touch. I shuddered in his lap despite my feigned bravery.

"Damn, you're feisty, and it's adorable. Not what I meant, though. Tell me you're never, ever, *ever* going to be in your room, alone, blaring your music so loud that no one would be able to hear your screaming, Freya."

"Wait, what? You're spanking me because my music was too loud? Is that... are you being serious right now?"

"Very. And also for teasing me with your perfect fucking tits and ass, and *running* from me. Don't ever run from me again, baby. *Ever.* You are mine, Freya. Mine. Do you understand me, Freya?"

His voice had gone from lighthearted to dark very quickly, and his grip tightened around me until it was almost painful. Guilt fluttered in my stomach weakly at the thought that I might have scared him, but then I realized how absurd it was and slammed the brakes on that particular topic before he threw me over his shoulder and found a cave nearby to fuck me inside of, all to establish his dominance, caveman style.

Totally wasn't going to admit that I was thrown into a vivid, twisted fantasy of him fucking me inside some cozy cave, dimly lit by the glow of the fire. The mammoth fur rug underneath me would feel slightly scratchy with that weird, leathery type of earthy smell while he grunted over me. His massive shoulders would be flexed like two bowling balls as he pounded into my widely spread thighs...

A blush spread over me and I was thankful he couldn't really see my face like this. I shook the dirty, ridiculous fantasy out of my extremely horny as fuck mind and answered him. I couldn't keep the breathless and whiny quality out of my voice.

"Yes, I won't run away, Brodie..."

He growled in approval and roughly squeezed the soft flesh of my hip. He sounded much less like a Neanderthal when he continued, which wasn't disappointing. Nope. Not at all.

"And as for the music, next time lower the volume to a safer level. For fuck's sake, babe, haven't you ever seen the movie *Taken?!* That's literally exactly what the little blond friend is doing when they break into her apartment and—"

His hands felt massive as they continued to pepper blow after blow against my ass. It was getting so hard to keep from coming that I was panting uncontrollably in between sobs.

"*Owww!* Okay, Brodie, please! I won't! I won't do it again, please stop spanking me, I can't..."

But he didn't stop. I laid across his lap and tried not to shudder at how freaking hot it made me to realize that he was in total and complete control. He was only going to stop when he wanted to, and not before. That thought almost made me come right then and there.

After a few minutes of alternating between very sharp spanks and light little slaps, I felt like all the blood flow in my entire body was directed on my clit.

The worst thing was that no matter how hard I tried to lean into the smacks, it wasn't enough to make me come. I wanted to come so badly, all I could think about was his hand stroking me right where all that blood was pooled and pulsating with every frantic heartbeat.

Finally he stopped, rubbing his massive hand up higher along my back. It felt so wonderfully hot and hard as he massaged me and sent the electric tingles from my sore ass all the way up my spine. I went limp in his lap as I continued to pant.

The transition from electric tingles to sharp, stinging pain kept making my pussy throb for more. I was so close to orgasm, but I knew it wouldn't be quite enough to get me there. It was such a delicious, agonizing sensation.

"Okay, baby. Your punishment is over. I went easy on you, so remember that, Freya. You did so good baby, you're so fucking hot when you beg me."

He'd thrown his arms under me and laid me back against the solid wall of his body. His clothing was still absolutely soaked, and I shivered as it sent chills down my body despite his heat. I could feel the thick bulge of him pressing against my overstimulated backside, and I shivered again. I was still terrifyingly close to falling apart, but the parts of my completely naked skin that were now very wet and a little bit chilled from his freaking *Aquaman* style entrance were a thankful distraction from the sinister pleasure.

I would rather be shot than admit it out loud, but another few minutes of that and I could have easily come harder than I ever thought was possible.

"And to be clear, you are completely allowed to wear that bathing suit in public again as long as you're okay with me ripping out the eyeballs of any man who sees you in it."

I couldn't help it and laughed. He was acting ridiculous, controlling, and possessive, but there was also a part of me that was weirdly flattered. Still, it was all unsettling and I shivered again. His wet clothes were starting to make me feel a little chilled and extremely restless.

I wanted him naked.

"Mmm, are you cold, baby? I need to get the fuck out of these wet clothes," he moved seamlessly as he spoke.

I couldn't believe how freaking strong this ginormous man was.

Without even straining his voice, he carefully stood up with me in his arms and somehow twisted around to lay me back down on the bed.

He grabbed my fluffy grey blanket from the chaise lounge by the bed and wrapped it around me before he turned toward the bathroom. I heard the sound of the steam jets coming on in the shower, and then he'd turned my way as he pulled off his tactical vest. Never taking his predatorial gaze off mine, he reached for his belt.

My mouth dropped open as he finished unbuckling his belt while he stalked back toward me on the bed.

The look in his eyes was hungry and violent, and it made my heart beat in triple time. I couldn't take my eyes away from the sexy way his muscles bunched and flexed as he pulled the tight, wet black shirt over his head. His pants were unbelted, unbuckled, and unzipped as they hung low over his hips. Only the very base of his crazily thick cock was visible as he kicked off each of his black boots.

He had the body of a Greek god.

From the massive width of his chiseled shoulders to the rock-solid barrel of his chest, his gigantic and powerfully masculine frame made me feel very *female*. There was literally nothing small about him.

I rarely came across men my own age whose thighs were larger than my own. I worked out, hard, dammit, and I was proud of my strength. Did it make me feel like an Amazonian sometimes?

Uggh, yes. Yes, it did.

But all I had to do was think about the sheer size of those pythons and the way it felt when they locked so tight around me, and I went weak in the knees.

I couldn't take my eyes off him as he stalked toward me on the bed. Suddenly I had the strangest sensation that my favorite grey blanket felt odd, almost scratchy. And hot, way too hot. I wanted it off; I wanted the warm rush of his gaze on me, everywhere.

I bit my lip as I let the blanket slide a little down my shoulder. He finally let his pants fall down his enormous thighs to reveal the thick, hard length of his bobbing and swaying erection. I dropped the rest of the blanket and leaned back onto the bed as he stalked toward me.

Lust, potent and hot, tore through me as I watched his masculine hand grip the base of his giant erection and pump up, down, up, down. His balls bounced with every stroke. It was obscene, and I couldn't look away from it.

"I have a surprise for you in the shower, baby. Come and find out," he kept stroking it as he spoke.

I looked up at his face and nodded hungrily as he kept walking toward me.

"Suck my cock while I take these off, baby; I want to see how wet that pussy is already," he reached for my black swim bottoms.

Without hesitation, I slid to the edge of the bed and put his thick cock into my mouth. I closed my lips around him and sucked, hard, right on the tip. At the same time, I swirled my tongue around and around, loving how it made the entire length of him twitch and jump while he was still inside my mouth.

I moaned in pleasure when he leaned down, his fingers toying with my nipples, giving them each a tiny pinch that was just short of pain before he moved down to my hips. Looping the thin black straps around each of his fingers, he pulled off my swim bottoms while I laid on the bed with my mouth full of his cock.

I felt the wetness coat the inside of my thighs all the way to my knees when he pulled them down. My heart raced and fell down into my stomach when I knew what he was going to do next.

He brought the tiny black piece of fabric up to his face, closing his eyes and inhaling vulgarly. He growled roughly and his eyes snapped open, his teal gaze searing into mine while he pumped softly into my mouth. My cheeks hollowed as I sucked in, hard.

"Fuck, baby. Your pussy is so sweet... I can't get enough of it, damn."

I moaned as I tasted the salty bit of precum on the smooth, wide tip of his cock.

"We need to get in the shower, Freya. Your surprise. But first I need to taste you," he gently pulled out of my mouth, dragging across my lower lip. "Spread those legs for me, Freya. Ask me to lick your pussy."

"Holy hell... yes, please! Please, lick my pussy, Brodie," the words were barely audible as they tumbled from my lips, which brushed against the tip of his cock as I spoke.

He jumped on me.

With a feral grunt he grabbed my hips and yanked me forward so that my pelvis was tilted up along the edge of the bed. Then, he knelt down and used his pythons to somehow wrap around my hips and pull me up to his mouth.

He looked into my eyes as he sucked directly on my clit, and I was instantly at fever pitch as I cried out in a strangled, high-pitched moan. Pleasure soared through me as he sucked and licked, his grip on my hips was so tight that I couldn't do anything but twist and moan as he feasted. The rough scrape of his beard against the sensitive skin of my upper thighs tickled in the most delicious way at the same time it made me even more aware of the wonderful way he was making my pussy feel. I was so close to orgasm again, it was almost painful.

When he pulled his head back and his eyes went directly to my pussy spread wide just inches from his face, I was so close to losing control that I tried to squeeze my legs together. It was useless, of course, and he growled low and tightened his grip. I didn't think I could come like that, so open and exposed. It terrified and thrilled me, but nothing prepared me for what he did next.

Kneeling down on the edge of the bed, he pumped one finger inside my soaking wet pussy as he sucked hard on my clit.

My body sang with the intense pleasure as he catapulted me off the ledge of sanity. I threw my head back and came screaming as I thrashed and twisted in his hands. I could feel his hot growls into my pussy and the vibrations only added to the potent and delicious pleasure. At the very height of my bliss, I felt him thrust into my...

"Holy... oh my, god, Brodie! Ohhh... uhhh-uhhh!"

Wave after wave of sensation poured over me. I felt the power of the orgasm in my entire body. I was so hot for him I had no chance to be insecure as he savagely pumped his fingers in and out of all of me while he sucked and licked my clit. It was the hardest, longest freaking orgasm I'd ever had in my life.

Every time we'd been together, he'd sent my body into a more powerful and soul-wrenching orgasm than the one before. At this rate every time he made me come, spontaneous combustion was entirely possible.

Worth it. Holy hell, was it worth it!

Afterward I lay panting on the bed, still too drunk on pleasure to overthink about how he'd put his finger in my ass and that it had made me come so hard I almost passed out. There wasn't much regular thinking going on at that point, let alone overthinking. My poor little melted, green, Swiss cheese brain clearly had no issues processing pleasure.

I didn't realize I was that kind of girl, but apparently, I was most *definitely* that kind of girl. I was so limp, satiated, and completely content that I didn't even bother to readjust the crazy position I was in, with my legs still spread open wide and mere inches from his gaze.

The feel of his rough palms caressing the inside of my thighs brought me out of the daze just enough to mull over whether or not I felt guilty about what we'd done.

I opened my eyes lazily and any indecision I had was gone when I saw the hot intensity of his gaze. He was absolutely stunning, the most attractive man I'd ever seen, and something deep inside me fluttered to life at the way he looked at me. He held out his hand, and I took it. He led me into the bathroom already full of warm steam.

That's when I saw all of them sitting on the bathroom counter, and I freaked. There was one sitting off by the side with a small bottle of what looked like it might be lubricant.

"Brodie, is that... I mean, are those what I think—"

"I don't know what you think they are, but if you were thinking that this," he pointed to one, "is an anal trainer with a cute pink heart on the tip, and some lubricant for your cute, tight little hole, then yes."

Chapter 39

Brodie

Once again, she did exactly what I'd thought she would and tried to bolt out of the bathroom when she saw the cute little butt plug. It wasn't even that big, made for a beginner.

I'd grabbed her before she'd taken a step, wrapping her in my arms as I chuckled darkly into her hair.

There was nothing that smelled as amazing as she did, even with her hair sun-soaked and windswept from a day at the pool. She relaxed a little in my arms and I caught a glimpse of her in the very foggy bathroom mirror.

I clicked the switch by the power outlet to activate the anti-fog feature, and within seconds our reflections were crystal clear.

Absolutely gorgeous.

My cock twitched hungrily against her hip as I feasted on the sight of her, totally naked and under my control.

The toy I'd selected to use on her first was small. The widest part of the tapered end was barely the size of a walnut. There was a cute little heart-shaped, hot-pink jewel on the tip. I couldn't wait to watch her cute little pucker turn pale pink around the edges as it swallowed my cock, but first I'd have to get her ass used to being stretched.

I felt how tight the little ring of muscle had choked down on my fingers when she'd come just now. It made me lightheaded imagining her asshole milking my cock frantically while she shattered and came all over me.

"Freya, baby. Why are you acting like you don't like how hard you come with I play with your pretty little asshole?"

I patted her ass, not hard, enjoying the way it jiggled enticingly.

"Oh... my god. It's, I dunno, it's—I've never done any of that before."

The fact that I was the first—and only, dammit—man to introduce this beautiful fucking creature to such a darkly erotic pleasure made me want to thump my fists over my chest. I couldn't wait to experience her body in such a purely satisfying and animalistic way.

The nervous flutter of her pulse along her neck told me I needed to get her a little hotter or she wouldn't feel bold enough to let go and enjoy the ride. And the process of getting her there was sexy as fuck. I was ripping at the seams of my self-control as more precum gathered at the tip of my cock.

I bit into the curve of her neck just hard enough to leave a little sting. She moaned in my arms as she melted even more against me. She was so responsive and sensual—especially when I talked dirty to her.

"Watch me, Freya. Watch me play with your nipples in the mirror. They get so long and puffy when I tease them, baby. Damn... so pretty. You make my dick so hard, Freya."

A blush erupted all over her. Seeing it spread across her body in the mirror so quickly was a heady rush. She was moaning and leaning back against me, still acting shy. I kept plucking on her nipples until they were long and distended, rolling them around between my thumb and forefinger.

I loved how they stuck out so far when she was this aroused, like they were begging to be pinched and sucked on. Her heavy breasts bounced in my hands as I kept teasing, . She moaned and whimpered, biting her lip.

I continued to torture her and myself, loving the perverted, sexy little show in the mirror.

"Watch me, baby. Watch me play with your pretty tits. You like that? You like when I make you watch how fucking sexy you are?"

"Oh, my god, yes... fuck, Brodie. That feels so—*yes!*"

I saw how she quickly closed her eyes after taking a peek at herself in the mirror.

I pinched her nipples just short of pain, loving the way her eyes opened instantly and locked into mine. They burned with an indigo fire that made me want to howl in victory. She started panting, rolling her hips and spreading her legs apart. The tip of my dick was throbbing, covered in precum.

"Play with your pussy, Freya. And look at me while you rub your clit," I wanted her to be so hot and needy for me that she was completely relaxed when I slipped the plug inside her.

When she reached between her legs and used two fingers to slowly spread her soaking wetness up to her clit, I almost passed out from pure sexual need. I grunted as I watched her play with her perfect body right in front of me. I was making sounds like I'd had the wind knocked out of me every time I tried to breathe.

I kind of had. Watching her rub that soaking fucking wet, pretty little pink pussy while I teased her nipples made me so fucking feral with lust for her it was hard to think about anything else.

Neither my brain nor my lungs were working because all the blood in my body was pulsing through my painfully swollen cock. I wasn't complaining. I was transfixed at the sexy show before me, trying to take in her slick pussy and her gorgeous face at the same time.

I lasted about thirty seconds before I growled like a maniac and turned toward the shower. I grabbed her arms and pulled her into the open enclosure with me. I'd only turned on the warm steam function and not the actual shower earlier. I knew it was going to be awhile before we'd be ready to use the water. Keeping one of my hands wrapped tightly around her upper arm, I turned on and adjusted the shower heads accordingly so they would spray on her without hitting her face.

The way she was biting her lip, gazing up at me and trying to look completely horrified despite her reluctant fascination made me want to forget the tiny little anal trainer and just ram into her virginal asshole with my cock. And I definitely would be doing that eventually, but not today.

I wanted her to be breathless with the need to come before I put the cute little toy into her naughty little hole.

It would make most of the slight discomfort these first few times much easier for her to handle, then it would be nothing but pleasure. I could already imagine the hot fucking sight of my cum dripping down out of her ass. The image had my temperature raising by the degree, and it had absolutely nothing to do with the steamy shower.

I held the side of her head and fisted her hair as I kissed her soundly, diving my tongue into her. She kissed me back as she relaxed into my embrace and allowed me to take complete control. I played with her body, touching her everywhere and keeping her at fever pitch.

Her moans were so primal and so fucking wild, and I caught all of them through her open mouth as I gripped her jaw. When she took my tongue in her own mouth and sucked, then gently nibbled on the tip before she swept her own tongue over mine, I almost came.

I'd never wanted a woman this badly, this completely, ever.

The things I wanted to do to her would probably send her screaming as she ran from me, but I'd chase her to the ends of the Earth to reclaim her.

Mine.

I grabbed the shower gel and a sponge and started to clean all over her body. After a few minutes I tossed it to the other side of the shower and used my hands. I couldn't tolerate any barrier between us. I started to massage the tense muscles of her lower back and hips. Every little groan and moan of pleasure she made as she relaxed against me had my dick bursting with the need to fill her with my cum.

When I reached for more shower gel and went to clean her between her legs, she squeaked and grabbed my hand.

"Brodie, wait. That's like, a lot right now... I'm overwhelmed," her voice was more breathless with her desire than fear. I was sure of it.

Almost every female I had been lucky enough to experience anal play with was at least a little bit nervous at first. I didn't mind, and there was probably something a little fucked up inside me that made me get a little harder when they were.

I was very rough in the bedroom, but I always made sure my partner was enjoying every single thing we did together. It also made their eventual submission that much sweeter; that such a beautiful creature would allow me to enjoy her body in such a way.

What seemed to upset females the most about anal play was the idea of it. How dirty and wrong it was. I'd always managed to erase their self-conscious concerns by my savage response to how fucking hot it was, and I was never shy about reassuring them.

My reasons were totally selfish; the more comfortable my partners were, the more they'd engage in the hot-as-fuck act. A win-win situation for me.

That being said, none of my previous experiences came even fucking close to how much I wanted this gorgeous woman in my arms. There was nothing I wouldn't do to be inside her, to feel either one of her hot, tight sheaths milking my dick as she screamed her release.

The shower part was for her benefit, not mine. It was way more comfortable for me to fuck on the bed.

The shower was my solution to the female excuse of *I'm worried it will be too messy.* Boom, problem solved. It was barely a sacrifice on my part considering the sweet reward of the darker side of pleasure.

Honestly, it was probably a good idea that women didn't find out how much some men were obsessed with everything to do with their asses. They already pretty much led us around by our damn balls anyway, unless it was our cocks making the calls at the time.

Instead of going between her thighs, I started rubbing the shower gel into the muscles along her neck and shoulders. I loved any excuse to put my hands on her body, anywhere.

"The only thing that should overwhelm you is how much I want to put my cock inside your ass tonight, and not just that tiny little plug," I nipped at her ear playfully.

I laughed when she let out a desperate sounding little whimper that she quickly tried to pass off as a nervous squeak.

"Brodie, it's not funny! You are absolutely not putting that freaking ball-bat cock of yours in my ass!"

"Oh, yes, I am, baby; just not tonight. Your cute little asshole is too tight to swallow up my cock. Why are you overwhelmed, Freya?"

I massaged her heavy breasts and pulled her in closer to me.

I knew my voice was deep and thick with need and that was probably making her more nervous, but I was having a very hard fucking time keeping the beast in his cage. I could feel her resistance fading under my hands, my naughty words, and the steamy warmth of the shower, but there was no way I'd push her. Not with this.

She took a long time to answer me, but I didn't mind. I was mesmerized by the feeling of her body so close to mine, the firm globes of her backside cradling my painfully hard dick. The feel of her waist as it flared out to her hips and the soft, feminine flesh of her lower abdomen.

I could feel every single curve when I held her like this, and thanks to the mutinous throbbing in my genitals, I knew it was an addiction I'd never be able to shake.

"I'm worried, I guess?"

Her voice was breathless, but it was very quiet.

Still too soon.

"Worried about what? I really was joking about fucking your ass with my cock tonight, Freya. But I think you'll really like the way the plug feels in that naughty little ass while I fuck your pussy. Mmmmm... you're going to scream and shatter all over my cock, baby."

Her breath hitched and she moaned. It was the sexiest sound I'd ever heard in my life until she did it again as her hips rolled into me and her body sagged against me.

I'd never fully understood what the word swoon had meant, but I was pretty damn sure that's what she just did and that it was hot as motherfucking hell.

I almost completely lost the very fragile and almost nonexistent hold on my self-control as she became totally pliant in my arms. I wrapped my arm around her from behind, placing my hand on her neck again. She leaned into me even more.

"Baby, I'm not going to last much longer. I need to be inside you, now."

I could have roared in relief when she moaned and nodded her head weakly, leaning into me as if she'd fall over without my arms around her. She was finally there. My heart hammered in my chest with the sudden force of my need.

I walked us over to the bench seat toward the back wall of the shower. It was just large enough to sit on, and I situated her on my lap facing me. The shorter style of seat worked so well for fucking in almost any position but missionary, of course. Her legs could fall down the sides of it in a more natural position as she rode me, either from front or behind.

My dick lengthened and my balls clenched thinking about the view of her bouncing up and down on my cock, reverse cowgirl style.

Her legs could rest across my thighs without hurting her knees while she bounced up and down on my cock until she came all over me.

I could also take complete control of her hips to fuck her hard if I wanted, also without worrying about banging her knees against a hard stone seat.

I'd already adjusted the shower heads so there was a pleasant flow of warm water that wouldn't hit above our shoulders. I grabbed the faucet right next to the bench and turned the sprayer on higher pressure, then aimed it between her cheeks. She gasped, then giggled as she leaned closer into the crook of my neck, offering her trust. Fucking adorable. I put the shower head back on the hook.

"I've wanted to do this to you since the first time I saw you, baby. I wanted to hold your thighs like this," I grabbed her upper thighs with my hands, squeezing the sensitive flesh with my palms and dragging my thumbs down along the crease between her pussy lips and her thigh. "And I wanted to spread your sweet little pussy lips like this," she moaned into my neck as I dragged my thumbs up higher, moving in closer to her core as I firmly parted her pussy lips.

My balls clenched and I growled when she gave me a little love bite of her own on my neck.

She instantly responded, panting and whimpering as her nipples beaded even tighter right in front of my face.

I couldn't resist and pulled one of the little rosy buds into my mouth. I loved the sounds she made when I sucked on her, especially when I toyed with and teased her nipples. With her thighs straddling mine, I could see her pussy fluttering hungrily as I licked and tugged on her nipples.

Reluctantly I released her perfect tits from my mouth, but I kept teasing her with the dirty sexual words that made her so fucking hot and flustered.

"And I wanted to tease your clit with my fingers, baby, just like this," my cock was so rock hard it was hard to think about anything but being deep inside her.

I straddled her legs even wider over my thighs, feasting on the sight of her pretty pink little cunt spread so wide for me, just waiting to be fucked. She moaned and whimpered as I teased her swollen little bud some more with my thumb. Her entire pussy was drenched with her arousal, and she was jerking and twitching on my lap from the pleasure. I spread the wetness up and around her clit again and again as I watched her squirm.

"*Fuck, Brodie!* Oh, god, Brodie that feels so good, I—"

She had no fucking clue how sexy she was like this.

"Yes, Freya. Tell me how good it feels when I play with your clit."

"Holy fucking shit... yes, it feels so good. Please keep doing that, Brodie!"

My hands were trembling when I finally grabbed the lubricated plug from the shower shelf.

Her clit was so puffy and swollen, her folds dripping wet and pulsing around my fingers. My body was on fire for her so badly I couldn't fucking see straight.

I positioned the small end of the tapered toy on her little pucker. It tightened instantly, but she whimpered and tucked herself further into my neck.

At this point I was a little scared to blow my load inside her.

There was no way it wouldn't bruise her from the massive orgasm I could feel waiting to burst up from the base of my spine, starting in my balls. Even the adorable little sounds she made while I teased her made me want to claim her so thoroughly that she'd never think to question our bond again.

"How do you want it, baby? Show me what you like. Play with your clit. Spread your pretty pussy nice and wide so I can see what you like."

She obeyed me shyly, biting her lip and shrugging her shoulder as she tucked her head down. Her eyes were closed and her lashes were fluttering. I wanted to see her need for me burning little violet fires around the deep blue depths of her eyes.

"Open your eyes, baby. I want to see your pretty blue eyes," I commanded her darkly, pumping my hips into her rounded ass to appease the violent demands of my painfully hard erection.

She opened her eyes at the sound of my voice, biting her lip as she tentatively held my gaze. She reached between her open thighs with one hand, using two fingers to spread her pussy wide for me just like I'd asked.

"Oh, my god, baby. Yes, *fuck yes*. Your pussy is so fucking pretty. Play with that clit, Freya. Show me how good it feels," I pushed the toy against the tightly closed pucker of her ass. I groaned, spanking her ass with my other hand and tried not to come.

"It feels so good, so... I'm so close, Brodie! Are you... are you sure you want to—*ow!*" I spanked her ass again, hard.

She threw her head back and rubbed her clit even harder, making a sound that was just short of a scream. Her breasts were bouncing deliciously between her arms as she rubbed her clit in furious little circles with one hand and kept herself spread open with the other.

Knowing I was only seconds away from the most powerful fucking orgasm I'd ever had in my life, I spread her ass apart wide and shoved the plug into her pucker in one slow and steady movement. I fucking loved the sound she made and the way her hips sagged toward me when the widest part passed through. Her asshole clenched frantically around it and I spanked both her cheeks again.

"Oh! Brodie, oh god! It feels... it's—"

"You like the way it feels to have your ass stretched, don't you baby? You're going to love how it feels with my cock inside you."

"*Fuck yes,* please, please Brodie! I need... I mean, I want..." some of her bravery faded away and her voice trailed off.

She whimpered in sexual frustration as she kept shyly teasing her clit.

"Tell me, Freya. What do you need, baby? You need me to shove my cock up inside your pussy so you can come all over it? Would you like that, baby?"

I was gripping my dick so hard to keep from coming, but I kept teasing her, rubbing her pussy juices all over the tip of my cock. The only regret I had in that moment was that I couldn't see the tight ring of her asshole stretch around and then swallow the toy up inside.

Mmmm, now *that* would be something.

That little hot-pink, heart shaped jewel would bob up and down at the tip of her asshole while her pussy pulsed with her orgasm.

Next time. I could play with her tight little pucker another time. Right now, if I didn't get inside her I was going to fucking explode.

"*Ohh, fuck! Yes!* Please... please make me come with your cock inside me, Brodie," she was breathless and wild with the power of her desire.

I'd never seen anything fucking prettier than the way she looked when she begged for my cock, her body flushed with need, her gorgeous thighs spread wide for me.

My growl echoed through the shower. I grabbed her hips with one hand and adjusted the angle of my cock so I could plow into her in one thrust. She screamed softly as she threw her head back, her pussy clenching down on my dick so tightly I have no fucking clue how I didn't come right then and there.

"Freya, *fuck*. I'm so damn close. Don't move, baby; your pussy feels too fucking good like that," I barely got the words out because she clenched her pussy again hungrily.

Growling again, I grabbed her face and held her as I looked into her eyes. They were like a dark blue storm of lust. The blood was roaring in my ears so savagely I barely heard what she said to me.

"Brodie; I need... I need you to fuck me hard. To hold me, and... I don't want to think about anything else. Just you. Please, I need..." her eyes were dazed, but the desperate need still shone through.

I didn't need to be told twice.

My hips pumped into her tight sheath with a primal force that made her glorious breasts bounce crazily in front of my face. I grabbed onto one of her nipples and sucked as I gently pinched and rolled her other one between my fingers. She moaned and moaned, one of her hands moving frantically between her legs, and her other propped on the tiled wall of the shower enclosure behind my back.

"Tell me, baby. Tell me how good that cock feels in your pretty fucking pussy."

"It's so good, it's so fucking good, *yes!*"

"Are you going to come all over that cock, baby?"

"Yes. Yes! Brodie, I—*ffffuuu—uuuck! Yes;* please, don't stop! Oh... my god!"

Her words became unintelligible as her orgasm ripped through her body.

I grabbed her face with one hand, holding her still to take my kiss while I pumped into her slick wet heat clenching frantically along the entire length of my dick. With my other arm I held her body crushed against mine, wanting to extract every bit of pleasure from her orgasm.

I wanted to taste every single scream as her pussy convulsed all over my cock.

Her moans were so primal and so fucking wild, and I caught all of them through her open mouth as I gripped her jaw. I wanted her to be pushed to the edge of sanity with the force of her release.

I'd never get enough of this woman.

After most of her orgasm seemed to fade, I pumped into her tight sheath in a savage rhythm.

I could feel the way her cunt started gripping my cock again and I growled into her neck. I sank my teeth into the spot that always made her melt, and I wasn't disappointed. She was so slick with the power of her release that I could feel it dripping down my furiously bouncing balls. The small toy still inside her naughty hole only added to the vice-like chokehold of her pussy around my cock.

It was absolute fucking bliss, and the fastest I'd ever come in my life.

My orgasm tore out from the base of my spine, making my balls tingle so hard that the corners of my vision faded. I let out such a savage groan of sexual satisfaction that there was no way the guards outside didn't hear.

Perversely, the beast inside made me roar even louder at that thought of me telling the entire world who this gorgeous creature belonged to. My pleasure soared even higher, and I pumped my cock into her like a madman.

She was mine.

I kept pumping into her until my orgasm erupted from the tip of my dick in electric spurts of pleasure. I felt it in my entire fucking body, my balls drawn up tight against the very base of my shaft and tingling with each spray of my cum up inside her.

Her pussy started spasming again greedily on my very oversensitive cock, and I grunted like a drunken ape when I realized what that meant.

She came again, this time so hard her eyes rolled back into her head. When her body was done jerking and twitching, she collapsed into my arms. I grunted with smug male triumph knowing the barbaric way I'd been fucking her had forced her into another orgasm.

I held her like that, my cock still buried inside her and my arms wrapped around her. My heart was hammering inside my chest like a jackhammer. I felt hers beating just as wildly, and I cuddled her in closer. The warm water sprayed over us as I wrapped her in my arms, and I realized I'd never felt more content in my entire life.

Her large, rounded breasts were so perfect, right at my eye level, and I couldn't help but take one of her pink nipples in my mouth. I knew it would probably be sensitive right after her orgasm.

She moaned at the contact and jerked within my grasp as she giggled softly, her expression soft and pleasure drunk. I growled in sexual satisfaction when I felt both of our releases drip from her pussy.

Before I even realized it, an image of her belly swollen from my seed made my still semi-hard cock jerk inside her and I groaned. Her glorious tits would be even more rounded and heavy with milk, her nipples even darker pink as she would feed our child lovingly in her arms.

I was still too consumed by the power of my own orgasm and the feel of her in my arms to freak the fuck out about what I'd just fantasized.

Even as a tiny fraction of my blood returned to my brain, I wasn't repulsed in the slightest. It made me wild when I pictured her like that, heavily pregnant from pumping my cum deep inside of her. If anything, it made my cock lengthen even harder as a ruth-less feeling of possession took root.

Mine.

• • • •

AFTER WE'D HAD SEX, I'd genuinely laughed with her in the shower, especially when I pulled out my best and most humiliating dance moves to the music still playing through the speakers.

"Didn't think a man my size could twerk so well, is that it? Huh?"

She'd laughed so hard at that one she'd snorted. Fucking adorable.

I enthusiastically made a total and complete jackass of myself while we rinsed off, just to hear her squeaky little giggles and see the dimples on her freckled cheeks. I couldn't stop smiling at how fucking cute she was, even her squeal of pretend alarm when she noticed my cock already hard and ready for her by the end of our shower.

I hadn't missed the way she kept sneaking glances at it, then getting all shy and smiley when I caught her. My cock was basically at a perpetual state of hardness anytime I was around her.

About an hour later, after I'd informed my idiot sister and little Miss Gia that Freya was otherwise occupied and would have to take a rain check on the movie night, I kept waiting for some kind of masculine panic to wash away the feeling of contentment.

It never happened.

The ridiculously shrill feminine giggles were the girls' only re-sponses to the change in plans. Even Gia's teasing parting comment about how she was definitely going to be the favorite Auntie didn't make me start sweating. It didn't make me feel like the walls were closing in around me, either, like I thought it would.

What surprised me even more is how much I wanted to be around Freya, period, after having sex. I'd felt like an asshole thinking it, but it was the truth. It didn't matter what we were doing, I just wanted to have her close. I'd been batshit crazy all fucking week being near her and not being able to touch her, but I was even more restless and volatile when I wasn't around her.

I hadn't felt anything like this since my last serious relationship, which ended abruptly back in my mid-twenties.

Finding out my fiancé was not only cheating on me, but was also four months pregnant, had turned her into an ex-fiancé pretty fucking quick. Especially because I hadn't seen her in six and a half months.

It'd taken me more time to forgive myself for judging her character so poorly than to mourn the relationship. While she'd been screwing another guy's brains out, wearing the engagement ring I'd given her, I'd been getting shot at and almost blown up carrying out a black op mission overseas.

Honestly, it's unsettling for most men to realize how little real control we had over so many choices in life because of the tyrannical, stubborn fuckers—literally—calling most of the shots from between our legs.

The word unsettling didn't even begin to cover what I felt as I realized that the pretty little redhead now curled up next to me in bed had me wrapped around her finger so tightly, it was bound to turn her candy-apple red nail polish into a cyanotic shade of blue. As I traced my hands over every inch of her gently sleeping form, paying close attention to my favorite pair of landmarks, I discovered that I couldn't fucking care less.

This woman had inserted herself into my life so completely and in such a short amount of time that it just made sense for us to move forward together. It was a simple decision for me, and I'd always been a man who knew exactly what he wanted.

I tucked her in closer to me, molding every inch of her against my front as I cradled the sweetness of her fleshy hips with my pelvis. I fell asleep faster than I had in years with her in my arms like that.

Something settled into place inside me while I held her, filling a void I didn't even know I had. With the intoxicating scent of her all around me and my hands cupping the roundness of her breasts, the feminine softness of her lower abdomen, and the sexy flare of her hips, I realized that there wasn't anything I wouldn't do to keep her safe and happy.

Chapter 40

Freya

I'd woken up from the deepest sleep I'd had in years, feeling refreshed but also sore in places that were already making me blush. I'd slept all night in pretty much the same position, and with none of the restless tossing and turning and dreaming like I had been lately.

It was just before dawn and already the concealing cover of night was starting to fade with the rising sun. I yawned sleepily, not ready to open my eyes yet and face the day.

Everything was so much easier from within the intimate bubble of last night. I'd never felt so connected with someone that also kind of terrified me, but in a really sexy "me, Tarzan; you, Jane" type of way. It was so beyond strange to have such a strong connection to someone I hadn't even known for two weeks.

Other than the insane chemistry between us, we were strangers living in the same room as if we were some sort of couple. He didn't know my favorite color, or that I used to write a secret letter to Santa Claus every Christmas until I'd turned fifteen, begging him to bring my parents back to me.

We'd had so few actual conversations. If it weren't for Laney, I'd hardly know anything about his personal life or his family.

However, none of that mattered at all when he was near me. My heart literally skipped a beat whenever I saw him or got of whiff of the sexy, mouth-watering sandalwood way he smelled. My stomach had done so many flippity-flips since I'd first met him that I'd probably need surgery soon to reattach whatever it was that kept your stomach from rolling around inside you. The way I felt when he held me was indescribable, but everything about it felt right.

329

I blushed a little when I remembered everything he'd made me do and the filthy, sexual things he made me say. But it was how much *he'd* liked it that had made me burn even hotter. Embarrassment had definitely been the last thing on my mind at the time.

Heat pooled between my thighs as I curled into the blankets a little tighter. I thought about the way we'd laughed and joked so easily after we finished the shower. His ridiculous and adorable and completely *naked* twerking to a song called *Ms. New Booty* had me literally snorting with laughter. The way I'd fallen asleep so fast in his arms after we'd finished eating off each other's plates like we were old roommates watching trash tv.

I'd felt so perfectly at ease around him, but at the same time he made my pulse race uncontrollably with terrifying and delectable lust.

Maybe it was just the quiet stillness of the pre-dawn light, but I couldn't summon much guilt about having sex with him, again, even though we weren't technically together. Honestly, that part was a little confusing, but everything was a little surreal in my life at the moment anyway.

I mentally shrugged as I closed my eyes, picturing the way he looked when he'd put his mouth directly between my legs and stared into my eyes like he'd devour me whole. I had to squeeze my thighs together to keep from touching myself right then and there.

With a quiet groan, I pulled the covers back and got up to face the day.

I felt a giddy little rush of nervous anticipation as I thought about seeing Brodie after last night. I was also trying to ignore the little pang of regret that I hadn't woken up in his arms. I knew I was being a little ridiculous; I'd noticed in the last almost two weeks that he was always up before the sun, apparently either working or working out.

I bit my lip as I thought about those massive arms wrapped around me, the solid wall of warm muscle all along my back and the delicious way he smelled. It was like I could shut out the whole world and just lie there, knowing he'd keep me safe.

Which was probably insane because he and I were essentially strangers.

Right?

It was all madness, every single bit of it, but my body definitely didn't give a damn.

I looked out toward the inviting water just outside the patio doors. It wasn't quite sunrise yet and the water looked too good to resist. When would I ever be able to wake up and go for a swim literally right out my bedroom window, if it weren't for my being here? Talk about a silver lining...

Grinning from ear to ear, I quickly brushed my teeth and used the bathroom. I threw on one of my one-piece swimsuits, ignoring the twisted thrill from seeing my still slightly pink backside in the mirror as I dressed.

The fresh breeze from the sea nearby greeted me as soon as I opened the sliding glass doors. I set my towel on one of the lounge chairs and stepped down into the pool. The temperature of the water was perfect. I'd taken a few laps back and forth along the entire stretch before I needed to stop and catch my breath.

Every time I thought I was in great shape, all I needed to do was start swimming laps and I was sucking wind like an asthmatic chain-smoker.

I pictured Brodie's colossal form, his rock-solid muscles flexed and glistening as he sped back and forth in the water like a hungry tiger shark. That image was making me even more breathless than the exercise was. I definitely wasn't mad about it.

I'd been swimming back and forth for a few more minutes when I'd heard yelling somewhere in the distance.

Men's voices, too far away and muffled to recognize. I wasn't even sure what language they were speaking. I looked around, but all I saw was Jim slash Bryan patrolling by the grounds toward the Parisi's private pool area like he usually did. He nodded to me solemnly and turned back to his job. He hadn't acted like there was anything to be concerned about, so I floated lazily right outside our patio steps.

Something made me think of my job back in New York.

With an odd feeling, I realized today should have been my ninety-day review. I could still remember the excitement I'd felt during my first week of work, could still remember drawing stars around today's date in my planner. I'd been told that if my review went well, I'd be eligible for a raise and additional benefits from the company.

What the hell was I going to do when it took six months, even a year, before it was safe to return back to my life? Was I really just going to waltz back into work like nothing had happened and it was completely normal to take an indefinite vacation after only two and a half months on the first "real" job I'd ever had?

Brodie and his team said that it might actually take a year or more to infiltrate the men who hunted me, but that was the worst-case scenario. But I also had a feeling Miles had only told me that because he'd seen the look of total shock on my face. He'd also probably noticed the tears gathering in my eyes.

These men voluntarily ran toward bombs and bullets but face them up against a few tears and they were all but shaking in their ginormous combat boots. It was totally ridiculous in a pathetically cute type of way.

It reminded me of the look on Brodie's face when he'd seen me get all weepy when he'd inadvertently reminded me of my parents. The memory of his abruptly nervous behavior made me smile. It was so stupidly adorable, and it made me feel that maybe there was more between us than just crazy-hot sex.

The crackhead butterflies were back again inside my stomach. I quickly dipped under the water to calm my rollercoaster thoughts.

It didn't help, because the one thing I'd kept thinking since I'd gotten out of bed this morning was *now what?*

So Brodie Magnuson, the insanely attractive, super-hot mega billionaire, bad-boy former super-marine and I were some kind of couple?

What, was he going to fly his private jet up to SoHo in between his multimillion-dollar business deals so he could watch *Netflix* shows with me in my queen-sized bed?

I was pretty sure my bed frame wouldn't even support his weight. I especially didn't think it was sturdy enough to withstand the force that he'd fucked me with last night, not that I was complaining. With orgasms like that, a girl could learn to sleep just about anywhere, broken bed frame or not.

I sighed as I floated onto my back in the soothing water, still trying to calm my thoughts. We literally had nothing in common. Nothing about this entire scenario made any sense.

Why me? Wouldn't they have just moved on to another "All-American" type of girl by now? I lived in a city with millions to choose from. Wouldn't it be more, I don't know, cost-efficient or something, to just move on to the next best option? Fixation with one particular female seemed like a very poor business venture in my humble opinion, but then again, I had a pretty strong bias.

I also assumed that someone who justifies the purchasing of another human being for their own sick, twisted purposes was a mind I *really* didn't want to understand.

I made myself smile; at least I'd have a super-steamy story to tell Kim someday when we were wrinkly old ladies, right?

I resurfaced and wiped the water from my eyes as I floated back over to the patio ledge outside the room. Everywhere I looked was luxury. This was a billionaire's playground, and I'd probably be happy if I made it to retirement with a million bucks after working into my sixties. It was just how it was for the vast majority of Americans.

But if Bryce McFuckerson and I were not in the same socioeconomic circle, then there was absolutely no way in hell that Brodie Magnuson aka *Magnuson Security* and I were. And I wasn't near vain or small-minded enough to assume that any kind of attractiveness would suddenly elevate me to be even close to that same level of wealth. It wasn't realistic; besides, looks faded.

I accepted the way I looked. Sometimes I even thought I was fairly attractive—with the right clothes, shoes, makeup, good hair day, lighting, and as long as I held my head at the perfect angle so that my slightly crooked front tooth wasn't as noticeable. But I was a real person, with real flaws, and I tried to accept them and embrace them just like anyone else should.

But every time I looked at Brodie Magnuson, I felt like an ugly, freckled duckling. He was so devastatingly handsome. I knew he'd caught me ogling him all week, and I couldn't help but feel as if he were annoyed when he'd realized what I'd been about.

In my defense, he was just too freaking insanely and totally *hot*, of course I was going to stare at him!

I was suddenly glad I was in the water to cover up my blush from head to toe remembering the sexy game he'd played with me in front of the mirror. Images of me naked, his darkly tanned and beautifully masculine, gigantic hands teasing my body made me feel distinctly un-duckling like.

He was too perfect to be a real person. He was absolutely the most attractive man I'd ever seen, and he was rich. Like, I-can-kill-people-and-get-away-with-it-rich. It was almost embarrassing that

I would assume he and I could have anything that remotely resembled a normal relationship.

I didn't even own a car. I took the train to work every morning. Or at least I had, before...

This. Whatever "this" was.

The prettiest, most luxurious, expensive, surreal, lonely, sometimes comforting and mostly terrifying vacation I'd ever been on? With a sort-of-friends-with-major-sexual-benefits relationship with my hot as hell super-soldier bodyguard with overly possessive and extremely arrogant and domineering tendencies?

Uggh.

One day at a time.

I'd been looking toward the coastline, waiting for the first light of the sun to peak over the horizon, when I heard Brodie's unmistakable bark. This time much louder.

Jim slash Bryan looked in the same direction the sounds had come from. When his entire demeanor changed wariness, I instantly got chills. He spoke into his headset a few times, seemed to relax, then turned back to patrol.

I'd seen the small smile on his face before he'd turned away, so I finally relaxed. Once again, he didn't seem concerned now, but I couldn't help the jumpy feeling that had replaced the giddy optimism I'd felt when I'd first woken up. I was just overthinking the situation because I didn't have enough things to occupy my mind, to give me some sense of purpose.

I'd been given access to a phone and computer that were supposed to be completely secure, but after the whole gym incident I'd been too scared to contact anyone from back home. Brodie and Marco had assured me that Kimberly and her father knew I was safe and understood the reason for any silence.

Trying not to draw any attention to myself, I swam over toward the sound of the voices on the other end of the pool. There were so many waterfalls and fountains in the pool design that it was hard to hear much else besides the sounds of running water. I noticed a darker section past the end of the pool that I hadn't ever noticed before. As I swam even closer, I realized there was another area just behind the largest fountain that looked like a tunnel, or some sort of hallway.

Sure, you might think you have money, but do you have a secret tunnel behind a waterfall fountain kind of money?

There was apparently no such thing as flashy or unnecessary when you were a Sicilian mafia king, I thought with a small smile.

My curiosity got the better of me and I crept closer. The men were talking loud enough I recognized Brodie and Marco's voices. I also recognized...

Peter Zakharov?!

Here in Sicily?!

My surprise turned into excitement; he was the closest thing to a father I'd ever known.

I couldn't believe he was here!

Suddenly I wanted nothing more than for him to give me a big hug like he'd done with Kimberly and I since we were little. I didn't realize how much I'd needed the comfort of a parent until my throat tightened with emotion. Good grief; was I almost twenty-five or almost five?!

Damn. I really needed to pull it together, I thought as I took a deep breath and kept listening quietly. I was going through the list of reasons why he might be here—some of them I quickly squelched because they scared me a little—when I heard Mikhail Bychkov's furious shouting.

Unfortunately, he was speaking Russian, so all I could understand was that he sounded pretty freaking pissed off.

"For the last damn time, Bychkov—English. We don't have time for this shit."

Definitely Brodie's deep, cranky voice.

It gave me a little flutter as I remembered how that deep voice felt as it tickled the side of my neck just like the rough scrape of his beard. I had to bite my lip to keep from smiling like a lovesick idiot.

"We aren't sending them a video of her in a fucking swimsuit, and I don't give a fuck what anyone says, dammit!"

Wait...

What?

Who was Mr. Zakharov talking about? I'd never even heard him swear before.

He was livid.

"There's footage of her a few days ago in a black one-piece. That's the one we would send them."

It was easy to pick out Marco's emotionless voice even without his accent.

More angry shouting back and forth in Russian. Mikhail sounded a little calmer; Peter sounded angrier.

"They are only going to take us seriously if we give them something unexpected."

Brodie grumbled something that I couldn't hear in response to Marco's comment. His voice was too low and raspy, not to mention all the water features surrounding me.

I tried to move closer but saw another guard right on the other side of the fountain. Something told me to stay hidden, so I sunk back into the water quietly.

Why were they talking about a "her" and sending a video in a swimsuit? I did not like how that question made me feel, but I asked myself anyway.

"And what about her being twenty-five before her trust fund money can be distributed? That's more than seven months from now!"

Seven months from now was very close to my twenty-fifth birthday.

Between the noisy water features and my escalating panic and denial, I couldn't hear much of what was said right after.

Then, there was an angry snort that sounded exactly like Peter when he wasn't getting his own way. I hadn't heard it very often, but I recognized it instantly.

"Since I'm the only one who knows about the damn account and I'm the designated trustee, it's pretty fucking easy for me to change things around so she can be awarded the money now. Or make it look like it's been in her custody since the first abduction attempt. There's a reason a fucking attorney was awarded that particular position, and they'd know that, dammit!"

Hair stood up on the back of my neck.

They were talking about me.

Me?

I had a trust fund? And Peter Zakharov was the trustee?

Is that why he'd always been so generous with me? Because he'd somehow known about money left to an orphaned six-year-old from her dead parents?

How the hell would he have been the trustee of my own trust fund, when he hadn't ever met me until a few years *after* my parents had died?

Had Peter Zakharov known my parents?! Or did he somehow insert himself into my life to be "awarded" the trustee position, like he'd just said?!

And why? How?

Why had no one, not him, not Kimberly, not either one of my grandparents, ever told me about the fund's existence?! I was no lawyer or financial whiz, but I was pretty freaking sure that intentionally hiding a trust fund from its designated beneficiary, in any way, was hella-illegal.

Why was Peter even in Sicily... and why hadn't he come to see me first?

How long had he been here, and without even saying anything to me?

A million questions soared inside my head, each one more terrifying and horrible than the last. I didn't even get a chance to listen to my own turbulent and chaotic thoughts because the next thing I heard almost made me pass out.

"If this is going to work, we have to think of every possible scenario. The sooner they give us a bid for her, the better. Things have gotten way too fucking dangerous. For fuck's sake, she's listed on their fucking auction site for two hundred million dollars!"

. . . .

I WAS NUMB.

The water felt cold, I felt cold all over. I felt sick.

...the sooner they give us a bid for her, the better...

...she's listed on their fucking auction site for two hundred million dollars!

Bid. Auction.

They weren't protecting me. They'd been holding me and waiting for a bigger cash payout!

That's why Brodie had been so angry. It wasn't some bullshit sexual frustration because he was 'trying to protect me.'

He was waiting for a payout and brainwashing me into trusting him so I wouldn't think to question them! They were probably all in it together; that was a life-changing amount of money, I didn't care who you were.

Motherfucking fuck, but I was such a damn idiot!

When the fuck was I going to learn?!

What hurt the most was Peter. He was like a father to me.

For that kind of money, a lot of people would pretend to be what-
ever they needed to be.

I don't know how long I stayed in the pool, but by the time I
realized I need to get out, *now,* and save myself, the sun was already
up over the horizon.

I sincerely hoped it wouldn't be the last sunrise I ever saw.

Panic threatened when I heard my own thoughts, and I knew I
had to leave. There was no other option. Somehow, I needed to get
out of this place and get to the American Embassy, or just out of
Sicily to start with.

"Hey, girl! What you doing up so early?! Gi and Laney are still
passed out cold from their little girly drinks," I hadn't even heard
Bridget walking up from behind me.

Could I even trust her?

Two hundred million dollars; what was her cut going to be?

Had these people done the same thing with Fiona Anderson?!
Pretending like she was being protected and then selling her to the
highest bidder when the price was high enough?!

"I just needed some space, we had a little bit of a fight last night
and I—" I didn't even get to finish the lie before she interrupted.

I had no idea what I was even saying. The words just came out
as if on autopilot.

"That arrogant bastard; is he still storming around throwing
furniture everywhere? I swear, that man is the most stubborn, bullheaded..." she looked at me, then sighed. "Look, he cares about you,
he really does. He's just being an idiot. I know this is all probably
really weird and probably scary, but... he's a good man, Brodie. He's
a damn arrogant bullheaded idiot, but he's a good man," she had
the nerve to smile at me like the man she praised wasn't currently
trying to fucking sell me for a cool two hundred million dollars.

Just another business transaction for a billionaire like him, Freya. You fell right into their trap, once again. All so you could feel like you belonged somewhere, to someone...

The voice of reason was a stingy bitch, but I'd take it over being lied to any day.

I let Bridget believe I was convinced, seeing a perfect opportunity for escape, and for the guards to hopefully leave me alone long enough so I could do so.

With a whole new rush of anger, I realized how stupid I'd been. No one here had any reason to think I'd run off on my own. I'd played along with them, every single order from every single guard. I had even felt comforted by them, for fuck's sakes! The anger and upset I felt was suddenly very genuine, and so potent it was hard to breathe.

"Yeah, I know... it's just a lot. I'm going to stay in today and rest, I think. And you're right about one thing, way too much alcohol! I think I just need a break from the sun and booze," I couldn't believe how fake my voice sounded to my own ears, but she seemed to buy it.

"Tell you what, I'll make sure he stays out of your way today so you can decompress. But seriously, girl, trust me—he's one of the good ones. He just has a really grumpy, arrogant, shitty way of showing it," she finished with an eye roll that looked a little too real.

Guess she didn't have to like him that much as long as they were all getting paid, I thought caustically.

No one had the kind of money these people did by doing anything commendable or respectable, not to mention legal! Blood money, all of it.

I needed to remember that if I wanted to live. Besides, this was a perfect excuse. I'd stay in the room then sneak out to the main pool area. It was much more public, and much closer to anything at all that wasn't under Marco Parisi's thumb. From there, hopefully I could make my way to the ferry and find a ride to somewhere, anywhere else but here.

I needed cash, and clothes.

I'd find both in Brodie's office in the hotel suite. I needed to move, and I needed to move *now*.

I waved to Bridget and thanked her for understanding with a smile so fake it would have made DevLynn "the-devil-lives-inside-me" Hartington swell with pride. I watched her walk away while I amazed myself at how easily I'd lied just now. What surprised me more was how little I cared.

I also wondered how much money the people who'd tried to take me at the hotel gym were offered before they realized they'd probably been played, too, by the same people who were trying to "protect" me. It made me sick.

Less than ten minutes later, I had packed and changed into another one-piece suit and a cute little thigh-length dress. I looked like I had every other day to go sit out by the pool with the girls, except today I had about nine thousand in cash in my small pool bag. It was all he'd had in his office drawer, but I hoped it was enough to get me to safety. I felt zero guilt in stealing that amount of money from Brodie; if there were more, I would have taken it.

These fuckers had stolen my life from me, and I was beyond terrified. The icing on the cake was how fucking stupid I felt because I'd truly felt like they cared about me.

I'd been a fool. I was done caring about any of them. I didn't sit around and wait to be saved, no. Fuck that. I'd save myself, just like I always had. I didn't need them, I didn't need Peter fucking Zakharov, I didn't need anyone.

The only person I could rely on was myself.

I stepped out of the room and let the door slam. The guards snapped their heads up, eying me warily. I'd never really slammed a door in my life that I could remember, let alone in the short time they'd known me.

"Brodie and I are fighting and he's in a horrible mood. Unless you want me to tell him that you walked in on me changing because you heard a loud noise in the room, I suggest you let me go over to the main side of the resort where I won't be bothered by any of you fuckwads. Is that understood, or should I let him take out his defenseless-sofa-throwing anger on you?"

I had no idea who was talking, but it sure didn't sound like me. Having your life in danger tended to do things to one's personality, I thought venomously.

When they just stared at me blankly, I lowered the strap of the one-piece off my shoulder for effect. The guard closest to me started shaking his head like a naughty toddler, holding his hands up in surrender. The other mimicked his actions exactly, if not more animatedly.

I mean really, I had to wonder why the hell I'd thought these over-tattooed G.I. Jerks were ever intimidating. Flash them a little collarbone and mention their boss, and they pissed themselves.

"No! That's not necessary. Enjoy your time at the pool, Ms. Daniels. I'll let the guards know where you'll be today."

Idiots, all of them.

I would use their own disgusting lust against them, the barbaric and overly possessive assholes.

As soon as I was around the corner, I darted into one of the restrooms by the pool. I changed into a floor length sundress. I took the black sarong I'd worn yesterday and wrapped it around my hair like a black scarf, tucking it here and there to make it look cute and intentional.

Honestly, I hadn't expected to pull off the look so well, but my mood had blackened so darkly that it was almost as if my own reflection had been altered along with it.

When I went to remove my sunglasses, I realized I didn't recognize the girl who looked back at me. Her eyes were dark, void,
burning with barely suppressed righteous anger and hatred. I
blinked, and so did she.

I replaced my shades with large, oversized ones to hide as much
of my face as I could. The sundress I changed into had long, flowy
sleeves in a crochet-knit pattern that still showed off a lot of my
freckled skin, but it was the best I could do without looking like
I was trying to disguise myself. I put the other much smaller dress
back into my bag and opened the door, heading toward the public
pool area. The wad of cash felt like a brick inside my purse, which I
tried not to cling too closely to my chest.

I'd been sitting in a cabana bed toward the edge of the pool for
a few hours, my mind racing and numb at the same time, when I
saw what looked like an American family heading toward the ferry.

They had snorkels and flippers and seemed to be in a hurry.
Two little ones were trotting along clumsily a little bit behind the
mother, each of their little hands held tightly by their father.

Before I'd realized what I was doing, I was walking toward
them, bag in hand.

"I'm so sorry, but are you and your family headed to go snorkeling? My husband is too hungover to go, but we bought tickets
from the concierge and of course they won't give me a refund," I'd
even managed to sound annoyed and rolled my eyes.

I'd seen the many excursions the resort had offered, but the
girls and I were not allowed to go. Too much attention because we
weren't allowed to go without the armed escort. Not that I'd even
asked—I didn't have any money for that, anyway—but Laney had
been dying to go.

Lies, all bullshit lies! They didn't want anyone to see me because they were the fucking ones trying to sell me like a used car!

Anger boiled just underneath the numbness, but I didn't let it surface. I still had on the same plastic smile from earlier. The woman seemed taken aback at first, her husband still walking behind her with their small children. He seemed distracted, and very stressed. He almost didn't realize his wife wasn't walking anymore and nearly ran into her.

"Oh, I—" she looked down at the snorkeling gear in her hand like it was the first time seeing it. "Oh, of course, dear! Sorry, we were in a big rush gettin' here; there's a big time difference between here and back home in Georgia!"

If my life weren't in complete danger, I would have thought her thick southern accent charming.

My relief was so strong at having found a possible way out that I almost fell over, but I somehow managed to keep it together as I followed them the short distance to the boat dock. When she chatted warmly with me, I responded automatically with such a solid fabrication of lies that I almost started to believe them myself.

Within a half hour, we were sailing away from the resort. It was such a beautiful place, but I now knew the beauty and luxury was tainted in blood and sacrifice, pain, and greed. Literal blood money. I turned away, never wanting to see any of it again.

The man was coming around for our tickets now that we were all on the boat—thank God it'd been so chaotic getting on board, because the boat staff had just assumed I'd been with the family from Georgia. Kathy was her name, and she had given me two different peach cobbler recipes on the walk to the boat. She seemed sweet and considerate, glancing at my fair skin and handing me her bottle of sunscreen with her eyebrows raised and a very motherly smile.

"I think they said the restrooms were down there over by those stairs. Your skin's too pretty to burn, sugah. Now go on down there and put some on 'fore it gets too bumpy, honey," she pointed to-ward the center of the boat.

Plastic smile still in place, I thanked her, took the sun block she handed me, and then turned toward the restrooms below deck.

Her apparent kindness toward a total stranger tried to shine through some of the darkness of my mood, but my survival in-stincts were calling all the shots.

The fighter inside me immediately roundhouse-kicked the feel-ing away faster than you could say *Chuck Norris,* and I mentally pulled the dark shield back up and around me as I walked stoically toward the stairs with the restroom sign hanging over them.

A wave of helplessness like I had never, ever known threatened against the protective armor of my dark black mood. I thought about collapsing and crying out for help, but reality won over in a heartbeat. The Parisi family was royalty here, and I was a very long ways from home.

I was about to duck into the bathroom below deck to apply the sunscreen—and avoid the very last of the ticketing rounds from the crew—when I saw a speedboat tailing behind our boat. There were a handful of men on board dressed in typical beachwear. Nothing was out of the ordinary, but nevertheless I got an uneasy feeling. The boat was moving fast, really fast. Did the Parisi's already dis-cover I'd escaped from the resort?!

I tried to calm my racing heart and churning stomach and went into the bathroom like nothing was wrong.

After about fifteen minutes, I'd applied a generous amount of sunscreen and by that time I assumed the ticketing was over, and it was safe to go back above deck. I didn't want to draw too much at-tention to myself, and my heart rate had returned to a more normal rate. Sort of.

I only made it a few steps when I saw Kathy at the top of the stairs.

Her motherly charm was gone, and she was pointing down at me. I recognized the Russian she was speaking in a daze, and then my entire body turned ice-cold.

Kathy from Georgia, my ass!

The men from the speedboat were just behind her, and they were coming down the stairs after me.

"Freya Daniels? My name is Paul Hudson," he sounded American, at least.

Every cell in my body felt on edge. Was there anyone that I could truly trust?

"This is Special Agent Tatiana Agofavona," he gestured to Kathy slash Tatiana, "and she's been working undercover as one of our scouts. Freya, I won't lie to you; you're in a lot of danger. You need to come with us at once. We are with the Embassy. We haven't been able to intercept you yet, it's been too dangerous. Please, there's not much time before they realize you've escaped," he was already ushering me up the stairs, his tone laced with quiet urgency.

The next thing I knew I was on their speedboat, and we were headed in the opposite direction at a breakneck speed. I was too numb to feel any relief; I wasn't safe yet. I wrapped my arms around my bag and pulled it tighter into myself, trying to stay calm and alert.

After a few minutes it became impossible to keep my eyes open. Exhaustion hit me like a ton of bricks, undoubtedly from all the shock and stress I'd just experienced.

The last thought I had before I closed my eyes was that we were headed in the same direction that the sun had come up, and according to the diorama in the opulent main lobby, the Parisi resort was on the easternmost side of Sicily.

There hadn't been anything east of the resort besides wide open ocean.

I hadn't eaten or drank anything since I'd left, other than the water jug I'd taken from the hotel suite. My mind and now my body were both simply too drained from the exhaustion, and I stopped trying to fight the fatigue as I closed my eyes and slipped into the darkness.

Chapter 41

Brodie

When my phone had gone off around four-thirty in the morning, I'd barely heard it. I was in such a deep state of sleep with Freya curled up beside me that it took me a few seconds to get my bearings.

I couldn't remember the last time I'd slept that soundly.

As quietly as I could, I crept from the bed where my little lioness still slept. Something very powerful tugged inside me when I saw her sleeping like that, with her long, dark red hair spread out along her back. She was even snoring a little, which was adorable. She was so vulnerable like that, and I was going to be the only man who'd ever get to see her in such a way again.

I felt a crazy surge of possessive energy as I answered Marco's call in the office.

"This better be fucking good, Parisi," I grumbled quietly into the phone.

I wanted to blow these fuckers to smithereens even more for tearing me away from Freya's still naked and very warm, soft body in the other room.

"Magnuson, it's so motherfucking far from good I don't even fucking know where to start."

Hair stood up along the back of my neck. His voice was barely audible. Fucking fantastic. Marco was in a towering state of rage, and my mind raced to compute all the possibilities as to why. I didn't like a single damn one of them.

"Where are you?"

"Corner room. Behind the *cascata*. You'll need your access code."

He disconnected the call and in the next few seconds I was dressed.

I walked quietly over to Freya's still sleeping form, standing over her like a dark shadow. I prevented myself from bending down to kiss her before I'd left because my cock was already rock-hard for her again.

For her sake, I couldn't afford to be distracted right now.

In a few more minutes I'd entered into Marco's private quarters. I heard men's voices coming softly from the back, where his massive office was located. Mikhail was here and speaking Russian with another man, but I couldn't quite place who it was. The second voice sounded strained and a little muffled.

As I turned the corner, I discovered why. It was Peter Zakharov and he looked like absolute shit.

He was holding an ice pack to his head and gesturing with one hand as he spoke in Russian to Mikhail, occasionally wincing as if his ribs were broken. He stopped talking when he saw me. It wasn't an outright hostile expression, but the man definitely didn't look happy to see me.

He could damn well kiss my ugly ass if he thought I gave a damn over his opinion of me.

I respected that he had a heavy presence in Freya's life as a substitute father figure, but she was mine, and mine she would stay. All decisions about her safety and well-being would be mine alone to make, and I didn't give a damn about who yanked whose chain in which Council Family. There was no one more capable than me to protect her, period and end of fucking story.

Mine.

He removed the icepack from his face gingerly, eventually giving me a respectful nod when I hadn't backed down from his one-eyed scowl. I returned his gesture of respect with a nod of my own, noting that his other eye was swollen shut and there were numerous stitches on his face.

"Damn, Zakharov; you look like hell. What happened? You get in a fight with one of your mountain lions or whatever you crazy Russian fucks keep as pets?"

"Dammit, Magnuson, you son of a bitch; don't make me laugh. Six broken ribs, seventeen stitches and feeling every fucking one of my fifty-two years. Explosion at one of our docks. Luka and myself. We barely got away alive, but our SUV was thrown from the blast," his expression turned even darker, "and if we hadn't left the site early because Irina was cussing Luka a blue streak about their new contractor, yet again, we'd both be sprayed all over the damn concrete right now."

"So is that why you needed to fly four thousand miles? To have Uncle Marco tend your wounds?"

Peter smiled darkly but didn't laugh.

I really needed to calm the hell down. This man was essentially going to be my father-in-law, but part of me couldn't resist baiting him. I still couldn't totally shake the feeling of insane jealousy from when he'd hugged Freya back in the hotel.

Marco's eyes crinkled in faint amusement as he poured some more Russian water into Mikhail's glass, who bowed his head and lifted the drink to him in silent thanks. He took a small drink before addressing me.

"My brother, Luka, is still in an induced coma. They were worried about his injuries and wanted him out for at least the next forty-eight hours," Mikhail swirled the clear contents of the glass tumbler, his expression stony.

Russians and their damn vodka. Give me a shot of the worst rot-gut whiskey any day over that swill. All of it tasted like rubbing alcohol, I didn't care how many thousands of dollars it was a glass. He downed the entire contents like it actually was water—I respected that—and propped himself against the back of the black leather sofa as he continued.

"As far as anyone else knows, I am still in our family's private hospital quarters back home. Peter is also assumed to be back in New York with me. Shortly after the explosion, my security team found a bomb in the Zakharov driver's *Range Rover*. If his daughter Kimberly hadn't been working late on a coworker's charity event, throwing off their usual schedule," his voice had gotten so quiet and his damn accent so thick it was hard to understand him. He closed his eyes briefly, then continued, "both she and their driver, Uncle Billie, would have gotten into that motherfucking car," Mikhail's voice was quiet and even, but there was murderous rage burning through his dark gray eyes.

Peter's black scowl turned even darker as Mikhail spoke, but he reached his hand out to pat the younger and much larger man's knee. Mikhail placed his own hand on top of his in a brief gesture of comfort between the two men.

"Any details on the explosion?" I scanned Mikhail's face for any reaction to my question but found none.

I didn't know Mikhail very well, but he seemed to express his anger just like Marco. Quietly.

"Other than a blatant data trail leading directly to Leonardo Parisi, nothing."

I looked from Marco to Mikhail, but neither man gave anything away in the expressionless masks they wore.

Leonardo was the eldest Parisi brother and three years older than Marco. From what I knew, he and Mikhail had a bit of a falling out a while back.

Leo wanted to open one of his new nightclubs too close to Bychkov turf in New York. The Council had gotten involved and ultimately sided with Mikhail. Marco told me that Leo had been a little hot for a few months, but quickly moved on. Leo had been too busy to care as he'd already immersed himself with the new build in Los Angeles, instead.

"So, is this the pre-game before the main event where y'all two duel each other to the death, or...?"

"No, Magnuson. Sorry to disappoint. That's been long since settled. Everything was fabricated. My arrival this morning is about Freya. There's been a rather... unfortunate... development in her case," Mikhail's jaw clenched and the vein in his temple enlarged, his voice almost like a whisper.

Any joking thought in my mind died the minute I heard my woman's name roll off his lips.

"Meaning what?"

Blood was pounding in my ears. It was getting harder and harder to keep the lid on my quickly escalating temper.

"Don't shoot the messenger, Magnuson. Freya is part of my extended family through Mr. Zakharov, and I don't tolerate any strike against my own. Which is why I flew out here to deliver this news in person. I intend to be involved in every part of the solution, however possible."

I didn't like this build up. It wasn't going to be good for either one of their lifespans if they didn't spill the fucking beans. Now.

Instead of telling them that, I crossed my arms over my chest and glared.

"I'm waiting."

Mikhail took his empty glass and returned back over to the bar where Marco had set out the chilled vodka, filling it half full. He drained it, poured another, and then returned back to his post. He propped himself against the back of the sofa, his relaxed stance at odds with the watchful glint in his eye. It was pretty clear that he was shielding the Zakharov man, and from me.

I hadn't thought about shooting my future father-in-law until he'd done that.

There was obviously a reason Mikhail expected me to lash out at Peter, even while the older man was clearly not in a condition for a brawl. Flying in a jet at speeds in excess of 720 mph with those kinds of injuries had probably just made him feel even worse.

I could speak from personal experiences, plural, on that one.

Still, I didn't like what their body language was implying.

"Bychkov, if you don't start talking I'm going to give you a real reason to be worried about his life," I gestured to them both in turn.

My hand was on the barrel of my gun inside its holster, and I gave them a smile that was anything but friendly.

Mikhail's eyes twitched at the corners, but Peter didn't flinch. He just looked utterly and totally furious, his own vein swelling up in his temple on the side of his face that wasn't already a puffy, multi-colored mess. Maybe he and I would get along just fine after all. The man seemed to have some stones.

Mikhail sighed quietly as he shifted and leaned forward in his seat, propping one of his elbows on the armrest as he scraped his hand roughly over his short beard. The other hand was resting on his knee, his hand gripped so tightly his knuckles were white underneath all his tattoos.

His movements were slow and controlled, but it was obvious he was furious.

"Freya Mae Daniels is not her real name. Her real name is Freya Maeve McDaniels, and she is one of the only surviving relatives associated with the McDougan crime family. The car crash that killed her parents wasn't an accident; it was a hit."

That was probably the last fucking thing in the world I thought he was going to say.

"Okay, Bychkov. I'm going to need the rest of the story there."

Mikhail studied me for a second or two, then continued.

"Her father, Blain Cathal McDaniels, and my father were associates, as well as close friends. They'd kept their relationship private for years due to the case brought against the McDougans back in the late '80s and early '90s. Her father had completely broken ties with the McDougans even before he met Freya's mother. He testified against the family, and was given complete immunity because of it. His testimony also cleared my father's name," he tossed back the rest of his Russian rubbing alcohol and looked at me blankly, waiting for any sign of reaction.

Mikhail nodded to Marco, who returned with the chilled crystal bottle of vodka. Marco surprised the hell out of me by pouring himself a glass, as well, and throwing it back with the Russians. I shared a look with him from across the room; he knew better than to offer that shit to me.

That being said, I was instantly prepared for the worst kind of news.

Marco only drank during working hours when he was seconds away from hurricane-force fury. And I'd sure as hell never seen the most Sicilian man I'd ever met throw back a shot of vodka like he was at a frat party.

Mikhail kept talking. I noticed his voice was getting quieter and his Russian accent thicker, and I assumed neither was a good sign.

"When she was barely five years old, her father contacted mine regarding several significant threats he'd received to not only him, but his family. Mr. McDaniels, Freya's father, had not been involved in any McDougan family business for almost ten years before Freya was even born. His father—her grandfather—was not well-liked within the Council and he'd made too many enemies, which you probably already knew.

"His legacy was passed onto a small group of McDougan insurgents. They have since been eliminated.

"But the car accident that killed her parents and almost killed her was not an accident. It was a hit ordered by the McDougan insurgents, and it was absolutely not approved by the Council.

"In fact, no one else on the Council knows Freya Mae Daniels is the same person as Freya Maeve McDaniels. Once my father was alerted, he'd made it known that the entire family had died in that car accident. The local papers even reported all three of them non-survivors in the crash. Her father wanted her protected, and for her new name to never be associated with his family's."

I couldn't believe what I was hearing.

"And I'm assuming that she has no knowledge about any of this, am I correct?"

"Yes. That was something her father requested explicitly, that she have no knowledge of her ties to the McDougans.

"When my father died from cancer five years ago, her well-being was handed over to myself along with Peter Zakharov. My father very much owed his life to Freya's father. Without his testimony against his own family, my father would have likely been dragged into the mess and found himself in prison. It would have brought down entirely too much heat on the Council, and inevitably he would have been eliminated."

Mikhail crossed his arms and leaned back a little against the sofa. He had one leg propped out to the side as if he were relaxed, but I wasn't fooled for a second. I could tell the worst of the news was yet to come by the way his eyes kept scanning me. I didn't like that one fucking bit.

"Okay. Give me the rest of it; I want to know what we're up against," my own voice was much calmer than I felt.

"Magnuson, it's not fucking good. The explosion at our warehouse over in Staten Island was just a small part of the security breach. Her grandparents weren't young when she came to live with them, and they were far from rich. Unfortunately, they'd had a falling out with their daughter, Freya's mother, some years before the car 'accident' that killed them.

"They'd been so upset at the news of their daughter's and son-in-law's deaths. They'd been easy to convince that changing Freya's name would keep her out of the foster system and in their custody. My father had set up a trust fund for her. It has been managed by Peter Zakharov and it will mature on her twenty-fifth birthday. The money is hers alone, and can never be transferred through marriage.

"There is now over one hundred million dollars in that account. The only place that Freya Maeve McDaniels still existed is buried within the trust fund documents. There were three fucking people, and three only, that knew of the fund's existence. After my father's passing, there were two: myself, and Mr. Zakharov."

Between his heavy Russian accent and my own growing anger, it was getting harder and harder to concentrate. My ears strained as I focused on breathing in and out, and not snapping necks and cracking skulls like I wanted to.

"My security team uncovered encrypted data from one of the same auction sites involved in the Anderson case," there was tension in every line of the Russian kingpin's face.

He clenched and unclenched his jaw as his scowl deepened, and when his eyes reached mine, I knew I wasn't going to like what came next.

His accent was so thick I could barely understand him as he continued, "and their newest addition is Freya Maeve McDaniels, the only living relative of the fallen McDougan empire, and the price has been fixed at two-hundred million dollars."

I tried, I really tried.

But as soon as the reality sank in of what that truly meant for my Freya, I launched one of the fancy fucking leather armchairs across the room practically one-handed. It landed it the center of the massive office space with a healthy series of cracks and thuds that nowhere near settled the savage rage simmering inside me.

Not only was my girl being targeted by some of the most vile and evil fucking humans on this Earth, but now she was apparently the next best thing to a fallen mafia princess. The McDougan name alone would call to the worst of the gutter rats who'd be itching to settle old scores with her innocent soul.

Blood roared in my ears. My heart hammered inside my chest. I couldn't think. I could feel the other men's stares, but I was so far gone to the power of my anger that I didn't give a rat's ass.

This was the absolute worst case fucking scenario.

In the previous twelve hours, our team had uncovered enough information to see exactly when Freya had been targeted.

The bounty hunters had been drooling when Freya's biodata had appeared on the live auction website approximately three weeks ago, and that price had only been set at fifty million dollars. When she'd essentially disappeared overnight from New York, that number had increased to seventy million dollars.

There were plenty of evil low-life degenerate bastards that would sell their beloved Grandma BettyLou to the fucking devil for that kind of money.

At two hundred million dollars, every sick fuck with more power and money than humanity would be after her like the hounds of hell. Just raising the price that much would draw out the pack mentality, likely resulting in an even bigger sale. Our time to act on the offensive instead of defensive had just been cut in motherfucking half.

For the first time in a long time, I couldn't pull myself up out of the spiral of my anger. The images of the other girls swam around in my head, but it wasn't their faces I could see.

It was hers.

I didn't realize I'd yelled so loud until I noticed my ears were ringing.

If these fuckers somehow managed to take her before we'd struck down some of their operation sites, she wouldn't ever be seen again. The things that those fucking monsters had done to those other women. Evil. Soulless.

I needed to kill them, now, every last one of them.

A few curse words followed by muffled laughter pulled me out of the tailspin like a bucket of ice water. Freya needed me, dammit. I was instantly disgusted with my lack of control.

And when I found out who the *fuck* was laughing at a time like this, they'd be minus a fucking heartbeat.

Marco smiled so rarely, let alone laughed, that it took me a few seconds to realize it was him. I started stalking toward him, growling, my fists clenched and ready to pummel his smug Sicilian face when he drew his gun on me.

He didn't even bother to look up from the wad of bills in his hand. I'd taken two more steps before he unclicked the safety and gestured to the dismembered furniture in the middle of the room.

"Calm down, you overgrown jarhead motherfucker," he waved the cash in front of me, still smiling darkly. "Call it an insurance policy for my office furniture. Fortunately for me, the Russians underestimated your temper. I also added in an extra ten grand for the one-handed throw."

"Jackass," I muttered.

He had a point. I was just too furious to give a shit at the moment.

I walked by the other men, one who was softly chuckling in between cuss words as he grabbed his painful ribs, and the other torn between perturbed annoyance and respectful disbelief.

Without a word I started toward the chair and started gathering pieces. Marco surprised me again by laughing, then walked toward me, "Magnuson, just leave it. We all needed to blow off some steam," he slapped me on the back and squeezed my shoulder in a brotherly gesture, then inclined his head back toward the sitting area, all traces of humor gone. "Gentlemen; we have some more hunting to do. Let's get to work."

. . . .

IT'D BEEN ALMOST SEVEN hours since I'd left Freya sleeping in bed. There wasn't any need to return to my private office when everything I needed to access was already here. We'd been working nonstop, and all I wanted to do was drag her back to our room and fuck her brains out. After that, I was actually, physically going to strap her down to the bed until all these fuckers were dead. But I couldn't do any of that, because every second that ticked by was like ten more seconds we were already behind the fucking game.

I was so restless I couldn't see straight, and my head was pounding from the effort it was taking me to stay focused within the confines of my rage.

As much as it tried the limits of my barely controlled temper, we'd set up a few false bids for her through their auction site. We knew only the dumbest players would even investigate, but that's what we were counting on. Once they accessed our bid, we reverse hacked their network and attained enough IP addresses to narrow down physical locations. From there, it was a constant scanning and cross referencing to see if anything matched to get us a bigger fish.

Less than an hour after our first fake bid went live, we'd already made some progress infiltrating into several areas of their operation sites. They ranged anywhere from weapons safehouses to resolute Albanian 'farms' with unassuming old barns stuffed to the brim with counterfeit Euros and millions of kilos of cocaine, heroin, and fentanyl.

Six operation sites we'd found, and two had already been leveled, nothing left but smoke. Four more to go, and I wasn't naïve enough to assume that was all there were. That's just what we'd found so far.

Hopefully it was going to send a loud enough message for the time being that if anyone even breathed my girl's name—either one of them—they'd fucking die.

Two of the last sites I would be visiting personally with my main team. It was too much risk for anyone but me and the most experienced. Of the two sites, one we now knew was where Fiona Anderson had been killed.

There were only a few of my men that I knew could handle that kind of evil without going to a place they'd not be able to return from.

I had been robotically sorting through our tactical gear and weapon stock for the thousandth fucking time when Marco had come around the corner. One look at his face and I dropped what I was doing immediately.

"She's not here, Magnuson. She's gone."

Chapter 42

Freya

It was the smell that I noticed first. I was so utterly exhausted that I couldn't open my eyes, could barely make my brain function. But that smell was *horrible*.

Stale, rotten, putrid, pungent.

The fatigue was so severe that I couldn't wake up completely, but I breathed through my mouth to avoid the horrible stench. Which turned out to be a huge mistake, because it seemed to coat the inside of my mouth in a sickening slime as soon as I'd opened my chapped lips.

The nausea hit me like a brick. I quickly tried to close my mouth, but it was already too late. I heaved and coughed on my side because I didn't even have enough energy to sit up. All I knew was the exhaustion and the dreadful odor. Like rotten eggs that had also been decomposed and fermented inside an outhouse, then sprayed all over the surrounding walls like paint.

My eyelids refused to open. My limbs felt heavy and drunk. I noticed something around my ankles which felt cold, rough, and very heavy.

Trying to sit up, I also felt something around my wrists. Both of my hands were tucked awkwardly underneath me and painfully I started to realize that both of my arms felt numb, as if I had been laying in that position for the entire night.

My brain was spinning and shifting through the fog, and I was trying to move my arms from under me when I heard a man's voice.

Fear like I had never known soared through every cell in my body.

My heart was like a jackhammer within my chest. I was sure it was pounding so strongly that it would chisel away at my ribcage and eventually burst its way free at any moment. It made it hard to focus on getting my arms moving, but my urge to flee was also fueled by the crippling fear.

I barely felt the painful cramping shooting up and down both of my arms as the blood returned. I had no idea how long I'd been in that position, but the way my muscles were clenching and protesting I assumed it was at least several hours or possibly an entire night.

There was a small window in the very corner of the room. It was difficult to tell what time of day it was, but it was definitely daytime. Early daytime, maybe morning.

There were heavy metal cuffs on my wrists and my ankles.

Shackles. I was in fucking shackles and handcuffs!

I looked around the room as my breaths came in and out in choked, uncontrollable sobs that quickly turned into ear-splitting screams. The fear was so potent, so overwhelming, that the last thing I knew was my frantically beating heart and the sickening flush throughout my body. My chest constricted with the force of my raging heartbeat as the terrifying scene around me turned back into darkness.

• • • •

"WAKE UP, STUPID BITCH!"

The same man's grating voice and the sound of metal clanking loudly snapped my eyes open. I jumped up, screaming. The sounds I was making were so terrifying and hoarse, screaming wasn't really an accurate description.

The light in the corner window made me think I hadn't passed out for very long.

A tall, lanky man stood above me as I lay on some kind of filthy mattress. He had what looked like a flimsy crowbar in one hand that he used to smack the metal chains noisily between my ankles.

His eyes were black, spaced so far apart that he looked more monster than human.

It also could have been his obnoxiously wide-set mouth and the way his unsymmetrical jaw took up over two-thirds of his slimy face. He looked like a demonic human toad.

My chaotic screeching got even more hysterical.

It was hurting my dry throat, but I couldn't stop the sounds. I was too fucking terrified; my body wasn't under my control anymore. The sound of the Frog Man's laughs as he beat on the chain links made bile rise in my throat again.

"Shut fuck up, whore!"

A loud shout from a disgustingly obese man behind Frog Man quieted my screeching into whimpering and uncontrollable hiccups.

The second man was so overweight that his eyes were barely visible between all the layers of fat trying to squeeze underneath the shiny, tightly stretched skin on his face. The stench hit me again as I took sobbing breaths, and I wasn't so sure it wasn't the Fat One who was making the entire place smell like the depths of a city sewer drain.

His shirt was filthy, grimy, disgusting. So was he.

In a former life, the shirt could have once been white. It was now a shade of putrid, grayish yellow. It looked damp in a disgusting, dark, V shape along the chest, repeated in a gradient of layers as if he were constantly sweating.

My swimsuit was still on me, thankfully, but it felt damp between my thighs, as if I'd pissed myself.

Awesome.

It was in that moment, as I looked from Frog Man to the Fat One, that my paralyzing fear turned into the most savage rage I had ever experienced in my life.

I looked at both of them in turn, wondering exactly what they wanted of me. My anger started picturing things like yanking their limbs from their bodies one by one. As angry as I was in that moment, I truly felt I was strong enough to accomplish that, and then some.

I embraced the unbridled fury with every shaking breath as I visualized all the different ways I could kill or seriously injure them, and then escape.

They spoke in some sort of guttural language back and forth to one another as I stared at them blankly. Apparently, something they said was motherfucking hilarious, because the Fat One laughed so hard I thought his pendulous potbelly was going to explode.

I was pretty upset when it didn't.

He was so disgusting and fat that his breath came out in choked, greasy sounding wheezes, even when he wasn't laughing.

Frog Man turned to leave the room, the smile on his face so wide and toad-like that I was surprised the man could actually speak words instead of croaks and ribbits.

My fear had completely consumed me earlier. Now, all that was left was a bloodthirsty fury that made me think of digging my fingernails into both of their eyes until they'd popped like gumdrops. The sound of my own screams still echoed in my head painfully.

I forced myself to imagine what their screams would sound like instead.

I wasn't anchored or tied down to anything. I could have danced with relief at that small miracle. That is, I could have if it weren't for the heavy iron shackles on my ankles and wrists.

The metal was thick and very rough. They were so tight that they were already digging into the flesh right above my ankle bone from my frantic thrashing earlier. Even with my dancer's flexibility,

I knew I couldn't point my toes enough to get them to slip off. Not without breaking my ankle or heel bone enough that I couldn't run.

My potent fury was raging inside me so wildly that I suspected even that kind of pain would likely only make me push harder. Become even angrier.

There was a keyhole on each cuff. Right next to each keyhole on my wrists and ankles were three painted dots. The paint was chipped and faded along the uneven surface of the metal, one dot almost scratched off. The same pattern was on both my wrists and ankle cuffs.

I noticed the jangling of the ring of keys around the Frog Man's belt. Each key had a different number and color pattern, except there were never more than three dots on one key.

It wouldn't surprise me in the least if these stupid fucks didn't know how to count higher than that. Or how to read.

Regardless, I took note and then concentrated on finding my own key. I noted several that could have been it, but there was too much movement to be sure. I didn't want him to realize what I was looking at, either.

All too soon the Fat One returned with the American Embassy agent from the speed boat.

He was beaten so badly he was barely recognizable. It was also hard to determine who was breathing harder, the poor man or the fat, slobbering bastard that drug him into the room. Maybe I'd get lucky and the Fat One would drop dead from a heart attack.

"Pay attention, bitch. This what happens if you try to run," Frog Man yanked on the rope around the man's neck, who let out a pitiful wail.

My stomach turned, but I refused to react.

I don't think I could have summoned a reaction even if I'd wanted to. The only thing I felt was rage, but it was so much better than the paralyzing fear. Frog Man pulled his gun out and aimed it at the man.

"No! No, no! Ti pregu! Pi favori!"

I'd heard enough Italian or Sicilian, whatever the hell the difference was, in the last few days to recognize that instantly.

"Yes, you beg for your worthless life, you Sicilian rat," Frog Man kept laughing as he used his other hand to yank on the man's neck, who continued to sob brokenly.

I felt a remnant of my humanity surface as his pitiful sounds filled the room. Before I knew it a tear had slipped from my eye. I was so dehydrated it felt as if it singed the corner of my eye as it fell.

A disgusting wheeze of laughter came from the Fat One who still hadn't caught his breath.

"Look at stupid whore, cries for man who deliver her to us like Christmas present!"

Sicilian rat.

"Yes, stupid bitch. Cry tears for poor American Embassy man!" Frog Man had started hitting the man in the stomach with his crowbar.

It was the way he'd said *American Embassy man.* It implied that this man was not, in fact, associated with anything American whatsoever.

"Tell her! Tell her who you are before you die!" Frog Man bellowed at the crumpled heap of man on the floor.

"No, no no—ti pregu! No!"

The man's words were barely recognizable.

"Who the fuck are you," I spat the words at him, my mouth barely able to move due to my fury.

Somehow that was even funnier to the two other men.

"She so stupid! Stupid spoiled American bitch!"

"WHO THE *FUCK* ARE YOU!"

I'd screamed so loud and ferally at the sobbing man on the ground, that the other men's manic laughing stopped immediately.

He didn't answer me, just continued to wail and moan on the floor, shaking his head weakly and rolling into a fetal position. The other two men started talking again back and forth, obviously arguing. The Fat One seemed to give in as he wobbled and slobbered his way over to the miserable man.

Sicilian rat.

Sicilian...

He's a fucking rat!

Special Agents, my ass!

They'd all played me like a fucking fool. All for money. That's all I was to them, money! A paycheck, a thing. Something to tease and torture and terrify for their own sick twisted entertainment.

I saw Fat One draw his gun on the Sicilian Rat. I raged at them all from my corner, prepared to fight with every cell in my body. Fat One turned to me and smiled, still wheeze-laughing at the sobbing man on the floor. My voice was hoarse from all my screaming and my throat burned like fire, but I couldn't stop.

I barely heard the soft *crack crack* from his gun as he shot the sobbing man twice. Still laughing and wheezing, he kicked the man's lifeless form as he wobbled out of the room.

I heard women's feeble, raspy cries getting closer and closer until finally there were four women standing in the doorway.

They were naked. Filthy. Skeletally thin. Chunks of their hair missing, and nothing but emptiness and terror in their pitiful eyes. Their skin was ashen.

Fat One made them take the dead man's body out of the room.

They were so weak that it took them probably ten minutes to move him to the doorway. Frog Man lit a cigarette and laughed every time he pretended to swing his crowbar at one of them and they fell over.

I felt every single tear burn a biting path down my face as I watched them, all the way until they were out of sight around the corner. I heard other men's voices and laughter coming from a distance, more than likely watching the show.

I hated them. I fucking hated all of them.

"Listen, stupid fucking bitch. You are nothing. You mean nothing. No one to save you," Frog Man turned toward me, waving his fucking crowbar baton back and forth like a demented circus freak.

I stared at him, too fucking furious to speak, too feral with rage to move.

"You will scream so loud, but all you good for is fuck. And suck cock. You die when they don't want you anymore, but we make money from you. So much fucking money!"

He was laughing so hard that his uneven black eyes bulged repulsively.

His phone rang. He was still laughing when he answered. Brandishing the crowbar at me, he went over to the filthy sofa on the other side of the room and continued his evil, jovial conversation.

The only thing I had left was my rage at that point. I clung to it, knowing that it was the only thing that would save me. As much as I tried, I couldn't stop the angry tears from falling.

Stop wasting your hydration and irritating your eyes. You can't escape if you can't see.

Fuck this *motherfucking* fuckery; I was going to save myself. I refused to see any other outcome.

Using every single ounce of my willpower, I only allowed myself to think about forming a plan to get out. Giving my brain constant "tasks" would help keep me from spiraling into fear, and I refused to be that scared ever again. With each breath, I concentrated on filling my lungs and fueling the fire of my rage. And escape.

Just when the beginning of a desperate plan was starting to form, a massive explosion sounded from the other side of the building.

It shook the very floor and rattled the frames of the window. My ears rang from it. The muffled sounds of men's angry shouting and women's frantic crying were barely audible through the ringing in my ears. The shouting was getting even louder and more chaotic. I strained my ears to figure out what in the hell had just happened, but it was useless.

Frog Man hopped up at once and headed toward the door, moving toward the sound of the blast.

Fear was etched into the slimy frown lines on his froggy little face. He barely seemed to notice when his boney shoulder hit the side of the door frame in his uncoordinated haste, but he righted himself and kept going. The muted thumping sound as he'd run into the frame was punctuated with the sweetest, most melodic jingling I'd ever heard in my life.

The ring of shackle keys had been ripped off his belt loop and was now lying on the floor just a few feet in front of me.

The keys felt like solid gold in my trembling hands as I frantically searched for the one that matched my colored dot pattern. My hands were fumbling terribly, and I dropped them a few times as the sharp *cracks* and *pops* of gunfire added to the muffled shouting and screaming from the floor below me.

I'd barely finished freeing myself, my hand still holding the heavy iron cuff that had been around my ankle, when I heard the slapping sounds of Frog Man's flat and probably webbed feet getting closer and closer.

Like a hungry, feral predator I crouched down in my corner closest to the door, keeping my feet wide for balance. The cold and rough edges of the metal chain links were heavy around the back of my neck and shoulders. I made sure the cuff was open, exposing the sharp edges of the clasp, and waited for the exact right moment.

Here, Froggy Froggy Froggy... let's play a game called I'm-going-to-smash-your-skull-open. I'll go first!

Chapter 43

Brodie

It was almost sunrise.

I was still so fucking angry I couldn't see straight; sleep was the furthest thing from my mind. The combination of sickening fear for my girl and the most potent rage I'd ever felt in my life had sharpened my mind just like the lethal Ka-Bar resting patiently in the knife sheath on my tactical belt.

In the almost twelve and a half hours since we'd realized she was gone, I'd aged a thousand years. Each time I closed my eyes I saw her pretty face twisted in fear, her gorgeous blue eyes bloodshot and swollen from tears. Or worse.

I'd never felt so sick and fucking furious at the same time.

I was an atomic bomb dropped into an abyss. Soaring endlessly through the air while forced to contain inside me the nuclear levels of furious, destructive energy while I awaited detonation, my target held maddeningly out of my reach.

Our team was awaiting Mikhail's return, ready to deploy and destroy as soon as he gave us her location. Every second it took for him to get his *fucking ass* back to Sicily made me want to sever his arrogant Russian head from his shoulders. Which I also recognized as being completely asinine because he was somehow the only person who knew exactly where Freya had been taken, and that she was alive.

He was damned lucky my gut instinct told me that he was telling the truth, or he'd already be dead.

I'd have launched a SAM to his private jet so quickly, he wouldn't even have time to shit himself before the missile would have vaporized him. Very fortunately for him, my instincts were rarely incorrect.

372

We still had no fucking clue how they'd hacked their way into this latest security breach with the Bychkovs. I understood Mikhail couldn't give her location over the phone, text, email, or literally any of our supposedly encrypted ways of communication. It could lead anyone else directly to her and it wasn't worth the risk.

At least, I had identified a very small compartment of my brain which reluctantly acknowledged his sound logic in spite of everything else I felt.

The rest of my mind was preoccupied by a combination of the most potent restlessness I'd ever felt in my damn life, and the need to shoot, strangle, slash, and smash until I'd gotten my beautiful baby girl back home safely. I just hoped she'd forgive me eventually.

I was mostly furious at myself for such a massive oversight.

I had been a damn fool, letting my guard slip so easily just because of the way we'd connected so strongly, only a few hours before. By the time I'd stomped into Marco's office and first saw the Russians, I'd been so arrogantly self-assured that she understood exactly what we were to each other. I hadn't thought to tighten her security for her own sake.

When we'd discovered she was gone, that for all accounts she'd *willingly* left the essentially impenetrable safety of the Parisi resort, I absolutely lost it.

I knew I didn't have the right to feel an ounce of betrayal after I'd fucked up so badly, but I'd be a fucking liar if I said that her leaving willingly hadn't cut me deeper than any knife wound I'd ever had.

We'd seen her on the security footage in the main pool area. It looked as if she'd tried to blend in with a family headed to the pier for a snorkeling excursion. At no point in the footage did it look as if she were forced or drugged whatsoever.

I had no idea what the fucking hell had gotten into her.

At some point earlier that night, I'd made the subconscious decision that she so clearly belonged in my arms that there was nothing and no one who would dare to take that away from me—even her. It absolutely didn't occur to me that she would *want* to leave.

The second I got her back, she was going to know exactly who she belonged with. She absolutely would not be leaving my side for the foreseeable future.

I'd already decided what the best course of action was now that her real name had been exposed. She'd never go back to being a Mc-Daniels—it was way too dangerous because of the reputation within the criminal world through their association to the McDougans.

The name Freya Maeve Magnuson had such a nice ring to it. Once I'd thought about it, that was it. I'd already contacted a judge back in the States. As soon as she got back here and was safe, her name was going to be on a marriage license right next to mine—whether she liked it or not.

She should have fucking thought about that before she ran from me, dammit.

We'd start by announcing our engagement on her social media accounts.

She could drag my ass to every single engagement party planning, cake tasting and napkin color and flower arrangement bullshit that she wanted. If she wanted a diamond big enough to sink a ship, I'd put it on her finger, bent down on one knee. If she wanted a year to plan a big white wedding, I'd make sure she had a whole team of professionals to make her every vision a reality.

But one way or another she was going to be my wife, going to be mine.

The danger was too fucking great, and her running away from me had only made me crazier with my possessive need to protect her. Once the word was put out that not only did Freya have my protection as my wife, but that of the Bychkov and Parisi families—no one would dare even think her name and live to tell about it.

My bullheaded brain had just decided there was no fucking danger anymore, just because it insisted upon her and I being a forever type of thing. No other scenario had existed for me since the first time I'd been with her. And *she* was the one paying the price for my fuck up. It was unforgivable.

There weren't enough evil cockroaches in the world to shoot, strangle, slash, or smash to erase that much self-disgust. Fortunately for me, I was about to be given the opportunity to try.

That is, if Mikhail would hurry his motherfucking ass up!

I was about to have a minor and therapeutic type of explosion when Marco jumped up from his spot beside Gia and Laney to answer his phone. It was an extremely short phone call.

"Mikhail will be here with us in less than three and a half minutes. Get all the transports booted up; I want wheels up in ten," Marco had returned to the couch and put his arm back around Gia's waist, then gave her hip a very unbrotherly squeeze. Interesting.

If I weren't expending so much energy to prevent myself from exploding, I would have laughed at the way Marco eyed his favorite black leather armchair warily when I'd jumped up immediately after hearing of Mikhail's arrival.

Both of the girls had been hysterical when they'd found out Freya was missing from the resort. I hadn't seen Laney cry in years, but both her and Gia now had a constant stream of silent tears as they sat with Marco. I felt every one of the salty drops stab at me like a knife; every single damn one that fell was another black mark on my soul.

It was my fault Freya had been taken, and when I'd sworn to protect her with my life. The only consolation I afforded to the darkest part of my fury-blackened heart was the offering of the torture and pain I'd inflict on anyone who'd dared to harm my beautiful little lioness.

"She's in Naples. Bagnoli district. An abandoned steel mill recently overrun by a bunch of Serbian *tarakany*," Mikhail stormed into the office, his face red and blotchy with anger as he approached me.

"Magnuson, I'm riding there with you. I have direct access to a completely harmless biological tracking device that will give us her global location to within a square meter. She is more than likely on the second floor. According to her data scans, she's likely dehydrated and probably scared fucking shitless, but very much alive. I have already sent a team of—"

"You put a fucking tracking device inside my girl?!"

"Yes, I did. After testing it extensively on myself first," Mikhail's narrow-eyed, furious gaze was unwavering as I stormed toward him. "Might I remind you that I have considered her part of my extended family since she was nothing more than a feisty, freckled little kitten, Magnuson. Save your rage for the *tarakany* who dared to take her. Do not forget that we are on the same team, soldier."

I nodded at him, too fucking furious for words. He returned the same murderous look I was giving him and hadn't flinched in the slightest when I had raged the accusation at him.

As much as I wanted to pummel the front of his face until it came out through his ears, I could have open mouth kissed the man for what it meant for Freya. It meant we were coming to get her, that in a few short hours or less I'd have her back in my arms where she'd damn well stay for the rest of her damn life. Dammit!

I settled for a rough slap against his shoulder that was honestly much harder than I'd meant it to be. For a split second I thought he was going to give me an excuse for the brawl I desperately needed, but then he threw his own fist into the side of my shoulder with a menacing and very Russian-sounding chortle.

"Ha! I like you, Brodie Magnuson! You're just as fucking bat-shit crazy as Parisi said you were. Now, let's go get your girl back before you turn into an angry green giant and kill us all," Mikhail's smile was dark, but his eyes burned brightly with the sinister promise of death.

"That's why we call him Smash, Bychkov. Speaking of that, what's your moniker, Russian?" Miles came up behind us with a giddy smile on his face as he handed Mikhail a set of his own personalized tactical equipment.

We were all headed toward the helicopter launchpad on the roof of the massive Parisi property where our transports were ready and waiting.

The location they'd taken her couldn't have been more perfect for an airborne launch to carry out an amphibious strike. The old steel mill was basically a big empty warehouse, located quite literally right off the coastline. Steel mills—especially the earliest ones—dumped toxic waste into the ocean, which is why it'd been shut down almost thirty years ago and was now abandoned. Unfortunately, the damage had been done to the surrounding environment and swimming wasn't permitted anywhere around the once beautiful coast.

That also meant a low chance of civilian involvement—something we always tried to avoid at all costs.

Besides the extremely unpleasant rotten egg smell, being in the water for even short periods could be terrible for health. Effects could be instantaneous in some areas, especially further away from the coastline—our entry point.

Fortunately, my men all had a very special pair of jet-propelled swim fins which automatically extended in the water. They reached speeds of around twenty miles per hour. I'd felt like *Aquaman* in the most badass way possible the first time I'd used them. My men also wore completely impenetrable, waterproof, and impact-resistant wet suits.

Surprisingly, the wet suits were also extremely fucking comfortable. I'd used them many times doing deep dives in Guam and The Maldives. Some of my company's best work. No one would appreciate that today more than Jim and Bryan, who would be swimming a little less than a mile after their jumps into the treacherous, turquoise-blue depths.

"Moniker?" Mikhail looked amused as he looked toward Miles, aka Raider.

"Yeah, your handle. Battle nickname. Magnuson goes by Smash because, well—I mean, you've met the guy. Angriest son-of-a-bitch you've ever met. Then there's Jim and Bryan, aka Reaper and Butcher, respectively; our MARSOC snipers," Miles made the final adjustments to Mikhail's communication equipment to align with the rest of our devices as we neared the launchpad.

"You Americans and your silly comic book characters," Mikhail was already changing out of his suit and into the field uniform we'd grabbed for him, but he sported a shit-eating grin as he threw the quip at Miles.

I'd had some doubts about the Russian's battle skills until I'd gotten a look at his tattoos.

You didn't run a multi-billion-dollar tactical and cyber security company without a reliable working knowledge of the notorious Russian criminal tattoo system.

Suffice it to say he had an extensive military and tactical resume to intertwine with his criminal one. It was written in slightly faded red and black ink all over most of his torso, back, neck, and arms. Some of the images had been partially disrupted by the jagged contours of starburst-shaped scars, created by what looked like bullets.

On closer look, a fair amount could have been from knife wounds or shrapnel exits.

I considered myself a bit of a crazy bastard, but I didn't have shit on these Russians. They were a whole other breed.

"I got it—Red Bull. It's perfect. You like, Bychkov?" Miles was very impressed with himself as he slapped his hand across the Russian's bulging, red and black shoulder.

"Red Bull? Like the energy drink?"

"Hell, yes; and Red Bull vodka. Because, well, you're Russian. And Bychkov, your last name. It means 'big angry bull,' or something, right? Red Bull. Perfect," Miles let out a low whistle and turned his head back to the rest of the team with his arm beckoning them to the copters. "Lock and load, gents!"

A sinister chorus of *"Raaah!" "Yut!"* and *"Kill!"* followed.

"Damn marines," Mikhail was still grinning from ear to ear.

Less than two hours later we were almost on site. Blood roared in my ears as I finally had a visual on the building where my baby girl was, alone and fucking terrified. It looked like a tiny beige dot right now, getting larger by the second.

Mikhail and I had been watching the monitoring device connected to Freya's tracker every few minutes during the trip to Naples. She'd been in the exact same location on the second floor since she'd arrived there.

I'd never been more ready to carry out a mission in my life.

My girl was in there, and it was all my fucking fault. I would never be able to take away this horrible experience from her, but I could make some cockroach and concrete soup out of the evil fucking scum who'd taken her. I considered it a good first step toward the path of redemption.

But that was just me.

Mikhail had already deployed his own surveillance team to assess the area. They'd been sent as soon as he'd realized Freya had left the Parisi territory, and they'd been on site in Naples for several hours by now. He'd sent three other teams to various locations around the region in an effort to confuse and disrupt anyone monitoring our activity. I had to admire Mikhail's ingenuity and attention to detail.

His surveillance team in Naples had already found a few of their lookouts in the area around the warehouse. If our operatives detected *any* movement on their part, they'd be dead before they could even think the word "snitch."

Finally, it was time to get into position.

Reaper and Butcher exited the copter first, doing HALO jumps with most of their sniper gear. They entered the water flawlessly a little way out from the coastline. The rest of their equipment was carefully hidden along their paths on land, coordinated by Parisi's contacts in Naples together with Mikhail's men already stationed nearby.

For as much as those two idiots messed around, their tactical, concealment, and especially marksmanship skills were among the best in the world, if not the best. In about a half hour they'd completed an entirely undetected amphibious insertion into the enemy territory. Both men were now essentially invisible hiding several hundred yards away on opposite sides of the abandoned warehouse.

No enemy had ever stood a chance once within the crosshairs of either man's telescopic sight. Today would be no different.

"Raider, this is Butcher, requesting fifteen Kilo confirmation, over."

"Butcher, this is Raider, affirmative fifteen Kilo, over."

The guards around the perimeter were killed one by one—all fifteen of them, as Raider had confirmed with both ground report and aerial surveillance. Outer perimeter shots were Butcher's particular specialty. I'd never seen another marksman drop successive targets so quickly while remaining invisible; it was exactly how he'd earned his moniker.

Reaper excelled in barricade shots, so he'd taken out the three men guarding the main room on the first floor, toward the center of the warehouse.

"Raider, this is Reaper, Kilo three, affirmative, over."

Reaper was usually the only one within confirmatory sight of his kills, so he gave us immediate affirmatory numbers.

"Smash, this is Raider, Alpha Foxtrot, over," Raider confirmed that phase A of our mission, or Alpha, was finished.

"Raider, this is Smash, Roger Alpha Foxtrot, over," I acknowledged that phase A was finished and that it would finally be my teams' turn next.

Hold on, Freya, baby, I'm coming for you...

"Smash, this is Raider, Bravo Oscar Mike in three, two, one, over."

Once Raider had confirmation that the rest of the fireteam was in position, he gave countdown for me to launch phase B of the operation.

His last "over" wasn't audible; it was just a formality at this point.

I fired my M320 grenade launcher toward the concrete wall on the northeastern side of the building. I knew it was the only area without any occupancy. It also wouldn't take out too much structural support while giving us our own custom-built entrance.

Less than thirty seconds later, my assault team and I were Oscar Mike—On the Move—entering through the perfectly created opening along the side of the building.

Room by room we dropped every one of the worthless fucking bastards in a pile of their own blood, piss, and shit.

A few of the rooms contained women, anywhere from groups of one or two to ten. They sobbed and screamed hoarsely as the bodies of the men jerked and twitched as they absorbed the blows.

Their guards were all dead before they'd hit the filthy floor; they'd never touch those women again.

One fucker had actually tried to use one of the women as a shield.

I'd put two bullets in his head about a centimeter apart before he'd even been able to draw his gun.

I didn't miss, and neither did any of my men.

We were forced to ignore the woman's terrified screaming and sobbing as we went to the next room. The poor girl had immediately collapsed on the floor, crawling away from us in fearful confusion.

Every single terrified sound those girls made poured gasoline over my already burning inferno of bloodthirsty rage. These women shouldn't have to see any more violence, but it couldn't be helped, dammit. Instead of guilt, I let the anger peak, sharpening my mind into the lethal killing machine I was trained to be.

Those girls would all be safe very soon, every single damn one of them, but there wasn't any time to explain that to them now. My job right now was to eviscerate this enemy and get the girls to safety, even if it scared them in the process.

Hopefully, they'd just realize what we were there to do when we killed the men and simply moved onto the next room, leaving them alone.

When we'd gotten to the center of the building where their "office" likely was, I had to admire the unparalleled and lethal skill that Reaper possessed.

Barricade shots—in my opinion—were some of the hardest as the targets were usually moving in and out of things like windows, doors, or solid concrete walls. So much additional input needed accounted for that might change the trajectory of the shot and reduce accuracy, as well as expose the location of the sniper. Reaper made it look like it was easy, as usual, to take out the three guards.

They'd been guarding the actual bosses on the other side of the door.

Two of the three guards were slumped over in their chairs, drinks unfinished on the filthy card table between them.

A cavernous dark red hole was between each pair of glassy, sightless eyes. Perched precariously between one of the men's now useless fingers was a still-burning cigarette, smoke furling lazily from the reddish-white glow of ash at its tip.

The third guard, probably the last one killed, wasn't far behind the table with an equally devastating and perfectly executed chest wound. His body lay in a boneless heap on the disgusting floor.

Reaper had made easy work of the little fuckers with his sniper rifle as soon as Butcher had dropped all fifteen of the ones guarding the front gate. I was almost pissed at two of our best men, only because their deadly efficiency had given all those spineless bastards an undeservingly humane death.

When room after room didn't contain my own girl, my beautiful, perfect little lioness, I could feel the rage start to not just take the driver's seat but hijack the entire fucking vehicle. I breathed through it, focused on the task at hand until we'd cleared the last room and killed every single one of the scumbag cockroach fuckers.

Freya was not in any of the rooms.

I was starting to actively lose the very fragile hold on my sanity. My men knew it, too; I could feel their wariness just like I could feel the heat coming off the metal barrel of my Mk18.

Finally, we cleared the entire building and had circled back to one of the front rooms, where we knew the five ringleaders, the bosses, were hiding. They were the only ones worth leaving alive to interrogate.

Raider's team had scouted them pissing and shitting down their legs in fear as soon as Reaper had killed the three guards outside their little man cave. The group had scurried back inside their fort to hide, and only fled when they'd realized we'd killed everyone else.

Raider had monitored their location throughout our sweep. They'd started fleeing to the side of the building we'd entered from, but the five little spineless fuckers were now trapped.

My team and I were getting closer and closer to those men with every one of my pounding heartbeats.

She had to be there, with them—the men who weren't dead yet, the leaders—or she was hidden somewhere.

Those spineless sons of bitches running and hiding were going to give us information, lots of it. Starting with where in the motherfucking fuck is my girl, and would they prefer I feed them their own fingers or toes first?

We knew they'd run; these fuckers were too stupid to be anything but predictable. They also had to know they'd be pumped full of hot lead as soon as they tried to escape through the hole I'd made in the side of the building earlier.

My heart was pounded even harder as we turned into the room where they were hiding.

No Freya, no women, just five fucking scumbags and a hand grenade.

"NO! You stop! You stop or I blow us all up! You listen! We all die unless you—"

Two in his chest and one to the head stopped the pseudo threat.

The dummy grenade slipped out of his lifeless hand to hit the floor with an insultingly hollow *tink-tonk-tinkitty-tink*.

I mean for fuck's sake, it looked like plastic and didn't even have a spoon! I just bet these dumbass scumbags had used it as a scare tactic for the girls. Fucking amateur hour bullshit!

A half second later, my fireteam and I descended on the remaining four men like the hounds of hell, guns drawn. I fired a few rounds behind their heads to prove a point. One man even dropped the gun he was holding and started sobbing as he crumpled. Fucking moron was lucky it hadn't fired, and Red Bull quickly kicked it to the side and out of reach.

Then again, I wondered if it was a fake plastic toy just like the 'hand grenade' had been.

"HANDS UP! GET DOWN! GET THE FUCK DOWN!"

"GET THE FUCK ON THE FLOOR! GET THE FUCK DOWN!"

"GET YOUR FUCKING FACE IN THE DIRT! I SAID GET THE FUCK DOWN NOW! I'LL BLOW YOUR FUCK-ING HEAD OFF, GET THE FUCK DOWN!"

The worthless bastards all pissed themselves and starting pleading in whatever stupid fucking language they spoke as we gunned them down to the dirt where they belonged. Our headsets all had language translators, but who knew what kind of Serbian trash these idiots conversed in.

The translator had probably been robotically offended at the way they'd butchered their own language.

We'd strongly suspected on the helicopter ride here that this place was only a last-minute holding cell before they planned to take Freya to the next site. This group was nothing but an extremely low-level trafficking organization that simply abducted women and kept them in places like this, whoring them out until they died from the conditions.

Still, they had apparently been in contact with someone much higher up the food chain at some point, and that information is the third thing we came for. First being my girl, and a close second being all the remaining girls, of course.

Those poor things. No innocent human being deserved to be treated so savagely.

The fucking bastards here had kept the poor girls starving and practically dying of thirst. Most were too weak to even stand up, which helped prevent them from escape. Getting them addicted on drugs like some of the other traffickers and pimps was too expensive for these cheap-ass bastards.

My savage growl was echoed by the other four men behind and alongside me, and I knew they knew exactly what I was thinking.

For many people there was a fine line between good and evil. I did what I did, and so did my men, so that people could go on believing that those two worlds never intersected. They could continue living in ignorance and blissful peace while men like us eliminated that evil.

And we didn't do so like a white knight in shining armor, but I knew that most people needed to think that way in order to make some kind of rose-colored sense of the world they lived in.

But that wasn't reality. Sometimes we became even more evil than the enemy, always one step ahead and outsmarting them at every turn. Violence was met with violence, and we didn't stop until we'd won. I was trained to never give up, no matter the price—and so were the men right beside me.

I'd be lying if I said there wasn't a part of me that craved it, but I also truly believed that violence without purpose was nothing but a direct path toward evil.

When people said I was arrogant, they would be correct.

I was as fucking arrogant as they came, but I always made sure I could back it up.

I was going to kill every last one of these shitbags, and how long it took depended on how much murderous rage was still left inside me by the time I reached my Freya.

The way I felt right now, I could saw off pieces of them with a steak knife a little bit at a time for a fucking year and it still wouldn't be enough. If they'd done anything, *anything* at all to her, they'd pray for death for a fucking decade before I'd even consider sending their worthless fucking souls to fester and burn in hell.

We let them sob and beg for a few more seconds on the ground. Let their new realities sink in.

Red Bull stepped forward as planned, putting the barrel of his gun inside the largest man's mouth. He spoke to the man in what sounded like the same slithering version of Serbian. Something Red Bull told him must have been even more terrifying than the smoking-hot 11-inch barrel of his M27 RWK, because the man started to sob and shake uncontrollably. Red Bull leaned in even closer, laughing in Russian.

I don't know how it was possible to laugh in Russian, but apparently it absolutely was.

It was also fucking hilarious how the terrified little fucker on the ground sharted through his pants. Disgusting, but hilarious. These scumbags were all the same; they only preyed on those who were weaker.

Red Bull nodded to me and motioned me over. Damn, the fucking smell of these rank bastards!

"I'm going to ask you one time, and one time only. Where is the beautiful redhead female you took from me?"

Red Bull translated what I'd said. The man's eyes got even wider as he shook his head back and forth and went back to the worthless blubbering.

I got out my Ka-Bar and sliced through his Achille's tendon.

That seemed to spark his memory.

Red Bull moved the barrel out of his mouth just enough so the man could reply. He glared down at him for a few seconds after he spoke. He surprised me by raging a short reply back to the man, and then shoving the barrel deeper between his lips. Murderous intent was all over his face.

Then, Red Bull turned and spoke to the other men who started sobbing and sharting.

For fuck's sakes, between the sulfuric acid smells of the old steel mill and these disgusting cockroach bastards, we were all going to smell like a damn sewer for a week!

Red Bull turned to me and translated the exchange right as Marco, aka Diavolo, came around the corner, also dressed in his own combat gear.

When the Sicilian mafia king spoke to them in what sounded like Serbian, I wasn't very surprised. The man knew at least five languages, that I knew of.

Apparently what he'd said was worse than what Red Bull had just told them, because they sobbed and blubbered even more.

"Smash, she's here. They weren't allowed to touch her, only secure her. They also specifically weren't allowed to... disrobe her," Diavolo's voice had the menacingly flat quality of a killer.

One of the cockroaches started sobbing and mumbling some kind of Serbian bullshit. It made Red Bull and Diavolo snap their heads over to him, share an extremely brief, homicidal look, then chuckle darkly as both their eyes met mine.

They gave me a brief translation, and I let out a maniacal bark of laughter.

This fucker had just offered to give us a *portion* of the bounty for my own future wife's *sale*.

He actually thought we'd let any of them live!

Now that shit was just about the funniest thing I'd heard all fucking day. I almost had to wipe the fake fucking tears from my eyes from my humorless barks of laughter, but instead I just started firing rounds into the man that had dared to speak, killing him instantly.

My team finished the rest of them off in a matter of seconds. We had all we'd ever need in their communications equipment anyway. There was no way these stupid imbeciles could give us any more information by being alive. They had all just been a decoy, a way to hide Freya in plain sight.

Besides, the words "she's here" were on replay in my head. The only thing I cared about after hearing that was finding her then holding her so tight that neither of us would be able to breathe.

Once they were all dead, I turned to my team.

"FIND HER! NOW!"

Like they needed to be told, but I was beyond control at that point.

"Raider, this is Smash, requesting status update, over."

I hadn't even gotten the call out on my radio when I saw a flash of messy, dark auburn waves dart from a pile of crates, boxes, and tarps.

"FREYA!" I didn't recognize the ear-splitting agony that was my voice.

In mere seconds I followed her out through the opening and was quickly closing the distance between us. Something dark and sinister snapped inside me when I realized she was running. She was *running away from me.*

I'd wanted to be gentle.

I knew she'd be fucking terrified, dehydrated, weak. There was nothing weak about the way she was running from me right now, but it didn't matter. I was stronger and faster and overtook her in a handful of strides.

I didn't realize I'd been screaming her name until I was close enough to finally touch her. She immediately started fighting my arms that wrapped around her. It didn't stop me from picking her up off the ground, holding her tight and rolling her on top of me as we both fell. Once we'd stopped moving, I had my arms wrapped around her tight enough to crack a rib, but I couldn't stop.

I let her hit me, only keeping a grip on her enough so that she couldn't get up and run. When I felt a particularly sharp blow to the side of my face, I snatched her wrists up immediately—there was no way I was going to let her break a wrist from punching my dumbass jaw.

But it felt good to let her beat up on me.

It felt even better to have her in my arms.

And for the first time in a very long time, I felt the hot sting of a handful of tears from my own eyes.

All I could do in that moment was hold her. The more she tried to get away, the tighter I held on. Eventually she gave in, sobbing quietly into my arms and letting me hold her. I knew in that moment that I was not only the luckiest damn man alive, but that I was never, ever, *ever* letting this beautiful woman out of my grasp.

Chapter 43

Freya

I woke up in the same bed I'd been sleeping in since we'd arrived in Sicily.

For a second I thought the whole thing might have been a dream, some kind of horrible nightmare, but the bandage on the back of my hand from where I'd been given yet another IV told me otherwise.

I had no idea how long I'd been asleep. The only light outside was that of the moon glowing faintly through the surface of the pool water through the patio doors. The quiet stillness of the moment suggested it was the middle of the night.

A warm, heavy weight shifted right behind me. I tried to sit up in bed, but before I knew it a very solid python-like rope had wrapped around me tightly from behind, completely preventing my escape. With its presence around my waist came a delicious and enticingly masculine, clean sandalwood scent that was now officially my favorite smell in the entire world.

"Don't. Even. *Think*. About it, baby. You aren't going anywhere. Ever. Not without me by your side, and I don't care if I have to handcuff us together."

Brodie's voice sounded even growlier and grumpier than usual, but I'd be lying if I said I didn't immediately melt back into the comforting weight of his body wrapped around mine. After what I'd been through, it felt so good to feel surrounded by his heat and larger than life strength.

I didn't really remember much of what happened after Brodie had intercepted me. It was probably only a few seconds after I'd leapt through the dusty hole in the concrete wall of the warehouse.

I'd never been more terrified in my life. I wouldn't have been able to keep myself from fighting him like a cornered wild animal, even if I'd known the whole time that they were coming to save me, that they were on my side.

The enormity of what they'd all done for me still got me pretty freaking choked up.

He'd let me hit him. He hadn't even tried to deflect any of the blows, that is, not until I'd contacted a particularly hard area of his chest plate.

Now that I thought about it, maybe it had just been one of his shoulder or bicep muscles. They'd both felt equally as hard as I'd pounded on him crazily, still lost within my own terror.

Even then, he'd only grabbed my hand tightly and brought it to his lips. By that point, his grip around me had become almost too tight for me to breathe, especially since I was still panting and gasping for air.

When his shoulders shook violently once, twice, three times, and I felt hot wetness on the inside of my wrist, I realized it was a tear. I let him hold me like that, his grip around me almost painful.

He seemed... terrified.

I'd felt it in the way he'd shuddered as he'd held me, and then like a flash, it was gone.

That's when I knew without a shadow of a doubt, that I'd almost made a *really* dumb mistake that could have cost me my life.

I'd been so quick to assume the worst that I'd inadvertently put myself in the direct path of evil. But to be fair, it had sounded really, really effing bad at the time.

When I'd seen the rest of the men, the entire crew of soldiers that had come to my rescue immediately, I had never felt more humbled in my entire life. They'd done it without question or complaint, like it was simply the right thing to do.

They had quite literally saved me and saved the lives of all the other women there. They'd also *literally* jumped out of a freaking helicopter, guns drawn and running toward the danger.

I actually had no idea if that's how it happened, but when I'd gotten the very brief summary earlier, that's exactly what it'd looked like inside my head. The jumping out of the helicopter part was something I was still trying to wrap my brain around. They talked about it like it was just another day in the office. *They'd said it was a 'boring' mission.*

I loved all of those men in that moment, even if they were all apparently more than a little nuts.

I'd never been inside a helicopter before, let alone jump from one in mid-air. I shivered again at the mere thought.

The ride back was so loud, and I was so exhausted. I felt like I'd closed my eyes for only a second and then we'd immediately landed in Sicily.

Brodie had taken me straight into the shower with him, both of us clothed and standing under the warm water. Well, I'd still had on the black swimsuit I'd been wearing for almost two days—*uggh!*—underneath the new clothes they'd so kindly brought for me to wear back home.

I cuddled into him a little tighter in bed as I remembered how absolutely gentle he'd been with me in the shower earlier. He'd taken off my clothes and his own shirt, but he kept my swimsuit and his own pants on.

He'd washed my hair. I'd taken the sponge and washed his back and shoulders while we held each other. We hadn't needed any words, just needed the grounding comfort of each other in that moment. It was so easy to be around him; it was like coming home.

After he'd rinsed my hair, I could tell he didn't know if he should remove my swimsuit or not.

It was when I noticed his wariness and hesitation that I realized I was absolutely and completely in love with Brodie Magnuson. I put my lips on his chest, kissing him under the spray of the water as I went to remove his pants.

"Freya, baby, are you sure you're okay if... if we're both naked right now?"

"How else are we going to get clean?"

He must have heard the smile in my voice because his entire body sagged with relief. He reached for the strap on my suit, then pulled his hand back. I frowned at him, confused.

"Maybe... maybe you should take it off?"

My heart melted even more for this arrogant, stubborn, selfless, and compassionate man mountain.

"But you do it so much better," I really couldn't keep the smile from my voice as I leaned into him and slid his pants further down, revealing more of his sexy as hell, massive hip muscles.

"Freya, if you keep that up, I'm going to be hard as a rock, and—"

"So you're saying I should keep it ... *up*?"

I knew it was probably wrong to be teasing him, but I couldn't help it.

I was here and with him, and we were both safe. All of those girls—every single one of them—were now safe, too. I figured I had every reason to smile.

When his deep, rough chuckle washed over me I felt like purring. His beautiful emerald green eyes had burned into mine as he slowly removed first one strap, and then the other. Still gazing intently at me, he'd pulled down the rest of the suit until it landed in a wet plop on the tiled shower floor.

I'd never shared such a moment of intimacy without actually having sex.

He had kissed my shoulder and neck, gently teasing me with his teeth. It sent delicious electric chills down my spine in spite of the steaming hot spray around us.

I had leaned into him, taking the pulsing, thick length of him and washing it in unhurried, back-and-forth strokes. By the time we'd finished washing each other and I'd rinsed the conditioner from my hair, I felt a little hot and bothered and a lot breathless.

Unfortunately, exhaustion had quickly overtaken me. In about five minutes I had applied lotion and combed out my wet hair, then covertly slipped into Brodie's slash my favorite *Texans* tee shirt. It was huge and perfectly worn, and somehow always smelled like him. Amazing.

It wasn't even a solid minute after my head hit the pillow that I'd fallen asleep in this exact same spot.

I vaguely remembered bits and pieces of Dr. Briggs and a few nurses coming into the room to take some more samples and administer another IV. I'd definitely slept through most of it, way too exhausted to fully wake up.

The one thing I did remember was Brodie's furious growl when Dr. Briggs and her team had discovered that it was the sunscreen from Russian Kathy that had drugged me so heavily, I'd passed out for almost twelve hours. I was actually pretty thankful for that in hindsight, I'd mused sleepily. The less I remembered, the less I'd need therapy for, so there was that.

The last thought I'd had before I'd fallen back asleep was that I was getting really mother-effing tired of being tired from being freaking drugged. Dammit.

I was still pretty tired, I realized as I curled up into Brodie a little more. He cuddled me back, bringing me in even closer and smelling my hair. I could feel his erection pushing up into the curve of my ass. I arched my back into him in blatant invitation.

I needed him to completely overwhelm me in that moment like he always had.

I needed him to push me to the edge of my sanity and then send me flying over that endless wave of pleasure.

He responded immediately, tightening his arms around me even more and kissing the sensitive skin along my neck. I moaned into him and pressed up against his solid and formidable heat, already at fever pitch.

"Baby, are you sure? I want you so fucking bad, Freya. But I'm not going to push you."

"Brodie, please. I want you to... take control, I... I like it. It makes me feel so safe when you hold me like that," my voice was breathless, my entire body flushed with desire.

He groaned into my neck, grabbing my hips and shoving them back against his. I loved the feel of his hands on me, his grip so rough and strong. I whimpered when I felt the scrape of his beard against my skin, followed by the sweetly stinging bite of his teeth.

"Do you like that, baby?"

"Hell, yes; that feels so good. Please, Brodie, I need..." my voice trailed off.

"Mmmm, yes, baby. What do you need?"

His words rumbled over the goosebumps along my collarbone and awakened every single nerve ending between there and the center of my thighs.

"I need... I need you to fuck me, Brodie. Now. I—I want to forget. Forget about everything," my voice cracked.

I could feel his sudden tension behind me as the solid wall of him became even more rigid. Then like a wave crashing over us both, I felt the tension leave his body as again he snuggled me even closer.

"Listen to me, Freya. You're fucking amazing, do you know that? You didn't do a damn thing wrong, and I don't care what you think about it. I'm sorry, but I don't. You are the bravest chick I know. Fearless, and you're strong as hell," he chuckled softly behind me and kissed my neck again. Tears fell as he kept talking. "And if it makes you feel better, you didn't actually kill that skinny, slimy looking fucker on the second floor. Although your methods were extremely effective. You were able to escape safely from him, and that's all that matters."

"How... how did you know about that?"

Despite my tears—again, I mean seriously I was *so* sick of crying already—I felt so safe with his solid heat surrounding me.

"Red Bu—I mean, Mikhail. He uh, took care of him. He's gone, baby. They're all gone, forever. Dust in the wind," he kept kissing me, his lips brushing over my shoulder and back down my neck.

"I wanted him dead."

He tensed for a second, then chuckled softly.

"I'm sure you did, baby. I would have, too."

"That's a horrible thing for me to think, but it's true. I wanted him dead. He'd been teasing the girls. They'd looked... it was awful. I couldn't do anything to help them. I'd been so mad, so fucking mad!"

I could feel my heart pounding and this time it wasn't from the pleasure. It was an adrenaline water slide, and not the enjoyable kind. It was the kind that dropped straight down and gave you a medical grade swimsuit wedgie.

Brodie literally shook me out of it. Gently, of course.

"Stop, Freya. It's done. He's gone, and there's nothing that's going to bring him back. He was evil, Freya, and I don't care what anyone says. There are some people in this world who are so damned evil," he took a calming breath as he squeezed me a little tighter. He went on very quietly, almost resolutely, "there really ain't nothin' left human inside them. Been that way since the dawn of time. Don't make it more than it is."

I was quiet for a little while, thinking of what he said. It was also cute as hell when his faint Texas accent came out with the occasional *ain't* and *y'all*.

That had never been something I'd believed before; I truly felt that all lives were equal and worth saving. I'd never believe that same thing again, because now I knew better, I had lived it.

Brodie was right.

There were some people whose souls had been stripped of anything good, anything human whatsoever. That's how it had felt to look into those men's eyes. Just... nothing. Emptiness. Hopeless disconnection to my own humanity.

I'd learned about sociopaths and psychopaths, gotten a bachelor's degree over all of that. An expensive degree, I might add.

There was nothing, absolutely nothing, that compared to being at the mercy of those kind of people. In the short time I'd been in such a situation—especially compared to those other women, I thought with a horrible shudder—I knew I never wanted to be in that state of mind ever again.

It was as if my own sense of humanity had literally whispered into my ear, *Nope, no human souls here. Go 'head, girl. Fire at will!*

But he was right about something else, too. I hadn't asked to be taken away or put in that situation. Neither had any of those girls, dammit.

He sighed as he pulled me in close again. His hands roamed up and down along my waist, hip, and thigh.

"You want to know what I think?" His tone was thoughtful.

"Yes, of course I do."

"I think I died a thousand deaths in the time it took for us to get to you. I think I could have killed every single one of them with my bare hands if they'd... done anything to you, Freya. I'm sorry,

I'm so sorry. I swear on my own life, Freya, nothing like that is ever going to happen to you again, baby. They'll have to kill me first. And I don't know if you've noticed, but I'm a pretty *hard* motherfucker to kill," he grunted softly as he paused on a particular word, and I pressed my hips back up against him, laughing quietly.

"No, Brodie. I'm sorry, too. I overheard you talking, and I was completely thrown. I lost it. I didn't know what to think, so I thought the worst," I sighed, embarrassed all over again for all the issues and unnecessary, ahem, excitement that I'd caused.

"Freya, I never want to hear you apologize for what happened ever again. Is that clear? None of it, at any point whatsoever, was your fucking fault."

I cowered just a little at the rough edge to his voice, but it was also weirdly reassuring that he felt so adamant about it. It was hard to doubt his sincerity when he put it that way and in that tone of voice. Absentmindedly I praised myself for not overreacting to the anger in his voice after what I'd just been through. Besides, I truly didn't feel that his anger was directed at me.

Then it hit me like a brick.

I hadn't overreacted because I understood, very truly understood now, how consuming and debilitating fear could become. I didn't care what anyone said, my anger is what had kept me somewhat sane during that situation. It had kept me far enough away from my paralyzing fear to give me strength when I'd had literally nothing else.

But what happened when the ultimate protector, the man unafraid of anything and stronger than everything, became afraid? Who would protect him when the inevitable human emotion of fear made its way past the unpassable?

The anger. The anger would pull him out of it.

This man that could literally explode with rage also had enough courage to not only run toward bullets and unimaginable danger, but consciously owned his behavior while he tried to do the right thing. I wondered if he embraced the rage in order to do things that would terrify and appall most people, all in order to protect others.

And every time, he had always found his way back from that anger.

That, more than anything, spoke to the strength of his soul, of his character.

That truly phenomenal show of strength—both physical and mental—had somehow cemented me to him almost instantly. He was truly so powerful that he could dance along the edge of evil, fight with it, conquer it, and destroy it, and then return to me with his arms open and ready to wrap around me.

Not even seconds after conquering that evil, this man had made the trip back to humanity and shown me the power of his strength through his vulnerable tears, even if it was only a handful of them.

I didn't need any more time to know how I felt. I knew there was no other man like this one, and I loved every single grumpy, growly inch of him.

I turned around to face him, immediately getting lost in his eyes.

"Will you have sex with me yet?"

I burst out laughing at the look on his face when I'd asked him point blank.

My heart felt lighter than it had in a very long time.

"Freya, baby, I... I don't know if you're ready for that yet. Not if you still feel like you need to forget about—"

"What about if I love you, and I want to be in this moment with you now, and not anywhere else?"

My heart started pounding a little as soon as I said it, but I didn't have time to be self-conscious. He pounced on me.

Chapter 44

Brodie

I pounced on her.

I hadn't realized how fucking much I'd needed to hear those words from her lips. My world pivoted, putting her at the complete center like the last piece of the puzzle finally falling into its rightful place.

The strongest surge of desire I'd ever known hit me like a tsunami. It was completely unleashed and wild lust, but not just for her body. I wanted her, all of her, every way, and right the fuck *now*.

In one motion I had yanked my favorite *Texans* shirt off of her, baring that beautiful body to my hungry gaze. She'd leaned into me, smiling and pulling her bottom lip between her teeth.

I couldn't get enough of her mouth, her skin, her curves. My hands roamed over her everywhere, enjoying every single moan and whimper from her lips. She kissed me back, pulling my tongue into her mouth and sucking on it. I dueled with her lips, capturing them between my teeth and gently pulling.

"Tell me again, baby. Tell me you love me, Freya," I was a man possessed.

"I love you, Brodie. I—" I couldn't even let her finish without descending back on her mouth.

I held her to me, kissing every inch of her neck and along her shoulder. Wrapping my arms around her and sitting us both up, I straddled her across my lap, facing me.

"You are so fucking beautiful, baby. You make me crazy," I growled against her neck before I reached up to hold one of her perfect tits.

I put my mouth on the other one, sucking on her gently. I loved the sounds she made when I teased her breasts. She was so damned responsive, so sensual.

She gasped, and then giggled. It was the sexiest sound I'd ever heard in my life until I heard the way she moaned when I circled her pebbled nipple with my tongue. She rocked her hips into me as I growled, moving my arms back around her. In a quick movement that had her squealing with surprise, I shifted to pin her underneath me.

I knew the way I was smiling down at her like a starving man was probably scaring her, but I couldn't help it. I wanted to devour her just like I always did whenever she was near. I looked right into her dark blue eyes as I grabbed her thighs and spread them wide. I loved the sound she made when she arched her back and rolled her hips up to me with blatant invitation.

"You have the prettiest pussy, baby. It's so fucking sexy when you spread your legs for me like that. Do you want me to play with your pussy, baby?"

"Oh my—yes, please!"

I used my thumbs to spread her cute pussy lips wide open. Her clit was so swollen it was already peeking out boldly, begging to be sucked on and teased. As I spread her even wider, her arousal glistened from her very center. My balls clenched painfully when I saw her cute little holes clench and flutter nervously. I used one thumb to tease the entrance to her pussy.

"Damn, baby. Keep those fucking legs spread and let me play with you."

I was having a hard time keeping the savage edge out of my voice, but being with her like this was like a drug. I'd never get enough of her.

Her breathy moan was like a whip of hot need across my brain. But the way she boldly rolled her hips up, legs spread wide for my eyes to see her most intimate and private places—fuck if it wasn't the hottest thing I'd ever seen in my life. I was so consumed by the need to possess her, make her scream and writhe in pleasure.

With one of my thumbs, I slowly moved in and out of her pussy, pausing every few thrusts to swirl the slickness of her arousal all over her center. She was absolutely drenched, her entire pussy was swollen with her desire. But it was the puffy little bundle of nerves at the top of her pussy that I especially wanted to play with.

I used the same thumb to drag her moisture up towards her clit, circling it and making it shine with her cum.

"Baby, fuck yes! Clench those holes for me, I love it when you do that. Do you like how it feels when I tease you like this?"

I tried to keep the beast out of my voice, but it was absolutely impossible, especially when her asshole and pussy were fluttering right in front of my face.

I moaned as a fresh wave of cum dripped from her pussy slowly, all the way down over her asshole. My balls were already drawn up so tightly against my body that it was almost painful. I couldn't look away, I could barely even breathe.

I used my other thumb to spread her arousal over her cute little pucker, chuckling darkly at the way she squealed in shocked surprise when I stuck my thumb inside to the first knuckle. She immediately tried to close her legs, but I held her open easily.

"Naughty girl, Freya. I said keep your legs spread so I can play with you. I want to play with your asshole and your pussy at the same time. I want to watch you lose control like this, baby."

"Oh my... umm, well I—oh, fuck! *Yes!*"

I kept fucking her ass with my thumb, almost passing out every time I felt the tight ring of her muscle close tautly. With my other thumb, I rubbed her clit in little circles and jiggled it back and forth, dipping into her soaking wet pussy to keep it slick.

"Your pussy is so wet, baby. I could watch you drip for me all day," I looked up at her face as I stroked her. "I'm going to play with your clit like this, with your pussy lips spread wide and dripping for me. I'm going to make you feel so good, Freya."

I felt precum oozing over the tip of my cock when her eyes met mine, heavy-lidded and dazed with her desire. They were the prettiest shade of indigo blue I'd ever seen when she was wild for me like this.

I rubbed her in bold circles as I watched her squirm, almost passing out every time her asshole clenched down around the tip of my thumb. When I continued to spread the slickness of her own cum back and forth across the sensitive bundle of nerves at the very top of her pussy, the sounds she made were desperate and primal. I felt every single one up and down the length of my cock.

I would never get enough of being with her like this. It was like a drug when she let me watch, when she didn't hide anything from me while she burned within the force of her desire. With her beautiful cunt spread wide for me and the rest of her on full display, I could feel every tremble and shiver of her body. I could see exactly where and how she liked to be touched.

Her cute little clit was so swollen and had turned the same dark pink as her nipples. She was so fucking beautiful everywhere that I didn't know where to look. The way her mouth curved in a smile right before she bit her lip, the way her hips rolled continuously toward me, the way her breasts bounced and jiggled with every shaky little moan. The dark copper of her hair was swept over one of her shoulders. Her cheeks were flushed a light pink, her lips swollen from sometimes hiding behind her teeth.

Even the faint stretch marks along her upper thighs made me want to growl with sexual, possessive need. They were exactly where I loved to grab onto her hips and squeeze, holding her still for my mouth or for my cock. I couldn't look at them without immediately needing to feel the firm softness of her hips under my hands. Every inch of her body screamed *female* just about as loud as it screamed *fuck me.*

My own body was growling *mine* and *fuck, yes* in response.

"Play with your tits, baby. I want to watch you tease your pretty nipples while I rub your soaking wet pussy and play with your ass."

"Ohhhh...!"

Her throaty moan made my dick throb so painfully that I felt like I was about to come with each of my own pounding heartbeats.

I lifted her hips up and pushed her back a little more against the pillows. I wanted to see every single inch of her, look into her eyes and watch the pleasure overtake her, and then glance down to feast my own eyes between her thighs while she shook with need.

She reached one hand shyly up to one of her breasts, barely cupping its weight. She let her head fall back, eyes closed, her mouth open in that adorable little "o" that always made me want to put my dick inside it.

"Roll your nipples around between your fingers, baby. Tease your nipples, I want to watch you make yourself feel good, baby."

I groaned when I felt a rush of wetness come dripping out of her swollen folds. This woman was absolute perfection, everything she did was hotter than fuck and made me feel seconds away from blowing my load.

She obeyed me almost instantly, the sexy and carefree smile on her face would have tempted a saint. I watched like a starving man as she played with her pretty, swollen pink nipples. It was so fucking sexy how much they poked out when she was really aroused.

My own arousal was quickly overtaking my consciousness; I had to taste her. Using my two fingers to spread her wide, I descended onto the needy little bundle of nerves. I sucked on her clit, rubbing my tongue back and forth across it. Soon it was so puffy that I didn't need to spread her pussy lips to suck on it.

I used two fingers to tease her pussy instead, quickly finding the swollen ridge of her G-spot. I kept teasing her asshole with my thumb, letting her own dripping wet arousal serve as lube. I couldn't wait to feel that taught little ring of muscle pulse frantically around my knuckle when she screamed her release, but my control was slipping.

I knew she was seconds away from orgasm when she whimpered loudly and arched up into my mouth. I flattened my tongue against her, rubbing up and down firmly.

"Fuck, Freya, you taste so good. Do you like it right there? Does that feel good, baby?" My mouth was so close to her that my lips brushed against her pussy lips when I spoke.

"Fuck, yes, please don't stop! That feels so good, Brodie!"

Her pussy was practically gushing under my mouth. I could feel it dripping around my chin. My balls clenched hungrily as I remembered how it felt when she came screaming while she bounced up and down on my cock. For a split second I was torn between making her come all over my mouth like this while I watched her play with her nipples, or pulling her back on top of me and feeling her wetness pour out of her pussy to drip all over my balls.

I smiled. Of course I'd make her come both ways, and then some.

"Keep playing with your tits, baby. I'm going to watch you come all over my mouth with your tits out."

"It feels... it feels better when you do it," she pouted sexily, and it was so damn cute it made my dick throb.

I changed position instantly so I could touch her exactly how she liked. It was sexy as fuck to hear how much she wanted my touch.

"Fuck yes, baby. I'll always give you what you want. You like it when I play with your nipples, Freya?" I was already reaching up to hold her amazing breasts.

"Yes, I love when you play with me like that! It feels so good... yes, fuck yes!"

I gently tugged on each one of her nipples while I pulled her pulsing clit further into my mouth, holding it between my lips. I flicked my tongue back and forth across it in a frantic rhythm at the same time I tugged gently on her pebbled nipples. I could feel her entire core clenching tightly, her orgasm getting closer and closer.

When her orgasm consumed her, I forced her body down tightly against the mattress and pillows as I made her ride out every single spike of pleasure. Wetness gushed from her wide-open pussy and I licked up every drop as I kept teasing her nipples, enjoying her soft screams of pleasure.

"Fuck yes, baby; I love when you come all over my mouth like that," I could still feel her pussy fluttering with satiated aftershocks.

I licked the sensitive skin between her upper thigh and her pussy, loving the way she squealed with pleasure. Her sex-drenched giggling was making my temperature rise so quickly I was already feeling a fine layer of sweat forming on my skin.

She was still smiling softly and whimpering as the last bits of her pleasure faded. As gently as I could, I twisted and shifted us again.

This time, I was going to lie back on the bed while she rode my face.

My dick throbbed painfully when she didn't even protest and started rolling her hips into my mouth.

She brought herself to another orgasm within a few minutes.

I'd never seen anything more beautiful than when I looked up at her bouncing breasts and gorgeous face twisted in tortured pleasure, with her legs spread in front of my mouth. Before the second orgasm faded, I reached up to roll her nipples around and around as I sucked down mercilessly on her puffy clit, drawing out a third orgasm from her almost instantly.

That time, I felt a wet rush drip down the sides of my jaw and along my neck. I growled into her pussy, shaking my head back and forth and lapping up every drop. Precum dripped from the tip of my dick in painful protest, but I couldn't stop.

Growling like a savage, I grabbed her around the waist as I switched us around again, this time laying her back on the pillows.

An emotion so powerful that I knew I'd never felt it before in my life grabbed all the air from my lungs as I gazed down at her.

I couldn't breathe from how absolutely fucking beautiful she was. Suddenly I knew if I didn't get my dick inside her, now, I wasn't going to make it.

I captured her lips again as I roughly shoved her thighs apart. I shoved my tongue into her mouth at the same time that I plunged every throbbing inch of my cock into her softness. When her entire wet, hot sheath clenched around me frantically, I felt sweat drip down from my neck to land right between her breasts. She moaned into my mouth, completely surrendering to the ferocity of my possession.

I pumped into her with a crazy and unyielding rhythm, driven almost to the brink of madness by the feeling of her little claws scraping lightly across my back.

Her pussy was so wet and I was fucking her so hard that there were obscenely wet, sloppy sounds coming from our joined bodies. They were mixed in between the other primal sounds we were making. I swallowed every gasp and moan and tried not to pass out from the feeling of her hips tilting and rising to meet every one of my thrusts.

"Oh, my god, Brodie! Yes! Oh, fuck, please keep doing that! Please, it feels so good Brodie, *ohhhh—uhhhh!*"

The force of her orgasm gripped every single inch of my cock inside her as her pussy clamped down.

I felt her claws scrape across my back. The sharp sting combined with the choke hold of her pussy on my cock sent me instantly into a powerful, mind-altering orgasm. The pleasure was so intense, my connection to her so fucking strong, so consuming.

My cum shot up into her pussy in hot spurts as absolute fucking bliss washed over me. I felt my balls tingling in almost unbearable pleasure with every single spasm as I held her. I kept pumping into her like a mad man, wanting to shove my cum as far into her pussy as it would go.

I would never fucking admit this out loud, but I was pretty sure I passed out from it for at least half a second. All the blood had been sequestered within my dick and my balls, so it was understandable that my brain was feeling neglected.

Afterward, I gently pulled out my still semi-hard cock—seriously, the fucker was trying to kill me at this rate—as I kissed her cheeks and down along her neck and collarbone. I wanted to hold her in my arms, tightly, when I told her what I was going to tell her.

"Freya, I love you, too. I know I haven't known you very long and that I probably drive you crazy sometimes, but I know all I'll ever need to know," I pulled her in closer, my world pivoting again as she giggled sexily at my admission.

There was something else I needed to take care of for her.

"Freya, baby. Will you please tell me what you heard? I am sure you have questions about... everything."

"I only heard about the trust fund and that you were going to send someone a picture in a bathing suit. Mikhail and Peter were yelling in Russian. Peter sounded furious. I got pretty upset after that, so I didn't really hear anything else. I think I sat there for about twenty minutes, but I honestly couldn't tell you what was said after that."

I gave her the summary of what Mikhail had told me earlier, being as gentle as I knew how while still telling her everything. I answered all of her questions as calmly as I could.

Afterward I held her while she briefly cried. I felt fucking helpless as I kissed the top of her hair.

I didn't *do* helpless, but it didn't matter. She needed me, and I'd get over it.

"So... what happens now? I mean, is it over? Can I go back to New York, back to my job?"

I sighed. I didn't want to talk about this part right now at all, but I'd never lie to her.

"No. Not yet. Unfortunately, that was just a sort of holding place, and we have yet to snag the bigger fish. However," I pulled her in even closer as I kept talking, "it's only a matter of time before we start making more connections. Now, we have communication devices from multiple people who were in direct contact with at least one buyer or distributor. Everything is heavily encrypted, and it's going to take some time, but we just made about two or three-months' progress in less than twelve hours. Although, there's no way in hell I'd ever fucking do it that way again."

I was practically growling by the time I'd finished talking. I took a deep breath, letting it out quietly as I held her tight. It was over, and she was safe.

I calmed quickly with her so close.

"And will we still be... dating... after the case is closed?"

I immediately hated the doubt that had crept into her voice. I tightened my arms around her a little more, knowing what I said next was probably going to piss her off. A lot.

I was already looking forward to the make-up sex.

"I was thinking something more serious," I said, trying to keep the joking tone out of my voice.

I felt her tense in my arms, suddenly aware and suspicious. She probably should be. I was acting like a control freak alpha male psycho, but I also didn't care after what we'd both just been through.

"What do you mean, something more serious? That sounds pretty vague."

Making an immediate judgement call based on the tone of her voice as well as the sudden tensing in her body, I altered the battle plan.

I wrapped my arms even tighter around her as I shifted her neck right to my lips. I licked her there, loving the sweetness of her skin, right before I lightly scraped her skin with my teeth. When her body had relaxed a little more, I started delivering the news.

"Freya, I love you. And I cannot tell you how fucking happy it makes me to hear you say you love me, too," I kept teasing her neck with tiny nips and light kisses.

She relaxed a little more. I took a little bit of a deep breath and blew it out along her neck at the same time I wrapped her up even tighter in my embrace.

"And when I say 'serious' I mean I'm not joking, and I promise I will explain and answer every question you have—" I felt her tense again but I was prepared, tightening my grip around her instantly.

I was never, ever, ever going to let this woman go. She might as well be informed of just how much she was, in fact, *mine*.

"Brodie, spit it out already! You're not making any sense," I heard the obvious wariness in her voice.

She'd find out in the next few hours, anyway. That is, as soon as she checked a particular social media account and saw her relationship status had been changed to *Engaged to Brodie Magnuson*.

But I wanted her to hear it from me first.

The danger was still out there, although we had made substantial progress in the last day. It would be some time yet before I could even consider lowering the current security protocol. I knew her well enough now to know she hated being kept in the dark, but especially after what happened I had a million other reasons for my decision.

Danger or not, there was not a life I could imagine for myself without her in it.

I would protect her from anything, and I think she knew that now, too.

"Freya, I don't know how to say this so I'm just going to say it. You and I are getting married. I filed paperwork before we knew you'd been taken. It was about an hour after we all discovered the danger associated with your birth name. I was planning on asking you at dinner that night, but obviously never got the chance."

"Are you out of your mind?!"

"No. Actually, what happened only confirmed what I already knew. Baby, I'm never fucking letting you go," I held her even tighter.

"Do I get a say in any of this?"

"Of course you do. I'm not a total monster."

"Okay, then I don't want to be engaged yet."

"That's unfortunate, because we already are."

Her teasing little pretend horrified outburst at my high-handedness would have been cuter if I weren't in such uncharted territory.

"I don't even get a romantic proposal?! That's like every girl's dream!"

"You can have any kind of proposal you want, as long as your answer is yes."

"That's kind of not the same thing, Brodie! You're supposed to actually ask!"

It was hard to take her complaining seriously when it was accompanied by such girly little giggles.

"You know, I'll admit; asking isn't something I'm great at. I prefer telling."

"I've noticed a time or two, now that you mention it."

I laughed at her good-natured and quick-witted sense of humor.

I never knew what was going to come out of her mouth next, but I loved how she always kept me on my toes with her playful banter. There wasn't anything I didn't love about this woman. Gently I cradled her face in my hand as I ran my other hand through her pretty hair.

I could look in this woman's eyes forever. Especially naked and in my arms, as she was right now.

What more could a man want?

"Freya, will you marry me? I promise we can have any kind of big fancy wedding you want. I'll buy you a diamond ring for every finger if you want it. I just need you. I can't be without you, and I'm not the kind of man who doesn't know what he wants. I want you, Freya. Forever. Especially now, it's too dangerous if your birth name gets leaked to the wrong people."

"So, you're proposing in relation to the job?"

"Absolutely not. It just happens to be a convenient excuse for what I've wanted since I first saw you."

"And what was that?"

I growled softly before I captured her lips in mine. We were both breathless after a few seconds.

"*That,*" I pulled her even closer next to me, "is only the beginning of what I want, Freya, and I want it every day for the rest of my life. All day long, baby," I kept kissing her because it drowned out the tiny little speck of fear I had that she might not actually say yes.

I mean, not that she really did have a choice, but still. Uncharted territory had always made me wary.

"I thought you said you were asking? It sort of still feels like I don't have a choice," the blissful smile on her face gave me a feeling I'd already won this battle.

But just to be sure...

"I am asking. Besides, I know you can't resist me. I saw you checking me out when I was twerking. These hips don't lie, baby," I gave her my corniest wink and kissy noises as I pressed my hips into her softness.

It worked. She burst into another fit of the squeaky little giggles.

"You're crazy!"

"What if I said please?"

Her giggles stopped quietly, but I could still feel the teasing laughter in her voice when she replied, "Well, I suppose since you're asking nicely..."

In a flash, I rolled her under me and kissed her. I smothered her squeals of laughter with my lips on hers.

"But I have a few terms of my own."

Her pretend stern voice was cuter than it had any right to be.

"Hmmm. I'll consider, but I'm not making promises."

"Can we go on a date first?"

I laughed, pulling her in close again.

"Baby, we can go anywhere you want. As long as it's with me."

"Then, yes, you big arrogant grizzly bear. I'll marry you. But only because you said please... and because I love you."

"I love you too, Freya."

Nothing had ever felt more right in my entire life than holding her in my arms as we drifted back to sleep.

Epilogue

(Some years later ...)

"**I**t was so nice to finally meet you, Dr. Magnuson!"

The pretty blond woman had a warm smile that lit up her face. I was still getting used to being called doctor, even though it'd been almost a year since I'd passed the EPPP and became a licensed psychologist. To be fair, it had been a very busy year—in many wonderful ways.

I took her hand in mine and returned the joy I felt in my own smile. Zaria was one of our newest guests at the retreat. She'd gone through the first phase of the recovery program wonderfully, making strides faster than any woman we'd seen yet. Our staff had been keeping me posted of her progress while I'd been on maternity leave the last few weeks, and I'd been so excited to finally meet her.

She'd been sold into a cleaning and maid service at the age of eight years old, by her own parents. At twelve years old, she'd been forced into sex work.

Now almost twenty-two years old, her life was finally her own again. The fact that our organization was able to help her regain her freedom and help rebuild her life, was something that would never take away the gratitude that perpetually lived in my heart.

Today was our semi-annual *Lawn, Pajama & Pool Party,* which was one of the guests' long-time favorite events.

It was basically a giant party all over the entire property, complete with pony rides, miniature Ferris wheel, inflatable unicorn water-polo, luxury spa services, and a bunch of whimsical, purely indulgent other things the women loved. It was an all-day event that the women also helped plan as part of the program.

We had a fairly massive budget, of course; being married to a billionaire had its perks.

"Zaria, it was my pleasure to meet you! I'm only sorry it took me so long. Now run along—remember, you're on strict doctor's orders. I want at least seventeen-thousand and forty-three more laughs out of you before the day is done!"

She gave me at least eight or nine more as she hugged me and ran off with her Sponsor and a small group of other women. Her charisma was contagious, and she loved to shine that light on others. She'd made friends quickly, especially with some of the more shy, hesitant girls.

A not so tiny scream made my heart stop for a half second, then fill again with overflowing joy and I chuckled quietly.

That little bundle of fury was going to be exactly like his father. Barely five-months old and he was already bellowing and carrying on like a tiny tyrant.

"See?! Momma's here, you're okay, bud. Just in time, huh little buddy? Were you famished?"

Thorsten Braeden Magnuson wailed dramatically as soon as he saw me. My heart spilled over with love instantly for both him and the sexy man mountain who held him.

"He seems to have his daddy's temperament when he's hungry," I kissed my arrogant alpha male caveman husband as he handed me our son.

"Or when he's separated from Momma for too long. He and I definitely have that in common," Brodie kissed me back soundly, but briefly, due to the screaming and apparently starving bundle of love between us.

Several hours later, after the little monster had been fed, changed, changed again, and passed out from an adorable little milk-induced coma, Brodie and I settled onto our balcony to watch the Movie on the Lawn.

I burst out laughing when I realized what the girls had chosen.

It was the same movie that Brodie and I had been to on our first date. That's what I'd called it, anyway, even though we'd been together for almost six months by that time.

It had taken even longer than that to finally catch the demented little puppet master pulling the strings behind the trafficking ring that had targeted me. No one would have ever guessed who the twisted little sicko was, or what their motives had been, but they'd still eventually met their fate at the end of the barrel of a smoking gun.

No one would have guessed who'd been the one to pull that trigger, either. But it didn't matter, as they were dead and gone all the same.

That horrible event had led me to the man who held me in his arms, and together we'd already started our little family. Tomorrow Kimberly and her husband would be in town for our friends' wedding—I couldn't wait to see her little girl again!

Being swept up in all that mess had also led me to this vision, and brought people into my life that helped me achieve that dream every day. Together, we'd started *Phoenix Foundation International* and had helped hundreds of women and families who'd been victims of human trafficking recover their freedom and find love and meaning in their lives.

A round of applause and laughter sounded from the women for the opening credits of the raunchy chick flick playing in the lawn over by the gardens.

I smiled as I remembered the huge tub of salty, butter-drunk popcorn on that first date, years ago, when we'd finally been able to leave Sicily. Brodie had taken me home to his ranch in Texas, and I'd fallen in love. With him, with the land, with everything.

"Baby, if you keep smiling like that, I'm gonna be giving Thorsten a little brother very soon," my husband growled at me as he playfully nipped my ear.

"Promise?" I asked him as I leaned into his embrace.

We didn't finish the rest of the movie.

Even knowing that I'd be woken up by a bellowing baby boy in a mere few hours, I couldn't contain my pure contented joy as I snuggled into my husband's arrogant, loving, and protective python arms.

For me, it was proof that everything happened for a reason. To think if I'd never walked into that naughty lingerie store and flung my vibrating panties at a total stranger, I'd have never met this man. He annoyed me, infuriated me, excited me, fiercely protected and loved me. He was my world, he and the sleeping love bug in the other room.

Brodie Magnuson, aka my husband, lover, protector, and best friend, *Mr. Panty Dropper* himself.

• • • •

The End